Part One

—

Men would be angels, angels would be gods.
—Alexander Pope

What's past is prologue.
—Shakespeare

DIVINE EVIL

Nora Roberts

Divine Evil

RANDOM HOUSE
LARGE PRINT

Grateful acknowledgment is made for permission to reprint the following:
"She Loves You" by Paul McCartney and John Lennon.
Copyright © 1963 Northern Songs, Ltd., London, England.
Copyright renewed. All rights for USA and Canada controlled by Gil Music Corp., New York, NY.

All rights reserved under International and Pan-American Copyright Conventions.
Published in the United States of America by Random House Large Print in association with Bantam Books, New York, and simultaneously in Canada by Random House of Canada Limited, Toronto.
Distributed by Random House, Inc., New York.

The Library of Congress has established a Cataloging-in-Publication record for this title.

0-375-43377-5

www.randomlargeprint.com

FIRST LARGE PRINT EDITION

10 9 8 7 6 5 4 3 2 1

This Large Print edition published in accord with the standards of the N.A.V.H.

Divine Evil

Chapter 1

THE RITE BEGAN *an hour after sunset. The circle had been prepared long ago, a perfect nine feet, by the clearing of trees and young saplings. The ground had been sprinkled with consecrated earth.*

Clouds, dark and secretive, danced over the pale moon.

Thirteen figures, in black cowls and cloaks, stood inside the protective circle. In the woods beyond, a lone owl began to scream, in lament or in sympathy. When the gong sounded, even he was silenced. For a moment, there was only the murmur of the wind through the early spring leaves.

In the pit at the left side of the circle, the fire already smoldered. Soon the flames would rise up, called by that same wind or other forces.

It was May Day Eve, the Sabbat of Roodmas. On

this night of high spring, both celebration and sacrifice would be given for the fertility of crops and for the power of men.

Two women dressed in red robes stepped into the circle. Their faces were not hooded and were very white, with a slash of scarlet over their lips. Like vampires who had already feasted.

One, following the careful instructions she had been given, shed her robe and stood naked in the light of a dozen black candles, then draped herself over a raised slab of polished wood.

She would be their altar of living flesh, the virgin on which they would worship. The fact that she was a prostitute and far from pure disturbed some of them. Others simply relished her lush curves and generously spread thighs.

The high priest, having donned his mask of the Goat of Mendes, began to chant in bastardized Latin. When he had finished his recitation, he raised his arms high toward the inverted pentagram above the altar. A bell was rung to purify the air.

From her hiding place in the brush, a young girl watched, her eyes wide with curiosity. There was a burning smell coming from the pit where flames crackled, sending sparks shooting high. Odd shapes had been carved in the trunks of the circling trees.

The young girl began wondering where her father was. She had hidden in his car, giggling to herself at the trick she was playing on him. When she had followed him through the woods, she hadn't been afraid *of the dark. She'd never been afraid. She had hidden, waiting for the right time to jump out and into his arms.*

But he had put on a long, dark coat, like the others, and now she wasn't sure which one was Daddy. Though the naked woman both embarrassed and fascinated her, what the grown-ups were doing no longer seemed like a game.

She felt her heart beating in her throat when the man in the mask began to chant again.

"We call on Ammon, the god of life and reproduction. On Pan, the god of lust."

After the calling of each name, the others repeated it. The list was long.

The group was swaying now, a deep hum rising up among them while the high priest drank from a silver chalice. Finished, he set the cup down between the breasts of the altar.

He took up a sword and pointing it south, east, north, and west, called up the four princes of hell.

> *Satan, lord of fire*
> *Lucifer, bringer of light*
> *Belial, who has no master*
> *Leviathan, serpent of the deep*

In the brush, the young girl shuddered and was afraid.

"Ave, Satan."

"I call upon you, Master, Prince of Darkness, King

of the Night, throw wide the Gates of Hell and hear us." The high priest shouted the words, not like a prayer, but a demand. As his voice rang out, he held up a parchment. The lights from the greedy flames washed through it like blood. *"We ask that our crops be bountiful, our cattle fruitful. Destroy our enemies, bring sickness and pain to those who would harm us. We, your faithful, demand fortune and pleasure."* He placed a hand on the breast of the altar. *"We take what we wish, in your name, Lord of the Flies. In your name, we speak: Death to the weak. Wealth to the strong. The rods of our sex grow hard, our blood hot. Let our women burn for us. Let them receive us lustfully."* He stroked down the altar's torso and between the thighs as the prostitute, well-schooled, moaned and began to move under his hand.

His voice rose as he continued his requests. He thrust the sword's point through the parchment and held it over the flame of a black candle until all that remained of it was the stink of smoke. The chant of the circle of twelve swelled behind him.

At some signal, two of the cloaked figures pulled a young goat into the circle. As its eyes rolled in fright, they chanted over it, nearly screaming now. The athamas was drawn, the ceremonial knife whose freshly whetted blade glimmered under the rising moon.

When the girl saw the blade slice across the white goat's throat, she tried to scream, but no sound passed her lips. She wanted to run, but her legs seemed rooted *to the ground. She covered her face with her hands, weeping and wanting to call for her father.*

When at last she looked again, the ground ran with blood. It dripped over the sides of a shallow silver bowl. The voices of the men were a roaring buzz in her ears as she watched them throw the headless carcass of the goat into the fire pit.

Now the stink of roasting flesh hung sickeningly in the air.

With a ululant cry, the man in the goat mask tore off his cloak. Beneath he was naked, his white, white skin glimmering with sweat, though the night was cool. Glinting on his chest was a silver amulet inscribed with old and secret symbols.

He straddled the altar, then drove himself hard between her thighs. With a howling scream, a second man fell on the other woman, dragging her to the ground, while the others tore off their cloaks to dance naked around the pit of fire.

She saw her father, her own father, dip his hands into the sacrificial blood. As he capered with the others, it dripped from his fingers. . . .

Clare woke, screaming.

Breathless, chilled with sweat, she huddled under the blankets. With one trembling hand, she fumbled for the switch on the bedside lamp. When that wasn't enough, she rose to flip on others until the small room was flooded with light. Her hands were still unsteady when she drew a cigarette from a pack and struck a match.

Sitting on the edge of the bed, she smoked in silence.

Why had the dream come back now?

Her therapist would say it was a knee-jerk reaction to her mother's recent marriage—subconsciously she felt her father had been betrayed.

That was bull.

Clare blew out a defiant stream of smoke. Her mother had been widowed for over twelve years. Any sane, loving daughter would want her mother's happiness. And she was a loving daughter. She just wasn't so sure about the sane part.

She remembered the first time she'd had the dream. She'd been six and had wakened screaming in her bed. Just as she had tonight. But then, her parents had rushed in to gather her up and soothe. Even her brother, Blair, had come in, wide-eyed and wailing. Her mother had carried him off while her father stayed with her, crooning in his calm, quiet voice, promising her over and over that it was only a dream, a bad dream that she would soon forget.

And she had, for long stretches of time. Then it would creep up on her, a grinning assassin, when she was tense or exhausted or vulnerable.

She stabbed out the cigarette and pressed her

fingers to her eyes. Well, she was tense now. Her one-woman show was less than a week away, and though she had personally chosen each piece of sculpture that would be shown, she was plagued with doubts.

Perhaps it was because the critics had been so enthusiastic two years before, at her debut. Now that she was enjoying success, there was so much more to lose. And she knew the work that would be shown was her best. If it was found to be mediocre, then she, as an artist, was mediocre.

Was there any label more damning?

Because she felt better having something tangible to worry about, she rose and opened the draperies. The sun was just coming up, giving the streets and sidewalks of downtown Manhattan an almost rosy hue. Pushing open the window, she shivered once in the chill of the spring morning.

It was almost quiet. From a few blocks up, she could hear the grind of a garbage truck finishing its rounds. Near the corner of Canal and Greene, she saw a bag lady pulling a cart with all her worldly possessions. The wheels squeaked and echoed hollowly.

There was a light in the bakery directly across and three stories down. Clare caught the faint strains of *Rigoletto* and the good yeasty scent of baking bread. A cab rumbled past, valves knocking. Then there was silence again. She might have been alone in the city.

Was that what she wanted? she wondered. To be alone, to find some spot and dig into solitude? There were times when she felt so terribly disconnected, yet unable to make a place just for herself.

Wasn't that why her marriage had failed? She had loved Rob, but she had never felt connected to him. When it was over, she'd felt regret but not remorse.

Or perhaps Dr. Janowski was right, and she was burying her remorse, all of it, every ounce of grief she had felt since her father died. Channeling it out through her art.

And what was wrong with that? She started to stuff her hands into the pockets of her robe when she discovered she wasn't wearing it. A woman had to be crazy to stand in an open window in SoHo wearing nothing but a flimsy Bill the Cat T-shirt. The hell with it, she thought and leaned out farther. Maybe she was crazy.

She stood, her bright red hair disheveled from restless sleep, her face pale and tired, watching the light grow and listening to the noise begin as the city woke.

Then she turned away, ready for work.

★ ★ ★

It was after two when Clare heard the buzzer. It sounded like an annoying bee over the hiss of the torch in her hand and the crash of Mozart booming from the stereo. She considered ignoring it, but the new piece wasn't going very well, and the interruption was a good excuse to stop. She turned off her torch. As she crossed her studio, she pulled off her safety gloves. Still wearing her goggles, skullcap, and apron, she flicked on the intercom.

"Yes?"

"Clare? Angie."

"Come on up." Clare punched in the security code and released the elevator. After pulling off her cap and goggles, she walked back to circle the half-formed sculpture.

It stood on her welding table in the rear of the loft, surrounded by tools—pliers, hammers, chisels, extra torch tips. Her tanks of acetylene and oxygen rested in their sturdy steel cart. Beneath it all was a twenty-foot square of sheet metal, to keep sparks and hot drippings off the floor.

Most of the loft space was taken over by Clare's work—chunks of granite, slabs of cherrywood and ash, hunks and tubes of steel. Tools for hacking, prying, sanding, welding. She'd always enjoyed living with her work.

Now she approached her current project, eyes

narrowed, lips pursed. It was holding out on her, she thought, and she didn't bother to look around when the doors of the elevator slid open.

"I should have known." Angie LeBeau tossed back her mane of black, corkscrew curls and tapped one scarlet Italian pump on the hardwood floor. "I've been calling you for over an hour."

"I turned off the bell. Machine's picking it up. What do you get from this, Angie?"

Blowing out a long breath, Angie studied the sculpture on the worktable. "Chaos."

"Yeah." With a nod, Clare stooped lower. "Yeah, you're right. I've been going at this the wrong way."

"Don't you dare pick up that torch." Tired of shouting, she stomped across the floor and switched off the stereo. "Damn it, Clare, we had a date for lunch at the Russian Tea Room at twelve-thirty."

Clare straightened and focused on her friend for the first time. Angie was, as always, the picture of elegance. Her toffee-colored skin and exotic features were set off to perfection by the navy Adolfo suit and oversize pearls.

Her handbag and shoes were identical shades of scarlet leather. Angie liked everything to match, everything to be in its place. In her closet, her shoes were neatly stacked in clear plastic boxes. Her blouses were arranged by color and fabric. Her handbags—a legendary collection—were tucked into individual slots on custom-built shelves.

As for herself, Clare was lucky if she could find both shoes of a pair in the black hole of her closet. Her handbag collection consisted of one good black evening bag and a huge canvas tote. More than once Clare had wondered how she and Angie had ever become, and remained, friends.

Right at the moment, that friendship seemed to be on the line, she noted. Angie's dark eyes were hot, and her long scarlet fingernails were tapping on her bag in time with her foot.

"Stand just like that." Clare bounded across the room to search through the confusion on the sofa for a sketch pad. She tossed aside a sweatshirt, a silk blouse, unopened mail, an empty bag of Fritos, a couple of paperback novels, and a plastic water pistol.

"Damn it, Clare—"

"No, don't move." Pad in hand, she heaved a cushion aside and found a chalk pencil. "You're beautiful when you're angry." Clare grinned.

"Bitch," Angie said and struggled with a laugh.

"That's it, that's it." Clare's pencil flew across the pad. "Christ, what cheekbones! Who would have thought if you mixed Cherokee, African, and French, you'd get such bone structure? Snarl a little bit, would you?"

"Put that stupid thing down. You're not going to flatter your way out of this. I sat in RTR for an hour drinking Perrier and gnawing on the tablecloth."

"Sorry. I forgot."

"What else is new?"

Clare set the sketch aside, knowing Angie would look at it the minute her back was turned. "Want some lunch?"

"I had a hot dog in the cab."

"Then I'll grab something, and you can tell me what we were supposed to talk about."

"The show, you imbecile!" Angie eyed the sketch and smothered a smile. Clare had drawn her with flames shooting out of her ears. Refusing to be amused, she glanced around for a clear spot to sit and finally settled on the arm of the sofa. God knew what else lurked under the cushions. "Are you ever going to hire somebody to shovel this place out?"

"No, I like it this way." Clare stepped into the kitchen, which was little more than an alcove in the corner of the studio. "It helps me create."

"You can pull that artistic temperament crap on someone else, Clare. I happen to know you're just a lazy slob."

"When you're right, you're right." She came

out again with a pint of Dutch chocolate ice cream and a tablespoon. "Want some?"

"No." It was a constant irritation to Angie that Clare could binge on junk food whenever the whim struck, which was often, and never add flesh to her willowy figure.

At five ten, Clare wasn't the stick figure she had been during her childhood, but still slender enough that she didn't check the scale each morning as Angie did. Angie watched her now as Clare, wearing her leather apron over bib overalls, shoveled in calories. In all likelihood, Angie mused, she wore nothing under the denim but skin.

Clare wore no makeup, either. Pale gold freckles were dusted across her skin. Her eyes, a slightly darker shade of amber-gold, were huge in her triangular face with its soft, generous mouth and small, undistinguished nose. Despite Clare's unruly crop of fiery hair, just long enough to form a stubby ponytail when it was pulled back with a rubber band, and her exceptional height, there was an air of fragility about her that made Angie, at thirty only two years her senior, feel maternal.

"Girl, when are you going to learn to sit down and eat a meal?"

Clare grinned and dug for more ice cream. "Now you're worried about me, so I guess I'm forgiven." She perched on a stool and tucked one booted foot under the rung. "I really am sorry about lunch."

"You always are. What about writing notes to yourself?"

"I do write them, then I forget where I've put them."

With her dripping spoon, she gestured around the huge, disordered space. The sofa where Angie sat was one of the few pieces of furniture, though there was a table under a pile of newspapers, magazines, and empty soft drink bottles. Another stool was shoved into a corner and held a bust of black marble. Paintings crowded the walls, and pieces of sculpture—some finished, some abandoned—sat, stood, or reclined as space allowed.

Up a clunky set of wrought-iron steps was the storeroom she'd converted into a bedroom. But the rest of the enormous space she'd lived in for five years had been taken over by her art.

For the first eighteen years of her life, Clare had struggled to live up to her mother's standards of neatness and order. It had taken her less than three weeks on her own to accept that turmoil was her natural milieu.

She offered Angie a bland grin. "How am I supposed to find anything in this mess?"

"Sometimes I wonder how you remember to get out of bed in the morning."

"You're just worried about the show." Clare

set the half-eaten carton of ice cream aside, where, Angie thought, it would probably melt. Clare picked up a pack of cigarettes and located a match. "Worrying about it is a lesson in futility. They're either going to like my stuff, or they're not."

"Right. Then why do you look like you've gotten about four hours' sleep?"

"Five," Clare corrected, but she didn't want to bring up the dream. "I'm tense, but I'm not worried. Between you and your sexy husband, there's enough worrying going on already."

"Jean-Paul's a wreck," Angie admitted. Married to the gallery owner for two years, she was powerfully attracted by his intelligence, his passion for art, and his magnificent body. "This is the first major show in the new gallery. It's not just your butt on the line."

"I know." Clare's eyes clouded briefly as she thought of all the money and time and hope the LeBeaus had invested in their new, much larger gallery. "I'm not going to let you down."

Angie saw that despite her claims, Clare was as scared as the rest of them. "We know that," she said, deliberately lightening the mood. "In fact, we expect to be *the* gallery on the West Side after your show. In the meantime, I'm here to remind you that you've got a ten A.M. interview with *New York* magazine, and a lunch interview tomorrow with the *Times*."

"Oh, Angie."

"No escape from it this time." Angie uncrossed her shapely legs. "You'll see the *New York* writer in our penthouse. I shudder to think of holding an interview here."

"You just want to keep an eye on me."

"There is that. Lunch at Le Cirque, one sharp."

"I wanted to go in and check on the setup at the gallery."

"There's time for that, too. I'll be here at nine to make sure you're up and dressed."

"I hate interviews," Clare mumbled.

"Tough." Angie took her by the shoulders and kissed both her cheeks. "Now go get some rest. You really do look tired."

Clare perched an elbow on her knee. "Aren't you going to lay out my clothes for me?" she asked as Angie walked to the elevator.

"It may come to that."

Alone, Clare sat brooding for a few minutes. She did detest interviews, all the pompous and personal questions. The process of being studied, measured, and dissected. As with most things she disliked but couldn't avoid, she pushed it out of her mind.

She was tired, too tired to concentrate well enough to fire up her torch again. In any case, nothing she'd begun in the past few weeks had turned out well. But she was much too restless to nap or to stretch out on the floor and devour some daytime television.

On impulse she rose and went to a large trunk that served as seat, table, and catch-all. Digging in, she riffled through an old prom dress, her graduation cap, her wedding veil, which aroused a trio of reactions—surprise, amusement, and regret—a pair of tennis shoes she'd thought were lost for good, and at last, a photo album.

She was lonely, Clare admitted as she took it with her to the window seat overlooking Canal Street. For her family. If they were all too far away to touch, at least she could reach them through old pictures.

The first snapshot made her smile. It was a muddy black-and-white Polaroid of herself and her twin brother, Blair, as infants. Blair and Clare, she thought with a sigh. How often had she and her twin groaned over their parents' decision to name cute? The shot was fuzzily out of focus, her father's handiwork. He'd never taken a clear picture in his life.

"I'm mechanically declined," he'd always said. "Put anything with a button or a gear in my hands, and I'll mess it up. But give me a handful of seeds and some dirt, and I'll grow you the biggest flowers in the county."

And it was true, Clare thought. Her mother was a natural tinkerer, fixing toasters and unstopping sinks, while Jack Kimball had wielded hoe and spade and clippers to turn their yard on the corner of Oak Leaf and Mountain View Lanes in Emmitsboro, Maryland, into a showplace.

There was proof here, in a picture her mother had taken. It was perfectly centered and in focus. The infant Kimball twins reclined on a blanket on close-cropped green grass. Behind them was a lush bank of spring blooms. Nodding columbine, bleeding hearts, lilies of the valley, impatiens, all orderly planted without being structured, all richly blossoming.

Here was a picture of her mother. With a jolt, Clare realized she was looking at a woman younger than herself. Rosemary Kimball's hair was a dark honey blond, worn poufed and lacquered in the style of the early sixties. She was smiling, on the verge of a laugh as she held a baby on either hip.

How pretty she was, Clare thought. Despite the bowling ball of a hairdo and the overdone makeup of the times, Rosemary Kimball had been—and was still—a lovely woman. Blond hair, blue eyes, a petite, curvy figure, and delicate features.

There was Clare's father, dressed in shorts with garden dirt on his knobby knees. He was leaning on his hoe, grinning self-consciously at the camera. His red hair was cropped in a crew cut, and his pale skin showed signs of sunburn. Though well out of adolescence, Jack Kimball had still been all legs and elbows. An awkward scarecrow of a man who had loved flowers.

Blinking back tears, Clare turned the next page in the album. There were Christmas pictures, she and Blair in front of a tilted Christmas tree. Toddlers on shiny red tricycles. Though they were twins, there was little family resemblance. Blair had taken his looks from their mother, Clare from their father, as though in the womb the babies had chosen sides. Blair was all angelic looks, from the top of his towhead to the tips of his red Keds. Clare's hair ribbon was dangling. Her white leggings bagged under the stiff skirts of her organdy dress. She was the ugly duckling who had never quite managed to turn into a swan.

There were other pictures, cataloging a family growing up. Birthdays and picnics, vacations and quiet moments. Here and there were pictures of friends and relatives. Blair, in his spiffy band uniform, marching down Main Street in the Memorial Day parade. Clare with her arm around Pudge, the fat beagle who had been their pet for more than a decade. Pictures of the twins together in the pup tent their mother had set up in the backyard. Of her parents, dressed in their Sunday finest outside church one Easter Sunday after her father had turned dramatically back to the Catholic faith.

There were newspaper clippings as well. Jack Kimball being presented a plaque by the mayor of Emmitsboro in appreciation for his work for the community. A write-up on her father and Kimball Realty, citing it as a sterling example of the American dream, a one-man operation that had grown and prospered into a statewide organization with four branches.

His biggest deal had been the sale of a one-hundred-fifty-acre farm to a building conglomerate that specialized in developing shopping centers. Some of the townspeople had griped about sacrificing the quiet seclusion of Emmitsboro to the coming of an eighty-unit motel, fast-food franchises, and department stores, but most had agreed that the growth was needed. More jobs, more conveniences.

Her father had been one of the town luminaries at the groundbreaking ceremony.

Then he had begun drinking.

Not enough to notice at first. True, the scent of whiskey had hovered around him, but he had continued to work, continued to garden. The closer the shopping center had come to completion, the more he drank.

Two days after its grand opening, on a hot

August night, he had emptied a bottle and tumbled, or jumped, from the third-story window.

No one had been home. Her mother had been enjoying her once-a-month girls' night out of dinner and a movie and gossip. Blair had been camping with friends in the woods to the east of town. And Clare had been flushed and dizzy with the excitement of her first date.

With her eyes closed and the album clutched in her hands, she was a girl of fifteen again, tall for her age and skinny with it, her oversize eyes bright and giddy with the thrill of her night at the local carnival.

She'd been kissed on the Ferris wheel, her hand held. In her arms she had carried the small stuffed elephant that cost Bobby Meese seven dollars and fifty cents to win by knocking over a trio of wooden bottles.

The image in her mind was clear. Clare stopped hearing the chug of traffic along Canal and heard instead the quiet, country sounds of summer.

She was certain her father would be waiting for her. His eyes had misted over when she walked out with Bobby. She hoped she and her father would sit together on the old porch swing, as they often did, with moths flapping against the yellow lights and crickets singing in the grass, while she told him all about the adventure.

She climbed the stairs, her sneakers soundless on the gleaming wood. Even now she could feel that flush of excitement. The bedroom door was open, and she peeked in, calling his name.

"Daddy?"

In the slant of moonlight, she saw that her parents' bed was still made. Turning, she started up to the third floor. He often worked late at night in his office. Or drank late at night. But she pushed that thought aside. If he'd been drinking, she would coax him downstairs, fix him coffee, and talk to him until his eyes lost that haunted look that had come into them lately. Before long he'd be laughing again, his arm slung around her shoulders.

She saw the light under his office door. She knocked first, an ingrained habit. As close a family as they were, they had been taught to respect the privacy of others.

"Daddy? I'm back."

The lack of response disturbed her. For some reason, as she stood, hesitating, she was gripped by an unreasonable need to turn and run. A coppery flavor had filled her mouth, a taste of fear she didn't recognize. She even took a step back before she shook off the feeling and reached for the doorknob.

"Dad?" She prayed she wouldn't find him slumped over his desk, snoring drunk. The image made her take a firmer grip on the knob, angry all at once that he would spoil this most perfect evening of her life with whiskey. He was her father. He was supposed to be there for her. He wasn't supposed to let her down. She shoved the door open.

At first she was only puzzled. The room was empty, though the light was on and the big portable fan stirred the hot air in the converted attic room. Her nose wrinkled at the smell—whiskey, strong and sour. As she stepped inside, her sneakers crunched over broken glass. She skirted around the remains of a bottle of Irish Mist.

Had he gone out? Had he drained the bottle, tossed it aside, then stumbled out of the house?

Her first reaction was acute embarrassment, the kind only a teenager can feel. Someone might see him—her friends, their parents. In a small town like Emmitsboro, everyone knew everyone. She would die of shame if someone happened across her father, drunk and weaving.

Clutching her prized elephant, her first gift from a suitor, she stood in the center of the sloped-ceilinged room and agonized over what to do.

If her mother had been home, she thought, suddenly furious, if her mother had been home, he wouldn't have wandered off. She would have soothed and calmed him and tucked him into bed. And Blair had gone off as well, camping with his jerky friends. Probably drinking Budweiser and reading *Playboy* by the campfire.

And she'd gone, too, she thought, near tears with the indecision. Should she stay and wait, or go out and search for him?

She would look. Her decision made, she moved to the desk to turn off the lamp. More glass crunched under her feet. It was odd, she thought. If the bottle had been broken by the door, how could there be so much glass here, behind the desk? Under the window?

Slowly, she looked up from the jagged shards at her feet to the tall, narrow window behind her father's desk. It was not open, but broken. Vicious slices of glass still clung to the frame. With watery legs she took a step forward, then another. And looked down to where her father lay faceup on the flagstone patio, impaled through the chest by the round of garden stakes he had set there that same afternoon.

She remembered running. The scream locked in her chest. Stumbling on the stairs, falling, scrambling up and running again, down the long hall, slamming into the swinging door at the kitchen, through the screen that led outside.

He was bleeding, broken, his mouth open as if he were about to speak. Or scream. Through his chest the sharp-ended stakes sliced, soaked with blood and gore.

His eyes stared at her, but he didn't see. She

shook him, shouted, tried to drag him up. She pleaded and begged and promised, but he only stared at her. She could smell the blood, his blood, and the heavy scent of summer roses he loved.

Then she screamed. She kept screaming until the neighbors found them.

Chapter 2

CAMERON RAFFERTY HATED CEMETER-
ies. It wasn't superstition. He wasn't the kind of
man who avoided black cats or knocked on
wood. It was the confrontation with his own
mortality he abhorred. He knew he couldn't
live forever—as a cop he was aware he took
more risks with death than most. That was a
job, just as life was a job and death was its re-
tirement.

But he was damned if he liked to be reminded
of it by granite headstones and bunches of with-
ered flowers.

He had come to look at a grave, however, and
most graves tended to draw in company and
turn into cemeteries. This one was attached to
Our Lady of Mercy Catholic Church and was

set on a rambling slope of land in the shadow of the old belfry. The stone church was small but sturdy, having survived weather and sin for a hundred and twenty-three years. The plot of land reserved for Catholics gone to glory was hugged by a wrought-iron fence. Most of the spikes were rusted, and many were missing. Nobody much noticed.

These days, most of the townspeople were split between the nondenominational Church of God on Main and the First Lutheran just around the corner on Poplar, with some holdouts for the Wayside Church of the Brethren on the south side of town and the Catholics—the Brethren having the edge.

Since the membership had fallen off in the seventies, Our Lady of Mercy had dropped back to one Sunday mass. The priests of St. Anne's in Hagerstown were on an informal rotation, and one of them popped down for religion classes and the nine o'clock mass that followed them. Otherwise, Our Lady didn't do a lot of business, except around Easter and Christmas. And, of course, weddings and funerals. No matter how far her faithful strayed, they came back to Our Lady to be planted.

It wasn't a thought that gave Cam, who'd been baptized at the font, right in front of the tall, serene statue of the Virgin, any comfort.

It was a pretty night, a little chill, a little

breezy, but the sky was diamond clear. He would have preferred to have been sitting on his deck with a cold bottle of Rolling Rock, looking at the stars through his telescope. The truth was, he would have preferred to have been chasing a homicidal junkie down a dark alley. When you were chasing down possible death with a gun in your hand, the adrenaline pumped fast and kept you from dwelling on the reality. But picking your way over decomposing bodies kind of knocked you over the head with your own ultimate destiny.

An owl hooted, causing Deputy Bud Hewitt, who walked beside Cam, to jolt. The deputy grinned sheepishly and cleared his throat.

"Spooky place, huh, Sheriff?"

Cam gave a noncommittal grunt. At thirty, he was only three years Bud's senior and had grown up on the same stretch of Dog Run Road. He'd dated Bud's sister, Sarah, for a wild and rocky three months during his senior year at Emmitsboro High and had been present when Bud had thrown up his first six-pack of beer. But he knew Bud got a charge out of calling him sheriff.

"Don't think too much of it during the day," Bud went on. He had a young, simple face, all curves and rosy skin. His hair was the color of straw and stuck up at odd angles no matter how often he wet his comb and fought it down. "But at night it makes you think about all those vampire movies."

"These people aren't undead, they're just dead."

"Right." But Bud wished he had a silver bullet instead of regulation .38 slugs in his revolver.

"It's over here, Sheriff."

The two teenagers who had chosen the cemetery to neck in gestured him along. They'd been spooked when they'd come squealing up his lane and banging on his door, but now they were running on panicked excitement. And loving it.

"Right here." The boy, seventeen and sporting a denim jacket and scuffed Air Jordans, pointed. He wore a small gold stud in his left ear—a sign of stupidity or bravery in a town like Emmitsboro. At his side the girl, a cuddly cheerleader with doe brown eyes, gave a little shudder. They both knew they'd be the stars of Emmitsboro High on Monday.

Cam shined his light on the overturned marker. The grave was that of John Robert Hardy, 1881–1882, an infant who had lived one brief year and been dead more than a hundred. Below the fallen marker, the grave yawned wide, a dark, empty pit.

"See? It's just like we told you." The boy swallowed audibly. The whites of his eyes gleamed in the shadowed light. "Somebody dug it up."

"I can see that, Josh." Cam stooped down to shine his light into the hole. There was nothing there but dirt and the smell of old death.

"You think it was grave robbers, Sheriff?" Excitement throbbed in Josh's voice. He was ashamed of the fact that he'd scrambled and bolted like a rabbit after he and Sally had all but tumbled into the yawning grave while rolling on the wild grass. He preferred to remember that he'd had his hand up her shirt. He wanted her to remember it too, so he spoke with authority. "I read about how they dig up graves looking for jewelry and body parts. They sell the body parts for experiments and stuff."

"I don't think they'd have found much here." Cam straightened. Though he considered himself a sensible man, peering into the open grave gave him the willies. "You run along, see Sally home. We'll take it from here."

Sally looked up at him with huge eyes. She had a secret crush on Sheriff Rafferty. She'd heard her mother gossiping about him with a neighbor, chattering about his wild days as a teenager in Emmitsboro when he'd worn a leather jacket and driven a motorcycle and busted up Clyde's Tavern in a fight over a girl.

He still had a motorcycle and looked to her as if he could still be wild if he wanted. He was six two with a ready, wiry build. He didn't wear a dumb khaki uniform like Bud Hewitt, but snug jeans and a cotton shirt rolled up to the elbows. His hair was jet black and curled over his ears and the collar of his shirt. His face was long and lean, and now the moonlight accented the fascinating shadows under his cheekbones and made her seventeen-year-old heart flutter. In Sally's opinion, he had the sexiest blue eyes—dark and deep and a little broody.

"Are you going to call in the FBI?" she asked him.

"We'll take it under advisement." God, to be seventeen again, he thought, then immediately: Unh-uh, no thanks. "Thanks for your help. The next time you want to make out, go someplace else."

Sally blushed prettily. The night wind ruffled her hair around her guileless face. "We were only talking, Sheriff."

And heifers jump over the moon. "Whatever. You go on home now."

He watched them walk away, among the headstones and markers, over plots of soft, sunken dirt and clumps of wild grass. Hip to hip, they were already talking in excited whispers. Sally let out a squeal and giggle, and glanced over her shoulder once to get a last look at Cam. Kids, he thought with a shake of his head as the wind flapped a loose shingle of the roof of the old church. Don't know a damn thing about ambience.

"I'm going to want some pictures of this, Bud. Tonight. And we'd best rope it off and post a sign or two. Come morning, everyone in town will have heard about it."

"Can't see grave robbers in Emmitsboro." Bud squinted his eyes and tried to look official. The graveyard was a pretty creepy place, but on the other hand, this was the most excitement they'd had since Billy Reardon had hot-wired his father's pickup and gone joyriding around the county with that big-breasted Gladhill girl and a six-pack of Miller. "Vandals, more like. Bunch of kids with a sick sense of humor."

"More than likely," Cam murmured, but he crouched by the grave again as Bud walked to the cruiser to get the camera. It didn't feel like vandals. Where was the graffiti, the senseless destruction?

The grave had been neatly—systematically, he thought—dug up. The surrounding headstones hadn't been disturbed. It was only this one small grave that had been touched.

And where the hell was the dirt? There were no piles of it around the hole. That meant it had been carted away. What in God's name would anyone want with a couple of wheelbarrow loads of dirt from an old grave?

The owl hooted again, then spread his wings

and glided over the churchyard. Cam shuddered as the shadow passed over his back.

The next morning being Saturday, Cam drove into town and parked outside of Martha's, a diner and long-standing gathering place in Emmitsboro. It had become his habit, since returning to his hometown as sheriff, to while away a Saturday morning there, over pancakes and coffee.

Work rarely interfered with the ritual. Most Saturdays he could linger from eight to ten with a second or third cup of coffee. He could chat with the waitresses and the regulars, listen to Loretta Lynn or Randy Travis on the tinny jukebox in the corner, scan the headlines on the *Herald Mail*, and dig into the sports section. There was the comforting scent of sausage and bacon frying, the clatter of dishes, the murmuring drone of old men at the counter talking baseball and brooding over the economy.

Life moved slow and calm in Emmitsboro, Maryland. That's why he had come back.

The town had grown some since his youth. With a population of nearly two thousand, counting the outlying farms and mountain homes, they had added on to the elementary school and five years before had converted from septic tanks to a sewage treatment plant. Such things were still big news in Emmitsboro, where the park off the square at Main and Poplar flew the flag from sunup to sunset daily.

It was a quiet, tidy little town that had been settled in 1782 by Samuel Q. Emmit. Tucked in a valley, it was ringed by sedate mountains and rolling farmland. On three of its four sides, it was flanked by fields of hay and alfalfa and corn. On the fourth was Dopper's Woods, so named because it adjoined the Dopper farm. The woods were deep, more than two hundred acres. On a crisp November day in 1958, Jerome Dopper's oldest son, Junior, had skipped school and headed into those woods with his 30–30 over his shoulder, hoping for a six-point buck.

They'd found him the next morning near the slippery banks of the creek. Most of his head was missing. It looked as though Junior had been careless with the safety, had slid on the slick carpet and blown himself, instead of that buck, to kingdom come.

Since then, kids had enjoyed scaring themselves over campfires with stories of Junior Dopper's ghost, headless and shambling, hunting forever in Dopper's Woods.

The Antietam Creek cut through the Doppers' south pasture, slashed through the woods, where Junior had taken that final slide, and meandered into town. After a good rain, it bubbled noisily under the stone bridge on Gopher Hole Lane.

A half mile out of town it widened, cutting a rough circle out of rock and trees. There the water moved slow and easy and let the sunlight dance on it through the shelter of leaves in the summer. A man could find himself a comfortable rock and sink a line, and if he wasn't too drunk or stupid, take home trout for supper.

Beyond the fishing hole, the land started its jagged upward climb. There was a limestone quarry on the second ridge where Cam had worked for two sweaty, backbreaking summers. On hot nights kids would ride up there, mostly high on beer or pot, and dive off the rocks into the deep, still water below. In seventy-eight, after three kids had drowned, the quarry was fenced off and posted. Kids still dived into the quarry on hot summer nights. They just climbed the fence first.

Emmitsboro was too far from the interstate for much traffic, and being a two-hour drive from D.C., it had never qualified as one of the city's bedroom communities. The changes that took place were few and far between, which suited the residents just fine.

It boasted a hardware store, four churches, an American Legion post, and a clutch of antique shops. There was a market that had been run by the same family for four generations and a service station that had changed hands more times than Cam could count. A branch of the county library stood at the square and was open two afternoons a week and Saturday mornings. They had their own sheriff, two deputies, a mayor, and a town council.

In the summer the trees were leafy, and if you strolled in the shade, you smelled fresh-cut grass rather than exhaust. People took pride in their homes, and flower and kitchen gardens were in evidence in even the tiniest yards.

Come autumn, the surrounding mountains went wild with color, and the scent of wood-smoke and wet leaves filtered along the streets.

In the winter it was a postcard, a scene from *It's a Wonderful Life*, with snow banking the stone walls and Christmas lights burning for weeks.

From a cop's point of view, it was a cakewalk. The occasional vandalism—kids soaping windows or breaking them—traffic violations, the weekly drunk-and-disorderly or domestic dispute. In the years he had been back, Cam had dealt with one assault-and-battery, some petty theft, a half dozen malicious mischiefs, occasional bar fights, and a handful of DWI's.

Not even enough to fill one good night of work in Washington, D.C., where he'd been a cop for more than seven years.

When he'd made the decision to resign in

D.C. and return to Emmitsboro, his associates had told him he'd be back in six months, screaming with boredom. He had a reputation for being a real street cop, by turns icy and explosive, accustomed, even acclimated, to facing down junkies and dealers.

And he'd liked it, liked the feeling of walking on the edge, cruising the streets, sweeping up bits and pieces of human garbage. He'd made detective, an ambition he'd held secret inside him since the day he joined the force. And he'd stayed on the streets because he felt at home there, because he felt right.

But then, one dripping summer afternoon, he and his partner had chased a twenty-year-old petty dealer and his screaming hostage into a crumbling building in South East.

Everything had changed.

"Cameron?" A hand on Cam's shoulder broke him out of his reverie. He looked up at Emmitsboro's mayor.

"Mr. Atherton."

"Mind if I join you?" With a quick smile, James Atherton settled his long, thin body into the vinyl seat opposite Cam. He was a man of angles, with a bony, slightly melancholy face and pale blue eyes—an Ichabod Crane of a man— white, freckled skin, sandy hair, long neck, long limbs.

There was a ballpoint pen and a pair of wire-rimmed reading glasses in the pocket of his sports coat. He always wore sports coats and shiny black, laced shoes. Cam couldn't recall seeing Atherton in tennis shoes, or jeans or shorts. He was fifty-two and looked like what he was, a high school science teacher and public servant. He had been mayor of Emmitsboro, hardly a full-time job, since Cam was a teenager. It was an arrangement that suited Atherton and the town perfectly.

"Coffee?" Cam asked and automatically signaled for the waitress, though she was already heading their way, pot in hand.

"Thank you, Alice," Atherton said as she poured.

"Get you some breakfast, Mayor?"

"No, I had mine already." But he eyed the plastic cake plate on the counter. "Those doughnuts fresh?"

"Just this morning."

He gave a little sigh as he added cream and two whopping spoons of sugar to his coffee. "I don't suppose you've got any of those apple-filled—with the cinnamon on top?"

"Got one with your name on it." Alice gave him a wink and walked off to fetch the doughnut.

"No willpower," Atherton said as he took his first delicate sip of coffee. "Between you, me, and the gatepost, it frustrates the wife that I can eat like a horse and never put on weight."

"How is Mrs. Atherton?"

"Min's just fine. Got a bake sale going this morning over at the middle school. Trying to raise money for new band uniforms." After Alice set his doughnut in front of him, Atherton picked up a knife and fork. His napkin was spread neatly over his lap.

Cam had to smile. No slurping up sticky apple chunks for the mayor. Atherton's neatness was as dependable as a sunrise.

"Heard you had an unusual disturbance last night."

"A nasty one." Cam could still see the dark, gaping grave. He picked up his cooling coffee. "We took pictures last night and roped off the site. I drove by early this morning. The ground was hard and dry. No footprints. The place was neat as a pin."

"Kids, perhaps, playing an early Halloween prank?"

"My first thought," Cam admitted. "But it doesn't feel right. Kids aren't usually so tidy."

"It's unfortunate and upsetting." Atherton ate his doughnut in small bites, chewing and swallowing before speaking. "In a town like ours, we don't expect this kind of nonsense. The fact that it was an old grave and there are no relatives around to be affected helps, of course." Atherton set down his fork, dusted his fingers on his napkin, then picked up his cup. "In a few days, the talk will die down, and people will forget. But I wouldn't like to see such an incident repeated." He smiled then, just as he did when a slow student managed to cop an A. "I know you'll handle it all with discretion, Cameron. Just let me know if I can help in any way."

"I'll do that."

After taking out his wallet, Atherton drew two crisp, uncreased singles out, then tucked the corners under the empty plate. "I'll be on my way, then. I have to put in an appearance at the bake sale."

Cam watched him stroll out, exchange waves with a few pedestrians, and walk down Main.

He spent the rest of the day with paperwork and routine patrols. But before sundown, he drove out to the cemetery again. For nearly thirty minutes, he stayed there, brooding down at the small, empty grave.

Carly Jamison was fifteen and mad at the world. Her parents were the first focus of her disgust. They didn't understand what it was like to be young. They were so dull, living in their stupid house in stupid Harrisburg, Pennsylvania. Good old Marge and Fred, she thought with a snort as she shifted her backpack and walked backward, thumb stuck out jauntily, on the verge of Route 15 South.

Why don't you wear pretty clothes like your sister? Why don't you study and get good grades like your sister? Why can't you keep your room clean like your sister?

Fuck, fuck, fuck!

She hated her sister, too, picture-perfect Jennifer with her holier-than-thou attitude and preppy clothes. Jennifer the A student who was going to freaking Harvard on a freaking scholarship to study freaking medicine.

As her red Converse high tops scrunched over gravel, she imagined a doll with pale blond hair that fell into perfect curves around a perfect heart-shaped face. The baby blue eyes stared blankly, and there was a superior smile on the full, lovely mouth.

Hi, I'm Jennifer, the doll would say when you pulled the string. *I'm perfect. I do whatever I'm told and do it just right.*

Then Carly imagined dropping the doll off a high building and watching its perfect face smash onto the concrete.

Shit, she didn't want to be like Jennifer. Digging in the pocket of her girdle-tight jeans, she hooked a crumpled pack of cigarettes. One

Marlboro left, she thought in disgust. Well, she had a hundred and fifty dollars, and there was bound to be a store somewhere along the route.

She lit the cigarette with a red disposable Bic—red was her signature color—stuffed the lighter back in her pocket, and carelessly tossed the empty pack aside. She cursed halfheartedly at the cars that rumbled past her. Her luck at hitching rides had been pretty good so far, and since the day was cloudless and pleasantly cool, she didn't mind the walk.

She would hitch all the way to Florida, to Fort Lauderdale, where her asshole parents had refused to let her go to enjoy spring break. She was too young. She was always either too young or too old, depending on her parents' mood, to do whatever the hell it was she wanted.

Christ, they don't know anything, she thought, tossing her head so her spiky cap of scarlet hair ruffled around her face. The three earrings she wore in her left ear danced in mad circles.

She wore a denim jacket nearly covered with patches and pins, and a red T-shirt with a Bon Jovi decal splashed across her chest. Her tight jeans were slashed liberally at the knees. A dozen slim bracelets jangled on one arm. Two Swatch watches adorned the other.

She was five-four and a hundred and ten pounds. Carly was proud of her body, which had only really begun to blossom the year before. She liked to show it off in tight clothes that scandalized and enraged her parents. But it gave her pleasure. Particularly since Jennifer was thin and flat-chested. Carly considered it a major triumph that she had beat her sister at something, even if it was only bust size.

They thought she was sexually active, with Justin Marks, in particular, and watched her like ghouls. Just waiting for her to pop up and say, hey, I'm pregnant. Sexually active, she thought and snorted. That was the term they liked to use to show they were up-to-date.

Well, she hadn't let Justin do it to her yet— not that he didn't want to. She just wasn't ready for the big one. Maybe once she got to Florida, she'd change her mind.

Turning to walk forward for a while, she adjusted her prescription sunglasses. She hated the fact that she was nearsighted and lately had refused to wear corrective lenses unless they were tinted. Since she had lost two pairs of contacts, her parents had nixed the idea of buying her more.

So, she'd get her own, Carly thought. She'd get a job in Florida, and she wouldn't ever go back to pissy PA. She'd get some of those Durasoft ones that would turn her dumb hazel eyes into a perfect sky blue.

She wondered if they were looking for her yet. Probably not. What did they care anyway? They had Jennifer the Great. Her eyes watered, and she blinked back tears furiously. It didn't matter. The hell with all of them.

Fuck, fuck, fuck.

They would think she was in school being bored shitless with U.S. history. Who the fuck cared what old farts signed the Declaration of Independence? Today, she was signing her own. She'd never have to sit in a classroom again or listen to lectures on cleaning her room or turning down her music or not wearing so much makeup.

What's wrong with you, Carly? her mother would always ask. *Why do you act this way? I don't understand you.*

Damn straight she didn't understand. No one did.

Carly turned around, sticking her thumb out again. But she wasn't feeling so cheerful. She'd been on the road four hours, and her defiance was rapidly turning to self-pity. As a tractor-trailer zoomed by, kicking dust in her face, she briefly considered moving across the asphalt and heading north, and home again.

The hell with that, she thought, straightening her slumping shoulders. She wasn't going back. Let them come looking for her. She wanted so badly for them to come looking for her.

With a little sigh, she moved off the gravel onto the grassy slope, toward some shade, where she sat down. There was a rusty barbed-wire fence behind which cows lolled lazily. In her pack with her bikini, her Levi's wallet, hot pink shorts, and extra T-shirt was a duo of Hostess cupcakes. She ate both, licking the chocolate and filling from her fingers as she watched the cows graze.

She wished she'd thought to stick a couple of cans of Coke in the pack. As soon as she found some little hick town, she would buy some, and more Marlboros. Glancing at her watches, she saw that it was just past noon. The school cafeteria would be crowded and noisy now. She wondered what the other kids would think when they found out she'd hitched all the way to Florida. Man, they'd be green. It was probably the coolest thing she'd ever done. They'd really pay attention then. Everyone would pay attention.

She dozed awhile and woke cramped and groggy. After swinging on her pack, she tromped back to the edge of the road and cocked her thumb.

Christ, she was dying of thirst. Crumbs from the cupcakes seemed to be lodged like pebbles in her throat. And she wanted another smoke. Her spirits lifted a bit when she hiked past a sign.

EMMITSBORO 8 MILES

Sounded like Hicksboro, but as long as they sold Coke Classic and Marlboros, it was fine by her.

She was delighted when, in less than ten minutes, a pickup slowed and pulled over. Earrings and bracelets jangling, she trotted to the passenger door. The guy inside looked like a farmer. He had big hands with thick fingers and wore a baseball-style cap with some feed-and-grain store advertised over the bill. The truck smelled pleasantly of hay and animals.

"Thanks, mister." She hopped into the cab of the truck.

"Where you heading?"

"South," she told him. "Florida."

"Long trip." His gaze skimmed her backpack before he pulled out on the road again.

"Yeah." She shrugged. "Well."

"Going to visit relatives?"

"No. Just going." She shot him a defiant look, but he smiled.

"Yeah, I know how that is. I can take you as far as Seventy, but I got to make a stop first."

"Hey, that's cool." Pleased with herself, Carly settled back.

Deep in the woods, deep into the night, the cold, clear note of a bell sounded. As the moon rode high in a black sky, the circle of thirteen chanted. They sang a song of death.

The altar writhed and strained. Her vision was blurred because they'd taken away her glasses and given her some kind of injection when they'd tied her up. Her mind seemed to be floating up and down. But deep inside it, there was an ice-cold fear.

She knew she was naked, that her arms and legs were spread wide and tied down. But she didn't know where she was, and her groggy mind couldn't pin down how she had gotten there.

The man in the truck, she thought, straining. He'd picked her up. He'd been a farmer. Hadn't he? They'd stopped by his farm. She was almost sure of that. Then he'd turned on her. She'd fought him, but he'd been strong, awfully strong. Then he'd hit her with something.

The rest was all a blur. Being tied up in a dark place. How long had she been there? An hour, a day? Men coming, talking in whispers. Then the prick of a needle in her arm.

She was outside again. She could see the moon and the stars. She could smell smoke. It rolled in her head, as did the silver ring of the bell. And the chanting. She couldn't make out the words, foreign maybe. They didn't make sense.

She wept a little, wanting her mother.

She turned her head and saw the black-clad figures. They had animal heads, like something out of a horror movie. Or a dream. It was a dream, she promised herself as her eyes heated with tears. She'd wake up. Her mother would come in and wake her for school any minute, and all of this would go away.

It had to be a dream. She knew there were no such things as creatures with men's bodies and animals' heads. Monsters only existed in movies and stuff, the kind she and Sharie Murray rented for the VCR when they had a sleep-over.

The thing with the goat's head put a silver cup between her breasts. In her drugged state she wondered how it could be that she could actually feel the cold metal against her flesh. Did you feel things when you were dreaming?

He lifted his arms high, and his voice boomed inside her head. He placed a black candle between her thighs.

She began to cry hard now, afraid she wasn't dreaming. Yet everything was shifting in and out of focus, and the sounds seemed to come from very far away. There were shouts and wails and keening, much too human a sound to come from those horrible animal heads.

He tipped the cup over, pouring the liquid in it down her body. It smelled like blood. She whimpered. He was touching her, drawing signs on her body with the red liquid. She could see his eyes gleam in the goat's head as he began to do things to her with his all too human hands, things her mother had warned her would happen if she hitched rides and teased boys.

Even through her fear, she felt shame, a hot, liquid sensation in her belly.

Then they were naked, the men beneath the cloaks and the heads of goats and wolves and lizards.

Even before the first one crouched above her, his penis hard and ready, she knew she would be raped. At the first thrust, she screamed. And the sound echoed, mocking and hollow, through the trees.

They sucked at her blood-spattered breasts, making horrible grunting sounds as they lapped and suckled. She gagged and struggled weakly as her mouth was savagely raped. Growling and keening, they pinched and nipped and pumped.

They were wild, all of them, dancing and capering and groaning as each one took his turn with her. Heartless, heedless, even as her screams turned to sobs and sobs to mindless mewling.

She went under, to some deep, secret place where she could hide from all the pain and all the fear. Hiding there, she never saw the knife.

Chapter 3

THE GALLERY WAS PACKED. An hour after the opening of Clare's show, people streamed through the lofty, three-storied space. Not just people, Clare thought as she sipped champagne, but People. Those capital *P* sorts who would expand Angie's heart to the size of Kansas. Representatives from the business world, the art world, the theater, the literati, the glitterati. From Madonna to the mayor, they came to look, to comment, and apparently to buy.

Reporters schmoozed their way through, gulping canapés and French bubbly. That old standby, *Entertainment Tonight*, had sent a crew who even now were doing a stand-up in front of Clare's three-foot iron-and-bronze work titled *Return of Power*. Controversial, they called it, because of the blatant sexuality and overt feminism in its image of three women, naked and armed with lance, bow, and pike, circled around a kneeling man.

For Clare, it was simply a symbol of her own feelings after her divorce, when she had yearned for a weapon to strike back and had found none.

Representatives from *Museums and Art* were discussing a small copper work, spouting words like "esoteric" and "stratified."

As successes went, you couldn't get much higher.

Then why was she so depressed?

Oh, she did her part, smiling and chatting until she thought her face would crack like flawed marble. She'd even worn the dress Angie had chosen for her. A sleek and glittery black number that plunged to a deep, wide vee in the back and had a skirt so tight that she had to walk like one of those poor Chinese women when feet binding had been in fashion. She'd worn her hair very straight and added some chunky copper jewelry she had designed herself, on a whim.

She knew the image was arty and sexy, but at the moment she didn't feel either.

She felt, Clare realized, small town and dazzled. Dorothy would have felt the same way, she was sure, when her farmhouse dropped down into the middle of Munchkinland. And like Dorothy, she was plagued by a deep and terrible longing to go home. All the way home.

Clare struggled to shake the feeling off, sipping champagne and reminding herself this was the realization of a lifelong dream. She'd worked hard for it, just as Angie and Jean-Paul had worked hard to create an atmosphere where art would be appreciated—and purchased for great quantities of money.

The gallery itself was elegant, a perfect backdrop for art and for the beautiful people who came there. It was done in stark whites, with a floating staircase that led to a second floor, then a third. Everything was open and curved and fluid. From the high ceiling above dripped two modernistic crystal chandeliers. Each of her pieces was carefully spotlighted. Around them hovered people in diamonds or designer denim.

The rooms were choked with expensive scents, each one layered over the others until they merged into one exclusive fragrance. Wealth.

"Clare, my dear." Tina Yongers, an art critic Clare knew and loathed, weaved her way over. She was a tiny sprite of a woman with wispy blond hair and sharp green eyes. Though past fifty, surgical nips and tucks kept her hovering deceptively at fortysomething.

She was wearing a misty floral caftan that reached her ankles. The opulent scent of Poison surrounded her. An appropriate scent, Clare thought, since Tina's reviews were often deadly. She could, with the lifting of one platinum brow, squash an artistic ego like a beetle. It was no secret that she did so, habitually, for the lively sense of power it gave her.

She brushed a kiss through the air over Clare's cheek, then fervently gripped her forearms.

"You've outdone yourself, haven't you?"

Clare smiled and called herself a cynical hypocrite. "Have I?"

"Don't be modest—it's boring. It's obvious to everyone here that you're going to be *the* artist of the nineties. The *woman* artist." She tossed her head and gave a tinkling laugh for the benefit of the film crew. "I'm pleased to say that I was one of the first to recognize it, at your first show."

And for the glowing review she had expected countless favors, invitations, and free rides. It was business. Clare could almost hear Angie's voice in her ear. *We all play the game.*

"I appreciate your support, Tina."

"No need. I only support the best. If the work is inferior, I'm the first to say so." She smiled, showing off small, kitten teeth. "Like poor Craig's show last month. Miserable stuff, incredibly dreary, not a soupçon of originality. But this . . ." She tipped a ringed hand toward a sculpture in white marble. It was the head of a wolf, thrown back in mid-howl, fangs sharp and gleaming. Its shoulders, the mere hint of them, were undoubtedly human. "This is powerful."

Clare glanced at the piece. It was one of her nightmare works, inspired by her own frightening dreams. Abruptly chilled, she turned her back on it. Play the game, she ordered herself, then gulped down the rest of her wine before setting the glass aside.

For the life of her, she couldn't figure out why the wine and the compliments were making her tense. "Thanks, Tina. Angie will breathe a lot easier when I pass your opinions along."

"Oh, I'll relay them myself, never fear." She tapped a finger on Clare's wrist. "I'd like to speak to you, at a less chaotic time, about addressing my art group."

"Of course," she said, though she hated public speaking even more than she hated interviews. "Give me a call." Maybe I can have my number changed first.

"Be sure that I will. Congratulations, Clare."

Clare took a step back, intending to slip off to Angie's private office for a moment of solitude. She bumped solidly into someone behind her.

"Oh, I'm sorry," she began as she turned. "It's so close in— Blair!" With her first genuine emotion of the evening, she threw her arms around him. "You came! I was afraid you wouldn't make it."

"Not make my sister's glitzy party?"

"It's an art showing."

"Yeah." He let his gaze skim the room. "Says who?"

"Thank God you're here." She grabbed his arm. "Come with me. And whatever you do, don't look back."

"Hey," he said when she'd dragged him outside, "the champagne's in there."

"I'll buy you a case." Ignoring the limo at her disposal, she hustled him down the street. Four blocks away, she walked into a deli, drawing in the scents of corned beef, pickles, and garlic.

"Thank you, God," Clare murmured and rushed over to the counter to stare at the display of potato salad, pickled eggs, smoked sturgeon, and blintzes.

Ten minutes later, they were sitting at a scarred linoleum table eating thick slabs of pumpernickel stuffed with layers of pastrami and Swiss.

"I bought a new suit and hopped a shuttle to sit in a deli and eat kosher pickles and cold meat?"

"We'll go back if you want," Clare said with her mouth full. "I had to get out for a minute."

"It's your show," he pointed out.

"Yeah. But is my sculpture on display, or am I?"

"Okay, kid." Leaning back in his chair, he crunched on a potato chip. "What gives?"

She was silent a moment, working it through. She hadn't realized just how much she'd needed to escape until she saw Blair, standing there, so real and solid, amid all the glitter and paste.

He was only slightly taller than she. His hair had darkened with age to a deep, reddish blond, and he combed it straight back from his face. He put many women in mind of a young Robert Redford, a fact that constantly embarrassed him. He'd never been conceited about his looks. Blair understood the frustration many beautiful women felt when they were categorized as brainless sex objects.

He had, despite the fact that he looked naive, pretty, and five years younger than his age, managed to claw his way up the journalism ladder. He was a political reporter for the *Washington Post*.

He was, Clare knew, sensible, logical, and earthbound, the direct opposite of her own personality. But there was no one with whom she felt more comfortable sharing her innermost thoughts.

"How's Mom?"

Blair sipped at his cream soda. He knew his twin would circle around whatever problem she had until she felt ready to dive into it. "She's good. I got a postcard the other day from Madrid. Didn't you get one?"

"Yeah." Clare nibbled at her sandwich. "She

and Jerry seem to be having the time of their lives."

"Honeymoons are supposed to be fun." He leaned forward, touched her hand. "She needs Jerry, Clare. She loves him and deserves some happiness."

"I know. I know." Impatient with herself, she pushed the plate aside and reached for a cigarette. Her appetite seemed to vacillate as quickly as her moods these days. "In my head I do. She worked hard after Daddy—after he died, to keep the family together, to keep the business from going under. And to keep herself sane, I guess. I know all that," she repeated, rubbing at her temple. "I know."

"But?"

She shook her head. "Jerry's a good guy. I like him, really. He's funny and he's sharp, and he's obviously crazy about Mom. It's not as if we're kids, wondering whether he's trying to take Daddy's place."

"But?"

"I keep feeling like he's taking Daddy's place." She laughed and drew deeply on the cigarette. "That's not really it, or not all of it. Christ, Blair, it just seems like we're so scattered now, so separate. Mom off in Europe for weeks on her honeymoon, you in D.C., me here. I keep thinking of the way it was before we lost Dad."

"That was a long time ago."

"I know. Jesus, I know." With her free hand she began to ball and unball her napkin. She wasn't certain she had the words. It was often easier to express emotions with steel and solder. "It's only that—well, even after . . . when it was only the three of us . . ." She shut her eyes a moment. "It was tough, the shock of the accident, then all that business about kickbacks and collusion and under-the-table deals for the shopping center. One minute we're a nice happy family, and the next Dad is dead and we're in the middle of a scandal. But we held on so tight, maybe too tight, then boom, we're scattered."

"I'm only a phone call away, Clare. An hour by plane."

"Yeah. I don't know what it is, Blair. Everything was going along just dandy. My work's great. I love what I'm doing—I love my life. And then . . . I had the dream again."

"Oh." He took her hand again, holding it this time. "I'm sorry. Want to talk about it?"

"The dream?" In jerky motions she tapped the cigarette out in a gaudy metal ashtray. She had never talked about the details, not even with him. Only the fear of it. "No, it's the same. Pretty awful when it's happening, but then it fades. Only this time, I haven't been able to get back into the groove. I've been working, but my heart doesn't seem to be in it, and it shows. I keep thinking about Dad, and the house, and,

Christ, Mrs. Negley's little black poodle. French toast at Martha's Diner after church on Sunday." She took a deep breath. "Blair, I think I want to go home."

"Home? To Emmitsboro?"

"Yes. Look, I know you told me you were in the middle of interviewing new tenants for the house, but you could hold off. Mom wouldn't care."

"No, of course she wouldn't." He saw her strain, felt it in the restless movements of her hand in his. "Clare, it's a long way from New York to Emmitsboro. I'm not talking about miles."

"I've already made the trip once."

"From there to here. Going back is a whole different thing. You haven't been there in . . ."

"Nine years," she told him. "Almost ten. I guess it was easier to just keep going after we started college. Then with Mom deciding to move to Virginia, there didn't seem to be any reasons to go back." She broke off a corner of her sandwich, eating more from nerves than hunger now. "But at least she kept the house."

"It's a good investment. Mortgage-free, low taxes. The rental income is—"

"Do you really believe that's the only reason she didn't sell? For rental income?"

Blair looked down at their joined hands. He wished he could tell her yes so that she might look for her peace of mind in the future instead of in the past. His own wounds were healed, but they could throb at unexpected moments, reminding him of his father's dishonesty and his own painful disillusionment.

"No. There are memories there, most of them good. I'm sure all of us feel an attachment."

"Do you?" she asked quietly.

His eyes met hers. There was understanding in them and the remnants of pain. "I haven't forgotten him, if that's what you mean."

"Or forgiven?"

"I've learned to live with it," he said briefly. "We all have."

"I want to go back, Blair. Though I'm not entirely sure why, I need to go back."

He hesitated, wanting to argue. Then with a shrug he gave it up. "Look, the house is empty. You could move in tomorrow if you want, but I'm not sure it's a good idea to go walking down memory lane if you're already feeling low."

"Like you said, most of the memories are good. Maybe it's time to deal with the bad ones."

"Still seeing that shrink, are you?"

She smiled a little. "Off and on. But my real therapy's work, and I don't seem able to work here anymore. I want to go home, Blair. That's the only thing I'm sure of."

★ ★ ★

"When's the last time you drove a car?" Angie demanded.

Clare loaded the last suitcase into the back of her brand-new Z, slammed down the hatch, and stood back. As cars went, this one was a work of art. "What?" she said as she noted Angie was tapping a foot, this time encased in teal blue snakeskin.

"I said, when was the last time you drove a car?"

"Oh, a couple of years ago. She's a honey, isn't she?" Affectionately, Clare stroked the shiny red fender.

"Oh, sure, a real honey. That's a five-speed in there, isn't it? And that speedometer goes up to about one-sixty. You haven't been behind the wheel in two years, then you go out and buy a machine with fangs?"

"I suppose you'd be happier if I'd bought a pokey old station wagon."

"I'd be happier if you'd unload that monster and get back upstairs where you belong."

"Angie, we've been round and round this for a week."

"And it still doesn't make any sense." Exasperated, Angie paced down the sidewalk and back again, instinctively avoiding the disaster of snagging her two-hundred-dollar heels in the cracks. "Girl, you can hardly remember to tie your shoelaces, how are you going to get this rocket launcher all the way to Maryland?"

"Didn't I mention the automatic pilot?" When Angie failed to see the humor, Clare took her by the shoulders and shook. "Stop worrying, will you! I'm a big girl. I'm going to go spend the next six months or so in a quiet little town with two stoplights, where the biggest crime problem is kids stealing lawn art from the neighboring yard."

"And what the hell are you supposed to do in a place like that?"

"Work."

"You can work here! Christ Almighty, Clare, you've got the critics eating out of your hand after the show. You can name your own price. If you need a vacation, take a cruise, fly to Cancun or Monte Carlo for a few weeks. What the hell's in Emmitsburg?"

"*Boro*. Emmitsboro. Peace, quiet, tranquility." Neither of them turned a hair when a cab driver jumped out of his hack and began screaming obscenities at another driver. "I need a change, Angie. Everything I've worked on in the last month is garbage."

"That's bull."

"You're my friend, and a good one, but you're also an art dealer. Be honest."

Angie opened her mouth but at Clare's steady stare let out only an impatient hiss of breath.

"Well, that's honest," Clare mumbled.

"If you haven't been producing your best work for the past couple of weeks, it's only because you've been pushing too hard. Everything you finished for the show was fabulous. You just need some time off."

"Maybe. Take my word for it, it's really tough to push too hard in Emmitsboro. Which is," she added, holding up a hand before Angie could argue, "only a five-hour drive. You and Jean-Paul can come down and check on me any time you like."

Angie backed off only because she knew there was no shaking Clare once her mind was set. "You'll call."

"I'll call, I'll write, I'll send up smoke signals. Now say good-bye."

Angie searched her brain for one final argument, but Clare simply stood smiling at her, in baggy jeans, screaming green high tops, and a purple sweatshirt with a huge yellow question mark down the front. Tears burned the backs of Angie's eyes as she held out her arms.

"Damn it, I'm going to miss you."

"I know, me too." She hugged Angie hard, drawing in the familiar scent of the Chanel that had been Angie's trademark since their art school days. "Look, I'm not joining the Foreign

Legion." She started around the car, then stopped and swore. "I forgot my purse, it's up-stairs. Don't say a word," she warned as she loped toward the entrance door.

"That girl will probably make a wrong turn and end up in Idaho," Angie muttered.

Five hours later, Clare was indeed lost. She knew she was in Pennsylvania—the signs said so. But how she had gotten there, when she should have been cutting through Delaware, she couldn't say. Determined to make the best of it, she stopped at a McDonald's and feasted on a quarter-pounder with cheese, large fries, and a Coke while she pored over her road map.

She figured out where she was well enough, but how she'd arrived there remained a mystery. Still, that was behind her now. Nibbling on a fry soaked in salt and catsup, she traced her route. All she had to do was get on that squiggly blue line and take it to that red one, turn right and keep going. True, she had added hours to her trip, but she wasn't on a deadline. Her equipment would be trucked down the next day. If worse came to worst, she could just pull off at a handy motel and get a fresh start in the morning.

Ninety minutes later, through blind luck, she found herself heading south on 81. She'd trav-

eled that route before, with her father, when
he'd gone to check out property on the Pennsylvania border, and with her family, when they'd
spent a weekend visiting relatives in Allentown.
Sooner or later, the route would take her into
Hagerstown, and from there, even with her
sense of direction, she would find her way.

It felt good to be behind the wheel. Though
it was true enough that the car seemed to have a
life of its own. She enjoyed the way it skimmed
the road, hugged the turns. Now that she was
driving, she wondered how she had managed to
do without the simple pleasure of being the captain of her own ship for so long.

An excellent analogy for marriage and divorce. Nope. She shook her head and drew a
deep breath. She wouldn't think of that.

The stereo was first class, and she had the volume up high. It had been too cool to remove
the T-tops—and her luggage took up all the
trunk space, in any case. But her windows were
down all the way so that a bouncy Pointer Sisters classic streamed out into the air. Her clutch
foot tapped in time on the floorboards.

She already felt better, more herself, more in
control. The fact that the sun was dropping low
and the shadows lengthening didn't concern
her. After all, spring was in the air. Daffodils and
dogwoods were blooming. And she was going
home.

On 81 South, halfway between Carlisle and Shippensburg, the sleek little car shuddered, hesitated, and stopped dead.

"What the hell?" Baffled, she sat, listening to the blaring music. Her eyes narrowed when she spotted the light on the dash with its symbol of a gas pump. "Shit."

Just after midnight, she made the last turn for Emmitsboro. The pack of teenagers who had stopped as she'd been pushing the Z to the shoulder of the road had been so impressed with her car that they'd all but begged her for the honor of procuring her a gallon of gas.

Then, of course, she'd felt obliged to let them sit in the car, discuss the car, stroke the car. The memory made her grin. She'd like to think if she'd been an ugly little man in a beat-up Ford, they'd have been just as helpful. But she doubted it.

In any case, her five-hour drive had taken nearly double that, and she was tired. "Almost there, baby," she murmured to the car. "Then I'm going to crawl into my sleeping bag and check out for eight hours."

The rural road was dark, her headlights the only relief. There wasn't another car in sight, so she hit the high beams. She could see fields on either side of the road. The shadow of a silo, the glint of moonlight on the aluminum roof of a barn. With the windows down, she could hear the song of peepers and crickets, a high-pitched symphony under a bright full moon. After what seemed like a lifetime in New York, the humming country silence was eerie.

She shivered once, then laughed at herself. Serene, the word was serene. But she turned up the radio a bit louder.

Then she saw the sign, the same tidy billboard that had sat on the side of the two-lane country road as long as she could remember.

WELCOME TO EMMITSBORO
Founded 1782

With a surge of excitement, she turned left, bumped over the stone bridge, then followed the lazy curve of the road that led into town.

No streetlights, no neon, no gangs posturing on street corners. It was barely midnight, but most of Emmitsboro was asleep. By the glow of the moon and her car's headlights, she could see the dark buildings—the market, its big plate glass windows blank, the parking lot empty; Miller's Hardware, its sign freshly painted, the shutters drawn. Across the street was the big brick house that had been converted into three apartment units when she was a girl. A light shone in the top window, faint and yellow behind its shade.

Houses, most of them old and built well off the road. Low stone walls and high curbs. Then a clutter of small businesses and more converted apartments with concrete or wooden porches and aluminum awnings.

Now the park. She could almost see the ghost of the child she had been, running toward the empty swings that moved a bit in the easy wind.

More houses, one or two with a light burning, most dark and silent. The occasional glare of a television against window glass. Cars parked against the curb. They would be unlocked, she thought, as the doors of most of the houses would be.

There was Martha's Diner, the bank, the sheriff's office. She remembered how Sheriff Parker had sat outside on the stoop, smoking Camels and keeping a beady eye on law and order. Did he still? she wondered. Did Maude Poffenburger still stand behind the counter at the post office, dispensing stamps and opinions? Would she still find old men playing checkers in the park and kids running across to Abbot's General Store for Popsicles and Milky Ways?

Or had it all changed?

In the morning would she wake up and find this vital slice of her childhood was now inhabited by strangers? Clare shook the idea away and drove slowly, drinking up memories like cool, clean wine.

More neat yards, daffodils bobbing, azaleas in bud. At Oak Leaf, she turned left. No shops here, only quiet homes and the occasional restless barking of a dog. She came to the corner of Mountain View and pulled into the sloping driveway her father had resurfaced every third year.

She'd traveled almost the length of town without passing another car.

Climbing out with the nightsong cheerful around her, she moved slowly, wanting to savor. The garage door had to be lifted by hand. No one had ever bothered to install one of those handy remotes. It opened with a loud keening of metal.

It wouldn't disturb the neighbors, she thought. The closest one was across the wide street and screened by a neat bayberry hedge. She went back to her idling car and pulled it inside.

She could have gone directly into the house from there, through the door that would lead into the laundry room, then the kitchen. But she wanted to make her entry more of an event.

Coming outside again, she lowered the garage door, then walked all the way down to the sloping sidewalk to look at the house.

She forgot her sleeping bag, her luggage, and

remembered her purse only because it held the keys to the front and back doors. Memories flooded her as she climbed the concrete steps from sidewalk to yard. The hyacinths were blooming. She could smell them, sweet and heartbreakingly fragile.

She stood on the flagstone walkway and looked at the house of her youth. It was three stories of wood and stone. Always the wood had been painted white with blue trim. The wide covered porch, or veranda, as her mother had called it, had open latticework at the eaves and long, slender columns. The porch swing, where she had spent so many summer evenings, was still there, at the end of the porch. Her father had always planted sweet peas nearby so that their spicy fragrance would reach out to you as you glided and dreamed.

Emotions, both pleasant and painful, choked her as she set the key in the old brass lock. The door opened with a creak and a groan.

She wasn't afraid of ghosts. If there were any here, they would be friendly. As if to welcome them, she stood in the dark for a full minute.

She turned on the hall light and watched it bounce and glare off the freshly painted walls and polished oak floor. Blair had already arranged for the house to be readied for new tenants, though he hadn't suspected that the tenant would be his sister.

It was so odd to see it empty. Somehow, she'd thought she would step inside and find it exactly as it had been, unchanged by the years—as if she'd walked home from school rather than returned after a long journey into adulthood.

For a moment she saw it as it had been, the pretty drop-leaf table against the wall holding a green glass bowl full of violets. The antique mirror over it, its brass frame gleaming. The many-armed coatrack in the corner. The long, slender oriental carpet over the wide-planked floor. The little hodgepodge shelf that held her mother's collection of porcelain thimbles.

But when she blinked, the hall was bare, with only a lone spider silently building a web in the corner.

Clutching her purse, she moved from room to room. The big front parlor, the den, the kitchen.

The appliances were new, she noted. Sparkling and ivory against the navy ceramic counters and the sky blue floor. She did not step out onto the terrace—she wasn't ready for that—but instead turned and walked down the hall to the stairs.

Her mother had always kept the newel post and railing polished to a gleam. The old mahogany was smooth as silk with age—countless palms and youthful bottoms had brushed over it.

She found her room, the first off the hall to

the right, where she had dreamed the dreams of childhood and adolescence. She had dressed for school there, shared secrets with friends, built her fantasies, and wept away her disappointments.

How could she have known that it would be so painful to open the door and find the room empty? As if nothing she had ever done within those walls had left a mark? She turned off the light but left the door open.

Directly across the hall was Blair's old room, where he had once hung posters of his heroes. Superman to Brooks Robinson, Brooks to John Lennon. There was the guest room her mother had furnished with eyelet lace and satin pillows. Granny, her father's mother, had stayed there for a week the year before she had died of a stroke.

Here was the bath with its pedestal sink and its soft green and white checkerboard tiles. Throughout their teens she and Blair had fought over possession of that room like dogs over a meaty bone.

Going back into the hall, she turned into the master bedroom, where her parents had slept and loved and talked night after night. Clare remembered sitting on the pretty pink and lavender rug, watching her mother use all the fascinating bottles and pots on the cherry vanity. Or studying her father as he'd stared into the cheval mirror, struggling to knot his tie. The room had always smelled of wisteria and Old Spice. Somehow, it still did.

Half-blind with grief, she stumbled into the master bath to turn on the faucet and splash her face with water. Maybe she should have taken it a room at a time, she thought. One room a day. With her hands pressed on the sides of the sink, she looked up and faced herself in the glass.

Too pale, she thought. Shadows under her eyes. Her hair was a mess. But then, it usually was since she was too lazy for hairdressers and almost always chopped away at it herself. She'd lost an earring somewhere, she noted. Or had forgotten to put it on in the first place.

She started to dry her face with her sleeve, remembered the jacket was suede, and decided to dig in her purse for a tissue. But she'd set it down somewhere along the tour.

"Doing great so far," she murmured to her reflection and nearly jolted at the echo of her own voice. "This is where I want to be," she said more firmly. "Where I have to be. But it's not going to be as easy as I thought."

Brushing away the excess water on her face with her hands, she turned away from the glass. She would go down, get her sleeping bag, and tune out for the night. She was tired and overemotional. In the morning she would go through the house again and see what she needed to make her stay more pleasant.

Just as she stepped back into her parents' bedroom, she heard the creak and groan of the front door.

Panic came first, quick and instinctive. Her always vivid imagination conjured up a pack of roving convicts newly escaped from the correctional institution that was only twenty miles away. She was alone, in an empty house, and for the life of her, she couldn't remember one move she'd learned in the self-defense course she and Angie had taken two years before.

Pressing both hands to her heart, she reminded herself she was in Emmitsboro. Convicts didn't tend to roam the streets of tiny rural communities. She took a step forward and heard the creak on the stairs.

Yes, they did, she thought again. Anyone who had ever watched a B movie knew that convicts and psychos always headed for out-of-the-way towns and quiet villages to spread their mayhem.

In the empty room, she looked around wildly for a weapon. There wasn't even a ball of dust. Heart thudding, she searched her jacket pockets and came up with three pennies, a half roll of Lifesavers, a broken comb, and her keys.

Brass knuckles, she thought, remembering how she'd been instructed to hold the keys with the pointed ends sticking out between the fingers of a closed fist. And the best defense was a good offense. So saying, she jumped forward toward the door, letting loose with the most hideous shriek she could summon.

"Jesus!" Cameron Rafferty stumbled back a step, one hand reaching for his weapon, the other gripping the flashlight like a club. He saw a woman with wild red hair and a kelly green suede jacket come leaping at him. He ducked her swing, tossed an arm around her waist, and used his weight to overbalance both of them. They landed with a thud on the hardwood floor.

"Bruno!" Clare shouted, inspired and terrified. "Someone's in the house! Bring the gun!" As she yelled, she tried to bring her knee up between her attacker's thighs and nearly succeeded.

Winded, Cam struggled to pin her arms above her head. "Hold on." He swore as she tried to take a bite out of him. "I said hold on. I'm the police. I said I'm the goddamn police."

It finally got through. She subsided enough to look at his face in the slant of light from the bedroom. She saw dark hair, a little curly, a little too long, the stubble of a beard over tanned skin that stretched taut over excellent cheekbones. A good mouth, she thought, artist to the last. Nice eyes, though in the dark she couldn't be sure of their color. There was a light scent of sweat about him, clean, clear sweat, not at all offensivc. His body, pressed hard into hers to keep her still, felt lean and muscled.

He didn't seem like a psychotic or a crazed felon. But . . .

She took her survey while she fought to regain her breath. "The police?"

"That's right."

Though she was flat on her back, she gained some satisfaction from the fact that he was breathless. "I want to see your badge."

He was still cautious. Though his grip on her wrist had caused her to drop the lethal keys, she still had nails and teeth. "I'm wearing it. At this rate, it should be imprinted on your chest."

Under different circumstances, she might have been amused by the exasperation in his voice. "I want to see it."

"Okay. I'm going to move, slowly." He was as good as his word. His eyes never left hers as he shifted back and dropped one hand to the badge pinned to his shirt.

Clare flicked a glance over the metal star. "I can buy one of those in the dimestore."

"I.D.'s in my wallet. Okay?"

She nodded, watching him as carefully as he watched her. With two fingers, he reached in his hip pocket and flipped open a wallet. Clare inched back, then reached out. She tilted the wallet toward the spill of light. She read the laminated identification, frowned at the name and picture.

"Cameron Rafferty?" She looked up at him then, squinting in the dark. "You're Cameron Rafferty?"

"That's right. I'm the sheriff here."

"Oh, God." She giggled, surprising him. "Then pigs must be flying." She laughed until tears ran down her cheeks. Baffled, Cam shined his light in her face. "Take a good look," she invited. "Come on, Rafferty, don't you recognize me?"

He played the light over her features. It was her eyes, gold and glowing with unholy amusement, that jogged his memory. "Clare? Clare Kimball?" He gave a shout of laughter. "I'll be a sonofabitch."

"Yeah, that's the truth."

He grinned at her. "Well, welcome home, Slim."

Chapter 4

"So HOW THE HELL are you, Clare?"

They were sitting on the front porch steps drinking two of the lukewarm Becks that Clare had picked up during her meanderings through Pennsylvania. Relaxed, she moved her shoulders as she tipped the bottle back. The beer and the cool night eased the driving kinks.

"I'm pretty good." She leveled her gaze to the badge on his shirt. Her eyes glowed with humor. "Sheriff."

Cam stretched out his booted feet, then crossed them. "I take it Blair didn't mention I'd moved into Parker's old job."

"Nope." She sipped again, then gestured with the bottle. "Brothers never tell their sisters the interesting gossip. It's the law."

"I'll write that down."

"So where is Parker? Spinning in his grave because it killed him to see you sitting in his chair?"

"Florida." He pulled out a pack of cigarettes and offered her one. "Took off his badge, packed up, and headed south." When he flicked on his lighter, Clare leaned over and touched the tip of her cigarette to the flame. In the glow they studied each other's faces.

"Just like that?" she said, expelling smoke.

"Yeah. I heard about the job and decided to give it a shot."

"You were living in D.C., right?"

"That's right."

Clare leaned back against the stair rail, her eyes amused and measuring. "A cop. I always figured Blair was pulling my chain. Who would have figured Cameron 'Wild Man' Rafferty on the side of law and order?"

"I always liked to do the unexpected." His eyes stayed on hers as he lifted his bottle and drank. "You look good, Slim. Real good."

She wrinkled her nose at the old nickname. While it didn't carry the same sting as some of the others—Beanpole, String, Gnat Ass—that had clung to her during her youth, it did remind her of the days when she had stuffed her woefully underfilled bra with tissues and consumed gallons of Weight-On.

"You don't have to sound so surprised."

"The last time I saw you you were what? Fifteen, sixteen?"

The autumn after her father had died, she thought. "About."

"You grew up nice." During their brief wrestling match inside, he'd noticed that while she was still on the skinny side she'd rounded out here and there. Despite the changes, she was still Blair Kimball's sister, and Cam couldn't resist teasing her. "You're painting or something, right?"

"I sculpt." She flipped her cigarette away. It was one of her pet peeves that so many people thought all artists were painters.

"Yeah, I knew it was some arty type thing up in New York. Blair mentioned it. So do you sell stuff—like birdbaths?"

Miffed, she studied his bland smile. "I said I was an artist."

"Yeah." All innocence, he sipped his beer while crickets chorused around them. "This guy I knew was really good at making birdbaths. He used to make this one with a fish on it—a carp, I think—and the water would come out the carp's mouth and fill the bowl."

"Oh, I see. Class work."

"You bet. He sold a bundle of them."

"Good for him. I don't work in concrete." She couldn't help it—it irked her that he wouldn't have heard of her work or seen her name. "I guess you guys don't get *People* or *Newsweek* around here."

"Get *Soldier of Fortune*," he said, tongue in cheek. "That's real popular." He watched her take another chug of beer. Her mouth, and he still remembered her mouth, was full and wide. Yeah, she'd grown up nice all right. Who would have thought that shy and skinny Clare Kimball would turn into the long, sexy woman sitting across from him. "Heard you were married."

"For a while." She shrugged off the memory. "Didn't work out. How about you?"

"No. Never made it. Came close once." He thought of Mary Ellen with a trace of sweet regret. "I guess some of us do better single file." He drained the beer and set the empty bottle on the step between them.

"Want another?"

"No, thanks. Wouldn't do to have one of my own deputies pick me up DWI. How's your mother?"

"She got married," Clare said flatly.

"No kidding? When?"

"Couple of months ago." Restless, she shifted and stared out at the dark, empty street. "How about your parents, do they still have the farm?"

"Most of it." Even after all these years, he couldn't think of his stepfather as a parent. Biff Stokey had never and would never replace the father Cam had lost at the tender age of ten. "They had a couple of bad years and sold off some acreage. Could have been worse. Old man Hawbaker had to sell off his whole place. They subdivided it and planted modulars instead of corn and hay."

Clare brooded into the last of her beer. "It's funny, when I was driving through town I kept thinking nothing had changed." She glanced back up. "I guess I didn't look close enough."

"We still have Martha's, the market, Dopper's Woods, and Crazy Annie."

"Crazy Annie? Does she still carry a burlap sack and scout the roadside for junk?"

"Every day. She must be sixty now. Strong as an ox even if she does have a few loose boards in the attic."

"The kids used to tease her."

"Still do."

"You gave her rides on your motorcycle."

"I liked her." He stretched once, lazily, then unfolded himself to stand at the base of the steps. Looking at her now, with the dark house brooding behind her, he thought she seemed lonely and a little sad. "I've got to get on. Are you going to be all right here?"

"Sure, why not?" She knew he was thinking of the attic room where her father had taken his final drink and final leap. "I've got a sleeping bag, some groceries, and the better part of a

six-pack of beer. That'll do me fine until I lo-
cate a couple of tables, a lamp, a bed."

His eyes narrowed. "You're staying?"

It wasn't precisely a welcome she heard in his
voice. She stood and kept to the stairs where
she was a head taller than he. "Yes, I'm staying.
At least for a few months. Is that a problem,
Sheriff?"

"No—not for me." He rocked back on his
heels, wondering why she looked so edgily defiant with the gingerbread veranda at her back.
"I guess I figured you were passing through or
opening the place up for new tenants."

"You thought wrong. I'm opening it up
for me."

"Why?"

She reached down and gathered up both
empty bottles by the neck. "I could have asked
you the same question. But I didn't."

"No, you didn't." He glanced at the house behind her, big and empty and whispering with
memories. "I guess you've got your reasons."
He smiled at her again. "See you around, Slim."

She waited until he got in his car and pulled
away. Reasons she had, Clare brooded. She
just wasn't completely certain what they were.
Turning, she carried the bottles into the empty
house.

★ ★ ★

By two o'clock the next afternoon, everyone in town knew that Clare Kimball was back. They talked about it over the counter in the post office, as sales were rung up in the market, while ham sandwiches and bean soup were consumed in Martha's Diner. The fact that the Kimball girl was back in town, back in the house on the corner of Oak Leaf Lane, touched off new gossip and speculation on the life and death of Jack Kimball.

"Sold me my house," Oscar Roody said as he slurped up soup. "Gave me a fair deal, too. Alice, how 'bout some more coffee down here?"

"That wife of his had one fine pair of legs." Less Gladhill leered, pushing back on the counter stool to get a load of Alice's. "Mighty fine pair. Never could figure why the man took to drinking when he had such a spiffy wife."

"Irish." Oscar pounded a fist on his chest and brought up a rumbling belch. "They gotta drink—it's in the blood. That girl of his is some kind of artist. Probably drinks like a fish too, *and* smokes drugs." He shook his head and slurped some more. He figured it was drugs, plain and simple, that was screwing up the country he'd fought for in Korea. Drugs and homos. "She was a nice girl once," he added, already condemning her for her choice of career. "Skinny as a rail and funny-looking, but a nice little girl. Was her who found Jack dead."

"Musta been a messy sight," Less put in.

"Oh, it was." Oscar nodded wisely, as if he'd been on the scene at the moment of impact. "Cracked his head clean open, blood everywhere where he'd stuck himself on that pile of garden stakes. Went right clean through him, you know. Speared him like a trout." Bean soup dripped on his grizzled chin before he swiped at it. "Don't think they ever got the blood all the way out of them flagstones."

"Haven't you two got anything better to talk about?" Alice Crampton topped off their coffee cups.

"You went to school with her, didn't you, Alice?" Kicking back in the stool, Less took out a pack of Drum and began to roll a cigarette with his stained and clever mechanic's fingers. A few flakes of tobacco drifted down to his khaki work pants as he let his gaze perch like a hungry bird on Alice's breasts.

"Yeah, I went to school with Clare—and her brother." Ignoring Less's glittery eyes, she picked up a damp cloth and began to wipe the counter. "They had brains enough to get out of this town. Clare's famous. Probably rich, too."

"Kimballs always had money." Oscar pushed back his frayed and battered cap with its lettered ROODY PLUMBING just above the brim. A few of the gray hairs he had left kinked out from below the sides. "Made a bundle on that sonofabitching shopping center. That's why Jack killed himself."

"The police said it was an accident," Alice reminded him. "And all that stuff happened more than ten years ago. People should forget it."

"Nobody forgets gettin' screwed," Less said with a wink. "Especially if they was screwed good." He tapped his cigarette into the thick glass ashtray and imagined putting it to the wide-hipped Alice right there on the lunch counter. "Old Jack Kimball pulled a fast shuffle with that land deal, all right, then he suicided himself." His mouth left a wet ring at the base of the rolled paper. He spat out a couple more flakes of tobacco that clung to his tongue. "Wonder how the girl feels about staying in the house where her daddy took his last jump. Hey, Bud." He waved with his cigarette as Bud Hewitt walked into the diner.

Alice automatically reached for a fresh cup and the pot.

"No, thanks, Alice, haven't got time." Trying to look official, Bud nodded to both men at the counter. "We just got this picture in this morning." He opened a manila folder. "Name's Carly Jamison, fifteen-year-old runaway from up in Harrisburg. She's been missing for about a week. She was spotted hitching south on Fifteen. Either one of you see her on the road, or around town?"

Both Oscar and Less leaned over the picture of a young, sulky-faced girl with dark, tumbled hair. "Can't recollect seeing her," Oscar said finally, and worked out another satisfying belch. "Would've if she'd come around here. Can't hide a new face in this town for long."

Bud turned the photo so Alice could get a good look. "She didn't come in here during my shift. I'll ask Molly and Reva."

"Thanks." The scent of coffee—and Alice's perfume—was tempting, but he remembered his duty. "I'll be showing the picture around. Let me know if you spot her."

"Sure will." Less crushed out his cigarette. "How's that pretty sister of yours, Bud?" He spat out a flake of tobacco, then licked his lips. "You gonna put in a good word for me?"

"If I could think of one."

This caused Oscar to choke over his coffee and slap his knee. With a good-humored grin, Less turned back to Alice as Bud walked out. "How about a piece of that lemon pie?" He winked, as his fantasies worked back to humping and pumping on Alice amid the bottles of catsup and mustard. "I like mine firm and tart."

Across town, Clare was polishing off the last of her supply of Ring-Dings while she turned the two-car garage into a studio. Mouth full of chocolate, she unpacked the fire bricks for her welding table. The ventilation would be good, she thought. Even when she wanted to close the garage doors, she had the rear window. Right now it was propped open with one of her ball-peen hammers.

She'd piled scrap metal in the corner and had shoved, pushed, and dragged a worktable beside it. She figured it would take her weeks to unpack and organize her tools, so she would work with the chaos she was used to.

In her own way, she was organized. Clay and stone were on one side of the garage, wood-blocks on another. Because her favored medium was metal, this took up the lion's share of space. The only thing that was missing, she thought, was a good, ear-busting stereo. And she would soon see to that.

Satisfied, she started across the concrete floor to the open laundry-room door. There was a mall only a half hour away that would supply a range of music equipment, and a pay phone where she could call and arrange for her own telephone service. She'd call Angie, too.

It was then she saw the group of women, marching like soldiers, Clare thought with a flutter of panic. Up her driveway, two by two. And all carrying covered dishes. Though she told herself it was ridiculous, her mouth went dry at the thought of Emmitsboro's version of the Welcome Wagon.

"Why, Clare Kimball." Streaming in front of the group like a flagship under full sail was a huge blonde in a flowered dress belted in wide lavender plastic. Rolls of fat peeked out from the cuffs of the sleeves and over the tucked waist. She was carrying a plate covered with aluminum foil. "You've hardly changed a bit." The tiny blue eyes blinked in the doughy face. "Has she, Marilou?"

"Hardly a bit." The opinion was whispered by a stick-framed woman with steel-rimmed glasses and hair as silver as the sheet metal in the corner of the garage. With some relief, Clare recognized the thin woman as the town librarian.

"Hello, Mrs. Negley. It's nice to see you again."

"You never brought back that copy of *Rebecca*." Behind her Coke-bottle lenses, her right eye winked. "Thought I'd forget. You remember Min Atherton, the mayor's wife."

Clare didn't allow her mouth to drop open. Min Atherton had put on a good fifty pounds in the last ten years and was hardly recognizable under the layers of flab. "Of course. Hi." Awkward, Clare rubbed her grimy hands over the thighs of her grimier jeans and hoped no one would want to shake.

"We wanted to give you the morning to settle." Min took over, as was her right as the mayor's wife—and president of the Ladies Club. "You remember Gladys Finch, Lenore Barlow, Jessie Misner, and Carolanne Gerheart."

"Ah . . ."

"The girl can't remember everybody all at once." Gladys Finch stepped forward and thrust a Tupperware bowl into Clare's hands. "I taught you in fourth grade—and I remember you well enough. Very tidy handwriting."

Nostalgia swam sweetly through Clare's mind. "You put colored stars on our papers."

"When you deserved them. We've got enough cakes and cookies here to rot every tooth in your head. Where would you like us to put them?"

"It's very nice of you." Clare gave a helpless glance toward the door that opened into the laundry room, then the kitchen. "We could put them inside. I haven't really . . ."

But her voice trailed off because Min was already sailing through the laundry room, anxious to see what was what.

"What pretty colors." Min's sharp little eyes darted everywhere. Personally, she didn't see how anyone could keep a dark blue countertop looking clean. She much preferred her white Formica with its little gold flecks. "The last tenants in here weren't very neighborly—didn't mix well—and can't say I'm sorry to see them gone. Flatlanders," Min said with a derisive sniff that put the absent tenants in their place. "We're glad to have a Kimball back in this house, aren't we, girls?"

There was a general murmur of agreement that nearly had Clare shuffling her feet.

"Well, I appreciate—"

"I made you up my special Jell-O mold," Min continued after drawing a breath. "Why don't I just put it right in the refrigerator for you?"

Beer, Min thought with a knowing frown after she wrenched open the door. Beer and soda pop and some kind of fancy chip dip. Couldn't expect any better from a girl who'd been living the high life up in New York City.

Neighbors, Clare thought as the women talked to her, around her, and through her. She hadn't had to speak to—or so much as look at—a neighbor in years. After clearing her throat, she tried a smile. "I'm sorry, I haven't had a chance to go shopping yet. I don't have any coffee." Or plates or cups or spoons, she thought.

"We didn't come for coffee." Mrs. Negley patted Clare's shoulder and smiled her wispy smile. "Just to welcome you home."

"That's so nice of you." Clare lifted her hands and let them fall. "Really, so nice. I don't even have a chair to offer you."

"Why don't we help you unpack?" Min was

poking around, brutally disappointed at the lack of boxes. "From the size of that moving truck that was here this morning, you must have a mess of things to deal with."

"No, actually, that was just my equipment. I didn't bring any furniture down with me." Intimidated by the curious eyes fixed on her, Clare stuck her hands in her pockets. It was worse, she decided, than a press interview. "I thought I'd just pick up what I needed as I went along."

"Young people." Min gave a quick, skipping laugh. "Flighty as birds. Now, what would your mama say if she knew you were here without a teaspoon or a seat cushion to your name?"

Clare yearned for a cigarette. "I imagine she'd tell me to go shopping."

"We'll just get out of your way so you can." Mrs. Finch rounded up the ladies as competently as she would a group of nine-year-olds. "You just return the dishes when you get around to it, Clare. They're all labeled."

"Thank you. I appreciate the trouble."

They filed out, leaving the scent of chocolate cookies and floral perfume behind.

"Not a dish in the cupboard," Min muttered to the group. "Not a single dish. But she had beer in the refrigerator and plenty of it. Like father like daughter, I say."

"Oh, hush up, Min," Gladys Finch said good-naturedly.

* * *

Crazy Annie liked to sing. As a child she'd been
a soprano in the church choir at First Lutheran.
Her high, sweet voice had changed little in
more than half a century. Nor had her skittish,
uncomplicated mind.

She liked bright colors and shiny objects. Often she would wear three blouses, one over the
other, and forget underpants. She would crowd
dangling bracelets on her arms and forget to
bathe. Since her mother's death twelve years before, there had been no one to take care of her,
to patiently, lovingly fix her meals and see that
she ate them.

But the town tended its own. Someone from
the Ladies Club or the Town Council dropped
by her rusty, ratpacked trailer every day to take
her a meal or look at her latest collection of
junk.

Her body was strong and solid, as if to make
up for her fragile mind. Though her hair had
gone steel gray, her face was remarkably smooth
and pretty, her hands and feet chubby and pink.
Every day, whatever the weather, she would
walk miles, dragging her burlap sack. Into
Martha's for a doughnut and a glass of cherry
fizz, to the post office for colorful flyers and oc-
cupant mail, by the Gift Emporium to study the
window display.

She moved along the roadside, singing and chattering to herself as her eyes scanned the ground for treasures. She stalked the fields and the woods, patient enough to stand for an hour and watch a squirrel nibble a nut.

She was happy, and her blank, smiling face concealed dozens of secrets she didn't understand.

There was a place, deep in the woods. A circular clearing with signs carved into trees. It had a pit beside it that sometimes smelled of burned wood and flesh. Walking there always made her skin crawl in a scary way. She knew she had gone there at night, after her mother had gone away and Annie had searched the hills and the woods for her. She had seen things there, things that had made her breathless with terror. Things that had given her bad dreams for weeks after. Until the memories faded.

All she remembered now was the nightmare vision of creatures with human bodies and animal heads. Dancing. Singing. Someone screaming. But she didn't like to remember, so she sang and doused the memory.

She never went there at night anymore. No sir, no indeedy, not at night. But there were days she felt pulled there. And today was one of them. She wasn't afraid when the sun was up.

"Shall we gather at the riiiv-er." Her girlish voice drifted through the air as she dragged her

sack along the edge of the circle. "The beautiful, the beautiful riiiv-er." With a little giggle,
she touched a toe inside the circle, like a child
on a dare. A rustle of leaves made her heart
pound, then she giggled again as she saw a rabbit scamper through the underbrush.

"Don't be afraid," she called after him. "Nobody here but Annie. Nobody here, nobody
here," she chanted, dipping and swaying in her
own private dance. "I come to the garden alone,
when the dew is still on the ro-ses."

Mr. Kimball had the prettiest roses, she
thought. He would pick her one sometimes and
warn her not to prick her finger on the thorns.
But he was dead now, she remembered. Dead
and buried. Like Mama.

The moment of grief was sharp and real.
Then it faded away to nothing as she saw a spar-
row glide overhead. She sat outside the circle,
lowering her thick body to the ground with
surprising grace. Inside her sack was a sandwich
wrapped in waxed paper that Alice had given
her that morning. Annie ate it neatly, in small,
polite bites, singing and talking to herself, scattering crumbs for some of God's little creatures.
When she was finished, she folded the waxed
paper precisely in half, in half again, and stored
it in the sack.

"No littering," she mumbled. "Fifty-dollar
fine. Waste not, want not. Yes, Jesus loves

meeee." She started to rise when she saw something glint in the brush. "Oh!" On her hands and knees, she crept over, pushing at vines and old damp leaves. "Pretty," she whispered, holding the slender, silver-plated bracelet to the sunlight. Her simple heart swelled as she watched the glint and glitter. "Pretty." There was carving on it that she recognized as letters, but couldn't read.

Carly

"Annie." She gave a satisfied nod. "A–N–N–I–E. Annie. Finders keepers, losers weepers. She loves you, yeah, yeah, yeah." Delighted with her treasure, she slipped it over her own thick wrist.

"Nobody saw her, Sheriff." Bud Hewitt set Carly Jamison's picture on Cam's desk. "I showed it all around town. If she came through here, she was invisible."

"Okay, Bud."

"Broke up a fight in the park."

"Oh?" Because he knew it was required, Cam looked up from his paperwork.

"Chip Lewis and Ken Barlow trading punches over some girl. Sent them both home with a bug in their ears."

"Good work."

"Got cornered by the mayor's wife."

Cam lifted a brow.

"Complaining about those kids skateboarding down Main again. And the Knight boy gunning his motorcycle. And—"

"I get the picture, Bud."

"She told me Clare Kimball was back. Got a garage full of junk and no dishes in the cupboards."

"Min's been busy."

"We read all about her in *People* magazine. Clare, I mean. She's famous."

"That so?" Amused, Cam shuffled papers.

"Oh, yeah. She's an artist or something. Makes statues. I saw a picture of one. Must'a been ten feet high." His pleasant face screwed up in thought. "Couldn't make out what it was. I dated her once, you know."

"No, I didn't."

"Yes, sir, took her to the movies and everything. That was the year after her dad died. Damn shame about all that." He used his sleeve to wipe a smudge from the glass of the gun cabinet. "My mom was friends with her mom. Fact is, they were out together the night he did it. Anyway, I thought I might go by the Kimball place sometime. See how Clare's doing."

Before Cam could comment, the phone rang. "Sheriff's office." He listened for a moment to the rapid, high-pitched voice. "Is anyone hurt?

Okay, I'll be right there." He hung up and pushed away from the desk. "Cecil Fogarty ran his car into the oak tree in Mrs. Negley's front yard."

"Want me to take it?"

"No, I'll handle it." Mrs. Negley's was just around the corner from Clare's, he thought as he went out. It would be downright unneighborly not to drop by.

Clare was just pulling into the drive when Cam cruised up. He took his time, watching her as she fumbled for the lever to pop the trunk. Hands tucked in his pockets, he strolled up behind her as she tugged at the bags and boxes heaped in the back of the car.

"Want some help?"

Startled, she rapped her head on the hatchback and swore as she rubbed the hurt. "Jesus, is it part of your job description to sneak around?"

"Yeah." He hefted out a box. "What's all this?"

"Things. I realized you need more than a sleeping bag and a bar of soap to survive." She dropped two bags on top of the box he held and gathered up the rest herself.

"You left your keys in the car."

"I'll get them later."

"Get them now."

On a long-suffering sigh, Clare walked around the car, juggling bags as she leaned inside to pull the keys out of the ignition. She went in through the open garage and left him to follow.

Cam took a look at the tools, several hundred dollars' worth, he estimated. The steel tanks, the stone and metal and lumber. "If you're going to keep all this stuff in here, you'd better start closing the garage door."

"Taking our job seriously, aren't we?" She stepped through the laundry room into the kitchen.

"That's right." He glanced at the counter loaded with covered dishes. "You want to make room for this?"

"Sorry." She pushed plates and bowls together. "The ladies came by this afternoon." She pried a plastic lid from a tub, took a sniff. "Want a brownie?"

"Yeah. Got any coffee to go with it?"

"No, but there's beer and Pepsi in the fridge. And somewhere in all of this is a coffeepot." She began to dig in the box, unraveling items wrapped in newspaper. "I hit a flea market on the way to the mall. It was great." She held up a slightly battered percolator. "It might even work."

"I'll take the Pepsi," he decided and helped himself.

"Just as well, I think I forgot to buy coffee. I got plates, though. This terrific old Fiestaware. And I got these great jelly glasses with Bugs

Bunny and Daffy Duck on them." She tossed back her hair, pushed up her sleeves, and smiled at him. "So, how was your day?"

"Cecil Fogarty ran his Plymouth into Mrs. Negley's oak tree."

"Pretty exciting."

"She thought so." He passed her the bottle of Pepsi. "So, you're going to set up shop in the garage."

"Um-hmm." She took a long sip and handed it back to him.

"Does that mean you're settling in, Slim?"

"That means I'm working while I'm here." She chose a brownie for herself, then scooted up to sit on the counter by the sink. The light of the fading sun glowed in her hair. "Can I ask you something I was too polite to ask you last night?"

"All right."

"Why did you come back?"

"I wanted a change," he said simply, and not completely truthfully.

"As I remember you couldn't wait to see the last of this place."

He had gone fast, not looking back, with two hundred and twenty-seven dollars in his pocket and all kinds of needs boiling in his blood. There had been freedom in that. "I was eighteen. Why are you back?"

She frowned, nibbling on the brownie.

"Maybe I'd had enough change. I've been thinking a lot about this place lately. This house, the town, the people. So here I am." Abruptly she smiled and changed the mood. "I had an incredible crush on you when I was fourteen."

He grinned back at her. "I know."

"Bull." She snatched the Pepsi from him. When he continued to grin, her eyes narrowed. "Blair told you. That weasely creep."

"He didn't have to." Surprising them both, he stepped forward and laid his hands beside her hips on the counter. Her head was above his so that his eyes were level with her mouth. "You used to watch me—and waste a lot of energy pretending like you weren't watching me. Whenever I'd talk to you, you'd blush. I thought it was real cute."

Cautious, she studied him as she tipped the bottle back and drank. She resisted the urge to squirm. She wasn't fourteen anymore. "At that age, girls think hoods are exciting. Then they grow up."

"I've still got a motorcycle."

She had to smile. "I'll bet you do."

"Why don't I take you for a ride on Sunday?"

She considered, polished off the brownie. "Why don't you?"

Chapter 5

THE COVEN OF THIRTEEN met at moonrise. Thunder grunted in the distance. In twos and threes they stood, chatting, gossiping, smoking tobacco or marijuana as the ceremonial candles were lit. Black wax softened and pooled. In the pit the fire caught and crackled and began to climb, digging greedy fingers into the dry wood. Hoods shadowed unmasked faces.

The bell was rung. Instantly voices were hushed, cigarettes extinguished. The circle was formed.

In the center the high priest stood, clad in his robe and his goat mask. Though they knew who he was, he never revealed his face during a rite. No one had the nerve to demand it.

He had brought them three whores, knowing

they required the release of sex to remain faithful—and silent. But that feasting would wait.

It was a time of baptism and beginnings. Tonight, two members who had proven themselves worthy would be given the mark of Satan. To brand them and bind them.

He began, lifting his arms high for the first invocation. The wind carried his call, and the power rushed into him like hot breath. The bell, the fire, the chant. The altar was ripe and lush and naked.

"Our Lord, our Master is the One. He is the All. We bring our brothers to Him so that they might be joined. We have taken His name into ourselves and so live as the beasts, rejoicing in the flesh. Behold the gods of the pits.

"Abaddon, the destroyer.

"Fenriz, Son of Loki.

"Euronymous, Prince of Death."

The flames rose higher. The gong echoed.

Behind the mask, the priest's eyes glittered, reddened by the light of the flames. "I am the Sayer of the Law. Come forth, those who would learn the Law."

Two figures stepped forward as lightning walked across the sky.

"We do not show our fangs to others. It is Law."

The coven repeated the words, and the bell was rung.

"We do not destroy what is ours. It is Law."

The response was chanted.

"We kill with cunning and with purpose, not with anger. It is Law."

"We worship the One."

"Satan is the One."

"His is the palace of Hell."

"*Ave*, Satan."

"What is His, is ours."

"Hail to Him."

"He is what we are."

"*Ave*, Satan."

"We shall know, and what we know is ours. There is no path back but death."

"Blessed be."

The Princes of Hell were called. And smoke billowed. There was incense to clog and mystify the air. Tainted holy water in a phallic-shaped shaker was dashed around the circle to purify. The hum of voices rose into one ecstatic song.

Again the leader raised his arms, and beneath his robe his heart gloated at the followers' weakness for imagery. "Cast off your robes and kneel before me, for I am your priest and only through me you will reach Him."

The initiates cast aside their robes and knelt, sex thrusting, eyes glazed. They had waited twelve months for this night, to belong, to take, and to feast. The altar rubbed her breasts and licked her slick red lips.

The priest, taking a candle from between the altar's thighs, circled the two, passing the flame before their eyes, their manhood, and the soles of their feet.

"This is Satan's flame. You have walked in Hell. The Gates have been flung wide for you, and His beasts rejoice. Hell's fire will make you free. We toll the bell in His name."

Again the bell rang out, its tone echoing, echoing until there was no sound. All the night creatures were hidden and silent.

"Now your path is set, and you must follow the flame or perish. The blood of those who fail is bright and will guide your steps to the power."

Turning, the priest reached into a silver bowl and drew out a handful of the graveyard dirt where an infant had rested for a century. He pressed the soil into the soles of the initiates' feet, sprinkled it over their heads, laid it gently on their tongues.

"Revel in this and stray not. You make your pact tonight with all who have gone before into His light. Seek and be glad as you obey the Law."

He took up a clear flask filled with holy water and urine. "Drink of this and ease the thirst. Drink deep of life so that He will shine within you."

Each man took the flask in turn and swallowed.

"Arise now, Brothers, to receive His mark."

The men rose, and others came forward to lock the first initiate's arms and legs in place. The ceremonial knife glinted under a full ghost moon.

"In the name of Satan, I mark you."

The man screamed once as the knife sliced delicately over his left testicle. Blood dripped as he wept.

"You are His, from now and through eternity."

The coven chanted. "*Ave*, Satan."

The second was marked. Drugged wine was given to both.

Their blood stained the knife as the priest lifted the blade high, swaying as he gave thanks to the Dark Lord. As the thunder rumbled closer, his voice rose to a shout.

"Raise your right hand in the Sign and take the oath."

Shuddering, faces glinting with tears, the men obeyed.

"You accept His pleasures, and His pains. You are returned from death into life by His mark. You have declared yourself a servant of Lucifer, the Bringer of Light. This act is of your own desire and by your own will."

"By our desire," the men repeated, in thick, dazed voices. "By our will."

Taking up the sword, the priest traced an inverted pentagram in the air over each new member's heart.

"Hail, Satan."

The sacrifice was brought out. A young black goat, not yet weaned. The priest looked at the altar, her legs spread wide, her breasts white and gleaming. She held a black candle in each hand, with another nestled at the juncture of her thighs.

Well paid and comfortably drugged, she smiled at him.

He thought of her as he raked the knife across the kid's neck.

The blood was mixed with the wine, then drunk. When he cast aside his robe, the silver medallion glinted against his sweaty chest. He mounted the altar himself, raking his stained hands down her breasts and torso while he imagined his fingers were talons.

As his seed spilled into her, he dreamed of killing again.

Clare woke in a cold sweat, her breath heaving, her face drenched with tears. Reaching out for the light, she found only empty space. There was one frozen instant of panic before she remembered where she was. Steadying herself, she climbed out of her sleeping bag. She counted her steps to the wall, then flicked on the overhead light and stood shivering.

She should have expected the dream to come again. After all, the first time she'd had it had been in this very room. But it was worse this time. Worse, because it had melded into the dream memory of the night she found her father sprawled on the flagstone patio.

She pressed the heels of her hands against her eyes and leaned back against the wall until both images faded. In the distance she heard a rooster heralding the new morning. Like dreams, fears faded with sunlight. Calmer, she stripped off the basketball jersey she had slept in and went to shower.

Over the next hour, she worked with more passion, more energy than she had felt in weeks. With steel and brass and flame, she began to create her own nightmare image in three dimensions. To create and to exorcise.

She puddled the metal, laying an even bead to fuse mass to mass. Controlling the motion with her shoulder muscles, she gave in to the rhythm. As moment by painstaking moment the form took shape, she felt the emotion of it, the power of it. But her hands did not shake. In her work there was rarely any need to remind herself of patience or caution. It was second nature to her to raise the torch from the work for a few moments when the metal became too hot. Always she watched the color and consistency of the metal, even as that freer part of her, her imagination, swam faster.

Behind her dark-lensed goggles, her eyes were intense, as if she were hypnotized. Sparks showered as she cut and layered and built.

By noon, she had worked for six hours without a rest, and her mind and arms were exhausted. After turning off her tanks, she set her torch aside. There was sweat skating down her back, but she ignored it, staring at the figure she'd created while she stripped off gloves, goggles, skullcap.

Cautiously she circled it, studying it from all sides, all angles. It was three feet in height, coldly black, apparently seamless. It had come from her deepest and most confused fears—an unmistakably human form with a head that was anything but human. The hint of horns, a snarl for a mouth. While the human part seemed to be bent over in supplication, the head was thrown back in triumph.

It gave her a chill to study it. A chill of both fear and pride.

It was good, she thought as she pressed a hand to her mouth. It was really good. For reasons she didn't understand, she sat on the concrete floor and wept.

★ ★ ★

Alice Crampton had lived in Emmitsboro all her life. She'd been out of state twice, once for a reckless weekend in Virginia Beach with Marshall Wickers right after he'd joined the navy and once for a week in New Jersey when she'd visited her cousin, Sheila, who had married an optometrist. Other than that, she'd spent nearly every day of her life in the town where she'd been born.

Sometimes she resented it. But mostly, she didn't think about it. Her dream was to save enough money to move to some big, anonymous city where the customers were strangers who tipped big. For now, she served coffee and country ham sandwiches to people she'd known all her life and who rarely gave her a tip at all.

She was a wide-hipped, full-breasted woman who filled out her pink and white uniform in a way the male clientele appreciated. Some, like Less Gladhill, might leer and gawk, but no one would have tried for a pinch. She went to church every Sunday and guarded the virtue she felt Marshall Wickers had trampled on.

No one had to tell her to keep the counters clean or to laugh at a customer's jokes. She was a good, conscientious waitress with tireless feet and an unshakable memory. If you ordered your burger rare once, you wouldn't have to remind her of it on your next visit to Martha's.

Alice Crampton didn't think about waitressing

as a bridge to another, more sophisticated career. She liked what she did, if she didn't always like where she did it.

In the reflection of the big coffeepot, she tidied her frizzed blond hair and wondered if she could manage a trip to Betty's Shop of Beauty the following week.

The order for table four came up, and she hefted her tray, carting it across the diner to the voice of Tammy Wynette.

When Clare walked into Martha's, the place was hopping, just as she remembered it from hundreds of Saturday afternoons. She could smell the fried onions, the hamburger grease, someone's florid perfume, and good, hot coffee.

The jukebox was the same one that had been in place more than ten years before. As Wynette entreated womenkind to stand by their men, Clare figured its selections hadn't changed, either. There was the clatter of flatware and the din of voices no one bothered to lower. Feeling just fine, she took a seat at the counter and opened the plastic menu.

"Yes, ma'am, what can I get you?"

She lowered the menu, then dropped it. "Alice? Alice, it's Clare."

Alice's polite smile opened to a wide *O* of astonishment. "Clare Kimball! I heard you were back. You look great. Oh, gosh, just great."

"It's so good to see you." Clare was already

gripping Alice's hard, capable hands in hers. "God, we have to talk. I want to know how you are, what you've been doing. Everything."

"I'm fine. And this is it." She laughed and gave Claire's hands a squeeze before releasing them. "What can I get you? You want coffee? We don't have any of that ex-presso stuff they drink in New York."

"I want a burger with everything, the greasiest fries you can come up with, and a chocolate shake."

"Your stomach hasn't changed. Hold on, let me put the order in." She called it back, picked up another order. "By the time Frank's finished burning the meat, I can take a break," she said, then scurried off.

Clare watched her serve, pour coffee, scribble down orders, and ring up bills. Fifteen minutes later, Clare had a plate of food and a well of admiration.

"Christ, you're really good at this." She doused her fries with catsup as Alice sat on the stool beside her.

"Well, everybody's got to be good at something." Alice smiled, wishing she'd had time to freshen her lipstick and brush her hair. "I saw you on *Entertainment Tonight*, at that show you had in New York with all those statues. You looked so glamorous."

Clare gave a snort and licked catsup from her finger. "Yep, that's me."

"They said you were the artist of the nineties. That your work was bold and . . . innovative."

"They say innovative when they don't understand it." She bit into the burger and closed her eyes. "Oh. Yes. Oh, yes. *This* is truly innovative. God, I bet it's just loaded with steroids. Martha's burgers." She took a second sloppy bite. "I dreamed about Martha's burgers. And they haven't changed."

"Nothing much does around here."

"I walked up from the house, just to look at everything." Clare pushed back her choppy bangs. "It probably sounds silly, but I didn't know how much I'd missed it until I saw it all again. I saw Mr. Roody's truck outside Clyde's Tavern, and the azaleas in front of the library. But, Jesus, Alice, you've got a video store now, and the pizza parlor delivers. And Bud Hewitt. I swear I saw Bud Hewitt drive by in the sheriff's car."

Tickled, Alice laughed. "Maybe a couple things have changed. Bud's a deputy now. Mitzi Hines—you remember, she was a year ahead of us in school? She married one of the Hawbaker boys, and they opened that video place. Doing real well, too. Got them a brick house off of Sider's Alley, a new car, and two babies."

"How about you? How's your family?"

"Okay. Drive me crazy half the time. Lynette got married and moved up to Williamsport. Pop talks about retiring, but he won't."

"How could he? It wouldn't be Emmitsboro without Doc Crampton."

"Every winter Mom nags him to move south. But he won't budge."

She picked up one of Clare's fries and slopped it around in the catsup. They had sat like this, they both remembered, countless times in their girlhood, sharing secrets and sorrows and joys. And, of course, doing what girls do best. Talking about boys.

"I guess you know Cam Rafferty's sheriff now."

Clare shook her head. "I can't figure out how he pulled it off."

"My mom liked to had a fit—so did some of the others who remembered him as hell on wheels. But he had all these commendations, and we were in a fix when Sheriff Parker took off like he did. 'Course now that it's worked out so well, everybody's patting themselves on the back." She gave Clare a knowing grin. "He's even better-looking than he used to be."

"I noticed." Clare frowned a bit as she sucked on her straw. "What about his stepfather?"

"Still gives me the creeps." Alice gave a little shiver and helped herself to more fries.

"Doesn't come into town much, and when he does, everybody pretty much leaves him alone. Rumor is he drinks up whatever profit the farm makes and whores around down in Frederick."

"Cam's mother still lives with him?"

"She either loves him or is scared shitless." Alice shrugged. "Cam doesn't talk about it. He had himself a house built up on Quarry Road, back in the woods. I heard it's got skylights and a sunken tub."

"Well, well. What'd he do, rob a bank?"

Alice leaned closer. "Inheritance," she whispered. "His real daddy's mother left the works to him. Pissed off his stepfather real good."

"I'll bet it did." Though Clare understood that gossip was served up in Martha's as regularly as the burgers, she preferred to have hers in a more private setting. "Listen, Alice, what time do you get off?"

"I have the eight to four-thirty shift today."

"Got a hot date?"

"I haven't had a hot date since 1989."

With a chuckle, Clare dug some bills out of her pocket and laid them on the counter. "Why don't you come by the house later, for pizza and catch-up?"

Alice grinned, noting without embarrassment that Clare had left her a generous tip. "That's the best offer I've had in six months."

★ ★ ★

In a corner booth two men sat, drinking coffee, smoking, and watching. One of them cut his eyes over toward Clare and nodded.

"People are talking a lot about Jack Kimball now that his girl's back in town."

"People're always talking about the dead." But he looked as well, shifting so he could stare without being noticed. "Don't figure there's anything to worry about. She was just a kid. She doesn't remember anything."

"Then why's she back?" Gesturing with his smoldering Marlboro, the man leaned forward. He kept his voice low so that k.d. lang crooned over his words. "How come some rich, fancy artist type comes back to a place like this? She's already talked to Rafferty. Twice, I hear."

He didn't want to think about problems. Didn't want to believe there could be any. Maybe some members of the coven were pulling away from the purity of the rites, getting a little careless, more than a little bloodthirsty. But it was just a phase. A new high priest was what was needed, and though he wasn't a brave man, he had attended two secret meetings on that particular problem. What was not needed was a flare of panic because Jack Kimball's daughter was back in town.

"She can't tell the sheriff what she doesn't

know," he insisted. He wished to hell he'd never mentioned the fact that Jack had gotten stewed one night and babbled about Clare watching a ritual. In the back of his mind, he was afraid Jack had died as much for that as for the shopping center deal.

"We might just have to find out what she does know." As he crushed out his cigarette, he studied her. Not a bad looker, he decided. Even if her ass was on the bony side. "We'll keep an eye on little Clare," he said and grinned. "We'll keep an eye right on her."

Ernie Butts spent most of his time thinking about death. He read about it, dreamed about it, and fantasized about it. He'd come to the conclusion that when a person was finished with life, they were just plain finished. There was no heaven or hell in Ernie Butts's scheme of things. That made death the ultimate rip-off, and life, with its average seventy-odd years, the only game in town.

He didn't believe in rules or in doing good deeds. He'd come to admire men like Charles Manson and David Berkowitz. Men who took what they wanted, lived as they chose, and flipped society the finger. Sure, that same society locked them up, but before the bars shut, these men had wielded incredible power. And, as Ernie Butts believed, they continued to wield it.

He was as fascinated by power as he was by death.

He'd read every word written by Anton LaVey, by Lovecraft, and Crowley. He'd pored over books of folklore and witchcraft and Satan worship, taking out of them all that he understood or agreed with and mixing them together into his own messy stew.

It made a lot more sense to him than sitting through life being pious, self-sacrificing, and humble. Or, like his parents, working eighteen frigging hours a day, sweating and scraping to make loan payments.

If all you were going to end up with was six feet of dirt, then it was logical to take whatever you could get, however you could get it, while you were still breathing.

He listened to the music of Mötley Crüe, Slayer, and Metallica, twisting the lyrics to suit his needs. The walls of his once airy attic room were lined with posters of his heroes, frozen into tortured screams or smiling evil.

He knew it drove his parents crazy, but at seventeen, Ernie didn't concern himself overmuch with the people who had created him. He felt little more than contempt for the man and woman who owned and operated Rocco's Pizza and were forever smelling of garlic and sweat.

The fact that he refused to work with them had fostered many family arguments. But he had taken a job at the Amoco, pumping gas. Reaching for independence was what his mother had called it, soothing his baffled and disappointed father. So they let him be.

Sometimes he fantasized about killing them, feeling their blood on his hands, experiencing the punch of their life force shooting from them at the moment of death and into him. And when he dreamed of murder, it frightened and fascinated him.

He was a stringy boy with dark hair and a surly face that excited a number of the high school girls. He dabbled in sex in the cab of his secondhand Toyota pickup but found most of his female contemporaries too stupid, too timid, or too boring. In the five years he'd lived in Emmitsboro, he'd made no close friends, male or female. There wasn't one with whom he could discuss the psychology of the sociopath, the meaning of the *Necronomicon*, or the symbolism of ancient rites.

Ernie thought of himself as an outsider, not a bad thing in his estimation. He kept his grades up because it was easy for him, and he took a great deal of pride in his mind. But he rejected outside activities like sports and dances that might have forged some bonds between him and the other kids in town.

He contented himself toying with the black candles and pentagrams and goat's blood he kept locked in his desk drawer. While his parents slept in their cozy bed, he worshipped deities they would never understand.

And he watched the town from his aerie-like perch atop the house, focusing his high-powered telescope. He saw a great deal.

His house stood diagonally across from the Kimball place. He'd seen Clare arrive and watched her regularly ever since. He knew the stories. Since she had come back to town they had all been dug up and opened—like an old casket, they breathed out sorrow and death. He'd waited to see when she would go up, when the light in the Kimball attic would go on. But she had yet to explore that room.

He wasn't very disappointed. For now, he could home his lens in on her bedroom window. He'd already watched her dress, pulling a shirt down her long, lean torso, hitching jeans over her narrow hips. Her body was very slender and very white, the triangle between her legs as red and glossy as the hair on her head. He imagined himself creeping through her back door, quietly climbing her steps. He would clamp a hand over her mouth before she screamed. Then he would tie her down, and while she writhed and bucked helplessly, he would do things to her—things that would make her sweat and strain and groan.

When he was done, she would beg him to come back.

It would be great, he thought, really great, to rape a woman in a house where someone had died violently.

Ernie heard the truck clatter down the street. He recognized Bob Meese's Ford from Yesterday's Treasures in town. The truck lumbered up the Kimball drive, belching carbon monoxide. He saw Clare jump out, and though he couldn't hear, he could see she was laughing and talking excitedly as the portly Meese heaved himself down from the cab.

"I appreciate this, Bob, really."

"No problemo." He figured it was the least he could do for old times' sake—even though he'd only dated Clare once. On the night her father died. In any case, when a customer plunked down fifteen hundred without haggling, he was more than willing to deliver the merchandise. "I'll give you a hand with the stuff." He hitched up his sagging belt, then hauled a drop leaf table out of the truck bed. "This is a nice piece. With some refinishing, you'll have a gem."

"I like it the way it is." It was' scarred and

stained and had plenty of character. Clare muscled out a ladder-back chair with a frayed rush seat. There was a matching one still on the truck, along with an iron standing lamp with a fringed shade, a rug in a faded floral pattern, and a sofa.

They carried the light loads inside, then wrestled the rug between them, chatting as they worked about old friends, new events. Bob was already panting when they walked back to the truck to study the curvy red brocade sofa.

"This is great. I'm crazy about the swans carved in the armrests."

"Weighs a ton," Bob said. He started to hoist himself up on the bed when he spotted Ernie loitering on the curb across the street. "Hey, Ernie Butts, what you doing?"

Ernie's sulky mouth turned down. His hands dove into his pockets. "Nothing."

"Well, get your ass over here and do something. Kid's creepy," Bob muttered to Clare, "but he's got a young back."

"Hi." Clare offered Ernie a sympathetic smile when he sauntered over. "I'm Clare."

"Yeah." He could smell her hair, fresh, clean with sexy undertones.

"Get on up there and help me haul this thing." Bob jerked his head toward the sofa.

"I'll help." Agile, Clare jumped up in the back beside Ernie.

"Don't need to." Before she could get a grip, Ernie had lifted the end of the sofa. She saw the muscles in his thin arms bunch. She immediately pictured them sculpted in dark oak. As they swung the sofa down, Bob grunting and swearing, she scrambled out of the way. Ernie walked backward, up the drive, over the walkway, through the door, his eyes on his own feet.

"Just plunk it down in the middle of the floor." She smiled as it thunked into place. It was a good sound—settling in. "That's great, thanks. Can I get you guys a cold drink?"

"I'll take one to go," Bob said. "I gotta get back." He offered Clare a friendly wink. "Wouldn't want Bonny Sue to get jealous."

Clare grinned back. Bobby Meese and Bonny Sue Wilson, she thought. It was still hard to imagine them seven years married and the parents of three.

"Ernie?"

He shrugged his thin shoulders. "Guess so."

She hustled to the kitchen and brought back three cold bottles of Pepsi. "I'll let you know about that chifforobe, Bob."

"You do that." He took a swig before he started toward the door. "We're open tomorrow twelve to five."

She let him out, then turned back to Ernie. "Sorry you got roped into that."

" 'S okay." He took a drink, then glanced around the room. "Is this all you've got?"

"For now. I'm having fun picking up a little here, a little there. Why don't we try it out?" She sat on one end of the sofa. "The cushions are sunk," she said with a sigh. "Just the way I like them. So, have you lived in town long?"

He didn't sit, but edged around the room— like a cat, she thought, taking stock of his territory. "Since I was a kid."

"You go to Emmitsboro High?"

"I'm a senior."

Her fingers itched for her sketch pad. There was tension in every inch of him—young, defiant, and restless tension. "Going to college?"

He only shrugged his shoulders. It was another bone of contention between him and his parents. *Education is your best chance.* Screw that. He was his best chance. "I'm going to California—Los Angeles—as soon as I save up enough."

"What do you want to do?"

"Make lots of money."

She laughed, but it was a friendly sound, not derisive. He nearly smiled back. "An honest ambition. Are you interested in modeling?"

Suspicion flickered in his eyes. They were very dark eyes, Clare noted. Like his hair. And not as young as they should have been.

"What for?"

"For me. I'd like to do your arms. They're thin and sinewy. You could come by after school sometime. I'd pay you scale."

He drank more Pepsi, wondering what she wore under her snug-fitting jeans. "Maybe."

When he left, he fingered the inverted pentagram he wore under his Black Sabbath T-shirt. Tonight, he would perform a private ritual. For sex.

Cam dropped by Clyde's after supper. He often did on Saturday nights. He could enjoy the single beer he allowed himself, some company, a game of pool. And he could keep an eye on anyone tossing back too many before pulling out car keys to head home.

He was greeted by shouts and waves as he walked out of the twilight and into the dim, smoky bar. Clyde, who grew wider and more grizzled year after year, poured him a Beck's draft. Cam nursed it at the ancient mahogany bar, one foot resting comfortably on the brass rail.

From the back room came music and the clatter of pool balls, an occasional ripe oath, and a snarl of laughter. Men and a scattering of women sat at the square uncovered tables with beer glasses, overflowing ashtrays, and mounds of peanut shells. Sarah Hewitt, Bud's sister, did what waitressing was required in a tight T-shirt and tighter jeans. She scooped up tips and propositions with equal relish.

Cam knew it was a ritual, coming here, nursing one dark beer and smoking too much. Listening to the same songs, hearing the same voices, smelling the same smells. And there was a comfort in it, knowing Clyde would always stand behind the bar, snarling at his customers. The Budweiser clock on the wall would always be ten minutes slow, and the potato chips would always be stale.

Sarah jiggled over, her eyes sooty, her skin drenched in come-hither perfume. She set her tray on the bar and rubbed her thigh lightly against his. Cam noticed, without much interest, that she'd done something different with her hair. It was a Jean Harlow blond since her latest trip to Betty's, and it drooped seductively over one eye.

"I wondered if you were coming in tonight."

He glanced over, remembering there had been a time he'd have chewed glass to get his hands on her. "How's it going, Sarah?"

"It's been worse." She shifted so that her breast brushed his arm. "Bud says you've been busy."

"Busy enough." Cam picked up his beer again and broke the inviting contact.

"Maybe you'd like to relax later. Like old times."

"We never relaxed."

She gave a low, throaty laugh. "Well, I'm glad to see you remember." Annoyed, she glanced over her shoulder when someone hailed her. She'd been aiming to get her hands into Cam's pants—and his wallet—since he'd come back to town. "I get off at two. Why don't I come by your place?"

"I appreciate the offer, Sarah, but I'd rather remember than repeat."

"Suit yourself." She shrugged as she picked up her tray again, but her voice had toughened with the rejection. "But I'm better than I used to be."

So everyone said, Cam thought and lighted a cigarette. She'd been a stunner once, stacked and sexy and seventeen. They'd fucked each other blind. And then, Cam remembered, she had slinked off to dispense the favor on as many other males as she could find.

"Sarah Hewitt'll do it" had become the battle cry of Emmitsboro High.

The pity of it was, he'd loved her—with all of his loins and at least half his heart. Now he only felt sorry for her. Which, he knew, was worse than hate.

The voices from the back grew in volume, and the curses became more colorful. Cam cocked a brow at Clyde.

"Leave 'em be." Clyde's voice was a froggy

rasp, as if he'd had his vocal cords wrapped in tinfoil. As he popped open two bottles of Bud, his face moved into a scowl that had his five chins swaying like Jell-O. "This ain't no nursery school."

"It's your place," Cam said casually, but he'd noticed that Clyde had glanced toward the back room a half-dozen times since Cam had ordered the beer.

"That's right, and having a badge in here makes my customers nervous. You going to drink that or play with it?"

Cam lifted his glass and drank. He picked up his cigarette, took a drag, then crushed it out. "Who's in the back, Clyde?"

Clyde's fleshy face pokered up. "Usual bums." When Cam continued to stare at him, Clyde picked up a sour-smelling rag and began to polish the dull surface of the bar. "Biff's back there, and I don't want no trouble."

Cam went very still at his stepfather's name, and the amusement faded from his eyes. Biff Stokey rarely did his drinking in town, and when he did, it wasn't friendly.

"How long's he been here?"

Clyde moved his shoulders and set off an avalanche ripple of flab beneath his stained apron. "I ain't got no stopwatch."

There was a quick, shrill feminine scream and the sound of crashing wood.

"Sounds like he's been here too long," Cam said and started back, shoving onlookers aside. "Back off." He elbowed his way through, toward the shouting. "I said back off, goddamn it."

In the rear room where customers gathered to play pool or dump quarters into the ancient pinball machine, he saw a woman cowering in the corner and Less Gladhill swaying beside the pool table with a cue held in both fists. There was already blood on his face. Biff stood a few feet away, holding the remains of a chair. He was a big, bulky man with arms like cinder blocks, liberally tattooed from his stint in the marines. His face, ruddy from sun and drinking, was set in a snarl. The eyes were as Cam always remembered them, dark and full of hate.

Oscar Roody was hopping from one leg to the other, standing out of harm's way while he played peacemaker.

"Come on, Biff, it was a friendly game."

"Fuck off," Biff muttered.

Cam set a hand on Oscar's shoulder and with a jerk of his head gestured him aside. "Take a walk, Less. Sober up." Cam spoke softly, his eyes on his stepfather.

"That sonofabitch hit me with the fucking chair." Less swiped at the blood pooling over his eye. "He owes me twenty bucks."

"Take a walk," Cam repeated. He curled his

fingers around the pool cue. He only had to tug once before Less released it.

"He's fucking crazy. It was assault. I got witnesses."

There was a general murmur of agreement, but no one stepped forward. "Fine. Go on over to the office. Give Doc Crampton a call. He'll take a look at you." He sent one sweeping glance around the room. "Clear out."

People moved back, muttering, but most crowded in the doorway to watch Cam face down his stepfather.

"Big man now, ain't you?" Biff's gravelly voice was slurred with drink. And he grinned, the way he had always grinned before he plowed into Cam. "Got yourself a badge and a shitload of money, but you're still a punk."

Cam's fingers tensed on the cue. He was ready. More than ready. "It's time you went home."

"I'm drinking. Clyde, you motherfucker, where's my whiskey?"

"You're finished drinking here," Cam said steadily. "You can go out walking through the front, or I can carry you out the back."

Biff's grin widened. He tossed the broken chair aside and lifted his ham-sized fists. He'd been set to kick Less's ass, but this was better yet. It had been years since he'd been able to beat

some respect into the boy. And Cam was over-
due.

"Why don't you just come and get me, then?"

When Biff lunged forward, Cam hesitated
only an instant. He imagined himself slamming
the cue hard against the side of Biff's head. He
could even hear the satisfying smack of wood
against bone. At the last minute, he tossed the
cue aside and took the first blow in the gut.

The air wheezed out between his teeth, but he
dodged the fist before it smashed into his jaw.
The glancing shot to his temple had stars ex-
ploding in front of his eyes. He heard the roar
of the crowd behind him, like pagans surrounding gladiators.

The first time his naked fist connected with
Biff's flesh, the shock sang up his arm and ended
with a riff of satisfaction. The punches that
rained on him were all but unfelt, like memory
blows of the dozens of beatings.

He'd been smaller once. Small and thin and
helpless. Then he'd had only two choices—to
run and hide, or to stand and take it. But that
had changed. This night had been a long time
coming. There was a wild kind of glory in it,
the kind soldiers feel as they suit up and storm
into battle. He watched his own fist slam into
Biff's sneering mouth, knuckles and lips ripping.

He smelled blood—his own and Biff's. Glass

crashed and shattered on the floor. His own control shattered with it. Like a madman, he threw himself into the fight, hammering his fists into the face he had learned to fear and despise since childhood.

He wanted to erase it. Destroy it. With hands that were bruised and bloodied, he grabbed Biff by the shirt and slammed that hated face, again and again, into the wall.

"Jesus, Cam. Come on, let up. Jesus."

The breath was racing out of his lungs, hot as fire. He struggled away when hands reached for his shoulders, and turning, he nearly rammed his fist into Bud's face.

The mist cleared from his eyes then, and he saw the white, strained face of his deputy, the huge, curious eyes of the crowd that had gathered. With the back of his hand, he wiped the blood from his mouth. Crumpled on the floor, beaten, broken, and unconscious in his own vomit, was Biff.

"Clyde called." Bud's voice was shaking. "He said things were out of hand." Wetting his lips, he looked at the destruction of the poolroom. "What do you want me to do?"

The breath wheezed out of Cam's lungs like an old man's. "Lock him up." Cam put a hand on the pool table to steady himself. He was beginning to feel the pain now from each individual blow, and a churning, aching nausea.

"Resisting arrest, assaulting an officer, disturbing the peace, drunk and disorderly."

Bud cleared his throat. "I could drive him on home if you want. You know——"

"Lock him up." He glanced up to see Sarah watching him with both approval and derision in her sooty eyes. "Get a statement from Less Gladhill and any witnesses."

"Let me get someone to drive you home, Sheriff."

"No." He kicked a broken glass aside, then stared down the people hovering in the doorway. His eyes were cold now, hard and cold, so that even the men who had been cheering him on averted theirs. "Fun's over."

He waited until the room had cleared before he left to drive to the farm and tell his mother her husband wouldn't be home that night.

Chapter 6

WHEN CAM SWUNG HIS HARLEY into Clare's driveway, it was just after noon. Every bone, every muscle of his body throbbed. He'd soaked in his whirlpool, tried ice packs, and downed three Nuprin, but the beating he'd taken and the sleepless night were hard to counteract.

Tougher yet had been his mother's reaction. She had looked at him with her big, tired, sad eyes and made him feel—as she always did— that he had somehow caused his stepfather's drunkenness and the fight that followed it.

It was small satisfaction that at least until Monday, and the judge's ruling, Biff would be nursing his own aches and pains in jail.

He turned his bike off and, leaning forward on the handlebars, watched Clare work.

She'd left the garage door open. On a large bricktopped worktable was a tall metal structure. She was bent toward it, guiding a welding torch. As he watched, a shower of sparks rained around her.

His reaction was instant and baffling. Desire— as hot and sharp as the flame she wielded.

Stupid, he thought, as he painfully swung his leg off the bike. There was nothing remotely sexy about a woman in workboots and overalls. Most of her face was hidden under a pair of dark goggles, and her hair was tucked under a leather skullcap. And though he liked women in leather, the thick apron she wore was a far cry from a tight skirt.

He set his helmet on the seat of the bike and walked into the garage.

She kept right on working. There was music blasting from a new portable stereo. Beethoven's Ninth competed with the hiss of flame. Cam walked over to turn it down, figuring it was the safest way to get her attention.

Clare glanced over briefly. "Just one more minute."

One became five before she straightened and switched off the flame. With competent hands she picked up a wrench and turned off her tanks.

"I just had a few finishing touches to put on it today." She blew out a breath and pushed up her

goggles. Energy was still vibrating in her fingertips. "What do you think?"

Taking his time, he walked around it. It
looked monstrous. And fascinating. Human,
and yet . . . other. He wondered what kind of
imagination, or what kind of need, drove her to
create something so disturbing.

"Well, I wouldn't want it in my living room
because I'd never be able to relax around it. It's
like a nightmare you could touch."

It was exactly the right thing to say. Clare
nodded as she stripped off her skullcap. "It's the
best work I've done in six months. Angie's going to dance on the ceiling."

"Angie?"

"She handles my work—she and her husband." She pushed at her flattened hair. "So,
what are you—oh my God." For the first time,
she focused on him. His left eye was discolored
and swollen, and there was a nasty gash along his
cheek. "What the hell happened to you?"

"Saturday night."

Quickly, she stripped off her gloves to run a
gentle finger over the cut. "I thought you grew
out of that. Have you had this looked at? Let me
get you some ice for that eye."

"It's all right," he began, but she was already
dashing into the kitchen.

"You're the sheriff, for Christ's sake," she said

as she searched for a cloth to wrap ice in. "You're not supposed to raise hell anymore. Sit down. Maybe we can get the swelling down. You're still a jerk, Rafferty."

"Thanks." He eased his aching body into the ladder-back chair she'd set in the kitchen.

"Here, hold this on your eye." She set a hip on the drop leaf table, then put a hand under his chin to turn his face to the sunlight and examine the cut. "You'll be lucky if this doesn't scar that pretty face of yours."

The ice felt like heaven, so he only grunted.

She smiled, but the concern remained in her eyes as she brushed at the hair on his forehead. She remembered Blair getting into fights, too many fights, over the last couple of years in high school. If memory served, a man wanted to be pampered—and praised—under these circumstances.

"So, should I ask what the other guy looks like?"

His lips quirked. "I broke his goddamn nose."

"God, I love this macho stuff." Taking the end of the cloth, she dabbed at the cut. "Who were you fighting with?"

"Biff."

The hand on his face stilled. Her eyes, full of understanding, came to his. "I'm sorry. I take it things haven't improved there."

"Official business. He was D and D in Clyde's—" Cam broke off and leaned back in the chair. "Fuck."

Her hand was gentle on his face again. "Hey, want a brownie?"

He smiled a little. "My grandmother always gave me milk and cookies whenever Biff beat the shit out of me."

Clare felt her stomach clench, but she made her lips curve as she took up one of his hands. "From the looks of these, I'd say he's in worse shape than you." On impulse she kissed the torn and bruised skin of his knuckles. He found the gesture incredibly endearing.

"It hurts here, too." He tapped a finger to his lips.

"Don't press your luck." Businesslike, she pulled the ice away and squinted at his eye. "Very colorful. How's your vision?"

"I can see you just fine. You're prettier than you used to be."

She tilted her head. "Considering I used to look like a scarecrow with an overbite, that's not saying much."

"I can probably do better once that painkiller kicks in."

"Okay. For now, why don't I run over to the pharmacy and get you some first aid cream?"

"I'll settle for the brownie."

He closed his eyes for a moment as he listened

to her moving around the kitchen, opening the refrigerator, the sound of liquid hitting glass, the muted music from the radio in the garage. He'd never gone in for classical, but it sounded pretty good just then. When she set the dishes and glasses on the table and took the seat across from him, he opened his eyes again. He could see patience, understanding, and the offer of a shoulder to lean on. It was so easy to open the wound.

"Christ, Slim, I wanted to kill him," Cam said quietly. There was a look in his eyes, a dark and dangerous look that contrasted with the calm control of his voice. "He was drunk and mean and looking at me the same way he looked at me when I was ten and couldn't fight back. And I wanted to kill him more than I ever wanted anything. What kind of cop does that make me?"

"A human one." She hesitated, pressing her lips together. "Cam, I used to hear my parents talking about—well, about your situation at home. Why didn't anyone ever do anything?"

"People don't like to interfere—especially in domestic problems. And my mother always backed him up. She still does. She'll post his bail as soon as it's set and take him home. Nothing he does will ever convince her that he's a worthless drunk. I used to wish he'd empty a bottle and kill himself." He cursed under his breath, thinking of Clare's father, knowing from the expression on her face that she was thinking of him as well. "I'm sorry."

"No, it's all right. I guess we both have first-hand experience of how destructive alcoholism can be. But Dad—he never hurt anyone when he was drinking. Except himself." She made the effort to shake off the mood. "You must be feeling pretty raw today. I can take a rain check on the ride."

"I am feeling raw." He flexed his stiff hands. "And I could use some company—if you can stand it."

She smiled and stood. "Let me get a jacket."

When she returned, Cam reminded her to turn off the radio—then reminded her to close the garage door. With her thumbs hooked in her pockets, she studied the motorcycle parked beside her car. It was big and brawny, a spartan black and silver without any fancy work. A machine, she thought with approval as she circled it. Not a toy.

"This is the real thing." She ran a respectful hand over the engine. With her tongue in her cheek, she picked up the helmet he'd set on the back as he unstrapped the spare. "Rafferty, you've mellowed."

As she laughed, he dropped the spare helmet over her head and fastened the strap. She slipped on the bike behind him, hooking her arms comfortably around his waist when he gunned the engine. Neither of them noticed the glint of the telescopic lens from the high window across the street when they swung out of the drive and cruised away.

She kept her hands loose and her head back. Years before, she had spent a spring and summer in Paris harmlessly in love with another art student. He'd been sweet and dreamy and broke. Together they had rented a motorbike and spent a weekend puttering through the streets.

Then she laughed at her own memory. This was nothing like that gentle interlude. Her young lover's body had been frail—nothing like the hard solid length she pressed against now.

Cam leaned into a turn, and she felt her heart race. A good burst of feeling, like the steady vibration of the bike beneath her. She could smell fumes rising from the muffler, grass newly mown, the leather of Cam's jacket, and the deeper, more secretive scent of his skin.

He liked the feel of her behind him, the unabashedly sexual sensation of her thighs spread and molded to his with the steady rhythm of the engine beneath them. Her hands rested lightly on his hips or crept more securely around his waist when he eased into a turn. On impulse he turned off the highway down a narrow, winding road. They swayed like dancers beneath an arch of trees. Shadow and light threw dizzy patterns on the asphalt. The air held the cool, fragrant breath of spring.

They stopped at a roadside store and bought icy soft drinks and huge cold-cut subs. With the picnic secured in the saddlebags, they drove farther into the woods to where a stream curved and widened.

"This is great." Clare took off the helmet and pulled a hand through her hair. Then she laughed and turned to Cam. "I don't even know where I am."

"We're only about ten miles north of town."

"But we've been riding for hours."

"I circled around." He took the bags of food and passed her one. "You were too busy singing to notice."

"The only trouble with a motorcycle is there's no radio to blast." She walked to the edge of the mossy bank where the stream was gurgling and tumbling over rocks. Overhead the leaves were still young and tender. Mountain laurel and wild dogwoods were bursts of white.

"I used to bring girls up here all the time," Cam said from behind her. "To fool around."

"Really?" She turned, smiling, and there was speculation in her eyes. He looked like a boxer who had gone the distance. Though she wasn't fond of blood sports, the analogy was appealing just then, and just there. "Is that still your standard operating procedure?" Tempted and curious, she leaned toward him. Then her eyes widened. "Oh, my God. Oh, my God, look at that!" Clare shoved the bag of sand-wiches at him and took off running.

By the time he caught her, she was standing in front of a huge old tree, her hands steepled at her lips, her eyes worshipful. "Do you believe it?" she whispered.

"I believe you took ten years off my life." He scowled at the old, misshapen tree. "What the hell got into you?"

"It's beautiful. Absolutely beautiful. I've got to have it."

"Have what?"

"The burl." She reached up, rose to her toes, but her fingertips were still several inches short of the swollen ring of wood and bark that marred the oak. "I've searched hours and never found one this good. For carving," she said when she dropped down to her flat feet. "The burl is scar tissue. When a tree is injured, it heals over, just like flesh."

"I know what a burl is, Slim."

"But this one is spectacular. I'd sell my soul for it." A calculating look came into her eyes, one that only appeared when she was preparing to haggle for material. "I've got to find out who owns this property."

"The mayor."

"Mayor Atherton owns land way out here?"

"He bought up several plots about ten, fifteen years ago when it was cheap. He owns about forty acres along here. If you want the tree, you'd probably only have to promise him your vote. That is, if you're staying."

"I'd promise him anything." She circled the tree, already considering it hers. "It must have been fate, your bringing me here."

"And I thought it was just so we could fool around."

She laughed, then eyed the bags he still carried. "Let's eat."

They settled on the ground near the stream where she had a good view of the tree, unwrapping the sandwiches and chips. Occasionally a car cruised by on the road, but for the most part there was silence.

"I've missed this," Clare said after she settled back against a rock. "The quiet."

"Is that why you came back?"

"Partly." She watched as he reached in the bag for a chip. He had beautiful hands, she realized, despite the raw and bruised knuckles. She would cast them in bronze, fisted on the hilt of a sword, or the butt of a gun. "What about you? If there was anyone I remember who was jumping to get out of Dodge, it was you. I still can't quite focus on your being back, and as a pillar of the community."

"Public servant," he corrected and took a

bite of the submarine sandwich. "Maybe I figured out finally that Emmitsboro wasn't the
problem—I was." It was part of the truth, he
thought. The rest had to do with the screams
tearing through an old building, the blast of
gunfire, blood, death.

"You were okay, Rafferty. You just took
teenage defiance one step further than most."
She grinned at him. "Every town needs its
bad boy."

"And you were always the good girl." He
laughed when disgust crossed her face. "That
smart Kimball girl, acing it through school,
heading up the student council. You probably
still hold the record for selling the most Girl
Scout cookies."

"All right, Rafferty, I don't have to sit here
and be insulted."

"I admired you," he said, but there was a glint
in his eyes. "Really. When you weren't making
me sick. Want some chips?"

She dug into the bag. "Just because I followed
the rules—"

"And you did," he agreed soberly. "You certainly did." He reached up to toy with the brass
hook of her overalls. "I guess I used to wonder
if you'd ever break out."

"You never used to wonder about me at all."

"I did." His gaze lifted to hers again. There
was still a smile in his eyes, but there was some-

thing behind it, a restlessness that put her on alert.

Uh-oh. That one quick thought slammed into her mind.

"It used to surprise me how often my mind wandered in your direction. You were only a kid, and bony with it, from a prominent family on the right side of the tracks. And everyone knew there wasn't a guy in town who could get past first base with you." When she brushed his hand away from her buckle, he only smiled. "I figured I was thinking about you because Blair and I had started hanging out."

"When he was going through his hoodlum stage."

"Right." He wasn't sure how she managed to make her throaty voice prim, but he liked it. "So did you ever break out, Slim?"

"I've had my moments." Irritated, she chomped down on her sandwich. "You know, people don't think about me as the skinny, well-behaved nerd from Dogpatch."

He hadn't realized it would give him such a kick to see her riled. "How do people think about you, Slim?"

"As a successful artist with talent and vision. At my last show, the critics—" She caught herself and scowled at him. "Damn you, Rafferty, you're making me talk like a nerd."

"That's okay. You're among friends." He

brushed some crumbs from her chin. "Is that how you think of yourself first, as an artist?"

"Don't you think of yourself as a cop first?"

"Yeah," he said after a moment. "I guess I do."

"So, is there much action in Emmitsboro these days?"

"Something crops up now and again." Because the cemetery incident was still on his mind, he told her about it.

"That's sick." She rubbed her arms against a sudden chill. "And it doesn't sound like something that would happen around here. Do you figure kids?"

"We haven't been able to prove otherwise, but no, I don't. It was too neat, too purposeful."

She looked around, taking in the quiet trees, hearing the musical water. "Too grisly."

He was sorry he'd brought it up and changed the subject to a do-you-remember-when mode.

He didn't think about his hurts and bruises. It was easy, maybe too easy, for his body to be distracted. He liked looking at her, the way her mussed cap of hair caught the sunlight. It was a wonder he hadn't noticed a decade before that her skin was so smooth, translucent, soft. It was her eyes he remembered most, the golden, almost witchlike glow of them.

Now he enjoyed listening to her voice, the rise and fall of it. Her laugh that rolled like fog. They talked the afternoon away, arguing over points of view, forging a friendship that had been tentative at best during childhood.

Though the stream played music, and sun and shade danced overhead, he sensed the timing was wrong for anything but friendship. When they climbed on the bike again, they were easy with each other.

The only mistake Cam figured he made that day was cutting through town on the way back. That gave Bud Hewitt the opportunity to flag him down as they rode past the sheriff's office.

"Hey, Sheriff." Though dressed in civvies, Bud put on his official face as he nodded at Clare. "Nice to have you back."

"Bud?" With a laugh, Clare hopped off the bike to give him a smacking kiss. "I spent last night eating pizza and getting sloppy drunk with Alice. She tells me you're the town deputy."

"One of 'em." He flushed with the pleasure of knowing his name had been mentioned. "You look real nice, Clare." In fact, his Adam's apple was bobbing a bit while he looked at her. Her cheeks were flushed from the wind, her eyes deep and gold. "Guess you two've been out riding."

"That's right." Cam wasn't as amused as he thought he should be by the puppy dog admiration in Bud's eyes. "Is there a problem?"

"Well, I figured you'd want to know—and

since you weren't home when I called and I saw you passing through, I stopped you."

Cam flicked a wrist and had the engine gunning impatiently. "I got that much, Bud."

"It's about that runaway. The kid from Harrisburg?"

"Has she been located?"

"No, but we got a call this morning from the State boys. Somebody spotted a kid with her description a few miles out of town on Route Fifteen, the same afternoon she took off. Heading towards Emmitsboro. Thought you'd want to know," he repeated.

"Did you get a name?"

"Got the name and phone number. Wrote them down inside."

"I'll take Clare home first."

"Can I wait?" She was already strapping her helmet to the back. "I haven't been in the sheriff's office since Parker used to sit behind the desk and belch."

"It's not as colorful as it used to be," Cam said, ushering her inside.

She recognized the man behind the desk as Mick Morgan. He'd been a fresh-faced deputy under Parker, and the years hadn't dealt kindly with him. He'd bloated and sagged, and the part in his dingy brown hair had widened as sadly as his waistline. He pushed a chaw in the side of his mouth and rose.

"Cam. Didn't think you were coming by." He focused on Clare and managed what passed for a smile. There was tobacco juice on his teeth. "Heard you were back."

"Hi, Mr. Morgan." She tried not to remember that he had been the first on the scene after her father's death. Or to blame him for being the one who had pried her away from the body.

"Guess you're rich and famous now." There was a crash and a curse from the back. Morgan cocked a brow, then spit expertly into the brass bucket in the corner. "Old Biff's been causing a ruckus most of the day. Got one godawful hangover."

"I'll deal with it." Cam glanced toward the back as a new wave of obscenities erupted. "Bud, why don't you run Clare home?"

She started to bow out graciously, then noticed the tension in Cam's face, his neck, his arms. "I'm fine." With a casual shrug, she began to study the papers stuck to the bulletin board. "I'll just hang around. Take your time."

Morgan patted the belly over his belt. "Since you're here, Cam, I'll take my dinner break."

With a curt nod, Cam strode over to the heavy door separating the cells from the office. The cursing went on after he shut the door behind him.

"Tough on him," Morgan said and spit again.

"Come on, Bud, buy you a cup of coffee down to Martha's."

"Ah . . . see you, Clare."

"Sure, Bud."

When they left, she wandered to the window to look out at the town. It was quiet as a portrait on a Sunday. A few kids were riding bikes down the Main Street slope. A couple of teenagers were sitting on the hood of an old Buick and flirting. Inside the houses, she imagined, people were sitting down to Sunday suppers of pot roast or baked ham.

From the room behind her, she could hear the vicious-tempered shouts of Biff, bullying and threatening his stepson. She couldn't hear Cam at all and wondered if he spoke or merely listened.

He spoke—in a low, controlled voice that held more power than all of Biff's ragings. Through the bars that separated them, he studied the man who had made his life hell for almost as long as he could remember. Doc Crampton had bandaged Biff up, but one eye was swollen closed, and his nose was a bruised mess against the white adhesive.

And he was old, Cam realized all at once. The man was old, used up, and pathetic.

"You'll stay in until bail's set tomorrow," Cam told him.

"You let me out of here now, or when I get out, I'll come for you. You understand me, boy?"

Cam looked at the battered face, realizing he'd done that with his own hands. Yet he couldn't remember it clearly. Every blow had been rammed through a blinding haze of hate. "I understand you. Stay out of my town, old man."

"Your town?" Biff's thick fingers wrapped around the bars and shook. "You're nothing but a pissant punk in this town, and you'll never be any different. Pin a fucking badge on your shirt and think you're big time. You're worthless, just like your old man was worthless."

Cam's hand snaked through the bars so quickly, Biff had no chance to evade. There was the sound of material ripping where Cam gripped Biff's shirt. "Just who do you think would give a shit if I found you dead in this cell?" He pulled, hard, and had Biff's face rapping into the bars. "Think about that, you bastard, and stay clear of me. And if I find out you went home and took out your little frustrations on my mother, I'll kill you. You understand me?"

"You ain't got the guts. You never did." Biff yanked himself away and swiped a hand under his freshly bleeding nose. "You think you know all there is to know, but you don't know shit. You don't run this town. You're going to pay for putting me in here. I know people who can make you pay."

Disgusted, Cam moved to the door. "You want to eat, then you watch your mouth. I'm leaving orders for Mick to hold back your dinner until you quiet down."

"I'll see you in hell, boy," Biff shouted through the bars, bashing them with his fists when Cam shut the door again. "If it's the last thing I do, I'll see you in hell."

Alone in the cell, he mopped at his face. And began to chant.

Clare waited until she heard the door close before she turned. One look at Cam's face had her heart going out to him, but she offered a casual smile instead.

"And I thought you had a boring job."

He avoided her by going to his desk. He wanted to touch her, hold on to her, but a part of him felt stained with filth. "You should have gone home."

She sat on the corner of his desk. "I'll wait until you take me."

He glanced down to read Bud's careful, grammar school handwriting. "I need to make this call."

"I'm in no hurry."

He pressed his thumb and forefinger on the

bridge of his nose, then picked up the phone. At least Biff had shut up, he thought.

"This is Sheriff Rafferty in Emmitsboro, I'd like to speak to Mr. or Mrs. Smithfield. Yes, Mrs. Smithfield. This is concerning the call you made to the state police regarding Carly Jamison." He listened for a moment, then began taking notes. "Do you remember what she was wearing? Yes, yes, I know that spot. What time of day was it? No, ma'am, I don't blame you for not picking up a hitchhiker. Yes, it can be dangerous. I really couldn't say. No, you and your husband did the right thing. We appreciate your cooperation. Thank you, yes, if I need anything else, I'll be sure to call."

When he hung up, Clare tilted her head down and smiled. "You sounded real official and diplomatic."

"Thanks a lot." Rising, he took her arm. "Let's get the hell out of here."

"So how old was the runaway?" she asked casually when they slipped back onto the bike.

"About fifteen—female from Harrisburg. Carrying a red knapsack and pissed at the world because her parents wouldn't let her go to Florida for spring break."

"How long has she been missing?"

"Too long." He gunned the motor and took off.

The sun was setting when she convinced him

to relax on the porch swing for a few minutes with a glass of wine. She'd poured the twenty-dollar French chardonnay into jelly glasses.

"My dad and I used to sit out on evenings like this and wait for the crickets to start." She stretched out her long legs and sighed. "You know, Cam, coming back home means coming back to a load of problems. That doesn't mean it was the wrong decision."

He sipped, wondering if the glasses made the wine taste jazzier, or the company. "Are we talking about you or me?"

She slanted him a look. "Word around town is that you're a pretty good sheriff."

"Since most people only have Parker for a yardstick, that isn't saying much." He touched a curl that lay against her neck. "Thanks. If I'd gone straight home, I'd have smashed a wall or something."

"Glad I could help. I also heard you have a nifty house." She watched him as she sipped. "Of course, I haven't been invited to see it."

"Looks like I owe you a tour."

"Looks like."

They drank in companionable silence, watching a car drive by, listening to a dog bark, breathing in the scent of hyacinths her father had planted years before.

The sun dropped lower, and the breeze shifted shadows over the lawn.

It seemed natural, almost familiar, when he touched a hand to her face, turned it toward his. His lips brushed over hers, sampling. With their eyes open, they leaned closer, soothed by the gentle movement of the swing. When he deepened the kiss, was compelled to deepen it, he tasted the quick release of her breath.

One glass of wine shouldn't make the head spin, she thought as she put a hand to his chest. Neither should one kiss, especially from a man she'd known most of her life.

Shaken, she drew away. "Cam, I think—"

"Think later," he muttered and pulled her against him again.

Exotic. It was strange that the shy, skinny girl from his childhood should taste so exotic. Feel so erotic. He knew his mouth was impatient, but he couldn't help it. He'd had no idea that one touch, one taste, would lead to a grinding need for more.

When she could breathe again, she shifted back an inch, then two, until her dazed eyes could focus on his face. The restless desire in his eyes had her heart racing.

"Oh," she managed, and he smiled.

"Is that good or bad?"

"Just—oh." With an unsteady hand she brought her glass to her lips. Wine helped cool the heat he had licked into her mouth. "I thought I was coming back for some quiet and relaxation."

"It's real quiet tonight."

"Yeah." And if he kissed her again, she was damn sure she'd go off like a rocket. "Cam, I've always thought in a place like this, things should move slow. Very slow."

"Okay." He brought her back, settling her head on his shoulder. He'd waited more than ten years to find out what it was like, he thought, as he set the swing back in motion. He figured that was slow enough.

As the crickets began to sing, neither of them realized they were caught in the lens of a telescope.

Chapter 7

THOUGH ERNIE BUTTS FIGURED school was, at best, a waste of time, he liked his advanced chemistry class. There was something fascinating about the Bunsen burners, the test tubes, and petri dishes. Memorizing the periodic chart of elements was a bore, but he'd never had any problem with retention. Nor did he have any trouble identifying unknowns in a mixture. Unknowns never failed to interest him.

Still, doing lab work was the best. There was something powerful about mixing chemicals, testing reactions. He always felt in control. He liked to measure and pour and create, and toyed with the idea of making a bomb. Not a stupid stink bomb like Denny Moyers had put together and set off during third period in the girls' locker room. That was kid stuff. Ernie wanted something that would flash and boom, busting out windows and setting off some real old-fashioned hysteria.

He could do it; school, and the books his parents had bought him, had given him the knowledge. He was certain he had the capability. And if he decided to do it, he wouldn't get caught like that jerk-off Moyers. Real power wasn't in bragging about what you did, but in having people wonder.

Doodling in his notebook, Ernie glanced up as James Atherton repeated his instructions. As far as Ernie was concerned, Atherton was a bigger asshole than most adults. He repeated everything in his quiet, tutorial voice, occasionally stretching and turning his long, skinny neck or polishing his glasses as he droned on and on.

Like a four-eyed giraffe, Ernie thought maliciously.

Everybody knew he'd made a nice little pile of money in real estate and didn't even have to teach. But here he was, semester after semester, in his dopey suits and ties, trying to teach chemical reactions to kids who mostly didn't give a fuck.

People said he was dedicated; Ernie figured he was just a dick.

The fact that he was mayor of Emmitsboro

only added to Ernie's bitter amusement. What did the mayor of Hicktown have to do anyway? Decide what color the benches in the park should be painted?

"This chemical bonding lab will count for one-quarter of your grade in this last marking period," Atherton continued, scanning the faces of his students with a little inward sigh. After nearly thirty years as a teacher, he had no trouble reading the outcome of this final experiment of the school year. At least ten percent of the class would fail and too many would barely skim by.

"Miss Simmons, perhaps you could put your compact down for a moment."

There was a ripple of giggles as Sally Simmons hastily stuffed her compact in her bag.

"You will be working in teams," Atherton continued, meticulously straightening a pile of papers before picking it up to distribute the sheets. "Lab partners are listed on this work sheet. I suggest you familiarize yourselves with the stages of the experiment. Written work will be due in two weeks."

As the papers made their way around the class, there were groans and grunts and whispered comments. Ernie noted, with little interest, that Sally Simmons was his lab partner.

"It will be up to each team to distribute the workload," Atherton said over the din. In his unassuming way, he studied each student. He knew each of them better than they would have guessed. "Remember, you are partners, and the grade, good or bad, will belong to both of you. You may go to your assigned stations and begin your planning." He held up a bony finger. "Quietly."

Atherton glanced at the clock and was as relieved as his students that only ten minutes remained in the period.

"I guess we're partners." Sally tried a bright smile. Though she'd known Ernie for years, from a distance, she still wasn't sure what to make of him. He was by turns wild and moody, and that appealed to her sympathy for rebels.

"Yeah." Ernie gave her a long, unnerving look that had her licking her lips.

"Well, I guess we could study and work on the written part after school some days. We can use my house if you want."

"I work after school."

"Well . . . after that, then. I could come over to your place if that's better."

He continued to look at her in a way that had her fussing with her hair, then the buttons of her shirt. Beneath the lacy black bra she'd swiped from her older sister, her heart pounded pleasantly.

"I'm usually finished about nine," Ernie told her. "We can use my place, nobody'll be around to bother us." He smiled then, letting his lips spread slowly away from his teeth. "Unless you figure Josh'll get pissed."

She smiled again, more comfortable on familiar ground. "We sort of broke up. Josh is cute and all, but he can really be a pain."

"Yeah? You two have been pretty tight the last few weeks."

She tossed back her rich fall of dark hair. "We just hung around some. People started putting us together after we found that empty grave. If you want, I can come by tonight, and we can get started."

He smiled a little. "Yeah, we'll get started." He wondered if she was a virgin.

After school Ernie drove to Clare's. He didn't mind the idea of having sex with Sally, but the hot, sweaty dreams he'd been having had centered on his new neighbor. He wondered how it would be to have both of them at once, the way he'd seen in the porno tape he'd copped from Less Gladhill at the gas station.

His hands were sweaty as he thought of it. He liked the idea of control, domination, power. Doing both of them would prove something. Would make him somebody.

He pulled into Clare's drive and shut off the engine. From there, he watched her work with hammer and snips. It was warmer today, and she was wearing shorts, snug ones frayed at the hem, and a big T-shirt that slipped over one shoulder.

What would it be like to walk in, to rip that shirt away? Right there, right now, in broad daylight. Her eyes would widen, the pupils dilating with fear and shock. He'd pull her down to the concrete. She'd whimper. But then . . . then she would be hot and wet and ready.

He didn't like the idea that Sheriff Rafferty was moving in on her, but he wasn't overly disturbed. Ernie figured he could take care of Rafferty if he had to.

He climbed out of the truck and walked toward her.

Intent on shaping the metal in her vise, Clare didn't notice him until he was almost beside her. She straightened, pressed a hand on her lower back, and smiled.

"Hi."

As she arched her back, her small, unencumbered breasts strained against the cotton T-shirt. He imagined squeezing them.

"You said I should come by after school sometime."

"So I did." She set the hammer aside. "I'm glad you decided to help me out." She took a moment to pull herself out of the project at hand and into a new one. "Listen, there's a chair inside the kitchen. Why don't you drag it out here? You can grab yourself a Pepsi if you want."

"Okay."

When he came back, she had cleared off a space on a worktable. "Just set it over there. You might want to rest your arm on that bench from time to time. Don't be afraid to tell me if you're getting tired." She hoisted herself up on the worktable, turned down the volume of the old Moody Blues number on her stereo, and gestured for him to sit. "I'm just going to do some sketches. I think if you set your elbow on that bench and make a fist . . . yeah." She smiled at him. "So how's school?"

"Okay."

"I guess you've only got a few weeks left." She was sketching on a pad as she spoke, and tried to put him at ease.

"Yeah."

A man of few words, she thought, and tried again. "You into sports or anything?"

"Not into sports."

"Got a girl?"

His gaze slid up her legs. "Not one in particular."

"Ah, a wise man. So, what do your folks do?"

He grimaced, from habit. "Run the pizza parlor."

"No kidding?" She stopped sketching. "I had

some the other night. It's terrific. I have to tell you, the idea of leaving New York pizza behind made the decision to come back here tough. Rocco's made up for it."

He shrugged, embarrassed to be pleased. "It's no big deal."

"Easy to say when you've grown up with it. Open your fist once and spread your fingers. Mmmm." With a frown of concentration, she continued to sketch. "So, where'd you live before here?"

"New Jersey."

"Oh, yeah? Why did you move here?"

The sulky look came back in his eyes. "Don't ask me. They didn't."

Sympathetic, she smiled at him. "It's not such a bad place."

"It's dead. I hate it. People sit around and watch the grass grow."

Three sentences in a row, she thought. He must have strong feelings. "I guess it's hard to believe there'd ever come a time when you'd actually appreciate watching the grass grow."

"Easy for you to say," he muttered, mimicking her. "You can go back to New York whenever you want."

"That's true." And children, she thought, no matter how hard they strained for independence, were stuck. "It won't be long before you can decide for yourself. L.A., right?"

"Yeah. I'm getting the hell out of here." He was staring at her legs again, at the way the frayed hem of her shorts cut high on her thighs. "Have you been there?"

"Yeah, once or twice. It's not really my style. You'll have to let me know what you think of it once you get there. Make a fist again." She turned a page in the sketchpad, then shook her head. "You know, what I think I want is from the shoulder up, kind of like a tree shooting up from the roots. You want to take your shirt off? It's warm enough."

He looked at her, secrets playing in his eyes as he slowly pulled the T-shirt over his head. She wanted him. He knew it.

What Clare saw was a slim, angry boy on the teetering brink of manhood. More, she saw a subject, a slender arm, surprisingly roped with muscle, its power still untapped.

"This is going to work." She scooted down from the table. "Let me pose it. I won't ask you to hold it long. It'll get uncomfortable."

She took his arm, cupping a hand under his elbow as she lifted it, bent it. Then she closed her fingers over his to make a fist again.

"Now, if you can hold it out at this angle. . . . Good, now put some tension into it. Terrific. You're a natural." As she stepped back, she glanced down to the pendant he wore. It was silver, in an odd geometric shape. Like a pentagram, she thought, and looked up at him. "What's this? A good luck charm?"

His free hand closed over it protectively. "Sort of."

Afraid she'd embarrassed him, she picked up her pad again and began to sketch.

She worked for an hour, letting him take frequent breaks to rest his arm. A time or two she caught him watching her speculatively, with a much too adult gleam in his eyes. She passed it off, a little amused, a little flattered that he might have developed a small crush on her.

"That's great, Ernie, really. I'd like to start working in clay whenever you've got another couple of hours to spare."

"Okay."

"I'll get you some money."

Alone, he flexed his arm and wandered around the garage. When he spotted the sculpture in the corner, he stopped short. Once again, his fingers closed around the inverted pentagram as he studied the half man, half beast she had created out of metal and nightmares.

It was a sign, he thought, his breath coming quickly. His fingers trembled slightly as he reached out to stroke it worshipfully. She had been brought here for him. The rituals, the offerings had met with favor. The Dark Lord had delivered her to him. Now he had only to wait for the right time and place to take her.

"What do you think of it?"

Cautiously, Ernie dragged on his shirt before he turned. Clare was standing behind him. She was staring, as he had been, at the sculpture. He could smell her, soap and sweat.

"It has power."

She was surprised to hear the opinion from a seventeen-year-old. Intrigued, she turned her head and stared at him. "Ever thought about becoming an art critic?"

"Why did you make this?"

"I couldn't seem to help myself."

The answer was perfect. "You'll do more."

She glanced back at the heap of metal on her welding table. "Yes, it seems that I will." Shaking herself, she held out some bills. "I really appreciate your posing for me."

"I liked it. I like you."

"Good. I like you, too." When the phone rang, she turned to the kitchen doorway. "Gotta go. See you soon, Ernie."

"Yeah." He wiped his damp palms on the thighs of his jeans. "I'll see you real soon."

Clare opened the refrigerator and picked up the phone simultaneously. "Hello."

As she rooted out a hot dog, mustard, pickles, and a soft drink, wet, heavy breathing sounded in her ear. She grinned, stuck the hot dog in the microwave, and began to breathe back, occasionally adding a husky "yes" or "oh yes!"

After setting the timer, she popped open the bottle. "Oh, my God, don't stop." She finished with a long, wavering moan.

"Was it good for you?" the low, masculine voice asked.

"Wonderful. Incredible. The best." She took a long swallow of Pepsi. "Jean-Paul, you give great phone." She took the hot dog out of the microwave, then wrapped it in a piece of Wonder bread, and began to slather on mustard. "If Angie ever finds out—"

"I'm on the extention, you idiot."

Chuckling, Clare added a row of dill pickle slices. "Oh, well, all is discovered. So what's up?"

"After that," Jean-Paul said, "I am."

"Behave yourself," Angie said mildly. "We wanted to see how you are."

"I'm good." Satisfied, Clare picked up the dripping sandwich and bit in. "Really good," she mumbled with a full mouth. "In fact, I just finished some sketches with a new model. The kid's got great arms."

"Oh, really?"

Amused by Angie's intonation, Clare shook her head. "I meant kid literally. He's sixteen, seventeen. I also took some sketches of this friend of mine who's a waitress. Competent poetry in motion. And I've got my eye on a fabulous set of hands." She thought of Cam and chewed thoughtfully. "Maybe the face, too. Or the whole damn body." Just how would he react if she suggested he pose nude? she wondered.

"You sound busy, *chérie.*" Jean-Paul picked up a chunk of amethyst from his desk.

"I am. Angie, you'll be pleased to know I've been working every day. Really working," she added, scooting up on the counter, then taking another bite of the hot dog. "I've actually got one piece finished."

"And?" Angie probed.

"I'd rather you see it for yourself. I'm too close to it."

With the phone cocked between his ear and shoulder, Jean-Paul passed the stone from hand to hand. "How is life in the boondicks?"

"Docks," Clare corrected. "Boondocks, and it's fine. Why don't you come see for yourself?"

"What about that, Angie? Would you like a few days in the country? We can smell the cows and make love in the hay."

"I'll think about it."

"A week in Emmitsboro is not like a year in the Outback." Warming to the idea, Clare polished off the hot dog. "We don't have wild boar or mad rapists."

"*Je suis desolé,*" Jean-Paul said, tongue in cheek. "What do you have, *chérie*?"

"Quiet, tranquility—even a comforting kind

of boredom." She thought of Ernie with his youthful restlessness and dissatisfaction. Boredom wasn't for everyone, she supposed. "After I show you the hot spots like Martha's Diner and Clyde's Tavern, we can sit on the porch, drink beer, and watch the grass grow."

"Sounds stimulating," Angie muttered.

"We'll see what we can shuffle in our schedule." Jean-Paul decided on the spot. "I would like to see Clyde's."

"Great." Clare lifted her bottle in an absent toast. "You'll love it. Really. It's the perfect American rural town. Nothing ever happens in Emmitsboro."

A thin spring drizzle was falling, muddying the earth in the circle. There was no fire in the pit, only the cold ash of wood and bone. Lanterns took the place of candles. Clouds choked the moon and smothered the stars.

But the decision had been made, and they would not wait. Tonight there were only five cloaked figures. The old guard. This meeting, this ritual, was secret to all but these chosen few.

"Christ, it's shitty out here tonight." Biff Stokey cupped his beefy hand around his cigarette to protect it from the rain. Tonight there were no drugs, no candles, no chanting, no prostitute. In the twenty years he had been a member of the coven, he had come to depend on, and require, the ritual as much as the fringe benefits.

But tonight, instead of an altar, there was only an empty slab and an inverted cross. Tonight, his companions seemed edgy and watchful. No one spoke as the rain pelted down.

"What the hell's this all about?" he demanded of no one in particular. "This isn't our usual night."

"There is business to tend to." The leader stepped out of the group, into the center, and turned toward them. The eyes of his mask looked dark and empty. Twin pits of hell. He lifted his arms, his long fingers splayed. "We are the few. We are the first. In our hands the power shines brighter. Our Master has given us the great gift to bring others to Him, to show them His glory."

Like a statue he stood, an eerie mirror image of Clare's nightmare sculpture. Body bent, head lifted, arms outstretched. Behind his mask, his eyes gleamed with anticipation, with appreciation of the power he held that the others would never understand.

They had come, like well-trained dogs, at his call. They would act, as mindless as sheep, at his command. And if one or two had a portion remaining of what some might call conscience, the thirst for power would overcome it.

"Our Master is displeased. His fangs drip with vengeance. Betrayed by one of His children, by one of His chosen. The Law is defiled, and we will avenge it. Tonight, there is death."

When he lowered his hands, one of the cloaked figures brought a baseball bat from beneath his robes. Even as Biff opened his mouth in surprise, it cracked over his skull.

When he regained consciousness, he was tied to the altar, and naked. The drizzling rain soaked and chilled his skin. But that was nothing, nothing compared to the frozen fear that squeezed his heart.

They stood around him, one at the feet, one at the head, one on each side at the hip. Four men he had known most of his life. Their eyes were the eyes of strangers. And he knew what they saw was death.

The fire had been lit, and rain splattered and sizzled on the logs. The sound was like meat frying.

"No!" He squirmed, straining his arms and legs as he writhed on the smooth slab. "Jesus Christ, no!" In his panic he called on the deity he had spent twenty years defiling. His mouth was filled with the taste of fear and the blood from where his teeth had sawed into his tongue. "You can't. You can't. I took the oath."

The leader looked down at Biff's scarred left testicle. The sign would have to be . . . erased.

"You are no longer one of the few. You have broken the oath. You have broken the Law."

"Never. I never broke the Law." The rope cut into his wrists as he strained. First blood stained the wood.

"We do not show our fangs in anger. That is the Law."

"That is the Law," the others chanted.

"I was drunk." His chest heaved as he began to weep, the thin, bitter tears of terror. There were faces he knew, shadowed by the hoods, hidden by masks. His eyes darted from one to the other, panicked and pleading. "Fucking Christ, I was drunk."

"You have defiled the Law," the leader repeated. His voice held no mercy and no passion—though the passion was rising in him, a black, boiling sea. "You have shown that you cannot hold to it. You are weak, and the weak shall be smote by the strong." The bell was rung. Over Biff's sobs and curses, the leader lifted his voice.

"O, Lord of the Dark Flame, give us power."

"Power for Your glory," the others chanted.

"O, Lord of the Ages, give us strength."

"Strength for your Law."

"In nomine Dei nostri Santanas Luciferi excelsi!"

"Ave, Satan."

He lifted a silver cup. "This is the wine of bitterness. I drink in despair for our lost brother."

He drank long and deep, pouring the wine through the gaping mouth hole of the mask. He set the cup aside, but still he thirsted. For blood.

"For he has been tried, and he has been judged, and he has been condemned."

"I'll kill you," Biff shouted, tearing flesh as he struggled against his bonds. "I'll kill you all. Please, God, don't do this."

"The die is cast. There is no mercy in the heart of the Prince of Hell. In his name I command the Dark Forces to bestow their infernal power upon me. By all the Gods of the Pit, I command that this thing I desire shall come to pass."

"Hear the names."

"Baphomet, Loki, Hecate, Beelzebub."

"We are Your children."

Blubbering with fear, Biff screamed, cursing them in turn, begging, threatening. The priest let Biff's terror fill him as he continued.

"The voices of my wrath smash the stillness. My vengeance is absolute. I am annihilation. I am revenge. I am infernal justice. I call upon the children of the Dark Lord to slash with grim delight our fallen brother. He has betrayed, and his shrieks of agony, his battered corpse shall serve as warning to those who would stray from the Law."

He paused, and behind his mask, he was smiling.

"Oh, brothers of the night, those who would ride upon the hot breath of Hell, begin."

As the first blow shattered his kneecap, Biff's scream tore through the air. They beat him mechanically. And if there was regret, it did not outweigh the need. It could not outweigh the Law.

The priest stood back, his arms lifted as he watched the slaughter. Twice before he had ordered the death of one of the brotherhood. And twice before the quick and merciless act had smothered the flickering flames of insurrection. He was well aware that some were discontented at the coven's veering away from its purer origins. Just as there were some who thirsted for more blood, more sex, more depravity.

Such things had happened before and were expected.

It was up to him to see that his children walked the line he'd created. It was up to him to be certain that those who didn't paid the price.

Biff screamed again, and the priest's pleasure soared.

They would not kill him quickly. It was not the way. With each nauseating crack of wood against bone, the priest's blood swam faster, hotter. The screaming continued, a high, keening, scarcely human sound.

A fool, the priest thought as his loins throbbed. The death of a fool was often a waste—if one discounted the sweetness of the kill. But this death would serve to warn the others of the full wrath. *His* wrath. For he had long ago come to understand that it was not Satan who ruled here, but himself.

He was the power.

The glory of the death was his.

The pleasure of the kill was his.

As the screaming faded to a wet, gurgling whimper, he stepped forward. Taking up the fourth bat, he stood over Biff. He saw that beyond the milky glaze of pain in his victim's anguished eyes, there was still fear. Even better, there was still hope.

"Please." Blood ran from Biff's mouth, choking him. He tried to lift a hand, but his fingers were as useless as broken twigs. He was beyond pain now, impaled on a jagged threshold no man was meant to endure. "Please don't kill me. I took the oath. I took the oath."

The priest merely watched him, knowing this moment, this triumph, was almost at an end. "He is the Judge. He is the Ruler. What we have done, we have done in His name." His eyes glittered down at Biff's face, still unmarked. "He who dies tonight will be thrown into torture, into misery. Into the void."

Biff's vision hazed and cleared, hazed and cleared. Blood dribbled from his mouth with each shallow breath. There would be no more screaming. He knew he was dead, and the prayers that raced through his numbed mind were mixed with incantations. To Christ. To Lucifer.

He coughed once, violently, and nearly passed out.

"I'll see you in hell," he managed.

The priest leaned over close, so that only Biff could hear. "This is hell." With shuddering delight, he delivered the coup de grace. His seed spilled hot on the ground.

While they burned the bats in the sacred pits, blood soaked into the muddy earth.

Chapter 8

CAM STOOD BY the fence bordering the east end of Matthew Dopper's cornfield. Dopper, his cap pulled down to shade his face and a chaw swelling his cheek, stayed on the tractor and kept it idling. Its motor putted smoothly, thanks to his oldest son, who preferred diddling with engines to plowing fields.

His plaid shirt was already streaked with sweat, though it was barely ten. Two fingers of his left hand were shaved off at the first knuckle, the result of a tangle with a combine. The impairment didn't affect his farming or his bowling average in his Wednesday night league. It had instilled a cautious respect for machinery.

The whites of his eyes were permanently red-streaked from fifty-odd years of wind and hay dust. He had a stubborn, closed-in look on his lined hangdog face.

He'd been born on the farm and had taken it over when his old man finally kicked off. Since his brother, the unlucky Junior, had blasted himself to hell in the adjoining woods, Matthew Dopper had inherited every sonofabitching stone on the eighty-five-acre farm. He'd lived there, worked there, and would die there. He didn't need Cameron Rafferty to come flashing his badge and telling him how to handle his business.

"Matt, it's the third complaint this month."

In answer, Dopper spat over the side of the tractor. "Them goddamn flatlanders move in, planting their goddamn houses on Hawbaker land, then they try to push me out. I ain't budging. This here's my land."

Cam set a boot on the bottom rung of the fence and prayed for patience. The ripe scent of fertilizer was making his nostrils quiver. "Nobody's trying to run you out, Matt. You've just got to chain up those dogs."

"Been dogs on this farm for a hundred years." He spat again. "Never been chained."

"Things change." Cam looked out over the field to where he could see the boxy modular homes in the distance. Once there had been only fields, meadows, pastures. If you'd driven by at dawn or at dusk, like as not you'd have seen deer grazing. Now people were putting up satellite dishes and planting ceramic deer in their front yards.

Was it any wonder his sympathies were with Matt? he thought. But sympathies aside, he had a job to do.

"Your dogs aren't staying on the farm, Matt. That's the problem."

Matt grinned. "They always liked to shit on Hawbaker land."

Cam couldn't help but smile back. There had been a running feud between the Doppers and the Hawbakers for three generations. It had kept them all happy. Lighting a cigarette, he leaned companionably on the fence.

"I miss seeing old man Hawbaker riding his hay baler."

Dopper pursed his lips. The fact was, he missed Hawbaker, too. Deeply. "I reckon he did what he thought he had to do. And made a pretty profit." He took out a dingy bandanna and blew his nose heartily. "But I'm staying put. As long as I'm breathing, I'm farming."

"I used to sneak over here and steal your corn."

"I know." The resentment faded a bit as Dopper remembered. "I grow the best Silver Queen in the county. Always did, always will."

"Can't argue with that. We'd camp out in the woods over there and roast it over the fire." He grinned up at Matt as he remembered the taste, sweet as sugar. "We thought we were putting one over on you."

"I know what goes on on my land." He adjusted his cap. For a moment, the eyes that shifted to the far, deep woods were wary. "Never minded you pinching a few ears. 'Round here we take care of our own."

"I'll remember that come July." He sighed a little. "Listen, Matt, there are kids over in the development. Lots of kids. Your three German shepherds are big bastards."

Dopper's jaw set again. "Ain't never bit nobody."

"Not yet." Cam blew out a breath. He knew he could bring up the county leash law until his tongue fell off. Nobody paid much attention to it. But as much as he felt empathy with Dopper, he wouldn't risk having one of the dogs turn and bite some kid. "Matt, I know you don't want anyone hurt." He held up a hand before Matt could protest. "I know, they're regular lapdogs. With you, maybe. But nobody can predict how they might react to strangers. If anything happens, your dogs go down, and your ass gets sued. Make it easy on everybody. Chain them up, build them a run, fence in part of your yard."

Dopper squinted at Cam, then spat. He had reasons for owning three big dogs. Good reasons. A man needed to protect himself and his family from . . . His gaze drifted toward the woods again, then away. From whatever they needed protection against.

He didn't like compromises. But he knew if he didn't make one, some snotty pissant from the ASPCA was going to come nosing around. Or some asshole flatlander was going to take him to court. He couldn't afford any shit-hole lawyer's fees.

"I'll think about it."

In six weeks of trying, it was the closest Cam had nudged him to an agreement. He smoked in silence as he measured the man on the tractor. The dogs would be chained, he thought, because old Matt wouldn't risk them, or his farm.

"How's the family?" Cam asked, wanting to end the interview on a friendly note.

"Good enough." Dopper relaxed in turn. "Sue Ellen done divorced that worthless car salesman she married." He grinned at Cam. "You missed the boat with her first time around. Might be she'd take a look at you now that you got some money and a steady job."

Unoffended, Cam grinned back. "How many kids does she have now?"

"Four. Fucker knocked her up every time she sneezed. Got herself a job, though. Clerking up to JC Penney's at that sonofabitching shopping center. Nancy's watching the youngest."

He glanced in the direction of the house, where his wife was busy with their youngest grand-child.

He talked for a few minutes more, about his oldest boy, who should have been back from the feed and grain an hour ago, and his youngest, who was in college.

"Imagine that boy figuring he had to go to school to learn how to farm." Dopper spat again contemplatively. "Guess things do change, whether you want them to or not. Got to get back to work."

"They got chains in the hardware," Cam said and pitched his cigarette. "Be seeing you, Matt."

Dopper watched him walk back toward his car, then shifted his gaze toward the huddle of houses in the distance. Fucking flatlanders, he thought, and revved up his tractor.

Cam turned his car around, spewing up dust and gravel. He drove by the edge of Dopper's Woods, where the leaves were thick and green. A part of his mind swung back to childhood, to adolescence.

He could see himself, a bundle of Dopper's corn in his arms, a couple of beer bottles clang-ing in the sack along with a pack of Marlboros and wooden matches. He might have been alone, running off to lick the wounds his stepfa-ther so gleefully handed out. Or he might have been with Blair Kimball, Bud Hewitt, Jesse Hawbaker, or one of the others he'd hung out with during those long gone days.

They would have sat by the fire, with the smell of roasting corn and hot dogs, guzzling beer, lying about girls, telling Junior Dopper stories designed to make the skin crawl.

Funny how often they'd gone there, even though the hairs on the back of their necks stood up. Probably because of it, he thought. It had been their place, haunted and eerie.

And sometimes, they had been sure that something walked through those deep and silent woods with them.

The involuntary shudder had him chuckling to himself. Some things don't change, he thought, grinning. Junior Dopper's faceless ghost could still bring a chill to the base of the spine.

He swung away from the woods, deciding to run by the development and assure the latest angry resident that Matt Dopper's dogs would be chained. The car purred up the slope, around the winding curves, making him think of his recent bike ride with Clare.

It had been fun, easy, an unexpected taste of childhood. Sitting with her by the stream, lazily talking, had been a homecoming.

Kissing her hadn't been like coming home at all. It hadn't been comforting or friendly or sweet. It had been like getting scorched by a lightning bolt. He wondered how in the hell he'd missed Clare Kimball the first time around. He didn't intend to let her slip by again.

When he was done here, he thought, he would just swing by her house—hoping she was welding—and see if she was interested in a meal and a movie in Hagerstown. If he had any luck, and his assessment of her reaction to him was anywhere close to target, he'd see about talking her into coming back to his house. Then they'd play it by ear.

She didn't want to be rushed, he reminded himself. It was too bad that patience had never been one of his strong suits.

Around the last curve, he spotted a couple of kids with bicycles. Hooking school, he thought, and had to appreciate the spirit of it on such a terrific May morning. It was with regret that he pulled over and prepared to give them the routine. He got out of the car and walked toward the boys.

He recognized both of them—the curse or blessing of small towns. Cy Abbot—younger brother of Josh, from the cemetery disturbance—and Brian Knight, Min Atherton's nephew. Though a part of Cam wanted to wink and grin and wish them well, he strode forward, sober-eyed. They were both a little green around the gills, he noted, and wondered if it was being caught by the law that had shaken them up or if they'd been practicing chewing tobacco.

"Well, now." Cam put a hand on the handlebars of the dirt bike the Abbot boy was straddling. "Little late for school this morning, aren't you?"

Cy opened his mouth, but only a wheeze came out. Turning a paler shade of green, he leaned over the side of the bike and vomited weakly.

"Oh, shit," Cam muttered, and put two hands on the bike to steady it. "What the hell have you two been up to?" He looked over at Brian since Cy was busy gagging.

"We were just fooling around. And we— we—" He scrubbed a hand over his mouth, hard, and Cam noticed there were tears welling in his eyes.

"Okay." He softened his tone and put an arm around the now shuddering Cy. "What happened?"

"We just found it." Brian swallowed deeply, and his spit tasted foul. "We were going to pull our bikes down and go wading in the creek, that's all. Then we saw it."

"What did you see?"

"The body." Despite the humiliation of being seen blubbering, Cy began to sob. "It was awful, Sheriff. Awful. All the blood."

"Okay, why don't you guys sit in the back of

the car? I'll go take a look. Come on, we'll put your bikes in the trunk." He led the two shaking boys to the rear of the car. Probably a deer, maybe a dog, he told himself. But his hands were icy—a symptom he recognized. "Relax." He opened the back door of the car and tried to lighten the mood. "You're not going to be sick all over the carpet, are you?"

Cy continued to weep as Brian shook his head. He gave his friend a little punch on the arm for comfort.

Beyond the gravelly shoulder of the road, the ground tapered down, carpeted with dead leaves from the previous autumns. With a last glance at the two white faces in the back of the car, Cam started down, sliding a bit on the ground, still slippery after the night of rain.

He could smell damp earth, damp leaves. There were deep skid marks where the boys had hustled down, and marks where they had scrambled back up again. He saw, as they must have, the smearing trail of blood. And he smelled it. Death.

An animal, he told himself as he regained his footing. Hit by a car, then crawled off to die. Sweet Jesus, there was a lot of blood. He had to stop a moment, shake off the image that rushed into his brain.

The walls of a tenement, splattered with red.

The stench of it. The screams that wouldn't stop.

He began to breathe through his mouth and curse himself.

That was over, goddamn it. That was done.

When he saw the body, his stomach didn't revolt as the boy's had. He had seen bodies before. Too many of them. What he felt first, vividly, was fury in finding one here. In his town. In his sanctuary.

Then came disgust and pity. Whoever this broken heap of flesh and bones had been, he had died horribly. Then regret, that two young boys had hooked school on a warm spring morning only to stumble across something they couldn't understand and would never forget.

He didn't understand it—after all the years on the force, all the senseless and small cruelties, he didn't understand it.

Carefully, not wanting to disturb the scene, he crouched down beside the body. Wet leaves clung to the naked flesh. It lay outflung, its broken arms and legs at impossible angles, its face buried in the dirt and wet leaves.

As he studied what was left, his eyes narrowed. Through the bruises and the blood, he made out a tattoo. His mouth dried. And he knew, before he cautiously lifted the battered head, before he looked into the ruined face.

Rising, he swore over what was left of Biff Stokey.

"Jesus, Cam." Bud felt bile rise up hot in his throat and choked it down. "Holy Jesus." He stared down at the body at his feet. With the sleeve of his shirt, he swiped at his mouth as sweat popped out on his face and ran cool and fast from his armpits. "Jesus, Jesus," he said hopelessly, then turned, stumbling away to be sick in the brush.

Calmer now, Cam stood where he was, waiting for Bud to get his system under control. From somewhere on the other side of the creek, a thrush began to trill. Squirrels scurried in the trees.

"Sorry," Bud managed, running a clammy palm over his clammy face. "I just couldn't— I've never seen—"

"Nothing to be sorry about. You going to be okay now?"

"Yeah." But Bud kept his gaze several inches above what lay on the leafy ground. "You think he got hit by a car? I guess he could've been hit by a car, then rolled on down here. People are always taking these turns too fast." He wiped his mouth again. "Too damn fast."

"No, I don't think he got hit by a car. Can't see a car breaking nearly every bone in his body." Eyes narrowed, Cam thought out loud. "Where are the skid marks? How the hell did he get out here? Where's his car? Where the hell are his clothes?"

"Well, I guess . . . I guess maybe, maybe he was shit-faced again. Could be we'll find his car, and his clothes, too, just down the road. And he was walking along, drunk, and a car came by and . . ." But he knew it was stupid even as he said it. Stupid and weak.

Cam turned until his eyes met Bud's panicked ones. "I think someone beat him to death."

"But that's murder. Christ Almighty, nobody gets murdered around here." In panic, Bud's voice rose an octave, then cracked. "We haven't had a homicide in this part of the county since T. R. Lewis went crazy and shot up his brother-in-law with his thirty-thirty. Hell, I wasn't no more than five or six years old then. People don't get murdered in Emmitsboro."

Judging by the waver in Bud's voice, Cam knew he could lose him if he didn't take it slow. "We'll wait for the coroner to get here. Meanwhile, we're going to have to rope this area off and start our investigation."

It would keep Bud busy, Cam mused, and little else. He was already certain Biff hadn't died here.

"We'll need pictures, Bud. Go up and get the camera." He caught the look in his deputy's eye and laid a hand on his shoulder. "I'll take the pictures," he said gently. "Just go on up and get me the camera."

"All right." He started up the slope, then turned back. "Sheriff, it's a damn mess, isn't it?"

"Yeah. It's a goddamn mess."

Once he had the camera, Cam sent Bud back up on the roadside again, to wait for the coroner. Making his mind a blank, Cam began his grisly task. He noted the raw and sawed flesh on the wrists and ankles, the lack of bruises on the back and buttocks.

Finished, he wished violently for a cigarette but only set the camera aside and picked up the can of spray paint he'd grabbed from the storeroom at his office. Crouched low, he pushed the sprayer, cursed when it only sputtered, then shook the can hard. He could hear the musical sound of the mixing beads jiggling inside.

He'd always liked that sound, he realized. The competence of it, the anticipation of it. But it wasn't something he would look forward to any time soon. Again, he aimed the can at the ground and pushed the nozzle.

He saw with grim amusement that he'd grabbed a can of canary yellow. Well, the lousy sonofabitch would get his death silhouette in a nice, cheerful color.

He started at the feet, forcing himself not to

cringe at the vulnerability of those bruised and broken toes.

You had that foot planted on your ass more times than you can count, he reminded himself. But his hand shook a bit as he continued the paint stream beside the naked left leg.

"Broke your fucking knees, didn't he?" Cam muttered. "I always hoped you'd die hard. Looks like I got my wish."

He gritted his teeth and continued. It wasn't until he stood again that he realized his jaw was aching. Very deliberately he capped the paint can, set it down, then took out a cigarette.

He remembered the last time he had stood and looked at death. Then it had been someone he cared about, someone he'd laughed with, felt responsible for. Had grieved for.

Cam closed his eyes, but only for a moment, because when he did, he could see the past all too clearly. Jake's body sprawled on that filthy stairway, the blood pumping out of him so fast they'd both known there hadn't been a chance. Not a chance in hell.

My fault, he thought as the sweat pooled at the base of his spine. My fault.

"Sheriff. Sheriff." Bud had to give him a shake on the shoulder before Cam snapped back and looked at him. "Coroner's here."

Cam nodded, then picked up the paint can

and the camera and handed them to Bud. Beside the deputy stood the county coroner, black bag in hand. He was a short, spare man with white, white skin and oddly Oriental eyes, dark, slightly slanted, and luxuriantly lashed. His salt-and-pepper hair was neatly combed, the part so straight it might have been surveyed. He was wearing a trim beige suit and a somewhat cocky bow tie. He was fiftyish, soft-spoken and shy. He felt more at home with his cadavers than with their living counterparts.

"Dr. Loomis. You made good time."

"Sheriff." Loomis offered a pale, fine-boned hand. "Apparently you've had some trouble."

"Apparently." Cam felt a ridiculous urge to chuckle at the understatement. "Some kids found the body about an hour ago. I've already taken pictures and outlined the body position, so you won't have to worry about disturbing the crime scene."

"Excellent." Loomis looked down at the body. His only reaction was a pursing of lips. With businesslike motions he opened his case and took out a pair of thin surgical gloves.

"You're not going to—" Bud took two steps back. "You're not going to do, like, an autopsy or anything right here?"

"Don't worry." Loomis gave a surprisingly rich chuckle. "We'll save that for later."

Cam took the camera back. They would need

it. "Bud, go on up to the road. Make sure nobody stops and gawks."

"Yes, sir." Relieved, Bud scrambled up the slope.

"Your deputy's a nervous fellow."

"He's young. It's his first homicide."

"Of course, of course." Loomis's mouth pursed again. "This paint is still a bit tacky."

"I'm sorry. I didn't have anything else handy."

"No trouble. I won't disturb it."

Loomis took out a small recorder, set it fussily on a rock. He spoke aloud, slowly and patiently, as he examined the body.

"We'll need to turn him over," Loomis said matter-of-factly.

Wordlessly, Cam set the camera aside to help the doctor lift and turn the corpse. The battered body shifted in their hold, reminding Cam of the way loose garbage moves in a Hefty bag. He bit back an oath as he heard bone rub against bone.

If it had been bad before, it was worse now with Biff's dead eyes staring up at him. Unlike the back, the front of the body was a nightmare vision of bruises and broken bones. The bull-like chest had been caved in, the manhood Biff had been so proud of was a jellied stump.

He'd been right about the knees, Cam thought, as he turned away to take a breath and pick up the camera again. As the doctor spoke his technical and meaningless terms, he took more pictures.

They both glanced up at the sound of an ambulance.

"There was no need for the siren," Loomis said, and all but clicked his tongue. "We'll be moving the body to the morgue, Sheriff, for a thorough examination. I believe it's safe to say that this man suffered a severe and prolonged beating. Death was probably caused by a strong blow to the head. From the progress of rigor, we can assume he died between ten and fifteen hours ago. I'll certainly be able to give you more precise details after the autopsy."

"Can you give me an idea when you'll be able to get back to me?"

"Forty-eight hours, perhaps a little more. Will we need dental records?"

"What?"

"Dental records." Loomis snapped off his gloves, rolled them, and tucked them in his bag. "As the body is nude and without identification, will you need dental records?"

"No, I know who it is."

"Well, then." He looked up as his attendants started down the slope with a thick plastic bag and a stretcher. Before he could speak again, they all heard a car squeal to a halt on the road above. Cam ignored it, trusting Bud to hurry any curiosity-seekers along. Then he recognized the voice that rose up suddenly in panic and demand: *"What do you mean Cam's down there?"*

Clare's legs nearly buckled. Every ounce of color drained from her face as she stared at the ambulance. "Oh, God, oh, my God, what happened?" She rushed forward, only to have Bud grab her arms and block her way.

"You can't go down there, Clare. You don't want to. Believe me."

"*No.*" Horrible, merciless visions streaked through her mind. She saw her father, sprawled on the flagstone. And now Cam. "No, not Cam, too. I want to see him. Damn you, I want to see him now." She fought her way clear, shoving Bud aside. Her blind rush forward took her skidding down the slope and into Cam's arms.

"What the hell are you doing?"

"You." She lifted a shaking hand to his face, pressing her fingers in hard. There were bruises, old bruises, but he was solid and real. "I thought— You're okay? Are you okay?"

"I'm dandy. Get the hell up on the road." He turned her so that she didn't see the scene below, then pushed her in front of him up to the shoulder. "I thought I told you to keep people out," he snapped at Bud.

"It's not his fault." She pressed a hand to her mouth and struggled for composure. "I got away from him."

"Now you can get away altogether. Get back in your car and go home."

"But, I—"

His eyes flared at her, hard and bright. "This doesn't concern you, and I haven't got time to hold your hand."

"Fine." She swung away, but the adrenaline drained quickly and had her leaning weakly against the hood of the car.

"Damn it, Clare, I said I haven't got time for this." All he could think of was getting her away, well away, before the body was brought up. He crossed over to take her arm and pull her to the driver's side.

"Fuck off." She jerked away, furious that she was near tears.

"Hey." He yanked up her head, frowning at the glitter in her eyes. "What's all this?"

"I thought it was you." After slapping his hand away, she fumbled for the latch of the door. "I don't know why it would have bothered me to think you were lying down there hurt or dead, but for some idiotic reason, it did."

His breath hissed out between his teeth. "I'm sorry." When she managed to wrench the door open, he merely slammed it shut again. "Damn it, Clare, I'm sorry. Come here." He pulled her against him, ignoring her struggle. "Give me a break, Slim. I've had a rough day." As she softened a bit, he pressed his lips to her hair, breathing in the clean scent of it after the rancid smell of death. "I'm sorry."

She shrugged, knowing the movement was bad tempered. "Forget it."

"You were worried about me."

"It was a brief moment of insanity. It's passed." But her arms went around him to give him one quick squeeze. She would think about her reaction later, she promised herself. For now, she eased away. "What happened here?"

"Not now." Over her head he saw the attendants struggling up the slope with their gruesome burden. "Go on home, Clare."

"I wasn't trying to pry into official business," she began. When she reached for the door handle, she looked back, intending to call an apology to Bud. And she saw the thick black plastic bag. "Who is it?" she whispered.

"Biff."

Slowly, she turned back to look at Cam. "What happened?"

His eyes weren't hot now, but flat and distant. "We haven't finished determining that."

She laid a hand over his. "I don't quite know what to say. What will you do now?"

"Now?" He rubbed a hand over his face. "Now I'll go out to the farm and tell my mother he's dead."

"I'll go with you."

"No, I don't want—"

"Maybe you don't, but your mother might need another woman." She remembered her own mother, coming home from a giddy evening with friends to find an ambulance in the drive, a crowd of people on the lawn, her husband in a body bag. "I know what it's like, Cam." Without waiting for agreement, she slipped into the car. "I'll follow you over."

Chapter 9

THE FARM WHERE CAM grew up had changed little in thirty years. In some ways it still held some of the charm he remembered from the years his father had been alive. Spotted cows still grazed on the sloping ground beyond the barn and milking parlor. A rolling field of hay waved in the light spring breeze. Rhode Island Reds pecked and squawked behind the chicken wire.

The house was a rambling three stories with a wide porch and narrow windows. But the paint was peeling and dingy. More than a few of the windowpanes were cracked, and there were shingles missing from the roof. Biff hadn't liked to open his wallet for anything that didn't offer a profit, unless it was a beer or a whore.

There were a few straggling daffodils, past their prime, along the rutted, muddy lane. Cam remembered that he'd given his mother money for a load of gravel two months before. He imagined she'd cashed the check, then handed the money over to Biff.

He knew her kitchen garden at the rear of the house would be planted and meticulously weeded. But there were no flowers in the beds she'd once fussed over. They were full of witch grass and choking vines.

He remembered a day, much like this one, when he'd been five or six—sitting beside her on the ground as she turned the earth for a flat of pansies. She'd been singing.

How long had it been since he'd heard her sing?

He parked the car at the end of the lane beside his mother's aging Buick station wagon and the rusty pickup. Biff's shiny new Caddy was nowhere in sight. He waited in silence for Clare to join him. She laid a hand on his arm and gave it a quick, supporting squeeze before they climbed the sagging steps to the porch.

He knocked, and that surprised her. She couldn't imagine knocking on the door of a house she'd grown up in, with her mother still living inside. She wondered if she'd feel obligated to knock before she entered the house her mother and Jerry would live in when they returned from Europe. The idea was painful, and she pushed it away.

Jane Stokey opened the door, wiping a damp hand on the front of her apron and blinking at the strong sunlight. She'd put on flesh in the middle over the last ten years. Cam supposed her figure would be called matronly. Her hair, once a sassy blond, had faded to a dull, neutral color. She had it permed twice a year at Betty's, paying out of her egg money, but now it was scraped back from her face with two big bobby pins.

She'd been pretty once. Cam could still re-member being proud and half in love with her as a young child. Everyone had said she was the prettiest girl in the county. She'd been Farm Queen the year before she'd married Mike Rafferty. There was a picture of her somewhere, in a white, frilly dress, with the winner's sash across her breasts, her young, triumphant face glowing with delight and promise.

Now she was old, Cam thought with a pang in his chest. Old, worn out, and used up. It was worse somehow because you could still see traces of that youthful beauty in the lined and tired face.

She wore no makeup. Biff had told her that he wouldn't tolerate his wife painted up like a whore. There were shadows under the eyes that had once been a bright, interested blue. Around the mouth that every boy in Emmitsboro had dreamed of kissing thirty-five years before, lines were dug deep.

"Mom."

"Cameron." The automatic twitch of fear faded when she remembered Biff wasn't home. When she saw Clare, she lifted a hand to her hair in that universal gesture of feminine embarrassment. "I didn't know you were coming by and bringing company."

"This is Clare Kimball."

"Yes, I know." She dredged up her manners and smiled. "I remember you—Jack and Rosemary's girl. And I've seen your picture in magazines. Would you like to come in?"

"Thank you."

They stepped into the living room with its faded furniture, starched doilies, and glossy big-screen TV. Biff had liked to stretch out with a six-pack and watch cop shows and ball games.

"Sit down." Jane was nervously wiping her hands on her apron again. "I can make some iced tea."

"We don't need any, Mom." Cam took her restless hands and led her to the sofa. It smelled of *him*, Cam thought, and gritted his teeth.

"It's no trouble." She shot Clare an uneasy smile as she sat in a chair across the room. "It's warm today. Humid, too, after that rain."

"Mom." Cam was still holding her hands, gently kneading them. "I need to talk to you."

Jane bit her lip. "What's wrong? Something's wrong. You've been fighting with Biff again. It's not right, Cam. It's not right that you fight with him. You should show him respect."

"I haven't been fighting with Biff, Mom." There was no gentle way, he thought. No easy way. "He's dead. We found him this morning."

"Dead?" She repeated the word as though she'd never heard it before. "Dead?"

"It happened sometime last night." He searched for words of sympathy that wouldn't scald his tongue. "I'm sorry I have to tell you."

Slowly, like a doll on a string, she pulled her hands from his and pressed them to her mouth. "You—you killed him. Oh, God, my God. You always said you would."

"Mom." He reached for her, but she jerked away and began to rock. "I didn't kill him," Cam said flatly.

"You hated him." She rocked faster, back and forth, back and forth, her faded eyes on him. "You always hated him. He was harsh with you, I know, but for your own good. For your own good." She was talking fast, words tumbling over each other as she wrung her hands. "Your daddy and I, we'd spoiled you. Biff could see that. He took care of us. You know he took care of us."

"Mrs. Stokey." Clare went over to sit on the edge of the couch and gather Cam's mother in her arms. "Cam's here to help you. We're both here to help you."

While she stroked Jane's hair and murmured, she watched Cam rise and pace to the window. "I'll call Dr. Crampton," he said.

"That's a good idea. Why don't you make some tea?"

"He hated Biff," Jane Stokey sobbed against Clare's shoulder. "He hated him, but Biff took care of us. What was I to do after Mike died? I couldn't run the farm all alone. I couldn't raise the child alone. I needed someone."

"I know." With her eyes on Cam, Clare continued to rock. Her heart was with him when he walked from the room. "I know."

"He wasn't a bad man. He wasn't. I know what people said. I know what they thought, but he wasn't bad. Maybe he liked to drink too much, but a man's entitled."

No, Clare thought. No one's entitled to be a drunk, but she continued to rock and soothe.

"He's dead. How can he be dead? He wasn't sick."

"It was an accident," Clare told her and hoped she wasn't lying. "Cam will explain it to you. Mrs. Stokey, is there someone you'd like me to call?"

"No." The tears welled and shimmered as

she stared at the wall. "I have no one. I have no one now."

"The doctor's on his way," Cam said as he set a cup and saucer on the coffee table. His face, his eyes were carefully blank. "I need to ask you a couple of questions."

"Cam, I don't think—"

"They need to be asked," he said, cutting Clare off. If he couldn't be a son to her, he thought, he'd damn well be a cop. "Do you know where Biff went last night?"

"He went out." Jane groped in her apron pocket for a tissue. "Down to Frederick, I think. He'd worked hard all day and needed to relax."

"Do you know where in Frederick?"

"Maybe the Am-Vets." A sudden thought seeped through, and she bit her lip again. "Did he have a car wreck?"

"No."

Clare shot Cam an exasperated look at his dispassionate questions and answers. "Drink some of this, Mrs. Stokey. It'll help a little." She brought the cup to Jane's lips herself.

"What time did he leave last night?"

" 'Bout nine, I guess."

"Was he with anyone? Was he going to meet anyone?"

"He was by himself. I don't know if he was going to meet someone."

"He took the Caddy?"

"Yes, he took his car. He loved his car." She pulled her apron up to her face and began to weep and rock again.

"Please, Cam." Clare slipped an arm over Jane's shoulders. She knew what it was like to be questioned, to be forced to think, after the violent death of a loved one. "Can't the rest wait?"

He doubted his mother could tell him anything helpful. Shrugging, he strode back to the window. The chickens were still pecking away, and the sun shone on the hay field.

"I'll stay with her until the doctor comes." Clare waited until Cam turned back. "If you want. I know you have things to . . . take care of."

He nodded and took a step toward his mother. There was nothing he could say to her, he realized. Nothing she would hear. He turned and left the house.

When Clare pulled up in front of the sheriff's office three hours later, she was wrung dry. Doc Crampton had come and with his habitual skill had soothed and sedated the grieving widow. Clare and the doctor agreed that Jane shouldn't be left alone, so Clare had stayed downstairs after he'd gone, and somehow the afternoon ticked by.

She bypassed the television and the radio,

afraid she might disturb Jane Stokey. There were no books in sight, so she paced until a combination of concern and restlessness had her creeping upstairs to check on Jane.

She was sleeping deeply, her tear-streaked face lax with the drug. Clare left her alone and wandered around the house.

It was scrupulously neat. She imagined Jane dusting and scrubbing day after day, going from room to room chasing down dirt. It was depressing. When she came across Biff's den, she hesitated at the doorway.

Don't handle death well, do you, Clare? she thought, and made herself step over the threshold.

It was obvious Jane wasn't allowed to wield her dust rag and broom in here. There was a deer head on the wall, cobwebs stringing from antler to antler. A glassy-eyed squirrel scampered up a log. A pheasant, its iridescent wings dusty, posed on a stand as if in midflight. A gun rack held rifles and shotguns. No dust on them, she thought with a grimace of distaste.

A leather Barcalounger sat in one corner beside a table that held an overflowing ashtray and a trio of Budweiser cans. In a glass display case was a collection of gleaming knives. A buck knife, a Bowie, another with a hooked and jagged edge. And oddly, she thought, a beautiful antique dagger with an enameled hilt.

There was a pile of pornographic magazines. The hardcore stuff. No *Playboy* for old Biff, she thought.

She saw a shelf of paperbacks, which surprised her. He hadn't seemed like a reader. Then she saw by the spines and covers that the books were merely an extension of the magazines. Hard porn, grisly murders, with a few lighter men's adventures. She thought she might be able to pass an hour with *Mercenaries from Hell*. As she slipped it from the shelf, she noted a book behind it.

The Satanic Bible. Nice stuff, she mused. Biff Stokey had been a real prince of a guy.

She set both books back, then rubbed her fingers clean on her jeans. It was with profound relief that she heard a knock on the door downstairs.

Now, relieved from her duties by Mrs. Finch and Mrs. Negley, she sat in her car in front of Cam's office and wondered what to say to him.

When nothing came, she climbed out of the car, hoping this was one of those times when planning wasn't necessary.

She found him at his desk, machine-gun typing with two fingers. Beside him a cigarette smoldered in the ashtray, and a chipped ceramic mug looked like it might hold coffee.

She could see by the rigid set of his shoulders how tense he was. If it hadn't been for the kiss they had shared on her front porch swing, she would have found it easy to walk over and massage the tension from his shoulders. But a kiss, that kind of kiss, changed things. She'd yet to work out if that was for the best.

Instead, she walked over, perched on the corner of the desk, and picked up his neglected cigarette. "Hi."

His fingers hesitated, continued. "Hi." Then stopped. He turned in the swivel chair to study her. She looked fresh, soft. Two things he needed badly just then. But her eyes were full of weariness and sympathy. "I'm sorry I dumped that on you."

"You didn't," she corrected and tried a sip of the coffee. It was stone cold. "I butted in."

"How is she?"

"The doc gave her a sedative. She's resting. Mrs. Finch and Mrs. Negley came by. They'll stay with her."

"That's good." He rubbed a hand over the back of his neck. Sighing, she tapped out the cigarette, then walked around the desk to massage his shoulders.

Grateful, he leaned back into her. "A man could get used to having you around, Slim."

"That's what they all say." Over his head she glanced at the paper in the typewriter. It was a police report, brutally frank and without compassion. She found herself swallowing as she read the condition of the body. Feeling her fingers stiffen, Cam glanced around. Without a word, he pulled the sheet out and set it face-down on the desk.

"You've done more than your share, Slim. Why don't you go home? Fire up your torch."

She let her hands fall to her sides. "He was murdered."

"We're not ready to release an official state-ment." He stood then, forcing her to take a step back. "And we don't want speculation running through the town."

"I wasn't planning on dashing over to Martha's and spouting off over a burger. Jesus Christ, Cam, if anyone knows what it's like to have death and scandal discussed in the beauty parlor and hardware store, it's me."

"Okay." He grabbed her hand before she could storm out. "Okay, I'm out of line. I'm in a pisser of a mood, Clare, but after what you did today, you're the last one I should be taking it out on."

"You're absolutely right," she snapped back, then relented a little. "Cam, your mother didn't mean those things she said."

"Yes, she did." To comfort himself, he rubbed the back of his hand over Clare's cheek.

"She was shocked and in pain. People say things—"

"She's blamed me since I was ten years old,"

he interrupted. "She knew I hated him, and maybe I hated her for marrying him, too. I couldn't tell her I was sorry he's dead because I'm not. I don't even know if I'm sorry he died the way he did."

"You don't have to be." She lifted her hand to close it over his. "You don't have to be sorry for anything. You'll do your job. You'll find out who killed him. That's enough."

"It'll have to be."

"Listen, you look like you could use a break. Why don't you come home with me? I'll fix you something to eat."

He glanced at the clock, then at the papers on his desk. "Give me ten minutes. I'll meet you there."

"Make it twenty," she said with a smile. "I don't think I have anything left but stale cookies."

Three men sat on a park bench. They watched Clare go into Cam's office. And watched her come out.

"I don't like how she's hanging around." Slowly, Less Gladhill brought the unfiltered cigarette to his lips. "Christ knows what she's telling the sheriff or what Jane Stokey said to her while they was out there all alone all that time."

"There's no need to worry about Clare." Less's companion spoke quietly, a voice of reason. Behind them, in the park, young children squealed on the swings. "Or about the sheriff, for that matter. We have more important, and certainly more immediate, concerns." He drew a deep breath as he studied both men beside him. "What happened last night could have been avoided."

"He deserved to die." Less had enjoyed every swing of the bat.

"Maybe he did, maybe he didn't." The third man didn't like to speak at all. He kept a weather eye on the traffic, both cars and pedestrians. Word could get around quickly that the three of them had met. "Thing is, it's done. I don't much care for killing our own."

"He broke the Law—" Less began, but the voice of reason raised his hand.

"A bar fight is foolish but nothing to be killed for. We joined together more than two decades ago for the rite, for the union, for the Master. Not to shed our own blood."

Less had joined for the sex, but he merely shrugged. "You shed plenty yourself last night."

"The vote was cast. I did what was necessary." And there was a part of him that had wallowed in the sick triumph of it. That was his weakness, and it shamed him. "There may come a time, and soon, for a shift of power."

The third man shook his head and moved his body away just enough to symbolize distance. "I won't take him on. I'm telling you straight out, I won't take him on. I'm not going to end up like Biff." He raised a hand in greeting as someone honked a horn. "You do what you want about him—" He nodded toward Less. "And the Kimball girl. I'm not having any part of it. Far as I can see, things're fine." He swallowed a little ball of unease. "I got work to do."

Less grinned and slapped his companion on the shoulder. "You go ahead and go for the top spot, buddy. I'm with you."

He smiled to himself as they parted. The way Less figured it, if the two of them battled it out, they would leave a nice clean spot for him to step into. As high priest, he'd have his pick of the whores.

After a quick trip to the market, Clare pulled up in her drive. Ernie was sitting on the low stone wall beside the garage. She waved, reached for the trunk release, and pressed the automatic seat-belt adjustment instead. After a brief struggle, she found the right switch.

"Hi, Ernie." She walked around the back to heft out two bags of groceries. He sauntered over and took one from her. "Thanks."

"You left your keys in the car," he told her.

She blew the hair out of her eyes. "Right." After leaning in the window and pulling them out, she smiled at him. "I'm always doing that." He let her lead the way inside so he could watch her hips sway.

"You said you wanted to work in clay," he said when she began pulling out groceries.

"What? Oh, yeah. Yeah, I do." She pulled out a bag of Oreos and offered it, but he shook his head. "Have you been waiting for me?"

"I thought I'd hang around."

"I appreciate it, but I'm not going to be able to work today. I'm tied up. Want a soda?"

He was annoyed but hid it with a careless shrug. He took the opened bottle she passed him and watched her search for a pan.

"I know I bought one, damn it. Oh, here we go." She set a dented pot, another prize from the flea market, on the stove. "You're not working today?"

"Not until six."

Listening with half an ear, she opened a jar of Ragu. It was the only sensible way she knew to make spaghetti. "Is it hard, juggling that with your schoolwork?"

"I get by." He moved a little closer, letting his eyes drop to where her tank top drooped over her breasts. "I'll be out of school in a few weeks."

"Hmmm." She set the burner on low. "You must have a prom coming up."

"I'm not into that."

"No?" Her hair fell over her face as she bent down to root out another pan for the pasta. "I remember my senior prom. I went with Robert Knight—you know, the family that runs the market? I just saw him a few minutes ago. He's got a bald spot as big as a dinner plate." She chuckled as she filled the pan with water. "I have to say, it made me feel old."

"You're not old." He lifted a hand to touch her hair but snatched it away when she turned to grin at him.

"Thanks."

He stepped toward her, and the look in his eyes surprised her more than a little. He didn't seem as much of a boy as he had a few minutes before when she'd seen him leaning on her stone wall, sulking. "Ah . . ." she began, wondering how to handle it without crushing his ego.

"Hey, Slim." Cam stepped into the kitchen doorway. He'd just seen the last maneuver and wasn't sure if he should be amused or annoyed.

"Cam." On a little breath of relief, she picked up a package of pasta. "Right on time."

"I like to be prompt when I'm offered a free meal. Hi. Ernie, right?"

"Yeah."

Cam was as surprised by the vicious flash of hate from the boy's eyes as Clare had been by the glimpse of mature desire. Then it was gone, and Ernie was only a sullen teenage boy again, dressed in a Slayer T-shirt and torn jeans.

"I gotta go," he muttered and bolted for the door.

"Ernie." Clare rushed after him, certain now that she'd misread that unnerving moment. "Look, thanks for helping me with the bags." She laid a friendly hand on his shoulder. "I should be able to start in clay tomorrow, if you have a chance to come by again."

"Maybe." He looked past her to where Cam poked a spoon into the sauce on the stove. "You making him dinner?"

"More or less. I'd better get back before I burn it. See you later."

His hands fisted hard in his pockets, he stalked off. He would take care of Cameron Rafferty, he promised himself. One way or the other.

"Hope I didn't—interrupt," Cam commented when Clare stepped back into the kitchen.

"Very funny." She plucked a loaf of Italian bread from a bag.

"No, I don't think it was. I've been wished dead on the spot before, but not so . . . skill-fully."

"Don't be stupid. He's just a boy." She rummaged through a drawer for a knife.

"That boy was about to take a chunk out of you when I walked in."

"He was not." But she gave a quick, involuntary shudder. That was exactly how it had seemed to her, that hungry, even predatory look in his eyes. Imagination, she told herself. "He's just lonely. I don't know if he has any friends, anyone to talk to."

"Not lonely. A loner. He's got a reputation for keeping to himself and for letting loose with a pretty wild temper. He's had two citations this month for speeding. Bud's come across him more than once bouncing on some girl in the cab of that truck he drives."

"Really?" She turned, poker-faced. "I wonder why that description reminds me of someone I used to know."

He had to grin. "I don't recall ever getting ready to slide my tongue down an older woman's throat."

"Ah, graciously put, Rafferty." Grinning, she sawed thick slices from the loaf. "You haven't lost your touch."

"Just watch your step with him, that's all."

"I'm using him as a model, not for Seduction 101."

"Good." He walked over and, taking her by

the shoulders, turned her to face him. "Because I'd just as soon I was the only one sliding my tongue down your throat."

"God, you're romantic."

"You want romance—put down the knife." When she only laughed, he took it away himself and set it aside. Slowly, his eyes on hers, he combed his fingers through her hair. Her smile faded. "I want you. I figure you should know that straight off."

"I think I already worked that out for myself." She tried to be casual but only succeeded in sounding breathless. "Listen, Cam, my track record's really lousy. I . . ." Her voice trailed off when he lowered his head and rubbed his open mouth against her throat. Frissons of fire and ice raced up her spine. "I don't want to make another mistake." She closed her eyes on a moan when he caught the lobe of her ear between his teeth. "I'm really bad at analyzing my feelings. My shrink says . . . oh, Jesus." His thumbs were circling slowly, lightly over her nipples.

"That's very profound," Cam murmured, then began a lazy, tortuous trail along her jaw-line with his tongue and nibbling teeth.

"No—he says that I use glibness and . . . oh, sarcasm to shield myself and only open up in my work. That's why I screwed up my marriage and the relationships that. . . . God, do you know what you're doing to my insides?"

He knew what was happening to his while he cupped her small, firm breasts in his hands and let his mouth roam her face. "How long are you going to keep talking?"

"I think I'm finished." Her hands were on his hips, fingers dug in. "For God's sake, kiss me."

"I thought you'd never ask."

He closed his wandering mouth over hers. He'd expected the punch, craved it. He let his body absorb the shock before he pressed himself hard against her.

Her lips parted hungrily, inviting him in so that she could scrape her teeth over his tongue, then soothe it with hers. His low groan of approval vibrated into her. He tasted dark, dangerous, and visions of wild, raging sex had her head spinning.

It had been long, too long, she thought, since she had felt a man's hands on her, since she had felt this churning frenzy to mate. But this was more, too much more, and it frightened her. The need sped beyond the hot, frantic sex she knew they could share. She knew, if she let herself, she could be in love.

"Cam—"

"Not yet." He caught her face in his hands, shaken by what she was doing to him. Body, mind, soul. He stared at her, searching for a reason, for an answer. Then with an oath, he crushed his mouth to hers again. When he realized he was crossing the line, he gentled his hold and rested his brow on hers.

"I guess we should be glad this didn't happen ten years ago."

"I guess," she said on a long breath. "Cam, I need to think about all of this."

He nodded and stepped back a pace. "I'm not going to tell you to take your time."

She passed a hand through her hair. "I wasn't kidding about mistakes. I've made too many of them."

"I imagine we both have." He tucked her hair behind her ear. "And though I don't think this is one, you're making a mistake right now."

"You lost me."

"The water's boiling over."

She turned around in time to see the water bubble up and sizzle on the burner. "Oh, shit."

Bud took his routine patrol up to the quarry, circling around while he munched on a bag of Fritos. As hard as he tried not to think about what he had seen that afternoon, his mind kept shooting back, flashing the image of Biff's mauled body behind his eyes like a personal movie projector. He was deeply ashamed that he'd thrown up at the scene, though Cam had made no fuss over it.

Bud firmly believed that a good cop—even if

he was only a small town deputy—required an iron will, iron integrity, and an iron stomach. He'd fallen flat on the third one that day.

News of Biff's death was all over town. Alice had stopped him on the street, pretty in her pink uniform and smelling of lilacs. It had done his ego considerable good to look sober-faced and quote the official line.

"Biff Stokey's body was found alongside Gossard Creek off of Gossard Creek Road. The cause of death has yet to be determined."

She'd looked impressed with that, Bud thought now, and he'd nearly screwed up the courage to ask her to the movies. Before he could, she'd rushed off, saying she'd be late for her shift.

Next time, he promised himself, and crunched down on a Frito. In fact, maybe when he'd finished his patrol, he'd stop by Martha's for a cup of coffee and some pie. Then he could offer to walk Alice home, slide an arm around her shoulder, and mention, real casual like, that the new Stallone movie was playing at the mall.

The more he thought about it, the better he liked the idea, so he sped up another five miles an hour. On his way down Quarry Road, he began to tap a foot on the floorboard, thinking how nice it would be to watch Stallone slaughter all the bad guys with Alice beside him in the darkened theater.

When he rounded a turn, a flash of metal caught his eye. He slowed, squinting against the rays of the lowering sun. It was a car bumper sure enough, he thought with some disgust. Damn kids didn't even wait until nighttime anymore.

He pulled to the shoulder and got out. Nothing embarrassed him more than having to poke his face into the window of a parked car and advise lovers to move along.

Just last week he'd seen Marci Gladhill without her blouse. Even though he'd averted his eyes quickly, he had a hard time adjusting to the fact that he'd seen Less Gladhill's oldest girl's tits. And they'd been whoppers. He imagined he'd have a harder time if Less ever got wind of it.

Resigned, he stepped off the shoulder and into the brush. It wasn't the first time he'd caught kids driving into bushes to do the backseat tango, but it was the first time he'd caught any in a Cadillac. Shaking his head, he took another step and froze.

Not any Caddy, he realized. Biff Stokey's Caddy. There wasn't a person in town who wouldn't recognize the glossy black car with its flashy red upholstery. He walked closer, his feet causing twigs and brush to crackle and crack.

It had been pulled halfway into the thicket of

wild blackberry, and the thorns had left nasty thin scratches along the gleaming black paint.

Biff would've had a shit-fit, Bud thought, and shuddered, remembering what had happened to Biff.

He tried not to think too hard about that, and spent some time cursing and picking thorns out of his pant legs. At the last minute, he remembered to use a handkerchief to open the door.

The stereo unit, complete with CD, that Biff had bragged about was gone. Neatly and skillfully removed, Bud noted. The glove box was open and empty. Most everybody knew that Biff had carried a .45 in there. The Caddy's keys were tossed on the seat. He decided against touching them.

He closed the door again. He was damn proud of himself. Only hours after the body had been discovered, and he'd come across the first clue. With a spring in his step, he walked back to his cruiser to radio in.

Chapter 10

CLARE DIDN'T KNOW what had awakened her. She had no lingering image of a dream, no aftershock of fear from a nightmare. Yet she had shot from sleep to full wakefulness in the dark, every muscle tensed. In the silence she heard nothing but the roar and pump of her heartbeat.

Slowly, she pushed the top of the sleeping bag aside. Despite its cocooning warmth, her legs were icy. Shivering, she groped for the sweatpants she had peeled off before climbing in.

She realized her jaw was locked tight, her head cocked to the side. Listening. What was she listening for? She'd grown up in this house with its nighttime moans and shudders and knew better than to jump at every creak.

But her skin remained chilled, her muscles rigid, her ears pricked.

Uneasy, she crept to the doorway and scanned the dark hall. There was nothing there. Of course there was nothing there. But she hit the light switch before rubbing the chill from her arms.

The light that flooded the room behind her only made her more aware that it was the middle of the night and she was awake and alone.

"What I need is a real bed." She spoke aloud to comfort herself with her own voice. As she stepped into the hall, she massaged the heel of her hand against her breastbone as if to calm her racing heart.

A cup of tea, she decided. She would go downstairs and fix herself a cup of tea, then curl up on the sofa. She'd probably have a better chance of getting some sleep if she pretended she was just going to take a nap.

She'd turn up the heat, too, as she had forgotten to do before climbing into bed. The spring nights were cool. That was why she was cold and shaky. The heat, the radio, and more lights, she thought. Then she'd sleep like the dead.

But at the top of the stairs, she stopped. Turning, she stared at the narrow steps that led to the attic room. There were fourteen worn treads leading to a locked wooden door. It was a short trip, but she had yet to make it. Had tried to believe she didn't have to make it. Yet it had been on her mind since she stepped into the house again.

No, she admitted, it had been on her mind long before she had come back to Emmitsboro, to the house where she had spent her childhood.

Her movements were stiff and drunkenly cautious as she walked back to the bedroom to get her keys. They jangled in her unsteady hand as she started toward the stairway, her eyes on the door above.

From the shadows of the first floor, Ernie watched her. Inside his thin chest his heart sledgehammered against his ribs. She was coming to him. Coming for him. When she changed directions, then reappeared to start up to the attic, his lips curved.

She wanted him. She wanted him to follow her to that room, a room of violent death. A room of secrets and shadows. His palm left a streak of sweat on the rail as he slowly started up.

There was pain, sharp and jabbing, like an icicle lodged in the pit of her stomach. It increased with each step. By the time she reached the door, her breath was whistling out of her lungs. She fumbled with the keys, then was forced to press one hand against the wall for balance as she rattled it into the lock.

"You have to face realities, Clare," Dr.

Janowski would say. "You have to accept them for what they are and deal with your feelings. Life hurts, and death is a part of life."

"Fuck you," she whispered. What did he know about pain?

The metal hinges keened as the door swung open. The scent of dust and cold, stale air filled the opening. Her eyes stung. She had hoped, somehow, to find some lingering scent of her father. A wisp of the English Leather he had splashed on every morning, a sweet trace of the cherry Lifesavers he'd been addicted to. Even the hot smell of whiskey. It had all been smothered by time. Nothing was left but dust. That was the most painful reality of all. She turned on the light.

The center of the room was empty, the floor coated with the thick gray powder of time. Clare knew her mother had given the office furniture away years before. She'd been right to do so. But Clare wished, how she wished, she could run a hand over the scarred surface of her father's desk or sit in the worn, squeaky chair.

There were boxes lined against a wall, neatly sealed with packing tape. More dust, layers of the passing years, clung softly to Clare's icy bare feet when she crossed to them. Using the keys still clutched in her hand, she cut through the tape and pried off a lid.

And there was her father.

With a sound that was half joy, half sorrow, she reached inside and drew out a gardening shirt. It had been laundered and neatly folded, but grass and earth stains remained. She could see him, the faded denim bagging over his thin torso as he whistled through his teeth and tended his flowers.

"Just look at the delphiniums, Clare." He'd grin and run his bony, dirt-crusted fingers over the deep blue blooms as gently as a man handling a newborn. "They're going to be even bigger than last year. Nothing like a little chicken poop to give a garden the edge."

She buried her face in the shirt, drawing breath after deep breath. And she could smell him, as clearly as if she'd been sitting beside him.

"Why did you leave me that way?" She kept the scent of him pressed hard against her skin as she rocked as if she could absorb what was left of him. And the anger came, hot waves of it that twisted tight around the smothering grief. "You had no right to leave me that way when I needed you so much. Damn you, I wanted you there. I needed you there. Daddy. Oh, Daddy, why?"

She lowered herself to the floor and let the tears come.

Ernie watched her. His body had been atremble with anticipation and power. Now the dark excitement ebbed, and a hot wave of shame, unexpected, unwanted, washed over him. He felt it burn his face and neck as her hard, wrenching sobs filled the room. As he crept away, the sounds of grief chased after him until he was running to escape them.

Dr. Loomis sat in the chair in front of Cam's desk, his hands neatly folded on his briefcase, his polished wingtips heel to heel. Cam wondered if the coroner would tap them together and whisk off to Kansas or wherever the hell home was.

"When I learned the deceased was your father—"

"Stepfather," Cam corrected.

"Yes." Loomis cleared his throat. "When I learned he had been your stepfather, I thought it best if I brought you my report personally."

"I appreciate it." Cam continued to read the autopsy report, word for grim word. "This confirms homicide."

"There's no doubt he was murdered." Loomis's fingers steepled up, then folded again. "The autopsy bears out my original theory. The deceased was beaten to death. From the bone fragments and the splinters of wood we found, I would say at least two clubs were used. One of natural pine and one that was stained, commercially, to an ebony color."

"Which means we have at least two murderers."

"Possibly. If I may?" Loomis picked up the pictures Cam had taken at the scene. After tapping their edges neatly together, he turned them as if he were about to show off family snapshots. "This blow to the base of the skull? It is the only wound on the back of the body. From the bruising and discoloration, this was delivered before death. It would be sufficient to render unconsciousness. Then you note the wrists and ankles."

"Someone clubbed him from behind, knocking him out. Then he was tied." Cam picked up his pack of cigarettes. "Flat on his back for the rest of it."

"Precisely." Pleased, Loomis nearly smiled. "From the depth of the wounds and the amount of fiber in them, he struggled violently."

"You would agree that he wasn't killed where we found him?"

"I would, most definitely."

Cam blew out a long stream of smoke. "We located his car. His stereo unit was removed, along with his gun and a case of beer from the trunk. The receipt for the beer was still there. He'd just bought it that afternoon." Studying

Loomis, he tapped the cigarette in an ashtray. "People have been killed for less."

"Indeed they have."

"How many homicides of this nature come through your office in a year?"

Loomis waited a moment. "I have never, in my eight years in this county, examined a body so viciously beaten."

Cam nodded. It was no less than what he'd expected. "I don't think Biff Stokey was killed for a stereo and a case of Bud."

Again Loomis steepled his hands. "I'm a pathologist, Sheriff. That makes me a detective in my way. I can give you the cause of death, the approximate time of death. I can tell you what the victim enjoyed as a last meal and if he had sex with a woman. But I can't give you motive."

Nodding, Cam crushed out his cigarette. "I appreciate you getting back to me personally, and so soon."

"Not at all." Loomis rose. "The body was released to the next of kin." Noting Cam's expression, Loomis felt a pang of sympathy. It hadn't taken long for the gossip to reach him. "Your mother requested that Griffith's Funeral Home here in Emmitsboro handle the arrangements."

"I see." She hadn't called him once for help, Cam thought, and stonily refused every offer he'd made. Smothering the hurt, he offered a hand. "Thank you, Dr. Loomis."

When the coroner left, Cam locked the reports and photographs in his desk drawer. He stepped outside and after a moment's debate decided against taking his car. The funeral parlor was only a few blocks away. He needed to walk.

People greeted him with nods and hellos. He knew without hearing that they whispered and murmured the moment they were out of earshot. Biff Stokey had been beaten to death. In a town that size, it wasn't possible to keep such an aberration secret. It was also no secret that Cameron Rafferty, Stokey's stepson and the town sheriff, had been the deceased's biggest enemy.

Giving a half laugh, Cam turned the corner at Main and Sunset. It was a hell of a note when the investigating officer and the chief suspect were one and the same—especially since the officer was the suspect's only alibi. He knew he'd been nursing a beer and reading a Koontz novel the night Biff had been killed. As his own witness, he could eliminate himself as a possible suspect. But there was bound to be speculation muttering around town.

He'd been in a fistfight with Biff and thrown him in jail only days before the murder. Everyone in the bar had seen just how much hate there was between them. The story had spread across town like brushfire, singeing the edges from

Dopper's Woods to Gopher Hole Lane. It would have been recounted and replayed over supper tables. Out-of-town relations would have heard the news on Sunday during discounted-rate phone calls.

It made him wonder if someone had used that very convenient timing.

Biff hadn't been killed for a car stereo and some beer. But he had been killed, viciously and purposefully. However much Cam had hated him, he would find out why. He would find out who.

There was a crowd of people outside Griffith's aged white brick building. Some were talking to each other, others were hanging back and watching. There was such a tangle of pickups and cars along the quiet street that anybody would have thought there was going to be a pa-rade. From a half block away, Cam could see that Mick Morgan was having trouble restoring order.

"Look now, there's nothing for y'all to see here, and you're just going to upset Miz Stokey."

"Did they bring him in the back, Mick?" someone wanted to know. "I heard he was carved up by some motorcycle gang from D.C."

"Hell's Angels," someone else chimed in.

"No, it was junkies from over the river."

There was a small, vicious argument over this.

"He got drunk and picked a fight again." This

came from Oscar Roody, who shouted over the din. "Got his head bashed clean in."

Some of the women who had poured out of Betty's House of Beauty next door added their own viewpoints.

"The man made poor Jane's life a misery." Betty herself wrapped her arms around her own expansive bosom and nodded sagely. "Why, she'd have to save up for six months before she could come in and get herself a perm. And he wouldn't let her have so much as a rinse put on."

"What Jane needs now is a woman's shoulder." Min, her hair rolled up in pink plastic curlers, stared at the front window of the funeral parlor with glittery eyes. If she could get in first, she might even get a peek at the body. *That* would be worth something at the next Ladies Club meeting. She elbowed her way through the crowd and started for the door.

"Now Miz Atherton, ma'am, you can't go in there."

"You move on aside, Mick." She brushed at him with the back of her chubby hand. "Why, I've been friends with Jane Stokey since before you were born."

"Why don't you go finish having your hair done, Mrs. Atherton?" Cam stepped forward, blocking her path. At his appearance, the arguments settled down to murmurs. Eyes narrowed against the sun, he scanned the crowd. Here were friends, men he might share a beer with, women who would stop him on the street to pass the time of day. Most of them looked away now. Across the street Sarah Hewitt leaned lazily against the trunk of a tree, smoking and smiling at him.

Min patted her curlers. In the excitement she'd forgotten about them, but it couldn't be helped. "Now, Cameron, I'm not the least bit concerned about my appearance at a time like this. I only want to offer your mother my support in this difficult time."

And you'd suck her dry, he thought, so that you can pass out her misery over manicures and on street corners. "I'll be sure to pass your sympathies along to her." Slowly, he looked from face to face, from eye to eye. Some backed away, others studied the fading bruises on Cam's jaw, around his eye. Bruises Biff had put there only days before.

"I'm sure my mother could use your support at the funeral." Christ, he wanted a cigarette. A *drink*. "But for now, I'd appreciate it if you left this to the family."

They filed off, some to their pickups, others to wander down to the post office or the market where they could discuss the situation in depth.

"I'm sorry about that, Cam." On a wheezy

sigh, Mick Morgan pulled a package of Red Indian chewing tobacco from his pocket.

"Nothing to be sorry about."

"They brought him in around the back. Oscar was working on a toilet inside. That's all it took. Old fart couldn't wait to get his tongue wagging." Mick stuffed the plug in his cheek. "They were just curious is all. I'd've had them on their way in a minute or two."

"I know. Is my mother inside?"

"That's what I heard."

"Do me a favor and keep an eye on the office for a while."

"Sure thing." He used his tongue to settle the chaw more cozily. "Ah . . . mighty sorry about your trouble, Cam. If you want to take a couple days off, stay with your mom, Bud and me can double up."

"Thanks. I appreciate it. But I don't think she'll need me." Wearily, he walked up to the door with its discreet brass knocker.

He stepped inside to the overwhelming scent of gladiolas and Lemon Pledge. There was a churchlike hush in the red-draped hallway. Why in the hell did funeral parlors always use red? he wondered. Was that the color of comfort?

Red plush, dark paneling, thick carpet, and ornate candlesticks. A bunch of plucky glads and lilies sat in a tall vase on a glossy table. Beside them was a stack of printed business cards.

WE'LL BE HERE IN YOUR TIME
OF NEED
Charles W. Griffith and Sons
Emmitsboro, Maryland
established 1839

It pays to advertise, Cam thought.

There was a carpeted stairway leading to the second floor. The viewing rooms. An entertaining term for a morbid tradition, he thought. Why the hell people wanted to stare at corpses he couldn't figure. But maybe that was because he'd had to look at more than his share.

He remembered climbing those steps as a child, to look at the dead face of his father. His mother had been weeping, walking ahead of him with Biff Stokey's beefy arm around her. He hadn't wasted any time moving in, Cam thought now. Mike Rafferty hadn't even been in the ground before Stokey put his hands on the widow.

Now they were full circle.

His hands jammed in his pockets, Cam started down the hallway. The double doors to the main parlor were shut. He hesitated, then pulled a hand free to knock. Within moments, the door opened silently.

Standing somber-eyed in one of his five black suits was Chuck Griffith. For more than a hundred and fifty years, the Griffiths had been undertakers in Emmitsboro. Chuck's son was already in training to take over the family business, but at forty, Chuck was in his prime.

As a boy he'd been as comfortable in the embalming room as on the baseball field, where he'd been the star pitcher. To the Griffiths, death was a business, a steady one. Chuck could afford to take his family on a two-week vacation every year and buy his wife a new car every third one.

They had a pretty house on the edge of town and an in-ground swimming pool, heated. People often joked about it being the pool that death built.

In his capacity as coach for Emmitsboro's Little League, Chuck was loud, boisterous, and competitive. As the town's only funeral director, he was somber, soft-spoken, and sympathetic. Immediately he extended one of his wide, capable hands to Cam.

"It's good you're here, Sheriff."

"Is my mother inside?"

"Yes." Chuck cast a quick glance behind him. "I'm having some trouble convincing her that, under the circumstances, a closed casket service would be advisable."

Cam had an instant and uncomfortable flash of what had been left of Biff's face. "I'll talk to her."

"Please, come in." He gestured Cam inside the dimly lit, flower-filled room. There was music playing quietly from hidden speakers. Something soft and soothing. "We're having some tea. I'll just get another cup."

Cam nodded, then walked toward his mother. She was sitting stiffly on the high-back sofa, a box of tissues within arm's reach. She was wearing a black dress, one he didn't recognize. He imagined she had borrowed it or had one of her lady friends buy it for her. She held the teacup in a white-knuckled grip. Her knees were pressed so tightly together, Cam thought they must ache with the pressure of bone to bone. At her feet was a small hard-sided suitcase with a broken strap.

"Mom." Cam sat beside her and after a moment put a hand awkwardly on her shoulder. She didn't look at him.

"Did you come to see him?"

"No, I came to stay with you."

"There's no need." Her voice was cold and steady as stone. "I've buried a husband before."

He took his hand away and had to fight the need to ball it into a fist and bash it against the glossy coffee table. "I'd like to help you make the arrangements. It's hard to make decisions at a time like this. And it's expensive. I'd like to take care of whatever bills there are."

"Why?" Her hand was rock steady as she lifted it, sipped her tea, then lowered it again. "You hated him."

"I'm offering to help you."

"Biff wouldn't want your help."

"Is he running your life now, too?"

Her head snapped around, and her eyes, reddened from hours and hours of weeping, burned into him. "Don't you speak ill of him. The man is dead, beaten to death. Beaten to death," she repeated in a harsh whisper. "You're the law here. If you want to help, then you find out who did this to my husband. You find out who killed him."

Chuck cleared his throat as he walked back into the room. "Mrs. Stokey, perhaps you'd like to—"

"I don't need any more tea." She rose and picked up the suitcase. "I don't need anything. I brought the clothes I want him buried in. Now you take me to see my husband."

"Mrs. Stokey, he hasn't been prepared."

"I lived with him for twenty years. I'll see him as he is."

"Mom—"

She whirled on her son. "I don't want you here now. Do you think I could stand and look at him with you beside me, knowing how you felt? Since you were ten years old, you made me stand between you, choose between you. Now he's dead, and I'm choosing him."

You always did, Cam thought, and let her go.

Alone, he sat again. It would do no good to wait for her, he knew, but he needed a moment before he went outside again to face the stares and whispers.

There was a Bible on the table, its leather cover worn smooth by countless hands. He wondered if his mother had found any verses inside to comfort her.

"Cameron."

He looked up and saw the mayor in the parlor doorway. "Mr. Atherton."

"I don't want to intrude during this difficult time. My wife called. She seemed to think your mother might need some support."

"She's with Chuck."

"I see." He started to back away, then changed his mind. "Is there anything I can do for you? I know people always say that at times like this, but . . ." He moved his thin shoulders and looked uncomfortable.

"Actually, my mother might need someone to drive her home when she's finished here. She doesn't want it to be me."

"I'd be glad to take her. Cameron, people react to grief in different ways."

"So I'm told." He rose then. "I have the autopsy report. I'll have a copy for you and the rest of my paperwork by tomorrow."

"Oh, yes." Atherton gave a weak smile. "I have to admit I'm out of my element."

"All you have to do is file them. Mayor, are there any gangs at school? Any of the tougher elements fusing together?"

Atherton's scholarly face creased as his brows drew together. "No. We have the usual trouble-makers, of course, and the misfits, some brawls in the hallway and fights over girls or ball games." His thoughtful eyes widened. "Surely you can't believe that Biff was killed by children?"

"I have to start somewhere."

"Sheriff—Cameron—we don't even have a drug problem at Emmitsboro High. You know that. We may have boys bloodying noses once in a while and girls pulling out some hair, but nothing that would lead to murder." He pulled out a carefully pressed handkerchief and dabbed at his upper lip. The thought of murder made him sweat. "I'm sure you're going to discover that someone out of town, a stranger, was re-sponsible."

"Funny that a stranger would know to dump the body where kids have been sneaking down to wade for years. And that a stranger would push the car halfway off the road just where Bud Hewitt drives by every night."

"But—whoever . . . I mean, doesn't that make my point? They couldn't have wanted the body found so quickly."

"I wonder," Cam murmured. "I appreciate your seeing my mother home, Mayor."

"What? Oh, yes. I'm happy to help." With his handkerchief still pressed to his lips, Atherton stared after Cam with fear dawning in his eyes.

Crazy Annie stood in front of Cam's car and patted the hood as though it were the family dog. She crooned to it, pleased with its shiny blue surface. If she looked close, she could see her face reflected in the wax. It made her giggle.

Mick Morgan spotted her through the window of the sheriff's office. Shaking his head, he opened the door.

"Hey there, Annie, you'll get Cam pissed if you put fingerprints all over his car."

"It's pretty." But she rubbed the hood with her dirty sleeve to remove the smudges. "I won't hurt it."

"Why don't you go down to Martha's for some supper?"

"I got a sandwich. Alice gave me a sandwich. A BLT on wheat toast, hold the mayo."

"She's all right." Cam stepped off the sidewalk. The walk back from the funeral parlor hadn't mellowed his mood. But seeing Annie stroking his car had his lips curving. "How's it going, Annie?"

She focused on him. Her bracelets jingled as she fussed with the buttons of her blouse. "Can I have a ride on your motorcycle?"

"I don't have it with me today." He watched her bottom lip poke out, a little girl gesture that was pathetic on the aged face. "How about a ride in the car? Want me to take you home?"

"I can sit in the front?"

"Sure."

When he bent to pick up her sack, she grabbed it and pressed it against her. "I can carry it. It's mine. I can carry it."

"Okay. Climb on in. Do you know how to put your seat belt on?"

"You showed me last time. You showed me." Hefting her bag and her hips into the car, she set her tongue between her teeth and went to work on the seat belt. She gave a little cry of pleasure when it snapped into place. "See? I did it myself. All by myself."

"That's good." Once inside, Cam let the windows down. Since Annie had skipped a few baths, he had to be grateful the evening was warm and breezy.

"The radio."

He pulled away from the sidewalk. "It's this button." He pointed, knowing she wanted to turn it herself. When Billy Joel rocked out, Annie clapped her hands. Bracelets slid up and down her arms. "I know this one." The wind ruffled her gray hair as she sang along.

He turned down Oak Leaf Lane. When they passed the Kimball house, he slowed automatically, but he didn't see Clare in the garage.

Annie stopped singing and craned her neck to keep the Kimball house in view. "I saw a light in the attic."

"There wasn't a light in the attic, Annie."

"Before there was. I couldn't sleep. Can't walk in the woods at night. It's bad at night in the woods. Walked into town. There was a light way up in the attic." She screwed her face tight, as one memory lapped over another. Had someone screamed? No, no, not this time. This time she hadn't hidden in the bushes and seen men hurry out and drive away. Hurry out and drive. She liked the rhythm of those words and began to hum them to herself.

"When did you see a light, Annie?"

"Don't remember." She began to play with the power window. "Do you think Mr. Kimball was working late? He works late sometimes. But he's dead," she remembered, pleased with herself for not getting mixed up. "Dead and buried, so he wasn't working. The girl's back. The girl with the pretty red hair."

"Clare?"

"Clare," Annie repeated. "Pretty hair." She twined her own around her finger. "She went away to New York, but she came back. Alice told me. Maybe she went up to the attic to look for her daddy. But he's not there."

"No, he's not."

"I used to look for my mama." She sighed and began to play with her bracelets, tracing the engraved letters on the silver one. "I like to walk. Sometimes I walk all the livelong day. I find things. Pretty things." She held up her arm. "See?"

"Mmm-hmm." But he was thinking of Clare and didn't look at the silver-plated bracelet with *Carly* engraved on it.

Clare felt foolishly shy as she walked around to the side entrance of the Cramptons' neat two-story brick house. The patient entrance, she thought sourly, then sighed. But she wasn't going to see Doc for a simple checkup, or a case of the sniffles. She just needed to see him, to hook one more link in the chain that led back to her father.

Still the memories came sneaking back, those childhood images of sitting in Doc's lemony-smelling waiting room with its paintings of ducks and flowers, reading tattered Golden Books, then ancient copies of *Seventeen*. Going into the examining room to sit on the padded bench and say "ah." Being rewarded with a balloon regardless of whether or not she'd cried at the prick of a needle.

There was comfort here, in the smell of freshly cut grass, in the gleam of new spring paint on the window trim, and in the quiet voice she heard singing, off key.

She saw him bent over his lilies of the valley, patiently weeding. Gardening was the obsession Doc Crampton had shared with her father—an obsession that had cemented their friendship in spite of Doc's being a good deal older than Jack Kimball.

"Hey, Doc."

He straightened quickly, wincing a little at the creak in his back. His round face brightened. Beneath a battered old hat, his white hair flowed, making her think of Mark Twain.

"Clare, I wondered when you were going to come by for a visit. We didn't have much time to get reacquainted the other day at Jane's."

"Alice told me you take a half day off now and then during the week. I was hoping to catch you when you weren't busy."

"You did. Just tending my ladies."

"Your flowers are lovely." It hurt a little to look at them and remember Doc and her father discussing pruning and fertilizer. "Just as always."

Though she was smiling, he saw trouble in her

eyes. A general practitioner in a small town learned to listen to problems as well as pulse rates. He patted the stone wall and sat. "Keep an old man company. I want to hear all about what you've been up to."

She sat and told him a little because they both knew it would help ease her into what she had come to say or to ask.

"So, Mom and Jerry should be back in Virginia in a couple of weeks. She likes it there."

"Since you're this far, maybe you'll go visit them before heading back."

"Maybe." Eyes lowered, she brushed at a smudge on her slacks. "I'm glad she's happy. I really am glad she's happy."

"Of course you are."

"I didn't know it would be so hard." Her voice shook, broke. She had to take two deep breaths to control it. "I went upstairs last night. Into the attic."

"Clare." He reached for her hand, tucked it comfortably between his. "You didn't have to do that alone."

"I'm not a child anymore, afraid of ghosts."

"You'll always be your father's child. You still miss him. I understand that. I miss him, too."

She gave a shaky sigh, then went on. "I know what a good friend you were to him. How you tried to help when he started drinking. And how you stood by us when the scandal came out."

"A friend doesn't turn his back because of hard times."

"Some do." She straightened and smiled at him. "But not you. Never you. I was hoping you were still his friend so that you'd help me."

Disturbed by the strain in her voice, he kept her hand in his. "Clare, you've been coming around here since you could toddle. Of course I'll help you. For Jack. And for you."

"I've made a mess out of my life."

His brows drew together. "How can you say that? You're a very successful young woman."

"Artist," she corrected. "Pretty successful there. But as a woman . . . You'll have heard I was married and divorced." The faintest trace of humor lit her eyes. "Come on, Doc, I know how you disapprove of divorce."

"Generally, yes." He huffed a bit, not wanting to sound pompous. "A vow is a vow, as far as I can see. But I'm not so set in my ways that I don't understand there are sometimes . . . circumstances."

"*I* was the circumstances." Reaching down, she plucked a blade of grass that grew close to the wall. "I couldn't love him enough, couldn't be what he wanted. Couldn't be what I wanted, I guess. So I messed it up."

Now he pursed his lips. "I would say that it takes two people to cause a marriage to succeed or to fail."

She nearly laughed. "Rob wouldn't agree, believe me. And when I look back over it and the other relationships I've had, or tried to have, I realize I keep holding something back."

"If you believe that, you must have an idea why."

"Yes. I—I need to understand how he could have done it," she blurted out. "Oh, I know all about addiction and alcoholism as an illness. But those are just generalities, and he was my father. He was mine. I have to understand, somehow, so I can . . ."

"Forgive him," Crampton said gently, and Clare closed her eyes.

"Yes." That was the one thing, the single thing, she had refused to admit no matter how Janowski had prodded. But the guilt wasn't so painful saying it here, with her hand clasped warmly in the hand of her father's closest friend. "Last night when I went up there, I realized I never had. I'm so afraid I never will."

Crampton was silent for a moment, smelling the smells of his garden, listening to the birdsong and the light ruffle of leaves in the spring breeze. "Jack and I talked about more than mulch and beetles in those long evenings. He used to tell me how proud he was of you, and

Blair. But you were special to him, the way I suppose you understand Blair's special to Rosemary."

"Yes." Her lips curved a little. "I know."

"He wanted the best for you. He wanted the world for you." Crampton sighed, remembering, regretting. "Perhaps he wanted too much, and that was why he made mistakes. I know this, Clare, that whatever he did, right or wrong, everything he did circled back to love for you. Don't blame him too much for being weak. Even in weakness he put you first."

"I don't want to blame him. But there are so many memories. They drown me."

He studied her with his solemn eyes. "Sometimes you can't go back, however much you'd like to. Trying to go back can hurt more than it can heal."

"I'm finding that out." She looked away, over the neatly trimmed lawn. "But I can't go forward, Doc. Not until I know."

Chapter 11

No AMOUNT OF REASON could sway Jane Stokey from having an open casket. When a man was dead, it was the duty of those who had known him to look one last time at his face, to remember him. To speak over him.

"He was a mean motherfucker," Oscar Roody commented, tugging on the knot of his tie. "After a couple of beers, old Biff would as soon punch you in the face as look at you."

"That's a fact." Less nodded wisely as he studied Biff's face. Rot in hell, you bastard, he thought. "Chuck sure knows his business now, don't he? From what I hear, Biff was messed up good and proper, but it just looks like he's taking a little snooze."

"Probably used a pile of makeup." Oscar took

out a bandanna and honked into it. "You ask me, it's gotta be creepy putting makeup on a dead man."

"I'd do it if it'd buy me a pool. I heard he got every bone in his body broke." Less shifted, looking for evidence and for the thrill. "Sure can't tell it."

They moved on and snuck outside for a smoke.

Jane was there, already seated in a chair at the front of the rows Griffith's had set up. Since Biff had had no church affiliation, the simple service would be held right there in the funeral parlor, with Chuck officiating. She wore the stiff black dress, her hair neatly pinned back, and accepted the condolences and awkward words of sympathy.

People filed by Biff to pay their last respects.

"He tried to get his fat hand up my skirt more times than I can count." Sarah Hewitt smirked down at the dead face.

"Come on, Sarah." Flushing, Bud looked right and left, hoping no one was close enough to have heard. "You can't talk that way here."

"It's stupid that we can say whatever we want about the living, but once someone's dead, we have to say what a nice guy he was—even if he was a bastard." She lifted a brow. "Did they really castrate him?"

"Jesus, Sarah." Bud took her arm and pulled her to the rear of the room.

"Well, look who's here." Sarah's smile became thoughtful as she watched Clare walk into the room. "The prodigal daughter." She skimmed her gaze up and down Clare's figure, envying the simple and expensive dark suit. "Never did fill out, did she?"

Clare's heart was a hot ball lodged in her throat. She hadn't known it would be so bad. The last time she had entered this room, had seen a coffin decked with flowers and flanked by townspeople, her father had been inside it. She would swear the same dreary recorded organ music had been playing.

The stench of gladiolas and roses spun in her head. There was horror in her eyes as she stared down the narrow center aisle between the rows of folding chairs and fought the urge to turn and bolt.

God, you're a grown woman, she reminded herself. Death is a part of life. One you've got to face up to. But she wanted to run, run out into the sunshine, so badly that her knees were vibrating.

"Clare?"

"Alice." She gripped her friend's hand and fought to steady herself. "Looks like half the town turned out."

"For Mrs. Stokey." Her gaze flicked over faces. "And for the entertainment." She was feeling awkward herself in her waitress's uniform, but she had only managed to steal twenty minutes away. Besides, the closest thing she had to funeral gear was a black sweatshirt. "They're going to start in a minute."

"I'm just going to sit in the back." Clare had no intention of marching up to the coffin and peeking in.

Hey, Biff, haven't seen you for years. Sorry you're dead.

The thought of it had her choking back a nervous laugh, then fighting off a wave of hot tears. What was she doing here? What the *hell* was she doing here? She was here for Cam, Clare reminded herself. And she was here to prove that she could sit in this little overheated room and get through a ritual like a responsible adult.

"You all right?" Alice whispered.

"Yes." She took a long, cleansing breath. "We'd better sit down."

As she and Alice took a seat, Clare scanned the room for Cam. She spotted Min Atherton in navy polyester, her face in solemn lines, her bright eyes gleeful. The mayor was beside her, his head bowed as if in prayer.

Farmers and merchants and mechanics stood in their Sunday suits and discussed business and the weather. Mrs. Stokey was flanked by townswomen. Cam stood to the side, a set, un-approachable look on his face as he watched his mother.

Chuck Griffith walked to the front of the room, turned, and waited. With murmurs and shuffles, people filed to the folding chairs.

Silence.

"Friends," he began, and Clare remembered.

The room had been packed both evenings during the viewing. There hadn't been a man, woman, or child in Emmitsboro who hadn't known Jack Kimball. All of them had come. The words they had spoken had blurred in her head, leaving only their meaning behind. Sorrow and regret. But no one, no one had known the depth of her own grief.

The church had been packed for the service, and the line of cars heading out to the cemetery at Quiet Knolls had stretched for blocks.

Some of the same people were here today. Older, with more flesh and less hair. They took their seats and held their silence and thought their thoughts.

Rosemary Kimball had been surrounded by townswomen, just as Jane Stokey was. They had stood by her, a unified line of support, filled with sympathy for her loss, filled with relief that their own widowhood was somewhere down the road of a murky future.

They had brought food to the house—ham,

potato salad, chicken—to feed the grieving. The food had meant nothing, but the kindness helped fill some of the empty spaces.

Days later—only days—the scandal had hit. Jack Kimball, well-loved member of the community, was now an opportunist charged with kickbacks, bribery, falsified documents. While her grief was still blood-fresh, she'd been told to accept the fact that her father had been a liar and a cheat.

But she had never accepted it. Nor had she accepted his suicide.

Cam saw her. He was surprised she was there and less than pleased when he noted that her face was too pale, her eyes too wide. She had a hand gripped in Alice's as she stared straight ahead. He wondered what it was she saw, what it was she heard. He was certain she wasn't listening to Chuck Griffith's words about eternal life and forgiveness any more than he was.

But others listened. With their faces blank and their hands still, they listened. And they feared. A warning had been given. When one of their number broke the Law, he would be plucked out, without mercy. The wrath of the few was no less than the wrath of the Dark Lord. So they listened, and they remembered. And behind their somber eyes and bent heads, they were afraid.

"I have to get back." Alice squeezed Clare's

hand. "I have to get back," she repeated. "Clare?"

"What?" She blinked. People were shuffling to their feet and filing out. "Oh."

"I could only get time off to come for the service. Are you driving out to the cemetery?"

"Yes." Clare had her own grave to visit. "I'll be driving out."

A half dozen cars slid into position in the back lot of Griffith's. There were farms to run and shops to open, and the fact was there weren't too many people willing to take the time to see Biff Stokey get plopped in the ground. Clare pulled in at the rear and settled into the short, stately drive. Ten miles out of town, the grim parade drove through the open iron gates.

Clare's fingers were clammy when she turned off the ignition. She waited in the car. The pall-bearers hefted their burden. She saw the mayor, Doc Crampton, Oscar Roody, Less Gladhill, Bob Meese, and Bud Hewitt. Cam walked beside his mother. They didn't touch.

Clare got out of her car and, turning away, walked up the slope of the hill. Birds were singing as birds do on warm May mornings. The grass smelled strong and sweet. Here and there among the stones and plaques were plastic flowers or wreaths. They wouldn't fade. Clare wondered if the people who had placed them there realized how much sadder their bright artificial colors were than drooping carnations or dying daisies.

There was family here. Her mother's mother and father, great-aunts and uncles, a young cousin who had died of polio long before Clare had been born. She walked among them while the sun stung her eyes and warmed her face.

She didn't kneel at her father's grave. She hadn't brought flowers. She didn't weep. Instead she stood, reading his headstone over and over, trying to find some sense of him there. But there was nothing but granite and grass.

As he stood beside his mother, Cam watched Clare. The sun turned her hair to copper. Bright and brilliant. Alive. His fingers flexed as he realized just how much he needed to touch life. Each time he put a hand on his mother's arm, her shoulder, her back, he was met with a cold wall. She had nothing for him, not even need.

Yet he couldn't leave her, couldn't turn away as he wanted to and go to Clare, put a hand on that bright, brilliant hair, absorb that life, that need.

He hated cemeteries, he thought, and remembered staring down into the empty grave of a child.

When Clare walked away, returned to her car, drove away, he knew what it was to be utterly alone.

★ ★ ★

Clare worked furiously for the rest of the day. Driven. Her second metal sculpture was almost done. When it was time to let the steel cool, she would turn off her torch, strip off her skullcap, and take up the clay model of Ernie's arm.

She couldn't bear to rest.

With knives and hands and wooden pallets, she carved and smoothed and formed. She could feel the defiance as she shaped the fist. The restlessness as she detailed the taut muscles of the forearm. Patiently, she carved away minute scraps of clay with thin wire, then smoothed and textured with a damp brush.

The music blared on her radio—the edgiest, grittiest rock she could find on the dial. Sparked with energy, she washed the clay from her hands, but she didn't rest. Couldn't. At another worktable sat a slab of cherry wood with much of its center already carved away. She took up her tools, mallet, chisels, calipers, and poured that nervous energy into her work.

She stopped only when the sun lowered enough to force her to switch on lights, then to turn the music from rock to classical, just as passionate, just as driving. Cars cruised by unheard. The phone rang, but she ignored it.

Her other projects faded completely from her mind. She was part of the wood now, part of its possibilities. And the wood absorbed her emotions. Cleansed them. She had no sketch, no model. Only memories and needs.

For the fine carving, her fingers were deft and sure. Her eyes burned, but she rubbed the back of her wrist over them and kept going. The fire in her, rather than banking, grew and grew.

Stars came out. The moon started its rise.

Cam saw her bent over her work, a wood file flashing in her hand. Overhead the bright, naked bulbs burned, drawing pale, wide-winged moths to their death dance. Music soared, all slashing strings and crashing bass.

There was a glow of triumph on her face, in her eyes. Every few moments, she would stroke her fingers over the curve of wood in a form of communication he recognized but couldn't understand.

There was something raw and powerful in the shape. It swept down, forming an open profile. As he stepped inside the garage, he could see that it was a face, eerily masculine, a head lifted back and up as if toward the sun.

He didn't speak and lost track of the time as he watched her. But he could feel the passion trembling out of her. It reached him and clashed almost painfully with his own.

Clare set the tools aside. Slowly, she slid from the stool to step back. Her breath was coming fast, so fast she instinctively pressed a hand to her heart. Pain mixed with pleasure as she studied what she had been driven to create.

Her father. As she remembered him. As she had loved him. Dynamic, energized, loving. Alive. Most of all alive. Tonight, finally, she had found a way to celebrate his life.

She turned and looked at Cam.

She didn't stop to wonder why she wasn't surprised to see him there. She didn't pause to ask herself if this new surge of excitement was dangerous or if she was ready for the needs she read in his eyes.

He reached up to pull the garage door down. Metal banged against concrete. She didn't move, didn't speak, but waited with every nerve in her body humming taut.

He crossed to her. The music was trapped with them, blasting from walls, ceiling, floor.

Then his hands were on her face, his rough palms shaping her, his thumbs rubbing across her lips, then her cheekbones, before his fingers dug into her hair. Her breath caught as he dragged her head back, as his body slammed into hers. But it wasn't fear that made her shudder. And the sound in her throat as his lips crushed to hers was one of triumph.

He'd never needed anyone more than he needed her at that moment. All the misery, all the pain, all the bitterness he had carried with him that day faded at the first hot taste of her. She was pure energy in his arms, snapping and pulsing with life. Starving, he dived deeper into her mouth while her heart pounded against his.

His hands moved down to grip her hips, then her thighs. If it had been possible, he would have pulled her inside him, so great was his need to possess. On an oath, he dragged her with him, stumbling blindly into the kitchen.

He thought of bed, of sinking with her onto the mattress. Of sinking into her.

Impatient, he tugged at her shirt, yanking it over her head and letting it fly. They rammed into a wall as he filled his hands with her breasts.

She laughed and reached for him, but could only moan when he bent low and suckled. Fisting her hands in his hair, she held on.

He seemed to be feasting on her. There was a wildness in him, a greed, a violence that staggered her. Her body arched, offering more. Straining for more. The prick of his teeth against her sensitive skin had her blood beating hotter. She could feel it, almost hear it, the primitive drumbeat rhythm just under her skin. She'd forgotten that she could feel passion like this for a man. This hunger that could only be sated by rough and frenzied joining. She wanted him to take her now, as they stood. Quickly, even viciously.

Then he was pulling her jeans down over her hips, and his clever, dangerous mouth was roaming lower.

He slid his tongue over the quivering skin of her torso. Her nails dug into his shoulders as her body rocked. She was naked beneath the denim, and his groan of pleasure shivered against her flesh. He could hear her quick, breathy murmurs but didn't know what she was asking. Didn't care. He caught her hips when her legs buckled, and his hands were rough. His mouth was demanding and greedy as it closed over her.

She was dying. She had to be dying. She couldn't be alive and feel so much. Her body was bombarded by sensation after sensation. His hands, those long, urgent fingers. And his mouth. God, his mouth. Lights seemed to dance behind her eyes. With each gasping breath, she gulped in hot, thick air until her system was too full and fighting for release. She cried out, dragging at him, pulling him back up to her, unable to bear what was happening to her. Frantic for more.

His breath was as ragged as hers as he hit the light switch beside her head. His hands were on her face again, holding her back against the wall.

"Look at me." He would have sworn the floor swayed under his feet. "Damn it, I want you to look at me."

She opened her eyes and stared into his. She

was trapped there, she thought with a flash of panic. Imprisoned in him. Her lips trembled open, but there were no words, nothing that could describe what she was feeling.

"I want to watch you." His mouth came down on hers again, devouring. "I want to see you."

She was falling. Endlessly. Helplessly. And he was there, his body shockingly hot over hers, the tiles icy cold against her own heated back.

Driven by her own needs, she pulled at his shirt, popping buttons in her rush to feel his flesh against hers. Out of control, she thought. She was out of control and glorying in it. As desperate as he, she ran her hands over his damp skin and fought to strip off the rest of the barrier.

He fought with her boots, cursing until she began to laugh. Rearing up, she hooked her arms around him, taking little nibbling bites along his throat and chest.

Hurry, hurry, hurry, was all she could think as they pulled and tugged and yanked.

Then they were rolling over the kitchen floor, the music crashing around them. He kicked clothing aside and sent a chair toppling. Her mouth was fused to his as they reversed positions once more. As she lay on top of him, he gripped her hips, lifting her up.

Now, she thought. Thank God. Now.

Arching back, she took him into her. Her

body shuddered, shuddered, as he filled her, as she opened herself and took more of him.

With her head flung back, her long, slender body curved, she began to rock. Slowly, then faster, still faster, driving him past reason with an ever quickening rhythm. He gripped her hands with his as he watched her ride above him.

Fearless. It was the only word his frantic mind found for her. She looked fearless, rising above him, joined to him, filled with him.

He felt her tighten around him as she reached her peak. His own release left him gasping.

She slid down to him, soft, boneless, and damp. His hand stroked lazily down her back as they caught their breath. He'd been waiting for this, he realized as he turned his head to kiss her hair, for a long time.

"I came by to ask you if you wanted a beer," he murmured.

She sighed, yawned, then settled. "No, thanks."

"You look so damn sexy when you're working."

She smiled. "Yeah?"

"Christ, yeah. I could have eaten you alive."

"I thought you had." She drummed up enough energy to brace a palm on the floor and look down at him. "I liked it."

"That's good because I've been wanting to get your clothes off ever since you tackled me in the upstairs hallway." He reached up to cup her breast, his thumb cruising over the nipple that was still pebble-hard and damp. "You sure grew up nice, Slim." He shifted so that he was sitting up with her across his lap. "You've still got a sock on."

She looked down and flexed her feet, one bare and the other covered with a thick purple sock. There might have been a moment in her life when she had felt better, but she couldn't remember it.

"Next time, maybe we should take off the boots before we get started." She leaned her head against his shoulder and thought, with some regret, that they would have to move eventually. "I guess the floor's getting hard."

"It started out hard." But he didn't feel like getting up just yet. She felt exactly right in his arms—something he'd hoped for but hadn't expected. "I saw you at the funeral. You looked tired."

"I need a bed."

"Mine's available."

She laughed but wondered if they were moving a bit too quickly. "How much do you want for it?"

He put a hand under her chin and turned her head. "I want you to come home with me, Clare."

"Cam—"

He shook his head and took a firmer grip. "I'd better make myself clear straight off. I don't share."

She felt the same skip of panic as she had when she'd looked in his eyes and saw her image trapped there. "It's not as if there's someone else—" she began.

"Good."

"But I don't want to take such a big jump that I end up on my face. What happened just now was—"

"What?"

When she looked into his eyes, she could see that he was smiling again. It made it easy to smile back. "Great. Absolutely great."

He figured he could handle a case of the jitters. Slowly, he skimmed his hand over her hip, up to her rib cage, and watched her eyes darken. Bending his head, he made love to her mouth with his until she was all but purring.

"I want you to come home with me, for tonight." Watching her, he caught her bottom lip between his teeth, nibbled, then released. "Okay?"

"Okay."

Ernie watched them come out of the house through the front door. Because his window was open, he heard Clare's laugh ripple up the quiet street. Their hands were linked as they walked to Cam's car. They stopped and kissed, long and slow and deep. She let him touch her, Ernie thought, while a fire began to burn in his belly.

He watched as they got into the car, then drove away.

While the rage was on him, he rose quietly to lock his door and to light the black candles.

In the woods the coven met. They did not stand in the magic circle. The ritual would wait. There were many among them who knew fear. The altar where one of the group had been executed stood before them. A reminder and a warning.

They had been called here tonight, hours after the burial, to prove their continued allegiance. During the rite to come, each would drink of blood-tainted wine.

"My brothers, one of our number lies tonight in the dirt." The priest spoke softly, but all the muted conversations ended instantly. "The Law was broken, and the weak one has been punished. Know that any who defy the Law, any who stray from the path will be struck down. The dead are dead."

He paused, turning his head slowly. "Are there any questions?"

No one would have dared. And he was pleased.

"Now we have need of another to fill out our number. Names will be considered and offered to the Master."

The men began to talk among themselves again, often arguing over choices like politicos over a favorite son. The priest let them ramble. He already had a candidate. Mindful of his timing, he walked into the circle and raised his hands.

Silence followed him.

"We require youth, strength, and loyalty. We require a mind still open for the possibilities, a body still strong enough to carry the burden of duty. Our Master craves the young, the lonely, the angry. I know of one who is already prepared, already seeking. He wants only direction and discipline. He will begin a new generation for the Dark Lord."

So the name was written on parchment to be offered to the four Princes of Hell.

Chapter 12

O<small>N</small> S<small>ATURDAYS</small> E<small>RNIE</small> <small>WORKED</small> the eight-to-four-thirty shift at the Amoco. And that was fine with him. It meant he was up and out of the house before his parents stumbled out of bed. They'd be busy making pizza at Rocco's when he came home. He could do as he pleased from the time he clocked out until his one o'clock curfew.

Tonight he planned to lure Sally Simmons up to his room, lock the door, turn on some AC/DC, and fuck her brains out.

He'd chosen to move on Sally with less concern than he felt when choosing what shirt to wear in the morning. She was at worst a substitute, at best a symbol of his real desire. The image of Clare rolling around between the sheets with Cameron Rafferty had haunted Ernie through the night. She had betrayed him and their joint destiny.

He would find a way to punish her, but in the meantime, he could vent his frustration with Sally.

He gassed up a milk truck. As the pump clicked off the dollars and gallons behind him, he looked vacantly around town. There was old Mr. Finch, his knobby white knees poking out below plaid Bermuda shorts, walking his two prissy Yorkshire terriers.

Finch was wearing an Orioles fielder's cap, mirrored sunglasses, and a T-shirt that said MARYLAND IS FOR CRABS. He clucked and crooned to the Yorkies as though they were a pair of toddlers. He would, Ernie knew, walk down Main, cut across the Amoco lot, and go inside for a doughnut and a piss. As he did every Saturday morning of his life.

"How's it going, young fella?" Finch asked as he asked every Saturday.

"All right."

"Got to get my girls some exercise."

Less Gladhill breezed in, late as usual. He carried the pasty, sulky look that said hangover in progress. With barely a grunt for Ernie, he went into the garage to change the plugs on a '75 Mustang.

Matt Dopper rumbled through in his aged

Ford pickup, his three dogs riding in the back. He bitched about the price of gas, picked up a pack of Bull Durham from the cigarette counter inside, and headed off to the feed and grain.

Doc Crampton, looking sleepy-eyed, pulled in to fill up his Buick, bought a book of raffle tickets, and commiserated with Finch about the man's bursitis.

Before ten, it seemed half the town had come through. Ernie moved from pump to pump, gassing up carloads of giggling teenage girls on their way to the mall. Young mothers and cranky toddlers, old men who blocked the pumps as they shouted to each other from car windows.

When he went in for his first break and a Coke, Skunk Haggerty, who ran the station, was sitting behind the counter, munching on a doughnut and flirting with Reva Williamson, the skinny, long-nosed waitress from Martha's.

"Well, I was planning on washing my hair and giving myself a facial tonight." Reva rolled strawberry-flavored bubble gum around her tongue and grinned.

"Your face looks just fine to me." Skunk came by his name honestly. No amount of soap, deodorant, or cologne could disguise the faint gym sock aroma that seeped through his pores. But he was single. And Reva was twice divorced and on the prowl.

She giggled, a sound that made Ernie roll his eyes. He could hear them continue their tease and shuffle as he walked into the back to relieve his bladder. The dispenser was out of paper towels. It was his job to keep the rest rooms stocked. Grumbling a bit, he wiped his hands on his jeans on the way to the storeroom. Reva let out a squealing laugh.

"Oh, Skunk, you are a case, you are."

"Shit," Ernie mumbled, and pulled down a box of paper towels. He saw the book, standing face out in the space behind the cardboard box. Licking his lips, Ernie reached for it.

The Magical Diaries of Aleister Crowley. As he flipped the pages, a single sheet of paper fell out. He scooped it up, glancing quickly over his shoulder.

Read. Believe. Belong.

His hands shook as he stuffed the note in his pocket. There was no doubt in his mind that it had been left for him. At last the invitation had come. He had seen things through his telescope. And he had suspected more. Seeing and suspecting, he had kept his silence and waited. Now he was being rewarded, being offered a place.

His young, lonely heart swelled as he slipped the book under his shirt. On impulse he pulled the pentagram out, letting it dangle free and in full view. That would be his sign, he thought. They would see that he had understood and was waiting.

Clare let the shower beat down on her head. Her body felt sore and weary and wonderful. Her eyes closed, she hummed and soaped her skin. It smelled like Cam, she thought, and caught herself grinning foolishly.

God, what a night.

Slowly, sinuously, she ran her hand over her body, remembering. She'd been certain she'd had her share of romantic encounters, but nothing had come close to what happened between them last night.

He'd made her feel like the sexiest woman alive. And the hungriest, the neediest. In one night they had given each other more than she and Rob had managed in . . .

Oops. She shook her head. No comparisons, she warned herself. Especially to ex-husbands.

She slicked her hair back and reminded herself she still had a long way to go. Wasn't she in the shower right now because she'd awakened beside Cam and wanted, too much, to snuggle up against him and cuddle? Even after the storm of lovemaking—or maybe because of it—the need just to be held and stroked had embarrassed her.

This was just sex, she told herself. Really great sex, but just sex. Letting her emotions run rampant would only mess things up. It always did.

So she would wallow in hot water and soap, rub herself dry and pink. Then she'd go in and jump all over his bones. Even as she started to smile at the idea, she opened her eyes and screamed.

Cam had his face plastered against the glass shower wall. His roar of laughter had her swearing at him as he pulled the door open and stepped under the spray with her.

"Scare you?"

"Jesus, you're an idiot. My heart stopped."

"Let me check." He put a hand between her breasts and grinned. "Nope, still ticking. Why aren't you in bed?"

"Because I'm in here." She tossed her hair out of her eyes.

His gaze slid down from the top of her head to her toes, then back again. She could feel her blood begin to pump even before his fingers spread and roamed. "You look good wet, Slim." He lowered his mouth to her slickened shoulder. "Taste good, too." He worked his way up her throat to her lips. "You dropped the soap."

"Mmmm. Most accidents in the home happen in the bathroom."

"They're death traps."

"I guess I'd better get it." She slid down his body, closing her hand over the soap, and her mouth over him. The hiss of his breath merged with the hiss of the shower.

He thought he'd emptied himself during the night, that the needs that had raged and clawed and torn at him had been put to rest. But they were only more desperate now, more violent. He dragged her up, pressed her back against the wet tiles. Her eyes were like melted gold. And he watched them as he plunged himself into her.

"Hungry?" Cam asked as Clare stood by the bedroom window finger-drying her hair.

"Starving," she said without turning around. As far as she could see, there were woods, dark and deep and green. He'd surrounded himself with them, hidden himself behind them. Distant, faintly purple, were the mountains in the west. She imagined what it would look like as the sun sank below them, showering the sky with color.

"Where did you find this place?"

"My grandmother." He finished buttoning his shirt and came to stand behind her. "It's been Rafferty land for a hundred years. She hung on to it, then left it to me."

"It's beautiful. I didn't really see it last night."

She smiled. "I guess I didn't see much of anything last night. I just got the impression of this house on a hill."

Then he'd tossed her over his shoulder, making her laugh as he hauled her inside, upstairs, and into his bed.

"When I came back, I decided I wanted a place where I could get away from town. I think part of Parker's problem was that he lived in that apartment over the liquor store and never got away from it."

"A badge hangs heavy on a man," Clare said somberly and earned a twisted ear. "You said something about food."

"I usually eat at Martha's on Saturday mornings." He checked his watch. "And I'm running behind. We could probably scare up something here."

It sounded much better to Clare. The gossip mills would start turning—there was no way to stop them. But for a morning, at least, they could be held at bay.

"Do I get a tour?"

So far all she'd seen had been the bedroom with his big platform bed, the random-width wooden floor, and ceiling. And the bathroom, she thought. The deep tiled bath with jets, the roomy glass and tile shower. She'd been pleased with his taste so far, the fact that he wasn't afraid to use color, but she wanted to see the rest.

Despite the events of the last twelve hours, she knew that man did not live by bed alone.

He took her hand and led her out.

"There are a couple of other bedrooms up here."

"Three bedrooms?" She cocked a brow. "Planning ahead?"

"You could say that."

He let her poke through the second floor, watching her nod and comment. She approved the skylights and the hardwood floors, the big windows and atrium doors that led to the wrap-around deck.

"You're awfully neat," she said as they started down.

"One person doesn't make very much mess."

She could only laugh and kiss him.

At the base of the steps, she stopped to take in the living area with its lofty ceilings, beams of sunlight, and Indian rugs. One wall was fashioned from river rock with a generous fireplace carved into it. The sofa was low and cushy, perfect for napping.

"Well, this is—" She stepped off the stairs, turned, and saw the sculpture. He had it set beside the open stairwell, positioned so that the sun would stream through the skylight above and pour onto it. So that anyone walking in the front door or standing in the living room would see it.

It was almost four feet high, a curving twist of brass and copper. It was an unmistakably sensual piece—a woman's form, tall, slender, naked. Her arms were lifted high, her copper hair streaming back. Clare had called it *Womanhood* and had sought to reproduce all the power, the wonder, and the magic.

At first she was flustered at finding one of her pieces in his home. Her hands fumbled into her pockets.

"I, ah—you said you thought I painted."

"I lied." He smiled at her. "It was fun getting you riled up and insulted."

She only frowned at that. "I guess you've had it for some time."

"A couple of years." He tucked her hair behind her ear. "I went into this gallery in D.C. They had some of your work, and I ended up walking out with this."

"Why?"

She was uncomfortable, he noted. Embarrassed. He slid his hand from her hair to cup her chin. "I didn't intend to buy it and could hardly afford to at that point. But I looked at it and knew it was mine. Just the way I walked into your garage last night and looked at you."

She moved back a little too quickly. "I'm not a piece of sculpture, Cam."

"No, you're not." Narrowing his eyes, he studied her. "You're upset because I saw this and recognized you. Because I understood you. You'd rather I didn't."

"I have a psychiatrist on call if I want analysis, thanks."

"You can get pissed off, Clare. It doesn't change anything."

"I'm not pissed off," she said between her teeth.

"Sure you are. We can stand here and yell at each other, I can haul your ass back upstairs to bed, or we can go in the kitchen and have coffee. I'll leave it to you."

It was a moment before she could close her mouth and speak. "Why, you arrogant sonofabitch."

"Looks like we yell."

"I'm not yelling," she shouted at him. "But I will make a point. You don't haul my ass anywhere. Understood, Rafferty? If I go to bed with you, it's my own choice. Maybe it's bypassed your snug little world, but we're into the nineties here. I don't need to be seduced, cajoled, or forced. Between responsible, unencumbered adults, sex is a matter of free choice."

"That's fine." He took her by the shirtfront and yanked her against him. Temper glittered in his eyes. "But what happened between you and me was more than sex. You're going to have to admit that."

"I don't have to do anything." She braced

herself when he lowered his head. She was expecting a hard, angry kiss, one ripe with frustration and demand. Instead, his mouth was whisper soft. The sudden and surprising tenderness left her reeling.

"Feel anything, Slim?"

Her eyes were too heavy to open. "Yes."

He brushed her mouth with his again. "Scared?"

She nodded, then sighed as he lowered his brow to hers.

"That makes two of us. Are you finished yelling?"

"I guess so."

He slipped an arm around her shoulders. "Let's get that coffee."

When he dropped her off an hour later, Clare's phone was ringing. She considered ignoring it and diving right back to work while her emotions were still heightened. But as it continued to shrill, she gave up and pulled the receiver from the kitchen hook.

"Hello."

"Jesus Christ, Clare." Angie's aggrieved voice stung Clare's ears. "Where have you been? I've been trying to get through to you since yesterday."

"I've been busy." Clare reached into a bag of cookies. "Working, and things."

"Do you realize that if I hadn't gotten in touch with you by noon, I was going to start down there?"

"Angie, I told you I'm fine. Nothing ever happens here." She thought of Biff Stokey. "Hardly ever. You know I rarely answer the phone when I'm working."

"And you were working at three this morning?"

She caught her bottom lip between her teeth. "I was certainly busy at three this morning. What's going on?"

"I've got news for you, girl. Big news."

Clare put down the cookie and reached for a cigarette. "How big?"

"Major. The Betadyne Institute in Chicago is building a new wing to be dedicated to women in the arts. They want to acquire three of your pieces for permanent display. And," she added as Clare let out a whistling breath, "there's more."

"More?"

"They want to commission you to create a sculpture that will stand outside the building to celebrate women's contribution to art."

"I'm going to sit down now."

"They expect the new addition to be completed in twelve to eighteen months. They'd like some sketches from you before September, and naturally they want you at the opening for press and photo opportunities. Jean-Paul and I will fill you in on all the details when we get there."

"Get there?"

"We're coming down." Angie let out a quick sigh. "I'd hoped you would come back up here to work, but Jean-Paul feels we ought to wait until we see what you've been up to."

Clare put a hand to her head. "Angie, I'm trying to take all this in."

"Just chill some champagne, Clare. We'll be there Monday afternoon. Is there anything we should bring besides contracts and blueprints?"

"Beds," Clare said weakly.

"What?"

"Nothing."

"Good. Jean-Paul will call you for directions tomorrow. Congratulations, girl."

"Thanks." Clare hung up, then scrubbed her hands over her face. This was the next step, she thought, the step she'd been working for, the step Angie had been pushing her toward. She only wished she could be sure she was ready.

She worked through the morning and late into the afternoon. When her hands began to cramp, she stopped. It was just as well, she thought. She needed to go shopping, for beds, sheets, towels. All the little niceties guests might expect. She could swing through town, and with luck, Cam would be able to go with her.

Wouldn't that prove she wasn't afraid of where their relationship was heading?

Sure. And burying herself in work all day proved that she wasn't afraid of being offered the biggest commission of her career.

She started upstairs to change and found herself climbing the attic steps again. The door was open, as she'd left it. She hadn't been able to lock it again, to lock the memories away again. Instead, she stood in the doorway and let herself go back. Back to when her father had kept his big ugly desk piled with papers and pictures and gardening books. There had been a cork bulletin board covered with photos of houses and newspaper listings, phone numbers of plumbers and roofers, carpenters and electricians. Jack Kimball had always tried to nudge work along to friends and townspeople.

He'd had an office in town, of course, tidy and organized. But he'd always preferred to work here, up in the top of the house, where he could be accessible to his family. And smell his flowers from the garden below.

There had been stacks of books, she remembered. Along the wall the shelves had been piled with them. Stepping into the room, Clare began to open other boxes, to go through all the things her mother had packed away but hadn't been able to toss out.

Real estate books, studies in architecture, her father's ratty old address book, novels of Steinbeck and Fitzgerald. There were heavy volumes on theology and religion. Jack Kimball had been both fascinated and repelled by religion. She pushed through them, wondering what had driven him to turn so fiercely back to his childhood faith near the end of his life.

Frowning, she dusted off a dog-eared paperback and tried to remember where she had seen the symbol drawn on its cover before. A pentagram, its center filled with the head of a goat. Its two top points held the horns, the sides the ears, and the bottom tip, the mouth and beard.

"*The Left-Hand Path*," she read aloud. She shuddered and started to open the book when a shadow fell over her.

"Clare?"

She jolted, dropping the book so that it fell facedown among the others. Without thinking, she moved her hand, shifting another book on top of it as she turned.

"I'm sorry." Cam stood in the doorway, searching for the right words. He knew being in this room had to cause her pain. "Your car was here—and the radio's on. I figured you were somewhere in the house."

"Yeah, I was just . . ." She rose and dusted off her knees. "Going through things."

"You okay?"

"Sure." She looked down at the books she'd scattered over the floor. "See, one person can make a mess."

He laid a hand on her cheek. "Hey, Slim. Do you want to talk about it?"

"Be careful." She closed her fingers over his wrist. "I'll start leaning on you."

"Go ahead." Gently, he drew her to him and rubbed a hand up and down her back.

"I loved him so much, Cam." She let out a long breath and watched the dust motes dance in the sunlight. "I've never been able to love anyone else like that. When I was little, I used to come up here after I was supposed to be in bed. He'd let me sit in the chair while he worked, then he'd carry me down. We could talk about anything, even when I got older."

She tightened her grip. "I hated it when he started drinking. I couldn't understand why he would make himself so unhappy, make all of us so unhappy. I would hear him crying some nights. And praying. So lonely, so miserable. But somehow, the next day, he'd pull it all together and get through. And you'd start to believe that it was all going to be okay again. But it wasn't." Sighing, she pulled away, and her eyes were dry.

"He was a good father, Clare. I spent a lot of

years envying you and Blair your father. The drinking was something he couldn't control."

"I know." She smiled a little and did what she hadn't been able to do alone. She moved to the window and looked down. The terrace was empty, swept clean. Edging it were the early roses her father had loved.

"I've been through all the groups, all the therapy. But there's one thing none of them could tell me. There's one thing I've asked myself again and again and never found an answer. Did he fall, Cam? Did he drink himself senseless and lose his balance? Or did he stand here, right here, and decide to stop fighting whatever demon was eating at him?"

"It was an accident." Cam put his hands on her shoulders and turned her to face him.

"I want to believe that. I've always tried to, because the other is too painful. The father I knew couldn't have killed himself, couldn't have hurt my mother or Blair or me that way. But you see, the father I knew couldn't have cheated, couldn't have bribed inspectors and falsified reports the way he did on the shopping center. He couldn't have lied and taken money and broken the law so arrogantly. But he did. And so I don't know what to believe."

"He loved you, and he made mistakes. There's nothing else you have to believe."

"You'd understand, better than anyone, what

it's like to lose a father when you need one so badly."

"Yes, I understand."

She tightened her fingers on his. "I know it might sound odd, but if I could be sure—even if I could be sure he had killed himself—it would be easier than wondering." She shook her head and managed a smile. "I warned you I'd lean." She linked her fingers with his, then brought his knuckles to her cheek.

"Any better?"

"Yeah. Thanks." Tilting her head, she touched her lips to his. "Really."

"Anytime. Really."

"Let's go downstairs." She started out ahead of him but put a hand out when he would have closed the door. "No, leave it open." Feeling foolish, she went too quickly down the steps. "Want a beer, Rafferty?"

"Actually, I was going to see how you felt about going into town for dinner, maybe a movie, then going back to my place and letting me make love with you for the rest of the night."

"Well." She ran her tongue over her lips. "It sounds pretty nice, all in all. One thing, I'm having guests next week, so I have to buy a couple of beds—and a chair, and a lamp or two, some sheets, food—"

He held up a hand. "You want to skip the movie and join the horde at the mall?"

"Well, the mall—and there's this flea market." She gave him a hopeful smile.

He would have done quite a bit to keep that smile on her face. "I'll call Bud and see if I can borrow his pickup."

"God, what a man." She threw her arms around him and kissed him, hard, then dodged before he could make the grab. "I'll go up and change." The phone rang as she headed for the stairs. "Get that, will you? Tell whoever it is I'll call back."

Cam picked up the phone. "Hello." There was a minute of humming silence, then a click. "They hung up," he shouted, then dialed Bud.

When Clare came down again, he was standing in the garage, studying the work she had done that day. Nervous, she stuck her hands in the pockets of the long gray skirt she wore.

"What do you think?"

"I think you're incredible." He rubbed a hand over the polished curve of wood. "These are all so different." He glanced from the completed metal sculptures to the fisted arm of clay. "And yet they're so unmistakably your work."

"I guess I should apologize for jumping all over you this morning for having the good taste to buy one of my pieces."

"I figured you'd get around to it." Idly, he paged through her sketchbook. "Oh, by the way, I got you that burl."

"You—the burl?"

"You did want it, didn't you?"

"Yes, yes, very much. I didn't think you remembered. How did you do it?"

"I just mentioned it to the mayor. He was so
flattered, he'd have paid you to cut it down."

She rewrapped the clay in its dampened cloth.
"You're being awfully nice to me, Rafferty."

He set her sketchbook aside. "Yeah, I am." He
turned, studied her. "You clean up good, Slim.
I hope to hell you're not a finicky shopper."

"I'll break the county record." She held out a
hand. "And I'll pop for the champagne we're
going to have with dinner."

"Are we celebrating?"

"I got some news today. I'll tell you about it
over dinner." She started to get into his car,
spotted Ernie across the street, and waved.
"Hey, Ernie."

He merely watched her, keeping one hand
closed over the pentagram around his neck.

Part Two

And the Lord said to Satan,
"Whence do you come?"
Then Satan answered the Lord and said,
"From roaming the earth and patrolling it."
—The Book of Job

Chapter 13

"WHAT IS THAT SMELL?"

"That, *ma belle*, is a sweet, pastoral bouquet." Jean-Paul's grin split his face from ear to ear as he sucked air in through his elegant nose. "Ah, *c'est incroyable.*"

"I'll say it's incredible," Angie muttered and scowled out of the car window. "It smells like horse shit."

"And when, my own true love, have you ever smelled the shit of a horse?"

"January 17, 1987, in a freezing carriage clopping around Central Park, the first time you proposed to me. Or maybe it was the second time."

He laughed and kissed her hand. "Then it should bring back beautiful memories."

Actually, it did, but she took out her purse bottle of Chanel spray and spritzed it in the air anyway.

Angie crossed her long legs and wondered why her husband got such a charge out of looking at grass and rocks and fat, fly-swishing cows. If this was pastoral bliss, give her Forty-second Street.

It wasn't that she didn't like scenery—the view of Cancun from a hotel balcony, the streets of Paris from a sidewalk café, the swell of the Atlantic from a deck chair. But this, while it had a kind of rough, rural charm best viewed in primitive paintings, wasn't her idea of visual stimulation.

"A seelo!"

She glanced over, sighed. "I think it's called a *silo*, though I have no idea why." Angie settled back while Jean-Paul practiced the pronunciation.

She hadn't minded the drive, really. Jean-Paul was deliciously sexy behind the wheel of a car. She smiled to herself—a purely feminine look of satisfaction. Jean-Paul was deliciously sexy anywhere. And he was all hers.

The fact was, she'd enjoyed driving down the turnpike, windows open, Cajun music blasting. She hadn't felt obliged to offer to take a turn at the wheel, knowing that her husband rarely had the opportunity to put on his cute little cap and leather gloves and let it rip.

Just past exit nine on the Jersey turnpike, they'd gotten a ticket, which Jean-Paul had cheerfully signed—right before he pulled out into traffic again and cranked the Jag up to ninety.

He was happy as a pig in slop, Angie thought, then closed her eyes. She was even thinking in rural analogies.

The last hour of the drive had made her nervous. All those fields, hills, trees. All that open space. She much preferred the steel and concrete canyons of Manhattan. A mugger she could handle—and had—but a rabbit dashing frantically across the road sent her into a panic.

Where was the noise, for God's sake? Where were the people? *Were* there any people, or had they crossed through the Twilight Zone into some version of Orwell's *Animal Farm*?

What the hell was Clare thinking of, actually choosing to live in a place where you had cows for neighbors?

She was restlessly twisting the thick gold links she wore around her neck when Jean-Paul gave a whoop and swung the car to the shoulder. Gravel splattered and smoked. "Look! A goat."

Angie dug in her bag for Excedrin. "Jesus, Jean-Paul, grow up."

He only laughed and leaned past her to stare through the passenger window at the ratty gray billy goat who was chewing grass. Billy looked as unimpressed as Angie. "You were very fond of goat when I gave you the angora wrap for Christmas."

"I like my suede jacket, too, but I don't want to pet a sheep."

He nuzzled his wife's ear, then sat back. "When is the next turn?"

Angie shot him a look. "Are we lost?"

"No." He watched her gulp down two painkillers and chase them with Perrier straight from the bottle. "I don't know where we are, but we can't be lost because we're here."

His logic made her wish she had Valium instead of Excedrin. "Don't be perky, Jean-Paul, it only depresses me."

Angie took out the map and Clare's directions so that they could study them. Her annoyance faded a bit as Jean-Paul massaged the back of her neck. As always, he sensed precisely the right spot to touch.

He was a patient man and an enthusiastic one. In all things. When he had met his wife, she had been the assistant of a rival art dealer with ambition glittering in her eyes. Cool and remote to the most casual of flirtations or the most overt of suggestions, she'd been an irresistible challenge to his ego. It had taken him six weeks to convince her to have dinner with him, another three frustrating months to ease her into his bed.

There she had not been cool; she had not been remote.

The sex had been the easiest hurdle. He had known she was attracted to him. Women were. He was artist enough to recognize that he was physically appealing, and man enough to play on it. He was tall with a body he cared for religiously with diet and training. The French accent—and his often deliberately awkward phrasing—only added to the attraction. His dark, curling hair was worn nearly shoulder length to frame his bony, intelligent face with its deep blue eyes and sculptured mouth. He wore a thin mustache to accent it and to keep it from appearing too feminine.

In addition to his looks, he had a deep and sincere affection for the female—all of them. He had come from a family of many women and had since childhood appreciated them for their softness, their strengths, their vanities, and their shrewdness. He was as sincerely interested in the elderly matron with blue-tinted hair as he was in the statuesque bombshell—though often for different reasons. It was this openness with women that had led to his success in bed and in business.

But Angie had been his one and only love, though not his only lover. Convincing her of that, and of the advantages of a traditional marriage, had taken him the better part of two years. He didn't regret a minute of it.

His hand closed lightly over hers as he cruised down the two-lane road again. "*Je t'aime*," he said, as he often did.

It made her smile and bring his hand to her lips. "I know." He was a precious man, she thought. Even if he could make her crazy. "Just warn me if you decide to pull over for any more goats or other animal life."

"Do you see the field there?"

Angie glanced out the window and sighed. "How could I miss it? That's all there is."

"I would make love with you there, in the sunlight. Slowly. With my mouth first, tasting you everywhere. And when you began to shudder, to cry out for me, I would use my hands. Just the fingertips. Over your lovely breasts, then down, inside you where it would be so hot, so wet."

Four years, she thought. Four years and he could still make her tremble. She slanted him a look and saw that he was smiling. She shifted her gaze downward and saw that he was quite sincere in his fantasy. The field no longer seemed so intimidating.

"Maybe Clare can direct us to a field that's not so close to the road."

He chuckled, settled back, and began to sing along with Beausoleil.

★ ★ ★

Because she was too nervous to work, Clare was planting petunias along the walkway. If Angie and Jean-Paul had left New York at ten, as discussed, they would be driving up any minute. She was delighted at the thought of seeing them, of taking them around the area. And she was terrified at the idea of showing them her work and discovering that she'd been wrong.

None of it was any good. She'd been deluding herself because she needed so badly to believe she could still make something important out of a hunk of wood or scraps of metal. It had come too easily at first, she thought. Both the work and the acceptance of it. The only place to go was down.

Do you fear failure, Clare, or success? Dr. Janowski's voice buzzed in her head.

Both—doesn't everyone? Go away, will you? Everyone's entitled to a little private neurosis.

She pushed all thoughts of her work aside and concentrated on turning the soil.

Her father had taught her how. How to baby the roots, mix in peat moss, fertilizer, water, and love. By his side she had learned how soothing, how fulfilling the planting of a living thing could be. In New York she'd forgotten the pleasure of that and the comfort of it.

Her mind wandered. She thought of Cam,

how intense their lovemaking was. Each time. Every time. It was like feeding on the most basic of levels. They went at each other like animals, hungry and feral. She'd never been so, well, lusty with anyone else.

And, God, she thought with a grin, what she'd been missing!

How long could it last? She shrugged and went on with her planting. She knew that the darkest and most intense of passions were supposed to fade the fastest. But she couldn't let it worry her. Wouldn't. However long it lasted would just have to be enough. Because right now it was hard for her to get through an hour without imagining getting her hands on him again.

Lovingly, she patted and firmed the dirt around the red and white petunias. The sun beat strong against her back as she covered the soil with mulch. They would grow, she thought, and spread and bloom until the first frost shriveled them. They wouldn't last forever, but while they did, it would give her pleasure to look at them.

She glanced up at the sound of an engine, then sat back on her heels as Bob Meese pulled his truck into her drive. "Hey, Clare."

"Bob." She stuck the spade into the dirt and rose.

"Nice flowers you got there."

"Thanks." She spread dirt from her palms to the hips of her jeans.

"Told you I'd bring the lamp on by if I got a minute."

Her brow wrinkled, then cleared as she remembered. "Oh, right. Your timing's perfect. My friends should be here anytime. Now they can actually have a lamp in their room."

And what a lamp, she thought, as he pulled it out of the back. It was about five feet high with a bell-shaped red shade, beaded and fringed, on a curving, gilded pole. It looked like something out of a nineteenth-century bordello. Clare sincerely hoped it was.

"It's even better than I remembered," she said, and tried to recall if she had paid him for it or not. "Could you take it on into the garage? I'll get it upstairs later."

"No problemo." He hefted it inside, then stood studying her tools and sculptures. "I guess people pay a bunch for stuff like this."

She smiled, deciding he was more baffled than critical. "Sometimes."

"The wife likes art," he said conversationally as he squinted at a brass and copper sculpture. Modern shit, he thought, sneering inwardly, but as an antique dealer, he knew there was no telling what people would plunk down hard cash for. "She's got this plaster donkey and cart out in the front yard. You do any stuff like that?"

Clare bit down on the tip of her tongue. "No," she said solemnly. "Not really."

"You can come on by and take a look at ours if you want some ideas."

"I appreciate that."

When he started back toward his truck without giving her a bill, Clare figured she must have paid in advance. He opened the door, then propped a foot on the running board. "I guess you heard Jane Stokey sold the farm."

"What?"

"Jane Stokey," he repeated, hitching a thumb in a belt loop. His mood lifted considerably when he saw he was the first to pass on the news. "Sold the farm—or she's gonna. Word is she might move on down to Tennessee. Got a sister down there."

"Does Cam know?"

"Can't say. If he don't, he'll know by suppertime." He wondered if there was any way he could mosey into the sheriff's office and drop the bombshell, real casual like.

"Who bought it?"

"Some hotshot realtor down to D.C.'s what I heard. Must've checked the obits and seen Biff's. Made her a good offer from what I heard. Hope to shit some developer don't plant more houses."

"Can they do that?"

He pursed his lips, lowered his brows. "Well, now, it's zoned agricultural, but you never know. Money greases the right palms, and that could change quick enough." He stopped, coughed, and looked away, remembering her father. "So, you, ah, settling in?"

She noted that his gaze had veered upward, toward the attic window. "More or less."

He looked back at her. "Not too spooky here for you, all alone?"

"It's hard to be spooked in a house you grew up in." And where all the ghosts were so familiar.

He rubbed at a spot on his side mirror. There'd been a light on in her attic once or twice. Certain people wanted to know why. "I guess with all the stuff you're buying, you're planning on being around awhile."

She'd nearly forgotten how important it was in small towns for everyone to know everything. "I don't really have any plans." She shrugged. "The beauty of being unfettered."

"I guess." He'd been fettered too long to understand. Casually, and cleverly, he thought, he wound his way around to his purpose for being there. "Funny having you back here. Makes me think about that first time I took you out. The carnival, right?"

Her eyes went flat, her cheeks paled. "Yes. The carnival."

"That sure was—" He broke off, as if he'd just remembered. "Jesus, Clare." Sincerity shone in his eyes as he blinked. "I'm awful sorry. Don't know how I could've forgotten."

"It's all right." Her cheeks hurt as she fought with a smile. "It was a long time ago."

"Yeah, a long time. Man, I feel like a jerk." Awkwardly, he reached for her hand. "It must be rough on you, having people remind you."

She didn't need anyone to remind her, but managed a restless movement with her shoulders. "Don't worry about it, Bob. I wouldn't be here if I couldn't handle it."

"Well, sure, but . . . well," he said again, "I guess you got plenty to keep you busy. Your statues." He gave her a sly wink. "And the sheriff."

"Word travels," she said dryly.

"That it does. I guess the two of you are hitting it off."

"I guess." With some amusement, she noted that his eyes kept cutting back into her garage, toward the sculpture she'd titled *The Inner Beast*. "Maybe Bonnie Sue'd like that to put next to her donkey."

Bob flushed and shifted his foot. "I don't think it's her style. Can't say I know anything about art, but—"

"You know what you like," she finished for

him. "It's all right if you don't like it, Bob. I'm not sure I do myself."

No, he didn't like it because it was all too familiar. "How come you made up something like that?"

She glanced back over her shoulder. "I'm not sure. You could say it just comes to me. In a dream," she added softly, almost to herself, and rubbed a chill from her arms.

His eyes narrowed, sharpened, but when she turned back, his face was bland. "I think I'll stick with donkey carts. You let me know if you have any trouble with that lamp."

"Yes. I will." He'd been the first boy to kiss her, she remembered, and smiled at him. "Tell Bonny Sue I said hello."

"I will." Satisfied with what he'd learned, he nodded and hitched at his belt. "I sure will." He turned. His eyes narrowed, then widened. "Christ in a handcart, look at that car."

Clare glanced over and spotted the Jaguar pulling up to the curb. Even as Jean-Paul jumped out, she was running down the slope of the drive to spring into his arms for a hard, exaggerated kiss.

"Mmmm." He kissed her again. "Licorice."

Laughing, she turned to hug Angie. "I can't believe you're here."

"Neither can I." Angie pushed her hair back as

she took a long, slow scan of the street. Her idea of country wear included nile green linen pants and matching jacket with a rose-colored silk blouse. She had worn flats—Bruno Magli. "So, this is Emmitsboro."

"It is indeed." Clare kissed her. "How was the drive down?"

"We only got one ticket."

"Jean-Paul must be mellowing." She watched him haul two suitcases and a leather tote from the car. "We'll go in and have some wine," she told him, and took the tote. She started up the drive, pausing beside Bob's truck to make introductions. "Bob Meese, Angie and Jean-Paul LeBeau, friends and art dealers from New York. Bob owns the best antique store in town."

"Ah." Jean-Paul set down a suitcase to offer a hand. "We must be sure to see your shop before we leave."

"Open ten to six, six days a week, twelve to five on Sunday." Bob took note of Jean Paul's alligator shoes and gold link bracelet. Imagine, a guy wearing a bracelet—even if he was a foreigner. Bob also noted his exotic-looking wife. His black wife. These were the little details he would dispense over the counter until closing time. "Well, got to get back."

"Thanks for bringing the lamp by."

"No problemo." With a quick salute, he

climbed into his truck and backed out of the drive.

"Did someone say wine?" Angie wanted to know.

"Absolutely." Clare hooked an arm through Angie's and started to steer her around to the walk leading to the front of the house. "In your honor, I went all the way into Frederick and stocked up on pouilly-fuissé."

"Wait." Jean-Paul headed in the opposite direction. "You're working here, in the garage?"

"Yes, but why don't we go in and get settled? How about these petunias? I just—"

Angie was already following her husband, pulling Clare with her. Clare blew a little breath between her teeth, closed her mouth, and waited. She'd wanted to put this moment off— foolishly, she supposed. Both Jean-Paul's and Angie's opinions meant a great deal. They loved her, she knew. And because they did they would be honest, even brutal if necessary. The pieces she had done here at home were vitally important to her. More than anything else she'd done, these had been ripped cleanly from her heart.

In silence she stood back, watching them study and circle. She could hear the gentle tap tap of Angie's foot on the concrete as she examined the wood carving from every angle. They didn't exchange a word, hardly a look. Jean-Paul pulled on his lower lip, a nervous habit Clare recognized, as he studied the metal sculpture Bob Meese had recently frowned over.

Where Bob had seen a tangle of metal, Jean-Paul saw a pit of fire, the flames boiling and streaking. It was a hungry and dangerous fire, he thought. It made his skin prickle. It made him wonder what had been consumed by it.

Saying nothing, he turned to the clay arm Clare had fired only the day before. Young, defiant, he mused. With the potential for brutality or heroics. He pulled on his lip again and continued on to the next piece.

Clare shifted from foot to foot, stuck her hands in her pockets, then pulled them out again. Why did she put herself through this? she wondered. Each time, every time, it felt as though she had ripped out her feelings, her fantasies and fears and put them on public display. And it never got better, never got easier, she thought, rubbing her damp palms against the thighs of her jeans. If she had any brains, she'd be selling appliances.

The LeBeaus huddled over the metal sculpture that had sprung from Clare's nightmare. They had yet to exchange a word. Whatever silent communication they shared was potent but was lost on Clare. She was holding her breath when Jean-Paul turned. His face was solemn when he put his hands on her shoulders. Bending, he kissed her cheeks in turn.

"Amazing."

Clare's breath whistled out. "Thank God."

"I hate to be wrong." Angie's voice was taut with excitement. "I really *hate* to have to admit I might be wrong. But coming here, working here was the best thing you could have done. Christ, Clare, you stagger me."

Clare put an arm around each of them, torn between the urge to weep and to howl with laughter. In her heart she'd known the sculptures were good. But her head had taken over with nasty, nagging doubts.

"Let's have the wine," she said.

Bob Meese hurried back to his shop, entering through the rear to avoid customers. He locked both the outside and inside doors before picking up the phone. As he dialed he tried to work up some saliva. Facing in the light of day what he did at night always dried up the spit in his mouth.

"I saw her," he said the moment the phone was answered.

"And?"

"She's thinking about her old man all right. You can see it." Bob took a moment to thank any deity that he'd been too young to be initiated when Jack Kimball had taken his last fall. "I don't think she knows what he was into—I mean, she acts too easy about it. I was right about that statue, though. I got a better look at it today."

"Tell me."

Bob wished he'd taken the time to get himself a nice, cold drink. "It looks like—I told you." He pressed his lips together. Here in his office, with the pictures of his wife and kids standing on his cluttered desk and the smell of linseed oil stinging his nostrils, it was hard to believe he was one of them.

Enjoyed being one of them.

"The ceremonial mask, the robes. A beast on a man's body." His voice lowered to a whisper, though there was no one to hear. "It could be any one of us—just like she'd seen. I don't think she remembers, exactly—or she doesn't know she remembers."

"A part of her does." The voice was flat and ice-cold. "And might be dangerous. We'll watch her. Perhaps give her a gentle warning."

Bob was only marginally relieved by the word *gentle*. "Listen, I don't think she remembers, really. Nothing to hurt us. She'd have told the sheriff. And from the look of things, those two are too busy squeaking bedsprings to talk about much of anything."

"Eloquently put." The cool disdain in the tone

made Bob wince. "I'll take your opinion under advisement."

"I don't want anything to happen to her. She's a friend."

"You have no friends but the brotherhood." It was no statement, but a warning. "If she needs to be dealt with, she will be. Remember your oath."

"I remember," Bob said as the phone clicked in his ear. "I remember."

Sarah Hewitt strolled down Main Street, delighted with the balmy evening. The mildness gave her a good excuse to wear shorts and watch the old farts in front of the post office go big-eyed. The thin denim was so tight she'd had to lie down on her bed to pull up the zipper. The material dug seductively into her crotch. Her full, firm breasts swayed lightly under a cropped T-shirt with WILD THING scrawled across the chest.

She'd doused herself with an Opium rip-off and painted her mouth a dark, dangerous red. She walked slowly, lazily, knowing that all eyes were trained on her jiggling ass. There was nothing Sarah liked better than drawing attention, and it didn't matter a damn to her if it was the shocked or approving kind.

She'd been drawing it since sixth grade, when she'd let Bucky Knight take off her shirt behind the bushes during the school picnic. Since Bucky was three years older, he'd gotten the brunt of old Gladys Finch's wrath. A fact that had amused Sarah no end, since the little experiment was her idea in the first place.

Three years later, she'd let little Marylou Wilson's daddy do a lot more than look. Sarah had baby-sat for Marylou most every Saturday night for fifty cents an hour. But when horny Sam Wilson drove Sarah home, he'd given her an extra twenty to keep her mouth shut if he copped a few feels.

She'd enjoyed the money but quickly got tired of Sam's sweaty hands and flabby belly. So she'd seduced a boy her own age, one of the Hawbaker boys—damned if she could remember which one.

It didn't matter, she thought. They were all married now to eagle-eyed, wide-assed women.

She was beginning to think of marriage herself—though not of fidelity. The idea of being stuck in bed with one man for the rest of her life was revolting. But she was past thirty, had less than three hundred dollars in the bank, and was tired of living in the single cramped room over Clyde's.

She liked the idea of having a house and a joint checking account. If she was going to take the plunge, she wanted it to be with someone who could stay hard long enough to bring her off and whom she could stand to look at in the morning. Barring that, she wanted it to be with someone who had pleasant things like stocks and bonds and a pocketful of credit cards.

With a little smile, she paused outside the sheriff's office. Inside was a man who filled all her requirements.

Cam glanced up as she came inside. He acknowledged her with a little nod and kept on talking into the phone. Her heavy perfume overwhelmed the smells of coffee and dust. He supposed he wouldn't have been human if his stomach hadn't clenched—if his gaze hadn't trailed along the naked length of her leg as she perched on the corner of his desk. She smiled, combed a hand slowly through her mane of hair—her roots shot through the platinum like dark snakes—then lighted a cigarette.

"It's registered to Earl B. Stokey, Route One, Box Twenty-two eleven, Emmitsboro. That's right. A forty-five-caliber Colt. I'd appreciate that, Sergeant." He hung up and glanced at the clock. He was already running late for dinner at Clare's. "Got a problem, Sarah?"

"That depends." She leaned over to toy with the badge pinned to his shirt. "Parker used to keep a bottle in the bottom drawer there. How about you?"

He didn't bother to ask how she knew what Parker had kept in his desk. "No."

"You sure are running straight these days, aren't you, Cam?" Her eyes, sharp and mocking, met his. "Here you sit, so serious and official." She rubbed the top of her foot along his thigh. "It sounds like you're actually investigating Biff's murder."

"That's my job." He didn't wince when she blew a light stream of smoke in his face, but waited.

"People are wondering if you might let a few things slide this time around." As she reached over to tap her cigarette in a glass ashtray, her breasts swayed beneath her shirt.

There was a flicker of anger in Cam's eyes, quickly controlled. "People can wonder what they want."

"Now, that sounds like the old Cam." She smiled, looking at him from beneath long, heavily mascaraed lashes. "Nobody knows better than me how much you hated Biff." She took his hand, set it on her thigh close, very close, to the edge of denim where her skin was firm and smooth and hot. "Remember? We'd sit in the woods, in the dark, and you'd tell me how you hated him, how you wished he was dead. How you'd kill him yourself. With a gun. With a knife. With your bare hands." She felt herself getting wet just thinking of it. "Then we'd have sex. Really incredible sex."

He felt something stir in his gut. Old memories. Old needs. Old lusts. "That was a long time ago." He started to remove his hand, but she laid hers on top of it, pressed it against her flesh.

"You never stopped hating him. The other night at Clyde's, you wanted to kill him. I got so hot watching you." She shifted so that his hand was caught snug in the vee of her thighs. "Just like old times."

"No." The heat was seductive, but he had a flash, a vivid one, of her vagina edged with teeth like a bear trap, ready to spring closed over an unwary penis. He kept his eyes on hers as he pulled his hand away. "No, it's not, Sarah."

Her eyes hardened, but she smiled as she slid over into his lap. "It could be. Remember the things we did to each other, Cam?" She reached down to cup him in her hand and felt a shudder of triumph when she found him stiff and throbbing.

He clamped a hand over her wrist. "Don't embarrass yourself, Sarah."

Her lips drew back over her teeth. "You want me. You bastard."

He took her by the shoulders, moving her up and back as he rose. "I stopped thinking with my dick ten years ago." But because he remembered, because he had once thought himself in love with her, he gave her a quick, impatient shake. "Why the hell do you do this to yourself? You've got looks, you've got brains. Do you think I don't know about the business you run upstairs in Clyde's? Twenty bucks to have some sweaty, cheating husband bounce on your bed? You don't need this, Sarah."

"Don't tell me what I need." For the first time in years, she felt a flush of shame. And hated him for it. "You're no better than I am, and never were. Just because you're screwing Clare Kimball for free, you think you've got class?"

"Leave her out of it."

That only made it worse. Fury flared, negating all the carefully applied cosmetics. In that instant she looked exactly like what she was—a slowly aging small-town hooker.

"Rich bitch Kimball with her fancy car and fancy house. Strange how money makes it all right that her old man was a drunk and a thief. She strolls on back into town, and the ladies cluck all over her with cakes and Jell-O molds."

"And their husbands come to you."

"That's right." Her smile was small and bitter. "And when Clare Kimball heads back to New York and leaves you dry, they'll still be coming to me. We're the same, you and me, we always have been. You're still Cameron Rafferty from the wrong side of the tracks, and you're as stuck in this stinking town as I am."

"There's a difference, Sarah. I came back because I wanted to, not because there was no place else to go."

She shrugged off his hands in two edgy moves. She wanted to pay him back, make him suffer. It didn't matter for what. "Must be handy, wearing that badge right now, when even your mother wonders if you were the one who beat Biff to death." She watched the heat leap into his eyes and fed off of it. "Won't be long before people start remembering that temper of yours and bad blood." She smiled again, eyes narrowed. "There are some who are going to want people to remember. You think you know this town, Cam, and all the good, solid citizens in it. But there are things you don't know. Things you couldn't even imagine. Maybe you should ask yourself why Parker picked up and ran. Why he moved his fat, lazy ass out before he even collected his pension."

"What the hell are you talking about?"

She was saying too much. It wouldn't do to let pride or temper push her further. Instead, she walked to the door, put a hand on the knob, then turned back. "We could have been good together, you and me." She gave him one last look, thinking that with a little help from her, he was already on his way to hell. "You're going to regret it."

When the door closed behind her, Cam rubbed his hands over his face. He already regretted it, he thought. Regretted that he hadn't gotten out of the office ten minutes sooner and avoided her altogether. Regretted that he hadn't handled the encounter better. Regretted that he remembered, all too clearly, those nights with her in the woods with the smell of pine and earth and sex.

She reminded him too well of what he had been at seventeen. What he could still be if he hadn't learned to strap down the more vicious of his impulses—of what he had nearly become again after his partner had been killed and the bottle had seemed the best and easiest answer.

Absently, he lifted a hand to touch the badge on his shirt. It was a small thing, something— as Clare had once said—he could pick up at any dime store. But it meant something to him, something he wasn't sure he could explain even to himself.

With it, he felt he belonged in the town, to the town, in a way he hadn't since his father had died. Sarah was wrong, he thought. He knew the people here. He understood them.

But what the hell had she meant with that re- mark about Parker? Suddenly tired, he rubbed the back of his neck. It wouldn't do any harm to put in a call to Florida. He glanced at the clock again, then picked up his keys.

He'd do it in the morning—just to satisfy his own curiosity.

He was too tired, Cam decided as he drove to Clare's, for putting on company manners and socializing with strangers. He would go by, make some excuse, then leave her alone with her friends.

Sarah's comments were rubbing against him, abrasive as sandpaper. He was stuck here. It might have been through choice, but it didn't change the bottom line. He could never again face living and working in the city, where every time he strapped on his gun or walked into an alley he'd be chased by his partner's ghost. Clare would go back to New York. In a week, a month, six months. He couldn't follow her. He remembered how empty he'd felt when he stood in the cemetery and watched her walk away.

It scared him right down to the bone.

Cam pulled up in back of a Jaguar, then stopped by Clare's car to pull out her keys before he walked through the garage to the door leading to the house. Music was blaring—jazz—hot and slick and sophisticated. He saw her standing at the counter, tearing open a bag of chips. Her feet were bare, and her hair was pulled back with a shoestring. Long amethyst wands swung from her ears, and her T-shirt was ripped under the armpit.

He realized he was desperately in love with her.

She turned, spotted him, and smiled as she poured chips into a cracked blue bowl.

"Hi. I was afraid you weren't going to—"

He cut her off, pulling her against him and savaging her mouth. Her hands went to his shoulders as her body absorbed the shock waves. She held tight—he seemed to need it—and let him feed whatever hunger gnawed at him.

Relief. Simple. Sweet. Stunning. It washed over him, flowed through him. Slowly, without even being aware of the change, he gentled the kiss, softened it, and savored. Her hands slid from his shoulders to cling weakly to his waist.

"Cam." She was surprised the sound was audible in the thick, syrupy air.

"Shh." He nibbled on her lips, once, twice, then slicked his tongue over hers. There was a lingering zip of wine overlaying the deeper, richer flavor he'd discovered was uniquely hers.

"Clare, Jean-Paul's not having any luck with the charcoal. I think we should—oh." Angie stopped, her hand still holding the screen door open. "I beg your pardon," she said when Cam and Clare drew a few inches apart.

"Oh." Clare lifted an unsteady hand to her hair. "Cam, this is—ah . . ."

"Angie." After letting the screen door slam, Angie held out a hand. "Angie LeBeau. It's nice to meet you."

"Cameron Rafferty." Cam kept an arm around Clare's shoulders in a gesture he knew was overly possessive.

"The sheriff, yes." Angie smiled at him and took his measure from the tips of his worn high tops all the way to his dark, tousled hair. "Clare's told us about you." Angie's brow cocked as she shot Clare a look. "Apparently she left a few things out."

"There's wine open," Clare said quickly. "Or beer if you'd rather."

"Whatever." Cam was taking his own measure. Angie LeBeau, he noted, was, like the jazz pouring out of the radio, very slick. She was also very suspicious. "You and Clare went to college together, right?"

"That's right. Now I'm her agent. What do you think of her work?"

"Have some more wine, Angie." Clare all but thrust a fresh glass in Angie's hand.

"Personally or professionally?"

"Excuse me?"

"I wondered if you were asking as her friend or as her agent." He watched Angie as he took a glass from Clare. "Because if it's as her agent, I'll have to watch my step. Since I want to buy the fire sculpture she's got sitting out in the garage." He flicked a glance at Clare. "You left the keys in your car again," he said, then dug them out of his pocket and tossed them to her.

Smiling, Angie sipped her wine. "We'll talk. Meanwhile, what do you know about starting charcoal?"

Chapter 14

JANE STOKEY DIDN'T CARE what was done to the farm. She was finished with it. She was done with Emmitsboro, too. She had two husbands lying in the cemetery, each one taken from her abruptly. The first one she had loved desperately, fully, happily. There were times, even after all these years, when she thought of him with longing—as she walked toward the fields he had plowed, the fields he had died in, or up the stairs toward the bed they had shared.

She remembered him as young and vibrant and beautiful. There had been a time when beauty had been a large part of her life, when such things as flowers in the garden or a pretty new dress had been vital and soothing.

But Michael was gone, more than twenty years gone, and she was an old woman at fifty.

She hadn't loved Biff, not in that heart-fluttery, giddy way. But she had needed him. She had depended on him. She had feared him. His loss was like an amputation. There was no one left to tell her what to do, when to do it, how to do it. There was no one to cook for, to clean for, no warm body breathing beside her in the night.

She had left her parents' home at eighteen and gone to her husband's, full of dreams and dizzy love and flowering hope. Mike had taken care of her, paid the bills, made the decisions, done all the worrying. She'd kept the house and planted the garden and borne the child.

That was what she had been taught. That was what she had known.

Six short months after his death, she had given herself, the farm, the house, to Biff. Even before that he had begun taking over the worries and details. She hadn't had to struggle with bank statements and budgets. If there hadn't been as much money, or as much serenity, as she'd had with Mike, at least she'd been a wife again. Perhaps Biff hadn't been kind, but he had been there.

Now, for the first time in her life, she was completely alone.

The loneliness was crushing, the house so big, so empty. She had almost asked Cam to come home with her, just to have a familiar male presence in the house. But that would have been disloyal to Biff, and he had ruled her life for so long, his death would not change her allegiances.

Besides, she had lost her boy somewhere along the way as completely as she had lost her boy's father. It wasn't possible for her to pinpoint when it happened, and she had long since given up the effort. He had stopped being her son and had become a restless, rebellious, defiant stranger.

He'd made her feel guilty, miserably guilty, about marrying Biff so soon after Mike died. He hadn't said a word, not one, but the way he'd looked at her with those dark, condemning eyes had done the damage.

She paused on her way to the huddle of outbuildings and set down the boxes she carried. The sun was bright, glinting on the green hay that would be cut and baled by strangers. A new calf scampered after its mama for milk, but Jane didn't notice. In her mind the farm was already gone, and the hope she'd had for it.

She'd loved it once, as she had once loved her son. But that feeling for the land and for her child seemed so distant now, as if experienced by another woman. She knew Biff had been hard on the farm, just as he'd been hard on the boy, as he'd been hard on her.

They had all needed it, she reminded herself as she hauled up the cardboard boxes again. Mike had pampered them. She felt her eyes welling as they did too often these days and didn't bother to blink back the tears. There was no one to see. No one to care.

In a few weeks she could take the money she earned from the sale of the farm and move to Tennessee, near her sister. She would buy a little house. And do what? she wondered as she leaned against the shed and sobbed. Please God, do what?

She had worked hard and long every day of her life, but she had never held a job. She didn't understand things like escrow and capital gains. She was baffled and frightened by the people she sometimes saw on *Oprah* or *Donahue* who talked about discovering self, starting over, coping with grief.

She didn't want to be liberated or capable. Most desperately of all, she didn't want to be alone.

When the weeping had run its course, she mopped her face with her apron. She had gotten through the days since Biff's death by filling them with chores, necessary and unnecessary. Already that morning she had dealt with the milking, the feeding, had gathered eggs and washed them. She had cleaned her already clean house. It was still short of noon, and the day stretched endlessly ahead, to be followed by yet another endless night.

She'd decided to start on the sheds. Most of the tools and farm machinery would be auctioned off, but she wanted to go through the outbuildings first, to examine and collect whatever bits and pieces might bring a higher price in direct sale. She was terrified of not having enough money, of being not only alone, but poor and alone.

Biff hadn't carried any life insurance. Why waste good money on premiums? She'd buried him on credit. Die now, pay later. The mortgage on the farm was nearly due, and the loan payment on the hay baler Biff had bought two years before. Then there was the feed payment, the market, the payments on the tractor and Biff's Caddy. Ethan Myers at the bank had told her they would extend her time until she had her affairs in order, but the payments gave her sleepless nights.

She couldn't bear the shame of owing. Before, she'd justified all the credit by thinking it was Biff who owed, Biff who paid or didn't. Now there was no one to stand between her and the reality of being in debt.

She couldn't sell the farm fast enough.

She took the keys out of her apron pocket.

Biff had never allowed her to enter this building. She had never questioned him. Had never dared. Even as she fit the key into the stout padlock, she felt a prickle of fear, as if he would leap up behind her, shouting and shoving. A thin line of sweat broke out over her top lip as the lock clicked open.

The old rooster crowed and made her jump.

The air inside was stale and overly sweet. As if something had crawled inside and died. Breathing through her mouth, Jane put both lock and keys in her apron pocket, then propped the door open with a rock.

She had a sudden, unreasoning fear of being trapped inside. Of beating on the door, pleading and screaming. Biff's laughter would snicker through the cracks as he shot the lock back into place.

She rubbed her cold hands over her cold arms as she started inside.

It wasn't a large area—ten by twelve and windowless—but the strong sunlight couldn't seem to reach the corners. She hadn't thought to bring a flashlight, was sure she would find one inside. How else had Biff been able to see? He'd spent hours in there, often at night.

Doing what? she wondered now as she hadn't allowed herself to wonder while he'd been alive and maybe able to read her thoughts.

Skin prickling, she stepped inside. In the

dimness she could make out a narrow cot, its mattress stained and bare. On the metal shelves where she had expected to find tools were stacks of the magazines he'd hoarded. She would have to burn them, Jane thought as heat stained her cheeks. She couldn't have endured it if the realtor or auctioneer had come through to snigger over them.

There was no flashlight that she could see, but there were candles. Black ones. It made her uneasy to light them, but the dim, secret light was worse. By their glow, she began to pull magazines off the shelves and into the box, averting her eyes from the titillating covers. Her fingers touched cloth. Curious, she dragged it out and discovered a long, hooded robe. It smelled of blood and smoke, and she dropped it hastily into the box.

She didn't wonder what it was—didn't allow herself to wonder. But her heart was beating too fast. Burn it, she told herself. Burn it all. The words repeated over and over in her head like a litany as she peered over her shoulder toward the doorway. Her mouth was dry, her hands unsteady.

Then she found the pictures.

There was a young girl, a child really, lying on the cot. She was naked, bound at the wrists and ankles. Her eyes were open, with a blind look in them. There were others—the same girl with her legs spread, her knees bent to expose her sex.

A different girl—a little older, very blond, propped up against the wall like a doll. And there was a candle—dear God, a candle was protruding obscenely from beneath the pale triangle of hair.

There were more, dozens of snapshots. But she couldn't look. Her stomach was heaving as she crumpled and tore them, as she scurried desperately on her hands and knees to gather every scrap. Her hand closed over an earring, a long column of beads. Jane tossed it in the box.

Panting, she blew out the candles, then tumbled them in with the rest. Her movements were jerky and rushed as she dragged the box outside. She blinked against the strong sunlight, scanning the farmyard and lane, wild-eyed.

What if someone came? She had to hurry, had to burn everything. She didn't stop to think what she was doing. She didn't ask herself what it was she was destroying. She ran to the barn for a can of gasoline, her chest constricting painfully. The breath was wheezing out of her lungs as she doused the box and its contents with fuel. Her rush had loosened the pins from her hair so that it fell in droopy tangles, giving her the look of a witch about to cast some secret spell.

Twice she tried to light a match and apply the

flame to the wick of one of the candles. Twice the flame flickered and died.

She was sobbing out loud when the wick finally sizzled and burned. She touched it to the gas-drenched box, her shaking hands nearly extinguishing the flame again. Then she stood back.

Cardboard and paper caught with a whoosh, shooting out hot flame and vapor. Inside, the photographs curled, and fire ate its way across Carly Jamison's face.

Jane covered her own with her hands and wept.

"I told you it was a quiet town." Clare had a satisfied smile on her face as she strolled down Main Street between Angie and Jean-Paul.

"I think the word 'town' is an exaggeration." Angie watched a dog trot, happy and unleashed, down the opposite sidewalk. He lifted his leg and casually peed on the base of an oak. "It might qualify for village."

"One bite of a Martha burger'll wipe that sneer off your face."

"That's what I'm afraid of."

"What's this?" Jean-Paul pointed to the red, white, and blue bunting strung high over the street.

"We're getting ready for the Memorial Day parade on Saturday."

"A parade." His face lit up. "With marching bands and pretty girls tossing batons?"

"All that and more. It's the biggest event in town." She nodded toward a house they passed where a woman was down on hands and knees, busily painting her porch. "Everybody spruces up and drags out their folding chairs. They'll put up a grandstand at the town square for the mayor and the councilmen and other dignitaries. We get school bands from all over the country, this year's Farm Queen, horses, the Little League."

"Whoopee," Angie said and earned a poke in the ribs.

"The Fire Department shines up the trucks or pumpers or whatever the hell they're called. We'll have balloons and concession stands. And," she added, looking up at Jean-Paul, "majorettes."

"Majorettes," he repeated with a sigh. "Do they wear those little white boots with tassels?"

"You bet."

"Jean-Paul, we're supposed to go back on Thursday."

He smiled at his wife. "Another day or two, in the vast scheme of things, can hardly matter. In any case, I want to arrange for Clare's finished work to be shipped to the gallery. I'd like to oversee the packing myself."

"You want to drool over little white boots," Angie muttered.

He kissed the tip of her nose. "There is that as well."

They stopped, waiting for a light stream of traffic before crossing the street. Glancing down, Angie noted a bumper sticker on a pickup.

GOD, GUNS, AND GUTS MADE AMERICA WHAT IT IS TODAY.

Jesus, she thought, closing her eyes. What was she doing here?

As they crossed, she listened with half an ear while Clare told Jean-Paul about past parades. If pressed, Angie would have to admit the town had a certain charm. If one was into country cute.

She certainly wouldn't want to live here and wasn't even certain how much of a visit she could tolerate before the quiet and the slow pace drove her crazy, but Jean-Paul was obviously delighted.

Of course, he didn't notice the stares, Angie mused. Though there were plenty of them. She doubted people were admiring her clothes or hair style. They sure as hell noticed her skin. There was a secret and—she couldn't help herself—superior smile on her face when she followed Clare into Martha's Diner.

There was music on the juke. What Angie always thought of as drunken cowboy songs. But the scents were as seductive as any Jewish deli in New York. Grilled onion, toasted bread, fat pickles, and some spicy soup. How bad could it be? Angie thought as Clare waved to a waitress and slid into a booth.

"A cherry Coke," Clare decided. "They still serve them here." She passed her friends plastic-coated menus. "Please don't ask for the pasta of the day."

Angie flipped the menu open. "I wouldn't dream of it." She scanned her options, tapping the menu with a long cerise-tipped finger. "Why don't we leave the verdict to you?"

"Burgers all around, then."

Alice stopped by the table, pad in hand, and did her best not to stare at the two people seated across from Clare. They looked as out of place in the diner as exotic birds, the man with his long, curling hair and big-sleeved shirt, the woman with her coffee-colored skin and light eyes.

"Did you come in for lunch?" she asked.

"Absolutely. Alice, these are my friends, the LeBeaus. Angie and Jean-Paul."

"Nice to meet you," Alice said. The man

smiled, putting her at ease. "You visiting from New York?"

"For a few days." Jean-Paul watched her eyes shift from him to his wife and back again. "Today Clare's giving us a tour of the town."

"I guess there's not a lot to see."

"I'm trying to talk them into staying on for the parade Saturday." Clare took out a cigarette, then pulled the metal ashtray in front of her.

"Oh, well, it's a pretty good one. Not like that one Macy's has on Thanksgiving or anything, but it's pretty good."

"Alice was a majorette," Clare told them and had the waitress flushing.

"About a hundred years ago. Are you ready to order, or would you like some time?"

"We're more than ready." Clare ordered for the table, then watched Alice hurry off. "Look at the way she moves. I really want to capture the motion, the competence of it. In clay, I think."

"I'm surprised you haven't convinced your sheriff to pose." Jean-Paul took out one of his slim black cigarettes.

"I'm working up to it."

"I liked him."

She smiled and touched his hand. "I know. I'm glad."

"He wasn't what I expected." Angie decided if the two men in the next booth were going to stare, she'd stare right back. "I had an image of a potbellied hick with sunglasses and an attitude."

"Listen here, boy," Clare mimicked in a slow Foghorn Leghorn drawl. "That's pretty close to the former sheriff. Cam's a different matter altogether. I think maybe—" She broke off when she noted Angie didn't appear to be listening. Following her friend's gaze, she spotted the two local men in the next booth. They were staring, and there was a belligerence in the look that put Clare's back up. Hoping to soothe, she placed a hand over Angie's. "We don't get too many urbanites around here."

Angie relaxed, smiled, and squeezed Clare's hand. "I noticed. I was hoping you'd tell me you also didn't get too many men in white sheets."

"Stuff like that doesn't happen in this part of the county."

"Right." Angie began to tap her fingers on the table. "Nothing much happens in Emmitsboro."

"We're not completely backward. Actually, we had a murder just last week."

"Only one?" Because Jean-Paul also sensed his wife's discomfort, he put a hand on her leg beneath the table.

"Only one," Clare agreed. "And the only one in Emmitsboro for as long as I can remember. It was pretty gruesome, really. Cam's stepfather was beaten to death and dumped off the road just outside of town."

"I'm sorry." Angie forgot the stares. "It must be difficult for Cam."

Restless, Clare put out her cigarette with quick, short taps. "It is difficult—though they were anything but close."

"Does he have any suspects?" Jean-Paul asked.

"I don't know. I doubt it." Clare glanced out the window at the slow-moving cars and slower-moving people. "It's hard to believe it could have been anyone from town." Then she shook her head and changed her phrasing. "No one wants to believe it could have been anyone from town."

It was after three when they returned home. Jean-Paul had scoured the antique stores and was toting three mahogany frames. To her surprise, Angie had come across a lovely Art Deco pin in sterling and had paid a small fraction of what the price would have been if the pin had found its way to Manhattan.

A big yellow school bus, pregnant with children, stopped at the corner with a belch and a wheeze to offload. The race was on for bikes, for cartoons, for catcher's mitts.

"There's Ernie." Clare spotted him standing at

the edge of her driveway. "The model for the arm," she explained.

"He seems to be waiting for you," Jean-Paul commented.

"He hangs around sometimes. He's lonely." She smiled and waved. "I don't think he gets along with his parents. They haven't even bothered to come take a look at the sculpture."

He watched her, annoyed that she wasn't alone. He knew the sheriff was busy out at Dopper's farm where two young calves had been slaughtered. Ernie knew, because he'd done the slaughtering in hopes that it would trigger his initiation into the cult.

"Hi, Ernie. Aren't you working today?"

"I got a few minutes."

"Good, I haven't seen you around the last few days."

"Been busy."

"Well, I'd like to show you the finished sculpture. These are my friends, Mr. and Mrs. LeBeau."

He acknowledged their greetings with a mumble but shook Jean-Paul's hand when it was offered.

"Come on into the garage. I'd like to know what you think." Clare led the way. "You haven't seen it since it was finished and fired," she continued. "Clay turned out to be the right medium, a little rougher and more primitive than wood. And since Mr. LeBeau plans to have it shipped up to New York soon, this might be your only chance." She gestured, then hooked her thumbs in her pockets. "So, what do you think?"

Studying it made Ernie feel strange and disjointed. Without thinking, he reached over to cup his left hand around his right forearm. She'd taken part of him somehow, more than his arm and hand and fingers. He couldn't explain it, didn't have the words. If he had, he might have chosen *essence*, for it seemed as though she'd stolen his essence and created it again in the defiant, disembodied arm and fist.

"I guess it's okay."

Clare laughed and put a hand on his shoulder. "That'll do, then. I really appreciate your helping me out."

"It was no big deal."

"To us it is a very big deal," Jean-Paul corrected. "Without you, Clare could not have created this. If she had not created it, we couldn't display it in our gallery so that other art dealers would pull out their hair in envy and frustration." He grinned down at the boy. "So you see, we are all in your debt."

Ernie only shrugged, sending the pendant around his neck swinging. Jean-Paul glanced down at it. Surprise came first, then amusement.

Teenagers, he thought, toying with what they couldn't possibly understand. He glanced back at Ernie, and the smile faded from his lips. A teenager, yes, a boy, but Jean-Paul had the uncomfortable feeling that this boy could understand all too well.

"Jean-Paul?" Angie stepped forward to lay a hand on his arm. "Are you all right?"

"Yes." He eased his wife slightly closer to him. "My mind was wandering. That's an interesting pendant," he said to Ernie.

"I like it."

"We must be keeping you." Jean-Paul's voice remained mild, but he kept a protective arm around his wife's shoulders.

"Yeah." Ernie's lip curled over his teeth. "I got things to do." Lightly, deliberately, he touched his fingers to the pentagram, closed his fist, and lifted the index and pinkie in the sign of the goat. "See you around."

"Don't use him again," Jean-Paul said as he watched Ernie walk away.

Clare's brows shot up. "Excuse me?"

"To model. Don't use him. He has bad eyes."

"Well, really—"

"Humor me." Smiling again, he kissed Clare's cheek. "They say my grandmother had the sight."

"I say you've had too much sun," Clare decided. "And need a drink."

"I wouldn't turn one down." He cast a last glance over his shoulder as he followed Angie and Clare into the kitchen. "Do you have cookies?"

"Always." She gestured him toward the refrigerator while she headed to the cupboard for a bag of Chips Ahoy. "Christ, listen to those flies. Sounds like a convention." Curious, she turned toward the screen door and peeked out. The burger she'd consumed with such relish threatened to bolt up. "God. Oh, God."

"Clare?" Angie was beside her in one leap. "Honey, what—" Then she saw for herself. Pressing the back of her hand to her mouth, she turned away. "Jean-Paul."

But he was already nudging them aside. On the stoop outside the screen door someone had flung a dead cat, a young black cat. Dark blood had poured and pooled where its head had once been. Black flies drank and buzzed busily.

He swore ripely in French before turning a pasty face to the women. "Go—in the other room. I'll deal with it."

"It's horrible." Hugging herself, Clare kept her back to the door. "All that blood." Still terribly fresh, too, she remembered, and swallowed hard. "It must have been a stray dog that killed it and dragged it here."

Jean-Paul thought of the pendant around

Ernie's neck and wondered. "The boy might have done it."

"Boy?" Clare steeled herself to hand Jean-Paul a plastic garbage bag. "Ernie? Don't be ridiculous. It was a dog."

"He wore a pentagram. A symbol of Satanism."

"Satanism?" Shuddering, Clare turned away again. "Let's not get carried away."

"Satanism?" Angie reached in the refrigerator for the wine. She thought they all would need it. "You read about it now and again. Hear about rites going on in Central Park."

"Cut it out." Clare fumbled for a cigarette. "Maybe the kid was wearing some kind of occult symbol—and he probably got a charge out of seeing Jean-Paul notice it. Christ, my father had a peace sign, that didn't make him a Communist." She dragged in smoke and let it out quickly. "Lots of people dabble in the occult, especially kids. It's a way of questioning authority."

"It can be dangerous," Jean-Paul insisted.

"That kid didn't behead some stray cat and leave it on my back doorstep. It's awful, I'll grant you, but you've been watching too many movies."

"Maybe." There was no use upsetting her or Angie any further, and he had to steel himself for the grisly task ahead. "But do something for me, *chérie*, and be careful of him. My grand-mother said that one should be wary of those who choose the left-hand path. Take the wine," he told them after a deep breath. "Go in the other room until I'm done here."

The left-hand path, Clare thought, and re-membered the book she had found in her father's office at the top of the stairs.

Chapter 15

WHAT THE HELL was going on? Cam settled back on the deck chair, a cold liter bottle of Pepsi at his side. He'd stripped down and showered since returning from the Dopper farm and now, wearing only jeans, watched the sun set, and wondered.

Two young Angus had been brutally butchered. Decapitated. Castrated. According to the vet who had examined the corpses with him, several of the internal organs had been cut out. And were missing.

Sick. Cam shrugged down Pepsi to wash the ugly taste from his mouth. Whoever had done it had wanted to shock and disgust—and had done a damn good job. Even Matt Dopper had been pale and pasty-faced beneath his fury. The calves had been only two months old and would have grown into hulking steers.

To be butchered, Cam thought, but not mutilated.

And Matt blamed him, at least partially. If the dogs hadn't been chained up, no one would have trespassed on the land, no one would have gotten to the stock, no one would have butchered his calves.

Cam leaned back, watching the twilight, feeling the light chill of it on his bare skin. There was a stillness that fascinated him, a lovely kind of hush as the light faded from pearly to dim. Into the silence, like a benediction, came a whippoorwill's hopeful call.

What was happening to his town, the town he thought he knew so well?

A baby's grave disturbed, a man hideously murdered, calves mutilated. All of these things had occurred within weeks of each other in a town where the biggest controversy was whether to have a rock or a country band at the Legion on Saturday nights.

Where was the connection? Did there have to be one?

Cam wasn't naive enough to ignore the fact that city problems, and city violence, could creep down the interstate and sneak into town. Emmitsboro wasn't Brigadoon. But it had been the next best thing.

Drugs. He took another swig from the bottle and watched the first star blink on. He would have said that whoever had taken a knife to the calves had to be wacked, or just crazy. And that person would have known Dopper's farm, and known too that the German shepherds were chained. So that someone belonged to Emmitsboro.

The town was close enough to D.C. that it had the potential for a drug drop-off point. The fact was the state police had raided a farmhouse about ten miles south and had confiscated a couple hundred pounds of coke, some automatic rifles, and about twenty thousand in cash. With almost ridiculous regularity, mules were picked up traveling on Interstate 70, stupid enough to speed with bags of coke under the hubcaps.

Could Biff have been picking up extra cash, screwed up a deal, or gotten greedy, then been taken out?

He'd been beaten by someone crazed with fury—or by someone making a point.

But neither of those incidents, nasty as they were, seemed to connect with the gruesome work in the cemetery.

So why were his instincts telling him to look for a connection?

Because he was tired, he thought. Because he'd come back here to escape from the ugliness and the guilt. And, he was forced to admit, the fears he had lived with since he'd held his dying partner in his arms.

He sat back, let his eyes close. Because he wanted a drink, badly wanted a drink, he refused to move. He let himself imagine what it would be like to pick up a bottle, lift it, set those seductive glass lips against his and swallow: hot liquid searing down his throat to burn in his gut and numb his brain. One drink, then two. What the fuck, let's drink the whole bottle. Life's too short to be stingy. Let's drown in it. Drip with it.

Then the misery of the morning after. Sick as a dog and wanting to die. Old Jack heaving back up while you sprawl in the bathroom and cling to the sweaty porcelain.

Hell of a good time.

It was just one of the mind games he played with himself since he'd broken off his friendship with good old Jack Daniels.

He wanted to believe he could get up in the morning and the urge to reach for the bottle would be gone. Vanished. He wanted to think he could get up, cruise into town, hand out a few traffic violations, lecture a few kids, fill out a few forms.

He didn't want a murder investigation or frantic farmers on his conscience. Most of all he didn't want to talk again to frightened, grieving parents like the Jamisons, who called every week, like clockwork.

But he knew he would get up the next day, check the urge to poison himself with Jack, then do his job. Because there was no place else for him to go and nothing else for him to do.

You think you know this town, but you don't.

Sarah Hewitt's bitter words played back in his head. What had she been telling him? What did she know about Parker?

Cam hadn't had any luck reaching the former sheriff. Parker had moved from Fort Lauderdale over a year before, without leaving a forwarding address. Now, Cam thought that he would add one more chore to his routine—trying to track Parker down. He only wished he knew why he felt compelled to bother.

He opened his eyes again to full dark, was soothed by it. He picked up the bottle and contented himself with the measly punch of sugar and caffeine. He lighted a cigarette, then swung his telescope around. It always soothed him to look at the stars.

He was studying Venus when he heard a car rattling up his lane. And he knew, with a certainty that surprised him, that it was Clare. More, he knew that he'd been waiting for her.

She'd needed to get out of the house. No, Clare admitted as she bolted out of the car, she'd been frantic to get out of the house. She knew

Angie and Jean-Paul would be fine on their own for an hour or two. In fact, she was sure they'd been waiting to have some time alone to discuss Jean-Paul's theories. She couldn't think about it. Wouldn't.

"Hey, Slim." Cam had walked to the end of the deck to lean over the rail. "Come on up."

Clare took the deck steps two at a time, then threw her arms around him. Before he could react, she had fastened her mouth hard to his.

"Well," he managed after a moment. "It's nice to see you, too." He stroked his hands up and down her rib cage, then settled them on her hips as he studied her in the backwash of light from the bedroom window. "What's wrong?"

"Nothing." She knew she had a bright smile on her face. She'd all but glued it there. "I was just restless." She combed her hands through his hair and pressed against him. "Or maybe it was horny."

He might have been flattered, even amused, if he'd believed her. He kissed her lightly on the forehead. "You can talk to me, Clare."

She knew he would listen. That he would care. But she couldn't tell him about the horror she'd found on her back stoop, or Jean-Paul's wild suspicions, or the book she had taken from her father's office and hidden under her mattress the way a teenage boy hides a porno magazine.

"It's nothing, really. I guess I'm wired—

commissions, contracts, great expectations." It was partially true, but she had a feeling he would sense more if she didn't wipe it from her mind. "So, what are you doing?" She pulled away from him to stroll along the deck to his telescope.

"Nothing much." He came up behind her to pick up the bottle of Pepsi. "Want a drink?"

"Yeah." She took it, sipped from the bottle. "I was hoping you'd call," she said, then was immediately annoyed with herself. "Forget I said that. What can you see through here?"

He put a hand on her shoulder before she could bend to the eyepiece of the scope. "I did call. Your line was busy."

"Oh." She couldn't stop the satisfied smile. "Angie's been on the line to New York. Got a cigarette, Rafferty? I must have left my purse in the car."

He took one out. "I like your friends," he said, striking a match.

"They're great. I guess it was stupid, but I was really nervous about your meeting them. It felt like I was showing you off to my parents or something. Oh, Christ." She plopped onto the arm of his chair. "I can't believe I said that. Pay no attention to me—pretend I just got here." She let out a long breath. "God, I feel like a teenager. I hate it."

"I like it." Cam put a hand under her chin to

lift her face. "In fact, I think I'm crazy about it. Ten minutes ago I was sitting here feeling sorry for myself. Now I can't figure out why."

She looked at him. His eyes seemed almost black in the dappled starlight. There was a faint, satisfied smile on his mouth. The pull was so strong her stomach trembled with the effort to hold back. "Rafferty, what have we got here?"

"What do you want to have?"

"I guess I haven't figured that out yet. I was hoping you had."

He'd figured it out all right, but he didn't want to make it easy on her. "Why don't you think about it for a while?" He sat in the chair next to hers. "I've got Venus in the scope. Want to take a look?"

She shifted into the chair and tilted her head. "I like being with you," she said as she studied the bright red star. "I mean like this—not just in bed."

"That's a good start."

"But the sex is great."

His lips quirked. "I can't argue with that."

"What I'm trying to say is that even though the sex is, well, incredible, that's not why I . . ." Care about you, dream about you, think about you. "That's not why I'm here."

"Okay." He took the hand that she was rapping against the arm of the Adirondack chair. "So, why are you here?"

"I just wanted to be with you." She kept looking through the scope, but she no longer saw anything. "Okay?"

"Yeah." He brought her hand to his lips, brushed a kiss over the knuckles in a quietly romantic gesture that brought tears to her eyes.

"I don't want to screw this up, Cam. I'm real good at screwing things up."

"We're doing fine, Slim. Just fine."

They looked at the stars for more than an hour. When she left, Clare had nearly forgotten about the book she'd secreted away.

Lisa MacDonald was pissed. She was also lost—in the middle of nowhere, as far as she could tell—and her car had definitely given up the ghost. Trying to be optimistic, she gave the engine one more shot. After all, it only had a hundred and sixty-two thousand miles on it. She turned the key and listened to the rattle—death rattle, she thought. The car vibrated beneath her, but didn't turn over.

Disgusted, she slammed the door on her '72 Volvo and rounded the hood. Since her forte was ballet and not auto mechanics, she knew ahead of time that it was a wasted effort.

The moon was nearly full, and the stars were brilliant. But the light they shed only cast shadows on the long length of dark road. All she could hear was the monotonous chorus of peepers and crickets. The hood screeched when she lifted it, then fumbled with the bar. Swearing, she went around to the passenger side to search in the glove compartment. Her brother, who was a nag, a pain, and her closest friend, had bought her a flashlight and emergency kit.

"Anyone who drives should be able to change a tire and do simple repairs," she muttered, mimicking Roy. "Up yours, bro," she added, but was relieved when the flashlight shot out a steady beam. Roy insisted on solid Duracell batteries.

If she hadn't been coming to see him—and if he hadn't insisted she take the train so that she'd felt *obliged* to drive from Philadelphia, just to irritate him—she wouldn't be in this fix.

Frowning, she tossed her waist-length blond hair behind her shoulders and aimed the beam on the engine. Looked fine to her, she thought. Everything was black and greasy. So why the hell didn't it run?

Why the hell hadn't she had the car tuned before the trip? Because she'd needed a new pair of pointe shoes and her budget hadn't allowed for both. Lisa had her priorities. Even now, standing in the dark, alone, beside her dead car, she wouldn't have done things differently. She would have bought dance shoes before food, and often did.

Tired, annoyed, and impatient, she turned a circle, shining the light as she went. She saw a fence and a field, and a scatter of lights that seemed at least two miles away. There were woods, thick and dark, and the black ribbon of road that disappeared around a curve.

Where were the gas stations, the phone booths? Where the hell was a McDonald's? How did people live like this? She slammed the hood and sat on it.

Maybe she should take a page out of the Boy Scout manual and stay put until someone found her. She stared up the road, then down the road, and gave a long, gusty sigh. At this rate, she'd be ready for social security before she got to civilization.

She could start walking. At five four and a hundred pounds, she might have looked frail and petite, but the rigors of dance had toughened her body. She had as much, maybe more endurance than your average quarterback. But which way—and for how long?

Resigned, she went back to the car for her map and the detailed directions Roy had given her—which she had somehow managed to mess up. She left the door open and sat sideways on the driver's seat as she tried to figure out where she had gone wrong.

She'd passed Hagerstown. That she was sure of, because she'd pulled off the interstate there for gas and a diet Coke. And a Hershey bar, she reminded herself guiltily. Then she'd come to Route 64, just as Roy had said. And she'd turned right.

Shit. She dropped her head in her hands. She'd turned left, she was all but sure of it. In her mind, she went back to the intersection, saw the convenience store on one side, the cornfield on the other. She'd stopped at the light, munching on chocolate and humming along with Chopin. The light had changed. She'd turned. Her brow furrowed in concentration. Lisa's mental block between right and left was the joke of the dance company. When she danced, she wore a rubber band on her right wrist.

Oh, yeah, she thought now. She'd turned left, all right.

The trouble was she'd been born left-handed, and her father had insisted she use her right. Twenty years later, she was still confused.

It was hard to blame dear old dad for the fact that she was sitting in a broken-down car in the middle of nowhere. But it helped.

So, she'd made a wrong turn. Lisa combed long, delicate fingers through her hair. That wasn't a big deal. All she had to do was figure out whether to walk up the road or down it.

She wasn't the kind of woman who panicked, but one who thoroughly, often stubbornly, worked her way through a situation. She did so now, backtracking on the map, pinpointing the area of her mistake, then moving forward toward the nearest town.

Emmitsboro, she decided. Unless she was completely brain damaged, she should be able to follow the road about two miles. She would come to the town, or with luck, to a house along the way where she could call Roy and confess to being stupid, inept, and irresponsible. At the moment, confession seemed better than spending the night in the car.

Lisa stuck her keys in the pocket of her sweats, grabbed her purse, and set off.

It wasn't exactly how she'd planned to spend the evening. She'd pictured herself landing on Roy's doorstep a good twelve hours before he'd be expecting her. She'd wanted to surprise him, then to open the bottle of champagne she'd brought with her.

It wasn't every day she could announce she'd just been handed the plum role of Dulcinea in the company's production of *Don Quixote*. Though she was the kind of woman who made friends easily and kept them, there was no one she wanted to share her news with more than her brother.

She could imagine his face lighting up when she told him, the way he would laugh and grab her and swing her around. It had been her mother who had dutifully taken her to dance classes, day after day. But it had been Roy who had understood her need, who had encouraged, who had believed.

Something rustled in the bushes. Being a city girl through and through, Lisa jolted, squealed, then swore. Where were the frigging streetlights? she wondered and was doubly grateful for the flashlight gripped in her hand.

To comfort herself, she started to imagine how much worse it could be. It could have been raining. It could have bccn cold. An owl hooted, making her quicken her steps. She could be attacked by a gang of mad rapists. She could have broken a leg. She shuddered. A broken leg was much worse than mad rapists.

She'd be going into rehearsals in a week. Lisa imagined herself flicking open the frilly black fan, spinning gracefully into a dozen *fouetté* turns.

She could see the lights, hear the music, feel the wonder. There was nothing, nothing more important than dance in her life. For sixteen years she had been waiting, working, praying for the chance to prove herself as a principal dancer.

Now she had it, she thought, and hugged herself before turning three pirouettes in the middle of the dark road. And every cramp, every bead of sweat, and every tear would have been worth it.

She was smiling when she spotted the car pulled off the shoulder of the road and heading into the woods. Her first thought was, salvation. Maybe there was a nice, clever man—she hated to be sexist, but now wasn't the time for sensitivity—who could fiddle with her car.

But she stopped on the side of the road, wondering why the car was pulled into the bush, half hidden from view. Uncertain, she took a few steps closer before she called, "Hello? Is anyone there?" She glanced up the road, that endless dark tunnel, and took another step, carefully avoiding a gully. "Hello? I could use some help." She shined the light at her feet, watching out for any ankle twisters as she started down the gentle slope. "Is anyone here?" She glanced up at the sound of rustling brush. "My car—" she began, then stopped.

They seemed to melt out of the trees. Two shadowy figures, draped in black. They were faceless, formless. The fear that rose up in her was instinctive and sharp. The beam of light shook as she aimed it at them. She took a step back, turned to run, but they moved quickly.

She screamed in pain and in terror as her hair was grabbed and ruthlessly wrenched. An arm came around her waist, lifting her up. Every woman's nightmare swam blackly in her brain. She kicked out, a vicious snap of her long legs, but met only air. Flailing with legs and arms, she slapped the flashlight against skull. There was a grunt, an oath, as the hold loosened. As she scrambled for freedom, she heard her shirt tear.

Something struck her face, making her reel, blurring her vision. Then she was running, blindly. She knew she was sobbing. She could feel each breath burn her throat. She tried to stop, her panicked mind focusing on the fact that they could hear and follow.

She realized she had run into the woods and lost all direction. Fallen logs turned into traps, leafy trees into barriers. She was the rabbit, fast but dazzled by fear, chased ruthlessly by the pack. Wild with terror, she plunged on. The roar of her heartbeat was so loud, she never heard the racing footsteps behind her.

He caught her in a vicious tackle, rapping her knee hard against a rock. Even through fear she heard the bone pop. Her leg twisted as her body hit the ground with a force that had pain singing through her. She tasted her own blood as her teeth sawed into her lip.

He was chanting. Dear God, was all she could think. He was chanting. And she could smell blood.

She heard more now, as he dragged her over. Bodies crashing through the trees. Shouts. Coming closer. Yet her captor didn't call to them. She could see his eyes, only his eyes. And she knew she would be fighting for her life.

He thought he had her cowed. She could see it. Indeed, she could smell her own fear. When he shifted to tear at her clothes, she raked her nails hard over his hand. She was fighting, with teeth and nails and every ounce of strength in her body.

But his hands were around her throat. He was growling, like an animal, she thought dizzily. She was choking, graying out, and her struggles weakened. The heels of her sneakers beat against the dirt.

She couldn't breathe—couldn't breathe. Her eyes were wide and bulging as he smiled down at her. Limp, boneless, her hands slid down the rough material of his cloak and shook on the carpet of leaves.

Dying. She was dying. And her hands clenched in the crackling leaves.

Her groping fingers closed over a rock. Her heart and lungs were ready to burst as she brought it up and smashed it against the back of his head. He grunted, and his fingers went lax. Even as she gulped in the first painful breath of air, she hit him again.

Gagging, she struggled out from under him. She'd never known such pain and wanted only to lie down and weep until it passed. But she heard voices, shouts, running. Fear barreled into her, pushing her up. She bit her lip when her leg buckled, when the agony of it shot up into her belly. In a limping run, she raced through the trees, knowing there were others close behind.

Clare felt better. Incredibly better, she thought. She was almost humming as she drove home from Cam's. She hadn't known that sitting out and looking at the stars, talking about nothing of particular importance could calm jangled nerves. She was sorry she couldn't have stayed, couldn't have snuggled up in bed beside him, to make love, or just to talk and drift into sleep.

Angie and Jean-Paul would have understood, she thought with a smile. But her mother had drummed manners into her a bit too successfully. In any case, she wanted to get back, to close herself off in her room and study the book from her father's office.

Hiding it away wouldn't solve anything. That was another conclusion her time with Cam had brought her to. She would read it, try to think it through. She would even go through the rest of the books that had been packed away.

"How about that, Dr. Janowski?" she muttered. "I didn't have to shell out a hundred and fifty dollars to figure out the best answer is to face the problem, then deal with it."

Besides, there wasn't going to be any problem. She tossed her head, and the wind sent her hair dancing around her face. Everything was going to be fine. Emmitsboro would have its parade, a few speeches, then would settle back to its quiet monotony. Just the way she liked it.

She saw the figure dash out of the woods. A deer, Clare thought as she pressed her foot down hard on the brake. The car skidded and swerved as she yanked at the wheel. Her headlights veered crazily and caught the figure—the figure of a woman, Clare realized with sick panic—just before the right fender bumped against flesh.

"Oh, Jesus. Oh, Jesus." Clare was out of the car in a flash, her limbs like Jell-O. The stink of rubber stung the air. Slumped beside the car was a woman. Blood stained the legs of her sweatpants, was smeared on her hands. "Oh, please. Please, God." Murmuring brokenly, Clare crouched down to gently brush back the fall of blond hair with shaking fingers.

Lisa blinked but could barely focus. Something had scraped her eye badly as she'd stumbled through the woods. "Help me." Her voice was a raspy whisper, barely audible.

"I will. I'm sorry. I'm so sorry. I didn't see you until it was too late."

"A car." Lisa pushed herself up, bracing a palm on the concrete and locking her elbow. Each word burned like acid in her throat, but she had to make herself understood before it was too late. "Thank God. Help me, please. I don't think I can get up alone."

"I don't think you should move." Wasn't there something about neck or spinal injuries? Christ, why hadn't she ever taken a first-aid course?

"They're coming! Hurry! For God's sake!" Lisa was already pulling herself up by the bumper. "For God's sake *hurry*!"

"All right. All right." She could hardly leave the woman lying in the middle of the road while she went for help. As gently as possible, Clare maneuvered Lisa into the passenger seat. "Here, let me—"

"Just drive." Lisa was terrified she would black out. With a hand clenched on the door handle, she peered out into the woods. Her good eye wheeled with panic. "Drive fast, before they find us."

"I'm taking you to a hospital."

"Anywhere." Lisa covered her bloody face with her hand. "Take me anywhere but here." She slumped in the seat as Clare drove away. Lisa's body began to shake as she swam toward unconsciousness. "His eyes," she murmured, fretful. "Oh, God, his eyes. Like the devil's."

Cam had his mouth full of toothpaste when the phone rang. He spat, swore halfheartedly, and didn't bother to rinse. The phone was on its third ring when he lifted it from the nightstand. "Hello?"

"Cam."

He needed only that one syllable to tell him something was wrong. "Clare, what is it?"

"I'm at the hospital. I—"

"What happened?" he demanded, grabbing the jeans he'd slung over the chair. "How bad are you hurt?"

"It's not me. I'm fine." Her hand trembled so violently the coffee in the Styrofoam cup splashed over the sides. "There was an accident—a woman. She ran out of the woods. I thought she was a deer. I tried to stop. Oh, God, Cam, I don't know how bad I hurt her. They won't tell me. I need—"

"I'm on my way. Just sit down, Slim, and close your eyes."

"Okay." She pressed a hand to her lips. "Thanks."

It seemed like hours. She sat in the Emergency Room, listening to the moans, the slap of feet on tile, the droning television. Leno was doing his monologue, and apparently knocking them dead. Clare kept staring down at the bloodstains on her blouse and jeans—reliving over and over that instant when she'd hit the brakes.

Had she hesitated? Had she been driving too fast? She'd been daydreaming. If she'd been paying closer attention, that woman wouldn't be in surgery.

God, she thought, I don't even know her name.

"Clare."

Dazed, she looked up just as Cam crouched beside her.

"I don't even know her name."

"It's okay." He brought her hands to his lips and held them there, assuring himself she was whole and safe. There was blood on her shirt, but after the first jolt of panic, he knew it wasn't hers. "Can you tell me what happened?"

"She ran in front of the car. I hit her."

He noted that her face was colorless, even her lips. Her pupils were dilated. When he put the back of his hand to her cheek, he found the skin clammy and cold. "Has anyone looked at you?"

She gave him a blank look. "I want to know what's happening. I have to know. They'll tell you, won't they? Please, Cam, I can't stand it."

"All right. Stay right here. I won't be long."

She watched him as he walked to a nurse, took out his identification. After a few moments, the nurse led him away down a hall. When he returned, he was carrying a blanket, which he tucked around her before he sat.

"She's in surgery." He took her hand, warming it between his. "It may be awhile. Her knee was badly damaged and her eye." He waited until Clare pressed her lips together and nodded. "There're some internal injuries and a lot of bruising around the throat. Clare, can you tell me how hard you hit her? How far the impact tossed her?"

"They asked me all that."

"Tell me."

"It seemed like kind of a bump. I was nearly stopped. I thought I'd be able to stop in time. I swung the car hard, to the left. I swear, it felt as though I'd be able to stop. But then, when I got out of the car, she was lying there, and there was blood."

Cam's eyes narrowed. "She was right beside the car?"

"Yes, she was almost under the damn tire." She pressed a hand to her mouth. "I didn't know what to do. She begged me to help her."

"She talked to you?"

Clare only nodded her head and rocked.

"Okay, take a minute." He put an arm around her shoulder, pressed a kiss to her temple. But he was thinking quickly. "Do you want some water?"

She shook her head. "I'm okay. It's only that I keep seeing her, in that instant she was caught in my headlights."

He would question her about that as well, but

he wanted to give her time. "Just listen. The intern on E.R. duty said her clothes were torn. There were leaves and twigs stuck to them and tangled in her hair. The bruises on her neck indicate attempted strangulation."

"But . . ."

"You said she ran out of the woods. Would you be able to show me where?"

"I won't forget it anytime soon."

"Okay." He smiled, noting some color was seeping back into her cheeks. "I'd like to take a look at your car before I take you home."

"I can't go. Not until I know."

"You're ragged out, Slim."

"Not until I know." She took a deep breath before she turned to look at him. "She was running away from someone. It didn't click in before. I was so scared. I didn't want to move her, but she tried to climb into the car. She was terrified, Cam. The pain must have been awful for her, but she was actually trying to crawl into the car. She said we had to get away before they found us."

He brushed a kiss over her brow. "I'm going to find you a bed."

"No, I don't want—"

"That's the condition, or I put you in the car and take you home. You need to relax." He sighed. "Clare, we'll have to take a blood test. For alcohol."

"Alcohol?" The color faded again. "Christ, Cam. I hadn't been drinking. You know. I'd just left—"

"Slim, it's for the record." He took her rigid hand in his again. "For your own protection."

"Right." She stared up at Leno, hooting over some sophisticated joke. "Do what you have to do, Sheriff."

"Fuck that." He wanted to shake her, but she looked as though she'd rattle apart at a touch. Patience, he warned himself. He wished it came easily to him. "Clare, I'm here to help you. There's a procedure, a necessary one. I'll make it as easy on you as I can."

"I know. Sorry." But she didn't look at him. "I'll cooperate. Just tell me what you want me to do."

I want you to lean on me again, he thought. "I want you to take the test. Try to relax. Try to trust me." She didn't respond, but she did look at him. "And I need you to give me a statement."

"Oh." She turned away again. "As a friend or as the sheriff?"

"I can be both." He took her face in his hands and turned it back to his. "Don't pull back on me, Slim. I'm getting used to you."

She pressed her lips together, afraid she would blubber and make things worse than they already were. "Are you going to leave after you get the statement?"

He studied her, brushing his thumbs gently over her cheekbones. "I figure you've had a rough night so you're entitled to one stupid question. But that's the last one."

As the relief worked its way through her, she nearly managed to smile. "I probably wouldn't think of any more if you'd just hold my hand for a while."

He cupped it in his. "How's that?"

"Better." She leaned her head against his shoulder and shut her eyes. "Lots better."

Chapter 16

SHE MUST HAVE DOZED OFF. When Clare dragged herself out of sleep, her heart was racing. The dry, sour taste of fear coated her mouth as she scrambled to sit up. For a moment, dream struggled against reality, and the hard table with the gauzy curtain surrounding it became a coffin, the image screaming through her brain.

Then she remembered Cam leading her back through the E.R., into the little cubicle, drawing the privacy curtain so that the light filtered weakly through. She could see shadows moving beyond it.

He had gotten his hands on a tape recorder and taken her briefly and thoroughly through the events that happened after she left his house.

She'd felt both sad and awkward answering his questions. He hadn't been wearing his badge, but she'd known it stood between them.

After he had put the recorder away, labeling and pocketing the tape, he had brought her a cup of tea and stayed with her until she drifted off.

She was relieved he wasn't there now, that she could take a moment to calm herself. The dream that had awakened her was still running through her mind like film on an endless loop.

Her old nightmare had mixed with a new one, one of herself running through the woods, crashing through brush and bursting out on the road. Behind her was the swell of chanting growing louder, louder. A smell of blood and smoke. It had been *her* white and terrified face caught in the hard glare of headlights. Behind the wheel of the car bearing down on her was the figure of a man with the head of a goat.

She had awakened on impact with the sickening thud echoing in her head.

Clare rubbed her hands over her face and could feel a wild pulsing in her fingertips. She was awake, she reminded herself, safe and unhurt. As her heartbeat quieted, she heard the beep of pages. Nearby she heard a hacking cough and someone moaning.

Nightmares fade, she thought. Reality doesn't. There was another woman lying in a bed somewhere upstairs. A woman she was responsible for.

Just as she started to swing her legs off the padded table, the curtain was parted.

"You're awake." Cam came forward to take her hand and study her face.

"How long did I sleep? Is she out of surgery? I want to—" She broke off, seeing that Cam was not alone. "Dr. Crampton."

He gave her a reassuring smile and patted her free hand. "Well, young lady, what have we got here?" he said as he took her pulse.

It was the same greeting he'd given her when he treated her for an ear infection fifteen years ago. It triggered the same reaction. "I'm fine. I don't need a shot or anything."

He chuckled, pushing his wire-rim glasses back up his prominent nose. "It's mighty depressing when people always look at you as though you've got a hypodermic in your pocket. Any dizziness?"

"No. Cam, you had no business bringing Dr. Crampton all the way up here."

"I figured you'd be more comfortable with Doc Crampton. Besides"—he grinned at her—"the intern on duty is too young and too good-looking." He turned to the doctor. "No offense."

"I don't need a doctor." How could he joke? How *could* he? "Tell me how she is."

"She's out of surgery." Cam kept Clare's hand in his while Crampton shined a light in her eyes. "She hasn't come around yet, but she's going to be okay." He couldn't bring himself to tell her that it was going to take at least one more operation to reconstruct the woman's knee.

"Thank God." She was so relieved she didn't object when Crampton fit a blood pressure cuff over her arm. "Can I see her?"

"Not until morning." He squeezed her hand before she could object. "Doctor's orders, Slim, not mine."

"You're carrying around a lot of stress, young lady," Dr. Crampton told her. "Entirely too much. You call the office and make an appointment for next week. No arguments, now."

"No, sir."

He smiled at her. "You're going to try to find a way to slip out of it."

She smiled back. "You bet."

"You always were one of my worst patients." He tapped a finger on the tip of her nose. "I want you to relax. I'm going to give you something to help you sleep." He caught the stubborn look in her eye and sent her one in return. "I'd do the same for my own girl."

It made her sigh. This was the man who'd seen her through chicken pox and that first, horribly embarrassing pelvic exam. His patient voice hadn't changed, nor the gentleness of his hands.

New and deeper lines were etched around his eyes since the last time Clare had been his patient. His hair was thinner, his waist thicker. But she remembered very clearly the way he had dispensed balloons from a china clown on his desk, for good girls and boys. "Don't I get a prize?"

He chuckled again and opened his bag. He pulled out a long red balloon to go with the sample of pills. "Nothing wrong with your memory."

She took it, the symbol of hope and childhood, and balled it in her hand. "It was good of you to come all this way, Doctor. I'm sorry Cam got you out of bed."

"It won't be the first time or the last." He winked at her. "You had a nasty shock, Clare, but I think rest will put you right. But you make that appointment, or I'll take back that balloon." He picked up his bag, then turned to Cam. "I can talk to the surgeon if you want, look in on the patient from time to time."

"I'd appreciate it."

He waved the thanks away, and they watched him go, tiredness slowing his steps.

"He hasn't changed," Clare said.

Cam brought her hand up to his cheek and held it there. "You gave me a scare, Slim."

"Sorry."

"Still mad at me?"

She shifted restlessly. "Not really. It's a little weird being interrogated by someone I'm sleeping with."

He let go of her hand, stepped back. "I can have Bud do the follow-up if you'd feel better about it."

She was screwing it up, Clare thought. Right on schedule. "No, I'll handle it." She tried a smile and almost made it. "So, what's the next step?"

"I can take you home so you can get some real sleep." That's what he wanted to do.

"Or?"

"If you're up to it, you can take me back to the scene, go through it with me." That's what he felt obliged to do.

She felt a skitter of panic inside her and ruthlessly squashed it. "Okay, we'll take door number two."

"I'll drive. We'll have your car picked up later." He wanted to examine it thoroughly, with more than a flashlight, for evidence of impact.

She slid off the table, then reached for his hand. "I think I left my keys in it."

Other wounds had been treated that night. Other decisions had been made. The twelve remaining children of Satan had closed ranks.

Their fears had been put to rest. On the night of the full moon, they would meet for the Esbat. To celebrate. To consecrate. To sacrifice.

The offering that had been sent to them had escaped. They had only to choose another.

"It was here." Clare closed her eyes as Cam steered his car to the shoulder. "I was coming the other way, but this is where . . ." A squeal of brakes, her own scream. "This is where I hit her."

"You want to stay in the car while I take a look?"

"No." She wrenched open the door and pushed herself out.

The moon had set. The stars were fading. It was the darkest, coldest part of night. Was there an hour, she wondered, when man was more vulnerable than this, the time that belonged to creatures who slept or hid by day? There was a rustle in the brush—the cry of the hunter, the scream of the prey. She saw the shadow of an owl as it glided away with its kill caught, bleeding, in its talons. The crickets continued their tireless music.

Clare wrapped her arms tight around her body. Cam was already playing his light on the skid marks that started up the road, then veered dramatically to the left.

From the length of them, he gauged that Clare hadn't been doing more than forty. And from the angle, she'd obviously reacted quickly, wheeling her car away. Judging by the evidence at his feet and Clare's statement, it appeared likely to him that the woman had run into Clare, rather than the other way around. But he kept his opinion to himself for the moment.

"She came out of the woods?" he prompted.

"Just there." She pointed, her artist's imagination recreating the scene vividly. "She was running, sort of a quick, stumbling gait. For just a fraction of a second, I thought she was a deer— the way she just burst out of the trees and kept going. My first thought was, shit, I'm going to run over Bambi. And Bambi's going to wreck my car. I remember Blair hitting a buck the first month we had our drivers' licenses, and totaling the Pinto."

She unwrapped her arms, then stuck her hands in her pockets. Inside were a couple of spare coins her nervous fingers could toy with. "I hit the brakes hard and dragged at the wheel. She was out on the road so fast. Then I saw her in the headlights."

"Tell me what you saw."

"A woman, very slim, lots of blond hair. There was blood on her face, on her shirt, on her pants. As if I'd already mowed her down."

Her spit seemed to dry up in her mouth as she spoke. "Got a cigarette?"

He took two out, lit them both, and handed her one. "Then what?"

The resentment eased back into her, like the smoke she inhaled. "Cam, I've already told you."

"Tell me here."

"I hit her." She snapped the words off and paced a few feet away. "There was this awful thud."

He played his light on the road again, following the trail of blood that ended beside the skid mark Clare's right tire had made.

"She was conscious?"

She dragged on the cigarette again, struggling not to hate him. "Yes, she asked me to help her. She was scared, really scared. Whatever she'd been running from was worse for her than her injuries."

"She had keys."

"What?"

"She had keys in her pocket." He pulled out a little plastic bag that contained them. "One's a car key." He scanned the road. "Let's take a ride."

As they drove, he was silent, thinking. She'd had no purse, no backpack, no I.D. Pretty blondes didn't go unnoticed in a small town like

Emmitsboro, so he was betting she wasn't a local. When he spotted the Volvo parked on the shoulder a mile from the accident site, he wasn't surprised.

Clare said nothing as she watched him work. He took out a bandanna, using it to cover his fingers as he opened the glove box and sifted through its contents.

"Lisa MacDonald." He read from the registration card before he glanced up at Clare. "Now we know her name."

"Lisa MacDonald," Clare repeated. It was a name she wouldn't forget.

He found a map as well, and neatly printed directions from Philadelphia to Williamsport, a town about fifteen miles from Emmitsboro. Still using the bandanna, he took the keys from the evidence bag and slid one into the ignition. The engine sputtered.

"Looks like she had a breakdown."

"But why would she have gone into the woods?"

Maybe someone took her there, Cam thought, and pocketed the registration. "That's what I'll have to find out." He closed the car door. The sun was beginning to rise above the mountains to the east. In its ghostly light, Clare looked pale and exhausted. "I'll take you home."

"Cam, I want to help. I want to *do* something."

"The best thing you can do now is take Doc's pills and get some sleep. They'll call me when she wakes up. I'll let you know."

He had shifted completely into his cop mode, and she didn't like it. "What are you going to do now?"

"Make some phone calls. File a report. Come on."

"I'll go with you," she said as he pulled her back to his car. "I can help."

"Clare, this is my job. I can't see you letting me hold your welding torch."

"This is different. I'm involved."

"The difference is this is official business." He pulled open the car door and nudged her inside. "And you're a witness."

"A witness to what?"

"I'll let you know." He closed the door.

The news spread like wildfire. Doc Crampton told his wife when he finally climbed into bed. His wife told Alice during their morning phone call. Alice hunted down Bud before the breakfast shift was over. By noon, when Cam arranged for George Howard to use his tow truck to bring the Volvo into the back lot of Jerry's Auto Sales and Repairs, the story was spreading through town like a fast-mutating virus.

Min Atherton didn't waste any time hustling over to the Kimball house with her prize-winning orange-and-marshmallow Jell-O mold and a nose itching for gossip. When she was turned away by an immovable Angie, who told her Clare was resting and couldn't be disturbed, she clumped off to Betty's House of Beauty to complain about that uppity black woman.

By the second lunch shift at Emmitsboro High, the rumor being passed out like the Steak Nuggets and Tater Rounds was that a psycho was loose in Dopper's Woods.

Others said the woman had run into Junior Dopper's ghost, but most favored the psycho.

They speculated in the market, over the ice-burg lettuce, about whether Sheriff Rafferty was covering up for Clare, seeing as they'd gotten so cozy. After all, he wasn't turning up much on Biff Stokey's murder either, though it was hard to blame him for that.

And wasn't it too bad about Jane Stokey selling her farm and getting ready to move down to Tennessee? The Rafferty place—it had been the Rafferty place for close to a hundred years and would always be the Rafferty place in local minds—would probably be sliced up for building lots. Just wait and see. Lord, look at the price on these tomatoes. Hothouse, too. Got no taste.

Wasn't it something about those calves of Matt

Dopper's? Had to be drug addicts from down in the city. Same ones that killed old Biff. Sheriff ought to be able to figure it out.

The buzzing went on, over the counters, through the telephone wires crisscrossing town, beside the swings in the park, where toddlers raced in the bright May sunshine.

Cam fielded dozens of calls and sent Bud or Mick out to ease the spreading anxiety from in and around town. People were jumpy enough to lock their doors, to peer out of dark windows before they climbed into bed. He could almost see the shotguns and hunting rifles standing oiled and loaded beside doorways, and hoped to God he wouldn't have to deal with a rash of accidental shootings.

It was bad enough during deer season when the lawyers and dentists and other desk jockeys from the city crowded the woods, shooting at one another more often than they shot at a buck, and mostly missing. But the people of Emmitsboro knew one end of a twenty gauge from the other.

If the town panicked, he'd have to go to the mayor about signing on another deputy, at least temporarily, to help handle the nail biters who would see Charles Manson every time a tree branch rattled a window.

He pushed away from his desk and went into the broom–closet–sized bathroom in the back of the office. It smelled—no, reeked, Cam thought—of Lysol. That was Bud's work. The germ-fighting deputy.

Bending over the bowl, he splashed cold water on his face, trying to rinse the rust out of his mouth and eyes. He hadn't slept in thirty-six hours, and his mind was almost as sluggish as his body.

There had been a time when he and his partner had stayed up as long, trapped in a freezing or sweaty car during a stakeout. Taking turns catching naps, drinking atomic coffee, making up stupid word games just to relieve the impossible tedium.

He lifted his head, face dripping, and stared into the spotty mirror. He wondered if there would ever come a time when he wouldn't remember. Or at least when those memories would dull a bit around the edges and become more comfortable to live with.

Christ in heaven, he wanted a drink.

Instead, he rubbed his face dry and went back into the office for more coffee. He'd just scalded his tongue when Clare walked in. She took one look at his shadowed eyes, the stubble of beard, and shook her head.

"You haven't been to bed at all."

He drank again, burning his already raw mouth. "What are you doing here?"

"I sent Angie down to make tea and snuck

out. She and Jean-Paul would make great war-
dens. I figured if I called you, you'd put me off.
This way it'll be tougher."

"She came around. She's a little vague on
what happened, but she knew her name, the
year, and her address."

"You said you'd call."

"I figured you were still asleep."

"Well, I'm not." Clare paced to his desk, then
to the window while she struggled with her
temper. It was a lost cause. "Damn it, Cam, official business or not, I have a right to know."

"And I'm telling you," he said evenly.

"I'm going to see her." She turned to the
door.

"Hold it."

"Fuck that." She whirled around again, ready
to fight. "I not only have a right to see her, I
have an obligation."

"You're not responsible. What happened to
her happened in the woods."

"Whether she was hurt before or after I ran
into her, I was there."

"You didn't run into her," he corrected.
"Your car doesn't have a mark on it. She may
have bumped into you, but that's as far as it
goes."

Her temper sizzled in spite of her relief.
"Damn it, I was there. And let's get something
straight," she continued before he could get in

a word. "I don't need or want to be coddled or patronized or protected. If I've given you that impression, well, too bad. I've been running my life for too long to let you tell me what I should or shouldn't do now."

Because he figured it was safer for both of them, Cam stayed where he was. "You get a hell of a lot across in a short time, Slim." He set down his coffee, very carefully. "I thought you'd like to know that I contacted Lisa's brother. He's on his way to the hospital, and when Bud gets back to take over here, so am I."

"Fine." She felt stupid, angry, and guilty but couldn't let it stop her. "I'll see you there." She slammed the door on her way out. She'd only taken two steps when she ran into Jean-Paul. "Oh, for Christ's sake."

"I thought you might be here."

"Listen, I appreciate your concern, but I'm in a hurry. I'm going up to the hospital to see Lisa MacDonald."

He knew her too well to argue, and only took her arm. "Then we'll go by the house first so Angie can stop tearing out her beautiful hair, and I'll drive you."

Pacing the hospital corridor for the better part of an hour had Clare's resentment rising all over again. Lisa MacDonald's room was off-limits except to immediate family and hospital staff. Sheriff's orders. So she would wait, Clare decided. If he thought she would go quietly to twiddle her thumbs at home, he obviously didn't know whom he was dealing with.

And maybe that was the problem. They really didn't know each other.

"I brought you some tea." Jean-Paul gave her a plastic cup. "To calm your nerves."

"Thanks, but it's going to take a hell of a lot more than tea."

"They didn't have vodka in the concession machine."

She gave a half laugh and sipped to please him. "Why won't he let me go in and see her? What does he think he's doing, Jean-Paul?"

"His job, *chérie.*"

A long breath hissed out between her teeth. "Don't go logical on me now."

She spotted Cam the moment he stepped off the elevator. There was a woman beside him carrying a briefcase. Clare pushed the cup back into Jean-Paul's hand and marched toward Cam. "What the hell's the idea, Rafferty? I have a right to see her."

Cam had just spent twenty minutes waiting for the attending physician to give him the go-ahead to take Lisa's statement. "Lisa MacDonald has rights," he said shortly. "If she wants to see you after I've talked to her, that's fine." He kept walking as he spoke, then, signaling to a nurse, went into Lisa's room and shut the door.

The tall, pale-haired man sitting beside Lisa's bed rose immediately. Roy MacDonald leaned over to murmur something to his sister, then crossed to Cam. He was about twenty-five, Cam judged, his serious face composed of finely drawn features. There were lines of strain around his eyes and mouth, and the hand he offered to Cam was cold but steady.

"You're Sheriff Rafferty."

"Yes. I've just spoken with Dr. Su, Mr. Mac-Donald. He's given me the nod to take a statement from your sister. This is Mrs. Lomax, the stenographer."

"I'll stay."

"I think that would be best." Cam gave a nod for the stenographer to set up. "This will probably be hard for her. And for you."

"Whatever it takes to find out who did this to her." Roy MacDonald's hands clenched and un-clenched. "The doctor said she wasn't raped."

"No, there was no indication of sexual assault."

"One small blessing," Roy murmured. "Her leg." He had to swallow and made certain he kept his voice low. "There's some artery damage—and the knee. She's a dancer." He glanced back at his sister while helplessness and rage battled. "She *was* a dancer."

"I can tell you that they got her into surgery very quickly and that the surgical staff here is as respected as any in the state."

"I'm holding on to that." He gave himself a moment, afraid, as he had been afraid since the sheriff's call that morning, that he would break down and do Lisa more harm than good. "She doesn't know that it's—that she probably won't dance again. Once she starts thinking . . ."

"I'll try to make it easy on her."

Roy went back to his sister, took her hand. When she spoke, her voice was a shaky croak. "Is it Mom and Dad?"

"No, not yet. They'll be here soon, Lisa. It's the sheriff. He wants to ask you some questions."

"I don't know." Her fingers curled tight around his. "Don't leave me."

"I'm not going anywhere. You don't have to talk if you don't want to." He pulled his chair closer to the bed and sat. "You don't have to do anything."

"It doesn't matter." She felt the tears burn her throat, but they wouldn't come. "It doesn't matter," she repeated in the same raw whisper.

"Miss MacDonald." Cam stood on the other side of the bed and waited for her to turn her head and focus her good eye on him. "I'm Sheriff Rafferty, from Emmitsboro. If you're feeling up to it, I'd like to ask you some questions. The stenographer will take everything down. We can go as slowly as you like and stop whenever you want."

There was pain, a grinding pain in her leg that played a merciless tug-of-war with the drugs they'd given her. She was afraid it would go on. She was afraid it would stop. Roy was wrong; she already knew she would never dance Dulcinea. "All right."

Cam glanced at Mrs. Lomax, who nodded, her hands poised over the keys. "Why don't you start by telling me as much as you remember about what happened?"

"I don't remember." The fingers in her brother's hand began to flex and flutter.

"Your car broke down?" Cam prompted.

"Yes. I was driving down from Philadelphia to see Roy. I wanted to . . ." But she couldn't speak of the ballet, of the company, of her dreams coming true. "I got lost, made a wrong turn." She sent Roy a wan smile. "Some things don't change."

Afraid he would weep, he squeezed her hand tighter but said nothing.

"I looked at the map and figured out that I was only a couple of miles from Emmits— Emmits—"

"Emmitsboro," Cam supplied.

"Yes. Emmitsboro. I thought I would start walking, maybe I would come to a house. I was walking . . ." She could see herself turning pirouettes in the center of the road.

"What happened then, Miss MacDonald?"

She shook her head. There was a black curtain between herself and her memory. Thin but opaque. "A car." She closed her eyes, shook her head. "A car," she repeated, but couldn't quite grasp it. "There was a woman." She could hear a voice in her head, frightened, shaking. Gentle fingers on her face. "I needed her to help me."

"Why?"

"I was afraid."

"Of what?"

Lisa shook her head again. "I only remember being afraid. She helped me into the car. We have to hurry. We have to get away."

"From what?"

Her eyes filled, and the salt burned the injured one. "I don't know. Was there a woman? Did I imagine it?"

"No, there was a woman." There were times he had to trust his instincts. "Hold on a minute," he said, then went to the door. "Clare?"

Clare whipped around quickly and started toward him. "Are you going to let me see her?"

"I want you to be prepared for two things. One, she's in bad shape. Two, everything that's said in that room is on the record."

"Okay."

"You don't have to go in." He continued to

block her way. "You can get a lawyer before you say anything."

She sent him a long, searching look. "I don't need a lawyer." Impatient, she moved past him, then hesitated when the man in Lisa MacDonald's room turned and looked hard at her.

Roy MacDonald knew. The moment he saw her he knew. This was the woman who had run his sister down. He rose quickly and came to the door.

"What the hell do you think you're doing? I don't want her anywhere near my sister."

"Mr. MacDonald—"

"I want her out." He cut Cam off with a hostile look. "Isn't it enough that she put my sister in that bed?"

"Mr. MacDonald, your sister was already hurt, running out of the woods, before the accident with Miss Kimball. Don't you want to know why?"

Roy reined in his temper, which was three quarters fear, and nodded grimly before he looked at Clare. "You say one thing, just one, to upset her, and I'll throw you out personally."

Sensing Cam's reaction, Clare put a hand on his arm. "You're entitled."

She'd wanted to see Lisa. Had insisted on it. But she hadn't known that crossing that tile floor to the hospital bed would be so difficult. Would be so frightening. The woman in the bed was almost as colorless as the bandages on her face and arms. Her one eye was covered with gauze, and her leg was surrounded by what looked to Clare like an erector set.

"Lisa." Clare pressed her lips together and gripped the bed guard. "I'm Clare Kimball."

As she stared at her, Lisa's breath began to come quickly. She shifted, tried to sit up further. Her brother was there to soothe and support her with pillows. "Don't worry, sweetie, no one's going to hurt you. She's going now."

"No." Lisa groped until her hand closed over Clare's. "I remember you."

"I'm sorry. So sorry." Sobs clogged in Clare's throat as she made a helpless gesture. "I know there's nothing I can do to make this up to you, to make it right. But I want you to know that anything you want, everything you want . . ."

"The lawyers will deal with that," Roy said. "This isn't the time to clear your conscience."

"No, it's not." Clare steadied herself. "Lisa—"

"I remember you," Lisa repeated. "You saved my life." Because her hand began to shake, she gripped Clare's harder. "You were there, on the road. They were going to kill me, those men. In the woods. Did you see them?"

Clare only shook her head.

"How did you get in the woods, Lisa?" Cam asked quietly.

"I don't know. I can't remember. I was run-ning. I lost my light, my flashlight." Her hand jumped. "I hit him with it, and I ran. They'd rape me, I thought. They'd rape me, and so I ran. It was so dark in the woods. I couldn't see. From behind me—I fell. He was on top of me. Oh, God, my leg. My knee. It hurt. Roy . . ."

"Right here, baby."

"It hurt. I smelled blood. *My* blood. I saw his eyes. He was going to kill me. He was singing, and he was going to kill me. He was choking me, and I couldn't breathe. I was dying. But I got away. There were more of them coming, and I ran. My leg hurt so bad. I knew I couldn't run much farther and they'd catch up to me. Find me. There was a light. I had to get to the light. Someone was screaming. Your car." She looked back at Clare.

"My headlights," Clare told her. "I hit you with my car."

"No, I ran to the car. I was afraid you'd drive away, and they were coming after me. So I ran in front of it to stop you. It knocked me down. You got me into your car. You got me away."

"Lisa." Cam kept his voice very low. "Did you see the man who attacked you?"

"Black."

"A black man?"

"No, I don't—I don't think so. He wore

black. Long black robe and a hood. His eyes. I saw his eyes."

"Anything else? The color of his hair, the shape of his face, his voice?"

"Just his eyes. I thought I was looking into hell." She began to weep then, covering her unbandaged eye.

"We'll leave it at that for now." Cam had already overrun the time the doctor had given him. "I'll come back tomorrow. If you remember anything else, anything at all, you just have to call me."

"Please." She tightened her grip on Clare's hand. "I want to thank you. I'll always remember looking up and seeing your face. It's going to help me. Will you come back?"

"Sure."

Clare's legs were watery as she walked out. She paused on the other side of the door to press her hands to her face and steady herself.

"Come on, Slim, let me get you a chair."

"I'm all right. Can you tell me how she is, physically?"

"Her cornea's scratched. They don't think there'll be any permanent damage, but it's a little early to say. Couple of ribs are bruised and her throat. It's going to be painful for her to talk over the next few days."

"Her leg." She noted that he was avoiding speaking of it. "How bad?"

"They don't know."

"Are you going to give me any trouble about seeing her?"

"That'll be for the doctor to say."

"Excuse me." Roy closed the door at his back. "Miss Kimball . . . I owe you an apology."

"No, you don't. I have a brother. Under similar circumstances, I think he'd react the same way. I'd like to leave my number at the nurses' station. You can call whenever she'd like to see me."

"Thank you." He turned to Cam. "I want to know every step of what you're doing, Sheriff. I want to know that whoever did this to my sister is going to pay." He stepped back into the room and closed the door.

"I have some things to tie up." Cam resisted the urge to rub at the headache that pounded in his temple. "Are you going to be all right?"

"I'll be fine."

"I may need to talk to you again. Officially."

She nodded. "You know where to find me. Sheriff." She walked away, leaving him standing alone.

Chapter 17

SALLY SIMMONS PULLED INTO the Amoco station, but she wasn't really interested in a fill-up and oil check. She was interested in Ernie Butts. It was an interest that often left her ashamed and confused. And excited.

In all the weeks that she had gone with Josh, she had only allowed him to touch her above the waist. Though she had let him take her shirt all the way off, even permitted him to close his hot, fumbling mouth over her breasts, she had cut things off each and every time his hands had wandered below the snap of her jeans.

It wasn't that she was a nerd or anything, and she knew that many of the other girls on the cheerleading squad had already done the big deed. But she was romantic, like the novels she read, and had always pictured herself falling wildly and uncontrollably in love with someone exciting, rebellious, and probably unsuitable.

Ernie filled all the requirements.

He was even sort of spookily good-looking and brooding, the way Sally had always pictured Heathcliff, her favorite tragic hero. The fact that she sensed a mean streak in him only added to the mystique. It had been a simple matter to convince herself she was in love with him. And he with her.

Her mother had talked to her very frankly about sex, birth control, responsibilities, consequences. The specters of AIDS, of unwanted pregnancies, of abortion, combined with her fevered desire to go to college and study journalism had been more than enough deterrent to make her keep her head with Josh.

Ernie Butts was a different matter.

When he had taken her into his room, all thoughts of responsibility, the future, her mother's caring and practical words faded.

He'd lit dark candles, had put on music that burned in her blood. He hadn't asked. He hadn't joked or fumbled like Josh. He'd been rough, and that frightened her at first. Then he had done things, things that her mother never told her about. Things that had made her cry out and sob and scream. And hunger.

Even thinking of it now had her wet and throbbing.

She had gone back to him, night after night, with the excuse of a chemistry project she no longer cared about. Mixed with the blind, terrible need she had for him was fear. She knew, as women do, that he was cooling toward her, that he was sometimes thinking of someone else when he buried himself inside her.

She wanted reassurance. Craved it.

She parked at the pump and got out, knowing she looked her best in the skimpy shorts and tank top. Sally was justifiably proud of her legs—the longest and shapeliest in the cheerleading squad. She'd dipped into her mother's hoarded cache of White Shoulders and spent an hour wrapping her hair in Benders to turn it into a mass of spiraling curls.

She felt very mature and sophisticated.

When Ernie strolled out, she leaned against the car door and smiled. "Hi."

"Hi. Need some gas?"

"Yeah." She tried not to be disappointed that he didn't kiss her. After all, he wouldn't even hold her hand in school. "I'm sure glad it's Friday." She watched him fit the nozzle into the tank, looking at his hands, his long, bony fingers, and remembering. "One more week, and we graduate."

"Yeah." Big fucking deal, Ernie thought.

She wiped her damp palms on her shorts. "Mary Alice Wesley's having a big graduation party. She said I could bring a date. Do you want to go?"

He looked at her in that odd, penetrating way he had. "I don't go to parties. How much gas do you want?"

"You might as well fill it." She licked her lips. "Are you going to the parade tomorrow?"

"I got better things to do than stand around and watch a bunch of jerks walk down the street."

She would be marching, too, and it hurt her that he didn't remember. Her grandfather was coming up, all the way from Richmond, with his video camera, to record her last stint as head cheerleader for Emmitsboro High. But she didn't feel like mentioning it now. "We're having a barbecue after, at my house. Just hamburgers and stuff. Maybe you could come over."

He wasn't even interested enough to snicker at the idea of sitting in Sally's backyard, munching burgers and drinking lemonade. "I got to work."

"Oh. Well, it goes on all day, so if you have time . . ." Her voice trailed off as she groped, humiliated. "I've got the car tonight, if you want to take a drive or something when you get off work."

He looked at her again as he pulled the nozzle

from the tank. Looked like Sally's tank was running on empty, too. He grinned. She was hot, all right. She'd probably drop to her knees and suck him off right then and there if he told her to.

"Why don't you come by around nine-thirty and see how I feel?"

"Okay."

"That's fifteen-fifty for the gas."

"Oh. I'll get my purse."

As she bent in the car window, Clare drove in. Ernie forgot Sally existed. "Hey, Ernie."

"Want me to fill it up?"

"Yeah." She smiled, carefully avoiding glancing down at his pendant. "Haven't seen you in a couple of days."

"Been busy."

"I bet." She rested her elbow on the window and pillowed her head. She'd just driven back from the hospital and another visit with Lisa MacDonald. She was tired but no longer guilty. "You must have a lot going, with graduation just a week away."

"Your friends are still here."

"They're going to stay for the parade tomorrow. You going?"

He only shrugged.

"I wouldn't miss it," Clare went on. "I hear they're going to be selling fried dough. I have a real weakness for fried dough."

"Ernie. Here's the money." Sally walked up to stand between them. She tossed back her long fall of hair and shot Clare a cool look. "I guess you've got customers to wait on, so I'll come by later."

"Sure."

Clare watched the girl go back to her car and rev the engine. "So, who was that?"

"Sally? She's nobody."

"Sally Simmons?" With a laugh, Clare reached in her purse for her wallet. "Christ, I used to baby-sit for her. I'd better go home and pull out the rocking chair." She paid him, feeling a lot lighter of heart. Surely there was nothing more normal than a kid with a jealous girlfriend. "See you later, Ernie."

"Yeah. See you." His hand closed over his pentagram as she drove away.

They needed information, desperately. How much did the MacDonald woman know? Whom had she seen? These were questions that burned in whispers from one to the other. Fear was growing, and the one who controlled them knew that fear was a weakness that led to mistakes.

The information would be gathered, as it always was.

There were those who murmured more about

Clare Kimball than about the offering who had escaped. Clare, who had interfered by taking away the woman chosen for sacrifice. Clare, who had ignored or failed to understand the warning left at her door. Clare, who as a child had broken the sanctuary of the circle and seen more than a young girl's mind could bear to remember.

And Clare, who had created an idol of the Master out of metal and fire.

Some argued for her, some against. But the outcome had already been decided.

The time of watching and warning was almost done. The time to act was approaching.

Some men might have tried roses. Cam figured clichés wouldn't work with Clare. It had taken him quite some time before he decided to try anything at all. That was a matter of pride. But there was nothing like depression to make a man kick pride aside and go for broke. It was becoming harder and harder to convince his gut that whatever was going wrong with the town was due to outside influences. Yet every time he drove through it, walked through it, stood on a corner, the idea of Emmitsboro's harboring a murderer, or worse, seemed preposterous.

But Lisa MacDonald was a reality, and his first solid lead. And he had the lab report. Not all of the blood on her clothing had been hers. Lisa was type O. Some of the blood had been type A. Under her nails had been traces of skin—male Caucasian—and some black cotton fiber.

With Bud and Mick he had combed the west end of Dopper's Woods, near the spot where Clare had found Lisa, and the three of them found the trail of blood, the signs of struggle and chase. It would require more lab work, and that meant he would have to ask the mayor for an emergency increase in budget.

He wanted a couple of hours in which he didn't have to think about evidence and procedure, didn't have to remind himself that he would have to go to the hospital again to probe and poke at Lisa MacDonald's memory.

Clare was working. He could see the light on in her garage, though it was barely dusk. He had driven by several times over the last couple of days and seen her there, bent over a worktable. But this time, he pulled into the drive.

Alice was with her, he noted, and they were chattering over the Beatles' "A Day in the Life."

"Go ahead and move around. It works better when you're moving."

"I thought people had to stand real still when they posed for an artist." Though flattered, Alice wished that Clare had asked her to pose in something other than her waitress uniform. "Is this going to be one of those modern things where nobody'll know it's me?"

"I'll know it's you." Patiently, Clare molded and caressed the clay. "I want it very fluid. I'll cast it in bronze when I'm done."

"My mama had Lynette's and my baby shoes bronzed." She glanced over and smiled. "Hi, Cam."

"Getting immortalized, Alice?"

She giggled. "Looks like."

Not trusting her hands, Clare took them from the clay. "Something I can do for you, Sheriff?"

Cool and slick as an ice cube, he thought, and cocked a brow. "Might be." He wrapped a hand around her arm and hauled her up. "Come on."

"What the hell do you think you're doing? I'm working." She shoved a clay-coated hand at him while he pulled her down the drive and Alice watched, wide-eyed. "Look, Rafferty, I don't have to tolerate this . . . police brutality."

"Don't be such a jerk, Slim." He yanked her around to the bed of Bud's pickup. "I brought you a present."

And there was the burl, even more spectacular than she remembered.

"Oh, God." Before he could give her a boost, she was clambering over the side of the truck and into the bed beside it. She stroked the bark reverently. "It's beautiful," she murmured, already imagining what she would find inside.

"It's a hunk of wood," Alice said from the other side of the truck. She was both baffled and disappointed.

"It's a mystery," Clare told her. "And a challenge, and a gift." She laughed at Alice's expression. "Tell you what, in a year or so when it's ready to work with, I'll make you a bowl."

"That'd be nice," Alice said politely, making Clare laugh again. "Wait until Angie gets a look at this." She sat back on her heels, stroking the burl, and sent a cautious look at Cam. He said nothing, just watched her with his hands curved lightly over the side of the truck. "This was a pretty sneaky thing to do, Rafferty."

"Desperate times, Slim. Desperate measures. I figured if I brought this along, you'd have to talk to me." He turned his hands over, palms up. "Want me to help you down?"

"I can manage."

But when she started to swing from the truck, he put his hands around her waist. He set her feet on the ground, turned her to face him, then waited a beat. "You've got mud on your hands."

"Clay." Damn it, this simple contact shouldn't make her so breathless. "You'd better back up, or it'll get all over your shirt."

"You already got it on my shirt." He edged

closer, scenting her the way a fox scented his mate. "How have you been?"

"I've been fine." Her heart was beating fast, entirely too fast, against his.

"I guess I'll be going." Alice cleared her throat. "I said I guess I'll run along."

"No!" Clare swiveled out of Cam's hold. "I mean, I'd like to get another hour in, unless you're too tired."

"I'm not too tired. But in a town this size, it doesn't pay to annoy the sheriff," Alice teased.

"That's some very clear thinking," Cam said and took Clare by the arm. "Why don't we step inside and talk?"

She was trying to decide whether to laugh or swear when a car drove up, horn beeping. "Hey." A man popped up out of the sunroof. "Can a guy get a room here for the night?"

"Blair!" Clare raced down the drive and threw her arms wide as her brother climbed out of the car. He took one look at her hands and backed up.

"God, don't touch me."

"What are you doing here?"

"Figured I'd take in a parade. Cam." He pulled a garment bag out of the backseat before starting up the drive. "You here for a visit, or is Clare under arrest?"

Putting her under house arrest didn't seem like

a bad idea, but Cam grinned and held out a hand. "Just making a delivery." He ran a finger down Blair's lapel. "Nice suit."

"I worked late, didn't want to take time to change. Alice, good to see you."

"Hi, Blair." She cursed herself for blushing. "Clare didn't say you were coming."

"She didn't know. So . . ." He tugged on his sister's hair. "How're you making out?"

Clare glanced at Cam, then away. "I guess you could say it's been an eventful few weeks. Angie and Jean-Paul are here."

"Here?" Blair's brows shot up. "In Emmitsboro?"

"For nearly a week. I think it's starting to grow on them. Listen, why don't I go in and fix some drinks?"

"I'm right behind you."

Cam put a hand on his shoulder before he could follow. "How about giving me a hand with this present first?"

"A present? Sure." He set his bag next to the truck and looked in. "It's a hunk of wood."

"Yep."

"A really big hunk of wood." He scowled over at Cam. "This suit is fifty percent silk."

Cam grinned, let down the tailgate, and jumped up. "Don't be a wuss, Kimball."

"Shit." Blair hauled himself up and put his

back into it. "What's this thing for? It's giving me splinters."

"It's a peace offering. Clare's ticked off at me."

"Oh?"

"It's a long story. Here, I'll go down first. Christ, get a grip, will you?" he muttered when Blair almost dropped the burl on his foot. "You might be interested in the story," he continued as they wrestled the burl out and carted it toward the side yard.

"Rafferty, stories are my life."

"Why don't you come by the office tomorrow after the parade?"

"Okay. Anything I should know now?"

"I'm sleeping with your sister." His eyes met Blair's stunned ones over the round of wood as it bobbled between them. "I figured we should get that out of the way first."

"Jesus, Cam, what do you expect me to say?"

"I guess congratulations might be a bit much. Let's put it here." He grunted as they set the burl beside the garage. He watched Blair dust off his suit. "Want to take a punch at me?"

"I'm thinking about it."

"Before you do, I'd better tell you something I haven't gotten around to telling her yet. I love her."

After a long stare, Blair stuck his hands in his pockets. "Well."

"I always said you had a real gift for words."

Feeling baffled and foolish, Blair ran a hand over his hair. "When the hell did all this happen?"

"Beats me."

Blair blew out a long breath. "Maybe we ought to go in and have that drink."

"You go ahead." Cam glanced toward the house. "She isn't ready for me yet." He started for the truck, pausing when Blair called his name.

"Cam—she's not Sarah Hewitt."

Cam wrenched open the truck door. "Nobody knows that better than I do."

But it was to Sarah that Cam had to go.

Clyde's was more subdued than usual for a Friday night. People were nervous. Wives were demanding that their husbands come home after work, end of the week or not. If a woman wasn't safe walking down the road, how could they know they were safe inside their own homes?

A few of the regulars remained. Less Gladhill hulked over the bar, nursing a brew and the indigestion he'd gotten from meatloaf at Martha's. A fight with his wife had sent him out looking for dinner and consolation elsewhere. Besides, everyone knew that Big Barb Gladhill could take care of herself and ten men besides.

Cam studied the familiar faces as he walked to the bar. He noted not only who was there but who was missing.

"Slow night," he said to Clyde.

The barman scowled. "You come in to point that out, or you want a drink?"

"Give me a Rolling Rock."

Skunk Haggerty was there, in his usual corner, nursing his usual shot of Johnnie Walker while he waited for Reva Williamson to finish her shift at Martha's. The Dopper boy, home from college for the holiday weekend, drank Budweiser and hoped he'd get lucky with Sarah Hewitt.

Nobody played the jukebox, and the clatter of pool balls came clearly from the back room.

Cam drank his beer while Less stood beside him and belched.

"Friggin' onions. Give me another beer, Clyde, goddamn it."

"Walking home?" Cam said easily.

"I can hold my beer."

"Another DUI'll go rough on you."

"Then I'll sonofabitchin' walk." Feeling sorry for himself, he slurped up beer. God knew he got enough nagging from his old lady. Was it any wonder he went out looking for other female companionship when he was married to a damn warhorse? "It's a fucking shame when a man can't enjoy a beer without being hounded."

"Hard day?" Cam sipped, but his eyes had fixed on the bandage wrapped around Less's right hand. "Hurt yourself?"

Grumbling, Less turned the hand from side to side. He'd been expecting the question and had already worked out an answer. "Burned the shit out of my hand on a fucking manifold."

Cam hated knowing he would check in the morning to corroborate Less's story. "That's tough."

Less guzzled down beer, burped, then sighed. "I guess I'm pissed 'cause we were supposed to have a poker game tonight. Roody's old lady won't let him out of her sight after sundown. Skunk's got his balls in an uproar over that skinny-assed Reva. Sam Poffenburger's sleeping in his ex-wife's living room until she calms down, and George Howard is patrolling his yard with his dogs, for Christ's sake. This business has screwed everything up."

"Can't deny that."

"That woman up to the hospital, she tell you anything you can use?"

"If I start discussing a witness, I'll get fired." He drank again. "Best I can tell you is that I've been hitting a lot of walls." He was studying Less like a cop, and they both knew it. "Thing is, when you keep hitting a wall, eventually you knock it down. You want to tell me where you were Tuesday night, between ten-thirty and eleven?"

"What the hell is this?"

"My job." Cam held up his mug. "Sometimes it's easier to do it over a beer than down at the office."

"Shit."

"It's routine, Less. You're not the first one I've talked to, and you won't be the last."

"I don't much like it." He snagged a bowl of peanuts off the bar and began cracking them with his good hand. He wanted to show he was pissed but not scared.

"Neither do I, so why don't you tell me so we can both get back to enjoying our beer?"

"If you got to know, I was over to Charlie Griffith's, working in his garage on his Cavalier." He glanced over his shoulder at Skunk. "I ain't supposed to do side jobs, and if it gets out, I could get canned."

"Nobody said it had to get out. I'll have to check with Charlie, though."

"Go right the fuck ahead. Now if you don't mind, Sheriff, I'd like to drink in peace."

Cam took his half-full mug and wandered toward the back room. Cops lost friends—he knew it too well. It was better to lose them this way than by a bullet.

Sarah was shooting pool with Davey Reeder,

a lanky, bucktoothed carpenter with good hands and a weak brain. Over the years Davey had joined Cam and Blair and some of the others on their jaunts into the woods. He was older by a couple of years and hadn't graduated until he was twenty. He'd knocked up one of the Lawrence girls and been married and divorced by the time he was twenty-two.

Cam was aware that Davey was one of Sarah's regular customers. He wasn't sure which of them he felt more sorry for.

"Hey, Davey."

"Hey." He smiled his beaver smile and kissed the three ball into the side pocket. "Want to play for beers?"

"Last time we did that, you got drunk and I got poor."

Davey whooped in the girlish way he had, then speared the four and five into opposing pockets. "I could spot you."

"I'll pass."

Sarah smiled and ran her hand deliberately, seductively, up and down her cue. "Got another game in mind?"

"Shit on Sunday." Davey missed his next shot. "You're up, Sarah."

"It's gloomy in here without the juke." Cam pulled some bills from his pocket. "Why don't you get some change, Davey, pick us out some tunes? Get another beer for yourself while you're at it."

"Sure." He sauntered out.

"Well . . ." Sarah leaned, long and slow, over the table, sighted in, and shot. "It's nice to know you'd spend five bucks to be alone with me." She tossed her hair back, tilted her head, then ran her tongue along her top lip. "Wanna play?"

"Straight questions, Sarah. And I want straight answers."

"Ooh, that official talk makes me hot."

"Cut it out." He grabbed her arm and jerked her upright. "What the hell did you mean the other day about me not knowing this town?"

She walked her fingers up the front of his shirt. "You were away a long time, baby. Things change."

"You're bullshitting me, Sarah. It didn't have anything to do with me being away."

When she shrugged and started to turn, he pulled her back.

Her eyes lit. "Go ahead. I like it rough. Remember?"

"You threw out that bone about Parker. What do you know about why he left?"

She slid her leg intimately between his. "What should I know?"

"Give me an answer, Sarah. Things are happening here that shouldn't be."

"Your stepfather gets himself beat to death. Your girlfriend runs a woman down. What's it to me?"

"Answers, damn it. Stick with Parker. Why did he leave?"

"Because he got sick of the town, I guess. How should I know?"

"You do know, and you were mad enough to almost tell me. Did he used to visit you upstairs?" He caught her hair and held her still. "Did he come up the back stairs for twenty a pop?"

"What if he did?" She shoved Cam away. "What's it to you who I fuck?"

"Did he talk to you—after he'd rolled his fat body off yours, did he tell you things?"

"Maybe." She pulled out a cigarette. When she struck a match, her hands were shaking. "Men tell women like me all kinds of things— like they'd tell a doctor or a priest." She laughed and blew out smoke. "Something *you* want to . . . tell me?"

"After almost sixty years in this town, more than twenty-five as sheriff, he packs up and leaves. Why?"

"Because the bitch he was married to wanted to move to Fort Lauderdale."

"He isn't in Fort Lauderdale. He isn't anywhere that I can find."

"Parker's old news." She picked up Cam's beer

and drank deeply. "Don't you have enough to worry about? You still got a murder on your hands, don't you? Or are you letting that slide?"

"What do you know?" he asked softly. "Who told you things he shouldn't have told you up-stairs in that bed?"

"I know all kinds of things." She set the beer down again. "I know who has trouble at the bank, who cheats the IRS, and whose wife won't do it more than once a week." She pulled on the cigarette, exhaled. "And I know that you're pissing a lot of people off by asking ques-tions when everybody thinks you should be looking for psychopaths under rocks in the woods. There's nothing I can tell you, Cam."

"Nothing you will tell me."

"I might have, once." She picked up the cue and gave him a playful poke. "I might have done a lot for you once. Could've made things easy for you. But a woman like me looks out for herself, and I figure you're on your way out. A murder, an attack, slaughtered cattle, all since you've been back." Her eyes were sly with se-crets. "Maybe somebody ought to ask you some questions."

He leaned close. "Figure this. If you know something you shouldn't, I'm your best chance."

"*I'm* my best chance," she corrected. "I always have been." She turned her back on him and leaned over the table again. She spared him one last glance. "I heard your mama was packing up, too. I wonder why?" Sarah shot the cue ball into the pack and scattered balls.

By the light of her bedside lamp, Clare leafed through her father's books. It wasn't the first time. Over the last few nights, she had read them again and again, trying to understand the connection they had with the father she had known and adored. Trying to understand at all.

She'd found six of them, in the boxes upstairs. Six that dealt with what Jean-Paul had called the left-hand path. A half-dozen books, most of them dog-eared, that touted, even celebrated, the freedoms of Satanism.

What frightened her most was that they were not the screaming ravings of uneducated lunatics. They were slickly, somehow persuasively written and published by reputable houses. As an artist she viewed freedom of expression the same way she did breathing: No soul could exist without it. And yet each time she opened a volume her skin felt soiled. Each time she read, she suffered. Yet she continued to read, as her father must have, in secret, in shame, and in sorrow.

He had been searching, she thought. Jack Kimball had been an open-minded man thirsty for knowledge, always ready to question the status quo. Perhaps he had developed an interest in the workings of Satanic cults in the same way he had honed his interest in politics, in art, in horticulture.

She sat smoking, then easing her raw throat with tepid tap water, wishing she could convince her heart as easily as she convinced her head.

He'd been a man who enjoyed being fascinated and challenged, being shown a different route. A rebel, she thought with a small smile, determined to break the strict mold in which his parents had struggled to enclose him. Raised by devout Catholics, he had often referred to his parents as Saint-Mom-and-Dad, as if they had been one holy entity.

Often he'd told Blair and her stories about rising at dawn to make it to mass before school every day during Lent—and dozing through the sermon until his mother would jab him with an elbow. He'd had a neverending supply of Catholic-school anecdotes, some hilarious, others a little scary. He'd told them how hurt and disappointed his parents had been when he refused to enter the priesthood. He had laughed when he related the way his mother had lit candle after candle, asking the Virgin to intercede so that her son would recognize his calling. But when he laughed, the bitterness had always come through.

And she had overheard other stories—ones not for her ears. About how his parents had come to detest each other, how they had lived under the same roof, shared the same bed, year after year, without love, often using him as a kind of seesaw on which they weighed their bitter unhappiness. But there was no divorce in the eyes of the church, and those were the only eyes through which his parents could see.

"Better to live in misery than in sin," he'd recalled in disgust. "Christ, what hypocrites they were."

By the time he married, Jack Kimball had turned completely away from the church.

Only to turn back, Clare thought now, almost as fanatically as his parents, some ten years later. And a few years after, he had picked up a bottle along with his rosary.

Why?

Was the answer somewhere in the books she had scattered over her bed?

She didn't want to believe that. Didn't think she could face it. The father she had known had been solid, ambitious, delightful. How could a man who fretted over a sick rosebush have connected himself with a sect that advocated the sacrificing of animals, the shedding of innocent blood?

It was inconceivable.

And yet, there was the dream, the dream that

had haunted her since childhood. She had only to close her eyes to see her father, glassy-eyed and naked, dancing around a fire pit with blood dripping from his fingers.

It was symbolic, she told herself and hastily began to pile up books. Dr. Janowski had said—over and over—that she had never accepted her father's death. The dream was simply a reminder of the horror, the grief, the terror of losing him.

But when she had switched off the light and lay sleepless in the dark, she knew that the dream had come to her long before her father died.

Chapter 18

$\mathcal{B}$Y TEN, EMMITSBORO WAS PACKED. Sidewalks teemed with people, children racing away from harried parents, teenagers hoping to be seen by other teenagers, concessionaires hawking lemonade, hot dogs, and balloons.

The older, or the wiser, of the crowd had their lawn chairs set up beside the curb, coolers of soft drinks close by. Since the road was closed off from Dog Run to Mousetown, people hiked in from their cars.

Those fortunate enough to live along Main Street—or to know someone who did—sat on their freshly painted porches, under the shade of awnings. They sipped cold drinks from cans, nibbled chips, and talked gleefully about their neighbors or about parades gone by.

In backyards picnics were already set—wooden tables covered with colorful paper cloths that fluttered in the light breeze. Grills had been scrubbed down, and beer and watermelon were chilling.

Emmitsboro High had a new young band director. The old-timers looked forward to criticizing. It was a small, human pleasure.

There was plenty of gossip. Talk about Biff Stokey's murder had been relegated to second place by the attack on the woman from Pennsylvania. Farmers considered the butchering of Dopper's cattle the number one topic of the day.

But with a communal sigh of relief, most of the townspeople had resolved to put tensions aside and settled in to celebrate.

The Hagerstown television station had sent a crew. Men sucked in their guts, and women patted their hair as the camera panned the crowd.

There were twelve who stood among the crowd, hiding behind the colorful banners and laughter to celebrate their own secret rite. Their eyes might meet; the sign would be given. Discontent might simmer among them, but for today the town was theirs, even though the town didn't know it.

The black armbands each wore were not an homage to the dead but a symbol of their alliance with the Dark Lord. Their Memorial Day celebration would begin here, among the gleaming brass and twirling batons, and end on another night, very soon, in the secret circle deep in the woods.

Someone would die, and the secret that had been held among the chosen few would continue to crouch in the darkness.

In the grandstand Min Atherton preened. She enjoyed sitting up there, looking down on friends and enemies. She'd bought a brand-new cotton dress for the occasion and thought the big purple irises spread across her breasts and hips gave her a girlish look. She was a bit sorry she'd belted it so tight—particularly after indulging in two plates of fried dough—but her mother had always told her beauty must suffer.

Her hair had been newly washed and set and sprayed so liberally it wouldn't have moved in a tornado, much less the light spring breeze. It sat like a lacquer helmet atop her wide face.

Nearby, her husband glad-handed with members of the town council. Min was pleased that he looked so grave and handsome in his buff-colored suit. He'd argued a bit about the red tie she'd chosen, but she convinced him it would look just right on TV. As always he had deferred to her.

Min considered herself the perfect politician's wife. The woman behind the man. And she enjoyed the power a woman could wield in secret. She fed him information she gleaned in the beauty parlor, in the market, over the backyard fence, and during bake sales. Often he would pat her hand and tell her she was better informed than the CIA.

She didn't need listening devices or hidden cameras. She had a nose for gossip the way a hound had a nose for blood. Min could masticate on a juicy morsel for days before swallowing it.

It was, after all, her right as the wife of the mayor to know all there was to know.

She scanned the noisy crowd with her greedy eyes.

There was Sue Ann Reeder—now Bowers, six months gone and only four months married. That marriage wouldn't last any longer than her first one had.

Peggy Knight was buying her three brats soda pop and cotton candy. Teeth would rot out for sure.

Mitzi Hawbaker had her youngest on her hip and was kissing her husband—tongue kissing, Min thought in disgust—right out on the street.

She huffed and turned away, not only from the open display of spit swapping but also from the children. All the children. Watching them made her feel empty inside, despite the two helpings of fried dough.

It wasn't fair—it wasn't right—that all those young sluts dropped babies the way a she-cat dropped kittens, year after year. And that she should have a sick and empty womb.

She hated them, all of them, for their careless fertility.

"Want a cold drink before it starts, Min?"

Atherton put a hand on his wife's shoulder. Min patted it—which was all the affection a wife need show in public—and smiled at him. "That'd be fine."

He loved her, she thought, as he hurried off to fetch the drink. And he was all the family she needed.

With a little help from one of the councilmen, Gladys Finch, in her role as president of the historical society, climbed up on the grandstand in her sensible shoes. "Sure is a nice day for it. Remember how it rained last year?"

"It's a little warm."

Gladys nodded but felt delightfully cool in her blue-striped seersucker. "Our band has a good chance of winning this year."

"Humph." Min didn't approve of the new director's notion of having the band play show tunes instead of Sousa. She spotted the Cramptons and waved, regally, she thought. "Lucy Crampton's looking peaked."

"New diet," Gladys said and irked Min because Min hadn't heard about it first.

"There's Sarah Hewitt. Would you look at that?" She put a white-gloved hand to her mouth—not in shock, but to disguise the words. "High heels and a skirt that barely covers her privates. I don't know how her poor mother holds her head up."

"Mary's done her best with the girl."

"Should have taken a strap to her a time or two— Why, that's Blair Kimball."

"So it is. My, doesn't he look nice?"

"Guess he came back because of his sister's trouble. Now that's a disgrace," she continued before Gladys could comment. "Bringing those people right into town."

"What people?" Gladys looked and saw the LeBeaus walking with Clare. "Oh now, Min."

"I tell you it's unnatural. You can spout off all you like, Gladys Finch, but if one of your chicks had taken it in their head to marry one, you'd have sung a different tune. Why, I remember the scandal when the Poffenburger boy brought that Vietnam woman back after the war."

"Their oldest girl's an A student," Gladys said dryly.

"And no better than she has to be, I'm sure." Min sniffed, then turned when her husband mounted the grandstand again. "Why now, thank you, James. I was just pointing Blair Kimball out to Gladys. Isn't it nice that he came up for the parade?"

"Yes, indeed. How are you this morning, Gladys?"

"Fit as a fiddle. Heard you have a big town meeting on Wednesday. People are mighty concerned now that the landfill's charging twenty-five dollars for a permit sticker. No doubt Poffenburger Refuse'll raise the rates, and that'll bump up taxes."

"The council and I are looking for solutions." He took out his glasses, polished them. "Better get the speech-making over with so these people can have their parade."

He approached the mike, tapping on it to see if it was on, clearing his throat. There was a scream of feedback that had the crowd laughing, then quieting down to listen.

He spoke about the valiant dead, the scourge of war, and the honor of God and country. There were those in the crowd who smiled secretly amid the cheers and applause. For the chosen dead, they thought, for the scourge of vengeance, for the honor of the Master.

Power sang in the air. Soon, there would be fresh blood.

Ernie didn't listen at all. He got enough of Mr. Atherton in school. Instead, he worked his way through the crowd, looking for Clare.

He was watched—as he had been watched, carefully, consistently over the last days. It had been agreed. And it had been written. His soul was ready for the taking.

"It starts down by the elementary school,"

Clare was explaining to her friends. "Believe me, right about now, it's utter chaos down there. Kids have lost their gloves or their boots. Some are throwing up in the bushes."

"Sounds delightful," Angie commented.

"Shut up, you jaded New Yorker," Clare said and swung an arm around her shoulder. "Word is the high school band has a shot at top honors this year."

"What about the majorettes?" Angie's husband asked.

"Dozens of them, Jean-Paul," Blair assured him. "A veritable bevy of high-stepping, nubile beauties. Pom-pom girls, too."

"Ah."

"Clare was almost a pom-pom girl."

"Blair, do you want to die?"

"Truly?" Eyes glinting, Jean-Paul studied her. "But *ma chère amie*, you never told me."

"That's because when she tried out, she tripped over her shoelaces."

"Betty Mesner untied them." Clare pouted, remembering. "You dumped her, and she took it out on me."

"Yeah." Blair grinned. "Those were the days. Why, hello, Annie."

Crazy Annie beamed. Parade day was her favorite day of the year, better even than Christmas or Easter. Already she'd had a grape snow cone. Her hands were purple and sticky from it.

"I know you," she said to Blair.

"Sure you do. I'm Blair Kimball."

"I know you," she repeated. "You used to play baseball down at the field. I would watch. I know you, too," she said to Clare.

"It's nice to see you, Annie. Some of the roses are blooming," she said, remembering how her father had often given Annie a flower.

"I like roses the best." She stared at Clare and saw Jack Kimball in her eyes, in the easy smile. "I'm sorry your daddy's dead," she said politely, as though it had just happened.

"Thank you."

Annie smiled, pleased she'd remembered to do the right thing. Then she looked at Angie. "I know you, too. You're the black woman who's living with Clare."

"This is my friend Angie and her husband, Jean-Paul. They live in New York."

"In New York?" Annie studied them with more interest. "Do you know Cliff Huxtable? He's black, too, and he lives in New York. I see him on TV."

"No." Angie's lips curved. "I haven't met him."

"You can watch him on the TV. He wears pretty sweaters. I like pretty things." She eyed Angie's gold panther link necklace. "Where did you find that?"

"I, ah . . ." A little uneasy, Angie lifted her hand to the necklace. "In New York."

"I find pretty things, right here." She stuck out her arm, jangling with bracelets. To rescue her friend, Clare took Annie's sticky hand and admired her jewelry.

"These are very nice." Curious, she ran a finger over the silver bracelet on which CARLY was engraved.

"That's my favorite." She beamed. "A-N-N-I-E. I wear it every day."

"It's lovely." But Clare frowned as some vague memory nearly surfaced.

"Okay, heads up," Blair announced. "Here comes the Farm Queen."

"I want to see!" Annie scrambled away through the crowd to get a closer view, and Clare lost the memory in the cheers from the sidewalks.

They watched the slow-moving caravan of convertibles. Listened to the wild cheers. The crowd shifted, rose on toes, hunched down. Young children were hoisted on shoulders. There was a scent of hot dogs grilling, of sweet, sugary drinks, of baby powder. In the distance Clare heard the first rumble of brass and drums. Her eyes filled.

Girls in glittery leotards turned handsprings, twisted into back bends, tossed silver batons high. If some bounced on the asphalt, the crowd still cheered. Behind them, between them, high-stepping through the town square, came the bands.

The sun glinted off brass and stunned the eyes. Trumpets, tubas, trombones. It glittered on the silver of flutes and piccolos. Beneath the roar of music was the click, click, click of heels on the roadbed. Drums added their magical rat-a-tat-tat.

Jean-Paul nearly swooned when a trio of girls in short, shiny skirts executed a snappy routine with white parade rifles.

The young and the hopeful marched by, in front of their peers, their parents, their grand-parents, their teachers, as the young had marched by for generations. They were the life-blood of the town. The old watched them, knowing.

Angie slipped an arm around her husband's waist. She'd expected to be bored, not touched. But she was touched. To her surprise, her blood was pumping to the rhythm of horns and drums. When she watched the Silver Star Junior Majorettes file by, some of them hardly bigger than their batons, her throat felt tight.

At that moment it didn't matter that she was an outsider. Clare had been right, she thought. It was a good parade. It was a good town. She turned to speak to her friend, then stopped when she saw Ernie standing just behind Clare.

He was toying with the pendant he wore. And there was something in his eyes, Angie thought, something too adult and very disturbing. She had a wild and foolish thought, that he would smile and show fangs just before he sank them into Clare's neck.

Instinctively, Angie put an arm around Clare and drew her forward a few inches. The crowd roared as the Emmitsboro High School Band strutted by, blaring out the theme from an Indiana Jones movie. Ernie glanced up. His eyes fixed on Angie. And he smiled. Though she saw only white, even teeth, the sensation of evil remained.

It took Cam and both deputies to deal with traffic control after the parade had ended. Bud Hewitt was at the south side of town, enthusiastically using a whistle and snappy hand signals. When the traffic thinned enough to muddle through on its own, Cam left the intersection. He'd just stepped onto the sidewalk when he heard the sound of applause.

"Nice job, Officer." Blair grinned at him. "You know, I have a hard time connecting the guy who chained Parker's rear axle to a telephone pole with this tin star."

"Does the brass at the *Post* know you once set a skunk loose in the girls' locker room, then stood outside with a Polaroid?"

"Sure. I put it on my resumé. Want to grab a cup of coffee at Martha's?"

"Let's live dangerously and try the poison at the office." Grinning at Blair, he started to walk. "So, did Clare say anything about me?"

"Not unless you count her asking me if you'd said anything about her."

"What did you tell her?"

"Christ, this feels like high school."

Cam opened his office door. "You're telling me." He went directly to the coffee machine and turned on the warming plate under the sludge already in the pot.

Blair eyed it with trepidation. "Can I have a tetanus shot first?"

"Pussy," Cam said mildly and rounded up two mugs.

"I heard about Biff." Blair waited while Cam lighted a cigarette. "Ugly business."

"He led an ugly life." When Blair only lifted a brow, Cam shrugged. "I don't have to like him to find who killed him. It's a job. My mother sold the farm," he added. He hadn't been able to tell anyone how much that hurt. The thing was, he wouldn't have to say it to Blair. Blair would know. "She's moving south as soon as the deal closes. I went by a couple days ago. She stood in the doorway. She wouldn't even let me in the goddamn house."

"I'm sorry, Cam."

"You know, I told myself I was coming back here, back to town to look out for her. It was mostly a lie, but not all the way. Guess I wasted my time."

"You get itchy feet here, D.C.P.D. would take you back in a heartbeat."

"I can't go back." He glanced down at the coffeepot. "This shit ought to be sterilized by now. Want some chemicals?" He lifted a jar of powdered milk.

"Sure, load it up." Blair wandered to the bulletin board, where pictures of felons at large were mixed with announcements for town meetings and a poster showing the Heimlich maneuver. "What can you tell me about Clare's accident?"

"That Lisa MacDonald was damn lucky Slim was driving down that road at that time." He handed Blair the coffee, then sat. Briefly, concisely, in the way of cops and journalists, he outlined what he knew.

By the time Cam finished, Blair had downed half the coffee without tasting it. "Jesus, if someone had attacked the woman, Clare was right there. If she hadn't gotten the woman in the car so quickly and driven away, they both could have been . . ."

"I've thought of it." All too often and all too clearly. "I'm just glad the idea hasn't occurred to her. The town's locking up and loading up. My main concern now is that some asshole is going to shoot his neighbor if he steps off the porch to piss in the bushes."

"And the woman didn't see the guy's face?"

"Not that she remembers."

"You don't figure it was a local?"

"I've got to figure it was a local." He drank some coffee, winced, then filled Blair in on everything that had happened since he discovered the disturbed grave the month before.

This time Blair got up and refilled his mug himself. "Things like this don't happen in a town like Emmitsboro."

"Not unless something triggers it." He sipped slowly now, watching Blair. "When I was on the force in D.C., we came across some dogs. Three big black Dobermans. They'd been mutilated in just about the same way as Dopper's cattle. We found a few other things there, though. Black candle wax, pentagrams painted on the trees. All in this nine-foot circle."

"Satanism?" Blair would have laughed, but Cam wasn't smiling. Slowly, he took his seat again. "Not here, Cam. That's really reaching."

"Did you know graveyard dirt's used in Satanic rites? I looked it up. It's even better if it's from the grave of a child. Nothing else was disturbed in that cemetery. And somebody had hauled the dirt away. Why?"

"Kids on a dare." But his reporter's instincts were humming.

"Maybe. It wasn't kids on a dare who clubbed Biff to death. And it wasn't kids on a dare who took a knife to those calves. The hearts were gone, Blair. Whoever did it took the hearts with him."

"Good Christ." He set the mug aside. "Have you told anyone else what you're working on?"

"No, mostly I'm just thinking out loud." Cam leaned forward. "But I've got to take into consideration that Lisa MacDonald says the guy who attacked her was chanting. She'd said singing before, but when I asked her about it again, she changed it to chanting. She said it sounded like Latin. You've got contacts on the paper, Blair, people who know a lot more about this cult business than I can dig up in a library."

"I'll see what I can find out." Blair rose, trying to pace off his unease. If they had been anywhere else but Emmitsboro, he would have bought into Cam's theory quickly. As a reporter he knew how pervasive cults had become, especially in cities and college towns. "You figure kids have experimented and gotten in too deep?"

"I can't say. I do know that drugs usually go hand in hand with this kind of thing, but other than a few kids rolling joints, we don't see much in this part of the county. There was more of that going on when we were in high school."

"Maybe you've got a renegade. One person who's wacked himself out reading Crowley or listening to Black Sabbath."

"It took more than one person to do what was done to Biff." He ground out a cigarette. "I don't believe for one minute that a couple of kids listening to black metal and doing a few chants psyched themselves up to do all this. In the books they're called dabblers because that's just what they do. What's happening here isn't dabbling."

"And I thought I'd come home for a nice relaxing weekend."

"Sorry. Listen, I'd appreciate it if you wouldn't mention any of this to Clare."

"Any reason?"

"Officially she's my only witness in the Mac-Donald case, and I don't want to influence her memory. Personally, I don't want her any more upset than she already is."

Blair tapped a finger against the coffee mug, considering. "She spent twenty minutes this morning examining every inch of that burl."

Cam's eyes cleared, and he smiled. "Oh, yeah?"

"And to think of the money I've wasted on flowers and jewelry whenever I've ticked a woman off."

"You never had my charm, Kimball. How about putting in a good word for me?"

"I never knew you to need anybody to do your talking."

"It was never this important before."

Blair couldn't come up with a joke and rose, jiggling change in his pockets. "You're really serious about her?"

"Deadly." He rubbed a hand over his heart. "Christ, it *feels* deadly."

"You know, that ex-husband of hers was a jerk. He wanted her to give swanky dinner parties and learn to decorate."

"I hate him already." He could ask Blair what he hadn't felt comfortable asking Clare. "Why'd she marry him?"

"Because she convinced herself she was in love and it was time to start a family. Turned out he wasn't interested in a family anyway. Before it was done, he'd convinced her everything that had gone wrong was her fault. She bought it, too. And she's still a little raw."

"I figured that out." Cam nearly smiled. "You want to ask me if my intentions are honorable?"

"Fuck you, Rafferty." He held up a hand quickly. "Don't say you'd rather fuck my sister."

"Right now I'd settle for sitting down and having a rational conversation with her."

Blair considered for a minute. "When do you get off duty?"

"In a town this size, you never get off duty. There's no telling when I'll have to chase off some kid skateboarding down Main or break up a fight over a checkers game in the park."

"Old Fogarty and McGrath still at it?"

"Every week."

"You can get to the park for round three just as quickly from our place. Why don't you give me a lift home, maybe hang around for some barbecued chicken?"

"That's neighborly of you," Cam said and grinned.

She wasn't upset that he was there, Clare thought. She glanced over at the echoing clank of metal on metal and noted that Cam had just missed tossing a ringer.

She wasn't angry with him. Not really. All she was trying to do was distance herself a bit, give herself some perspective. She'd let things get out of hand much too quickly as far as Cam was concerned. The proof was the way they'd grated on each other since the accident.

Rob had always said she played dirty in a fight, tossing out illogical arguments and past grudges or retreating into frigid silence. Of course, the arguments had seemed perfectly logical to her, and . . .

She was doing it again, Clare thought, and

poked viciously at the grilling chicken with her barbecue fork. Rob was old business, and if she didn't stop carrying around that particular baggage, she'd be right back on Janowski's couch.

If that wasn't enough to straighten her out, nothing was.

Cam was new business, she decided. She hadn't liked the fact that he'd questioned her like a cop one minute, then tried to bundle her off into a safe corner like a concerned lover the next. And she would tell him so. Eventually.

In the meantime, she'd just wanted some room to reevaluate. Then he'd shown up. First with the burl that he'd damn well known would weaken her. Then today, waltzing into the backyard with Blair. Showing off his wonderful body in snug jeans and a shirt rolled up over his tanned and muscled arms.

She poked at the chicken, turned it, and forced herself not to look up when she heard the shouts and masculine laughter, the ringing of horseshoes.

"He's got terrific buns," Angie commented and offered Clare a glass of the wine she'd just poured.

"I've *always* admired Jean-Paul's butt."

"Not his. Though God knows it's fine." She sniffed at the sizzling chicken. "This is a talent you've hidden well, girl."

"It's hard to barbecue in the loft."

"This from a woman who welds in her living room. Are you going to let him get away?"

"You're full of non sequiturs today, Angie."

"Are you?"

"I'm just taking time out to think." She glanced up and smiled. "Look, poor Bud is making cow's eyes at Alice, and Alice is making them at Blair."

"Who's your money on?"

"Bud. He's slow but steady. Blair will never be anything but a visitor in Emmitsboro."

"How about you?"

Clare said nothing for a moment, only slathered sauce on the browning chicken. She could smell lilacs from the big gnarled tree as the light breeze loosened some of the petals and had them drifting like snow. Sun and shadow played over the patio. The music crooning from the radio was old tunes from those sweet and happy years before she had had to make decisions or think of futures.

"Did you see the sculpture I was working on last night?"

"The brass piece. It made me think of a woman stretched out on an altar about to be sacrificed."

"It's almost scary how easy it is to work here. How compelled I am to pull it out of my head. I always thought I was made for New York."

She looked at her friend. "Now, I'm not so sure."

"Because of the work or because of those grade-A buns over there?"

"I guess I'll have to figure that out."

"Sonofabitch." Blair jogged over to snag a beer out of the cooler. "Jean-Paul must think we're playing bocce. When do we eat? I'm tired of being humiliated by a couple of hick cops."

"I'll let you know once you guys have shucked that corn."

They complained, but they did it. When everyone settled down at the old picnic table on the terrace to a meal of grilled chicken and corn, with Alice's potato salad and chilled French wine, the mood was easy. There was no talk of murder investigations, but a rehash of horseshoe games.

Along the edging stones, the early roses bloomed, fronted by the impatiens Clare had planted. There was the scent of lilacs and spicy sauce. Bud had positioned himself beside Alice and was making her laugh so often that her gaze hardly ever drifted toward Blair. Afternoon melded into the golden, fragrant, endless evening that is exclusive to spring.

Cam outlined his strategy, maneuvering Alice into his place in the horseshoe tournament and slipping into the kitchen behind Clare.

"Great chicken, Slim."

"Thanks." She kept her head in the refrigerator, rearranging plates of leftovers. He took her arm and pulled her out.

"Not that I wasn't enjoying the view, but I like to look at your face when I talk to you."

"Potato salad goes rancid fast."

"You're awful pretty when you're domestic. Hold it." He slapped his hands on the refrigerator, caging her in before she could slip away.

"Look, Cam, I have company."

"And they're having a hell of a time on their own."

Jean-Paul let out a yell of triumph that was followed by a heated but jovial argument. The raised voices came clearly through the kitchen windows.

"See?"

"You're boxing me in, Rafferty."

"Looks that way. Okay, I'd be more than willing to apologize, if you'd just tell me what I'm supposed to be sorry for."

"Nothing." She dragged a hand through her hair. "There's nothing."

"Don't wimp out on me now, Slim."

"I don't want to argue with you."

"Okay then." He dipped his head, but she slammed a hand against his chest before he could kiss her.

"That's not the answer."

"Seemed like a damn good one to me." He did his best to adjust both libido and ego. "Give me yours, then."

"You acted like a cop." She hooked her thumbs in her pockets. "Interrogating me, taking your damn blood tests, and filing your reports. Then you turned right around and acted like a concerned lover, holding my hand and bringing me tea."

"Well, I guess we've got a real problem, because I'm both." He put a hand firmly under her chin. "And I intend to go on being both."

Along with the frisson of excitement came annoyance. "That's another thing. What you intend. I feel as though this whole relationship has evolved as you intended. Will you move?"

He shifted. After all, she was talking to him now, and he didn't think she was going to stop until she'd spit it all out. "I have to plead guilty on that one. I wanted to take you to bed, and I did. I wanted you to want me, and you do."

It was hard to argue with basic facts. "So, now you're going to be reasonable."

He smiled, brushing a fingertip over her bangs. "Figured it wouldn't hurt to give it a shot. If I don't get my hands on you again soon, I'm going to go crazy."

She began rummaging through drawers for a loose cigarette. "I don't like getting swept off my feet. It makes me nervous."

"How about that? And here I thought it was the other way around."

She looked up then, and saw something in his eyes. Her hands froze as the bubble of panic worked its way toward her throat. "Don't say it," she managed. "Don't. I'm not ready to hear it."

He rocked back on his heels, struggling for patience. "If telling you how I feel about you is going to make you bolt for the door, I'll wait."

She didn't move away when he walked toward her, when he took her hand and drew her close. With a sigh, she settled into his arms, her cheek against his, her eyes closed.

"That feels a lot better," he murmured.

"Yes. Yes, it does."

"Listen. Remember this one?"

From the radio outside she heard the slow, shuffling music. " 'Under the Boardwalk.' The Drifters."

"Summer's almost here." He swayed her into a dance, and they were both reminded of the first time they had made love, there in that same room. "I've missed you, Slim."

"I've missed you, too." Content to let him lead, she twined her arms around his neck. He nipped lightly at her earlobe and made her shudder. Maybe it could be simple, she thought. If she would just let it. "I heard you were playing pool with Sarah Hewitt last night, and I imagined how it would feel to cut her eyes out with my metal snips."

Brows lifted, he drew back to study her face. She wore a very small, very smug smile. "You're a dangerous woman with a revolting imagination."

"You bet. I'd imagined using my snips somewhere else too, on an entirely different part of your anatomy. You wouldn't have liked it."

He pulled her back. "Do you know the penalty for threatening an officer?"

"Nope."

"Come home with me, and I'll show you."

Chapter 19

*T*HE STRONG MOONLIGHT streamed over the bed. Cold and silver, it bathed their heated bodies. They hadn't tumbled right into sex but had shared another dance, gliding slowly, silently together in the moonglow. He'd liked the way she had stood on tiptoe so that their eyes and mouths lined up. The way she slid her body against his and smiled. Or laughed when he spun her out and pulled her back, in the teasingly sexual way dances were meant for.

Still linked, they had swayed from the deck to the bedroom, the music playing.

Undressing lazily, kissing long and deep, touching gently. Patient now, with the night around them and ahead of them. Sighs and whispers to add to the music.

Their loving had been a continuation of the dance.

Smooth, sinuous rhythms.

Step, counterstep.

A bold, sensuous beat.

Turns.

Bodies brushing, parting, teasing.

Break.

Hands clasping.

That final sighing note.

Now, though the dance was over, Clare listened to the music that vibrated through the air and through her blood. "I should have threatened you several days ago."

"I wish you had."

"I was scared."

"I know. Me, too."

The mattress gave, the sheets whispered as she shifted to look down at him. And smiled. "But I'm feeling much better now."

"Yeah?" He tugged her hair to bring her mouth close enough to kiss. "Me, too."

"I like your face." Eyes narrowed, she traced a fingertip over his jawline, up to his cheekbones, along his nose and down to his mouth. "I'd really like to sculpt your face."

He only laughed and bit down gently on her finger.

"I mean it. It's a good face. Very strong bones. How about it?"

Vaguely embarrassed, he shrugged. "I don't know."

"And your hands," she said, more to herself than him as she turned them over, examining the palms, the ridges of callus, the length of the fingers. "Nothing delicate here," she mused. "They're all business."

"You ought to know."

She chuckled but shook her head. "From an artist's viewpoint, peasant! Then there's the rest of you. You've got a terrific body. Elegantly masculine. Lean through the hips, good shoulders, nicely defined pecs, tight abdominals, excellent thighs and calves."

Embarrassment became acute. "Come on, Clare."

"I was really considering asking you to pose nude, before we became so . . . intimately acquainted."

"Nude?" With a half laugh, he put his hands on her shoulders and drew her back. The rest of the laugh didn't surface because he could see she was dead serious. "No way am I posing naked."

"Nude," she corrected. "Naked's for sex and showers, nude's for art."

"I'm not posing naked or nude."

"Why not?" Warming to the idea, she scooted up, straddling him. Ah, yes, she thought, truly excellent abs. "I've already seen you naked, from a variety of angles. Nude's entirely impersonal."

"Nude's entirely undressed."

"You'd look great in copper, Cam."

"Not even for you."

She only smiled. "Okay, I'll just do the sketches from memory. Maybe I should just measure . . ." She slid a hand down, between their bodies.

"Cut it out."

She collapsed with laughter. "Who would have thought Cameron Rafferty, bad boy turned lawman, would be shy."

"I'm not shy, I'm just—discreet."

"My ass."

"I thought we were talking about mine."

Giving a snort, she shifted again, bundling pillows under her head. Where had all this energy come from? she wondered. Ten minutes ago she hadn't been certain she would ever move again. Now she felt like . . . well, dancing.

"I guess we could use a loincloth. You could pin your star to it if it made you feel better. I could title it *The Long Arm of the Law*."

"I'm going to slug you in a minute."

After a long, contented sigh, she turned her head to look at him. "I might as well tell you, I'm really stubborn when it comes to my work. I once hounded a bag lady for two weeks so

I could sketch her hands. What are you smiling at?"

"You're pretty."

"You're trying to change the subject."

"Yeah. But you are pretty. You've got these freckles on your nose. They're just about the same color as your eyes."

"Okay, you can sculpt me if you want, but I get to do you first."

He pushed a pillow into her face.

"You know." She slid it off and stuck it with the others under her head. "If we were in New York, I'd make you get dressed so we could go out. To a club." Smiling, she closed her eyes. "Hot music, too many people, overpriced drinks served by rude waitresses."

He picked up her hand to play with her fingers. "Do you miss it?"

"Hmmm?" She lifted a shoulder and let it fall. "I haven't thought about it much. It's tough not having a bakery across the street, but the market has pretty good doughnuts."

He was frowning now, studying her fingers instead of toying with them. They were long, slender and artistic, like her. "Where do you live up there?"

"I've got a loft in SoHo."

A loft in SoHo. That, too, was like her. Exotic and funky.

"Have you ever been to New York?"

"Couple of times." He looked from her hand to her face. She was utterly relaxed, eyes closed, lips just parted, skin faintly flushed in the afterglow of sex. She hadn't bothered to pull up the sheet as some women would have, but lay over it, comfortably naked. He slid a hand over her breast, down her rib cage, more to reassure himself than to arouse.

"Did you like it?"

"Like what?"

She smiled again. "New York."

"It was okay. Like a fast ride in a crowded and overpriced amusement park."

His description made her smile widen. "A long way from the Emmitsboro annual carnival."

"Yeah. A long way. It's funny the way things work out—that you and I would both come back here and end up together." He reached over to stroke her cheek. "I don't want you to go back to New York, Clare." She opened her eyes again, and they were wary. "Don't tell me I'm moving too fast, because I feel like my life's on the line here."

"I wasn't going to say that. I don't know what to say."

"I don't want to lose you, and if you went back to New York, I couldn't go with you. I can't go back on the force."

"You're doing police work here."

"Yeah." He sat up, reached for a cigarette. She wouldn't settle for half-truths or ultimatums. Why should she? he thought. He was going to have to tell her everything. "Nice, quiet little town. Or at least it was, and that's what I wanted." He struck a match. That, too, was quiet, even harmless, with just the right friction. He watched the flame flare before he shook it out. "What I had to have. I came back here because I couldn't function as a cop in the city. I couldn't trust myself to go through the door with anyone again."

"Through the door?"

"With a partner," he said. "I couldn't trust myself to back up a partner."

She put a hand over his. "Why?"

"I had a partner. We worked together for over three years. He was a good cop. And a good friend."

"Was?" she said and brought his hand to her lips. "I'm sorry. What happened?"

"I fucked up, and he died."

"Nothing's that simple." Suddenly cold, she picked up his shirt and pushed her arms through it. She knew what it was like to hold tight to hidden hurts, grow proprietary over them, nurse them inside like a miser with a dark, secret treasure. "Can you tell me?"

"It's more like I have to." But he was silent for a moment while a whippoorwill joined its song

to the music of Johnnie Ray. "We were out doing some legwork on a case, and a call came
through for a unit to respond to a disturbance."
He could hear the squawk of the radio, Jake's
good-natured oath.

Looks like you and me, Tonto.

"An armed man taking potshots at parked cars
and apartment windows in South East. We were
only a couple of blocks away, so we took it.
When we got there, the guy had some woman
around the neck with a forty-five to her head.
She was screaming."

He paused to take a pull on his cigarette. The
moonlight flashed into high summer sun. Hazy
heat. The stink of garbage.

He could see it clearly, much too clearly. The
color of the woman's shirt, the wild look in the
gunman's eyes, the glitter of glass on the sidewalk.

"He was on PCP, really raving. He dragged
her into this building. It was abandoned, slated
for demolition. We called for backup, and we
went in. Jake didn't come out."

"Oh, Cam."

"The guy was pulling her up the steps. She'd
lost a shoe," he said softly. "Funny what you remember. She'd lost a shoe, and her heels were
thudding on the steps as he dragged her up. Her
eyes . . ." She had looked right at him, dark,
dark eyes filled with terror and hope and plead-

ing. "She wasn't screaming anymore, just crying. Begging. But he was screaming.

I AM THE WAY, THE TRUTH AND THE LIGHT! I AM SALVATION! IF THINE EYE OFFENDS THEE, THEN PLUCK THE FUCKER OUT!

"We went up the first landing." He could hear the screams and sobs echoing off the scarred and crumbling walls. The smell of dust, the fetid, sweaty stench of terror. "It was at the top of the second floor. A step broke. I went through it, up to my goddamn knee." The unexpected give, the flash of pain and frustration. And fear. "Jake was three steps ahead of me. Three steps. I hauled myself out of the damn hole.

THE WHORE OF BABYLON! WHO'S GONNA CAST THE FIRST STONE? WHO'S GOT THE GUTS? WHO'S GOT THE GLORY?

"The crazy bastard shot the woman. I'm on my fucking hands and knees scrambling up, and he shot her. She bounced off the wall like a doll, and before she hit he'd already pumped three bullets into Jake. I killed him."

The scream as the bullets slapped into flesh. Blood blossoming on a torn T-shirt.

"I killed him," Cam repeated. "Just a couple of seconds too late. I was still on my knees, and Jake was tumbling down those steps when I did it. If I hadn't been three steps behind, he'd be alive."

"You can't know that."

"I can know that. He was my partner, and he died at the bottom of those steps because I wasn't there to back him up."

"He died because a maniac killed him and an innocent woman." She put her arms around him, folding herself around his rigid body. "Maybe if the steps hadn't been rotted, maybe if your partner had fallen through them instead of you, maybe if that man had gone crazy in another part of town—maybe then, it wouldn't have happened. There was nothing you could have done to change it."

"I've replayed it in my mind hundreds of times, thousands." He pressed his lips against her neck, taking comfort in the taste and scent of her skin. "And I'm never in time. Afterwards, I got into the bottle." He pulled away again because he wanted her to look at him. "Real deep into the bottle. I'd still be there if it had helped any. I turned in my shield and my gun, and I came back here because I figured I wouldn't have to do anything more than give out citations and break up a few bar fights."

"You do a good job here." She sat back to take his hands. "You belong here. Whatever happened to bring you back doesn't change the truth of that." Grieving for him, she pressed his fingers to her lips. "I know what it's like to lose someone important to you, what it is to wonder if you could have done something, anything to stop it from happening. I wish I could tell you that it goes away, but I'm not sure it does. All I know is that you have to forgive yourself and go on."

"Maybe I'd started to do that. Maybe. Then in the last few weeks, with everything that's been happening to this town, I've wondered if I'm the one who should be handling it. No. No, I guess I've wondered if I can handle it."

She smiled a little, hoping it would help. "I can tell you that you sounded like a pretty tough cop when you interrogated me."

"I didn't mean to be rough on you."

"You weren't. I think the word is 'thorough.'" She combed a hand through his hair. Yes, she liked his face, she thought. All the more now that she could see the vulnerability. "I remember you, Rafferty, ten, twelve years ago, strutting through Emmitsboro with a chip on your shoulder the size of a redwood. Nobody messed with you. I also remember you giving Annie rides on your bike. Talking to her. Being kind to her. It was a hell of a combination then, and it still is. This town needs you, and whatever's wrong with it, there's nobody better suited to fixing it than you."

He rubbed his hands up and down her arms. "You're good for me."

"Yeah." She leaned forward and kissed him. "I think I am." She kissed him again. "I think I love you."

"Hold it." He gripped her arms tighter and pulled her back. "Run that by me again."

"I think—"

"No, leave that part out."

She looked at him, saw what he wanted, and let out a long breath. "Okay. I love you."

"That's good." His lips curved when they met hers. "That's real good, Slim. I love you, too."

She framed his face, drawing away enough to see his eyes. "I know. I want to believe we've got a shot at this, Cam."

"We've got more than a shot." He settled her against his shoulder. She fit, just as the pieces of his life seemed to fit now that she had been added. "I've got to think that sometimes things happen because they just have to happen. After ten years we both end up back where we started. You came here because you needed to find some answers. And I was running away."

Her eyes closed, and she smiled. "So the reasons why don't matter so much as the result."

"That's the way I figure it."

"I still think you've got one point wrong. You were running to, not away." Her eyes shot open. "Oh, my God."

"What is it?" he asked as she struggled out of his arms.

"Running away. The girl you were looking for when I first came to town. The runaway from—"

"Harrisburg?"

"Yes, from Harrisburg. What was her name?"

"Jamison," he said. "Carly Jamison. Why?"

"Jesus." She shut her eyes again. It couldn't be a coincidence. "Spelled how?"

"C-a-r-l-y. Clare, what is it?"

"Annie. I saw Annie at the parade this morning, and she was showing off her jewelry. She had a bracelet on her arm, a silver bracelet with a name engraved on it. The name was Carly. I couldn't think why it bothered me so much until now."

The feeling of dread settled in his stomach. He glanced at the clock and saw it was after one. "I'll go talk to Annie first thing in the morning."

"Let me go with you. I'm not trying to interfere," she said quickly. "I think I can help. She said the bracelet was her favorite because it had her name on it. She read the letters wrong. If you give me an hour, I can make her another, then talk her into trading."

"All right. I hope to Christ she found it out on the shoulder of Fifteen and that the kid dropped it while she was out there hitching."

"That's probably just what happened." But she had grown cold. "Kids are careless. She probably didn't notice it was missing until she was halfway to Florida."

"Yeah." But something in his gut wouldn't let him believe it.

"It doesn't have to be your best work," Cam said, trying to hurry her.

"Everything has to be my best work." With infinite care, Clare soldered the link together. She was rather pleased with the design, the slim silver band that widened into an oval. She would engrave Annie's name there in big, bold script. If Cam didn't stop distracting her with complaints.

He paced the garage, picking up tools and setting them down again. "I want to get out to her trailer before she takes off for the day."

"All right, all right." He was going to bitch if she took the time to file the solder joint down. Clare examined it and decided he'd just have to bitch. She didn't pass out inferior work. "Don't play with my calipers."

"What the hell's going on?" Blair came to the doorway sporting a pair of jogging shorts and a major league hangover.

"Clare's making a bracelet."

"Making a bracelet?" He threw up a hand against the light and was careful not to scowl. Scowling only made his head pound more severely. "It's seven o'clock in the morning. Sunday morning."

Cam glanced at his watch. "Ten after."

"Oh, well then." Blair made an expansive rolling motion with his arms and instantly regretted it.

"I'm on police business," Clare told him while she searched through her engraving tools.

"Making a bracelet is police business?"

"Yep. If you're just going to stand there, why don't you make coffee?"

"We don't have time," Cam put in.

"We can take it with us."

"I'll buy you a goddamn gallon of coffee when we're finished."

"You need it now," she said, settling on the tool. "You're cranky."

"I'm past cranky and working my way rapidly to pissed."

"See?"

"Listen," Blair began and put both hands on his head to keep it bolted to his shoulders. "Why don't you two work this out, and I'll just go back to bed?"

Neither of them bothered to glance over.

"How much longer?"

"Couple minutes." The fine point skimmed into the silver. "If I'd had more time, I could've—"

"Clare, it's shiny. She'll love it."

"I'm an artist," she said, adding neat little flourishes with the engraving tool. "My work is my soul."

"Oh, Christ."

She bit her lip to stop the laugh and exchanged the tool for a polishing cloth. "There now. A bit primitive, but fine."

"Take your soul out of the vise and let's go."

Instead, she picked up a file. "Five more minutes. I just have to smooth down the joint."

"Do it in the car." He unscrewed the vise himself.

"Remind me to mention your lack of appreciation for the creative process." She spoke on the run as Cam pulled her out of the garage. "Let's take my car. It'll seem less official and more like a visit."

"All right. I'll drive."

"Be my guest. The keys are in it." She took the bracelet back, settled in the passenger seat, and began to file. "What will you do after you get the bracelet from her?"

He backed out of the drive. "Hope to God she can remember where she found it. Then I'll call the Jamisons. They'll have to identify it."

"It must be awful for them. Not knowing where she is, how she is."

If she is, Cam thought.

Annie's trailer was on the edge of town, on a small, overgrown plot of land known as Muddy Ridge. No one knew why, since the soil was so thin and the rocks so plentiful that there hadn't been any appreciable mud there since the summer of seventy-two, when Hurricane Agnes had hit.

But Muddy Ridge it was, and the scattering of trailers that shared it accepted the title with a kind of pride.

At this hour, on a Sunday, the only inhabitants out and about were a pair of slack-hipped, skinny dogs busy holding a pissing contest on the tires of a pickup. From one of the trailers came the slick, oily voice of a broadcast evangelist, selling God.

There was no mistaking Annie's trailer. She had painted one side of it a bright purple with some paint she'd found in the dumpster behind the hardware store. The rest of it was a faded metallic green, with the exception of the steps Davey Reeder had recently repaired and which Annie had painted a violent yellow. The result was a visual rendering of indigestion, but Annie loved it.

"I remember the last time I was here," Clare said. "It was just before Thanksgiving, when I was—oh—fourteen, fifteen, and I rode out with my mother to deliver some pumpkin pies." She set the file down on the armrest between them. "Do you know what I love about this town, Cam? People take care of their Annies, and they don't even think about it. They just do it."

Clare slipped the bracelet into her pocket. They could hear Annie singing "Amazing Grace" inside the trailer. Her voice in the still morning air was haunting, and so much truer, purer, than the practiced rise and fall of the evangelist's.

"Wait." Clare put a hand on his arm before Cam could knock. "Let her finish."

" 'I once was lost, but now I'm found. Was blind, but now I see.' "

Cam knocked on the metal door. He noted that the screen had holes in it and made a mental note to have it repaired before summer. There were sounds of shuffling and murmuring inside before Annie opened the door, blinked, then beamed.

"Hello. Hello." She had put on one blouse over another, and some of the buttons from the bottom one were pushed through the holes of the one on top. Her tennis shoes were neatly tied, and her arms and chest clinked with jewelry. "You can come in. You can come right on in and sit down."

"Thank you, Annie." Cam stepped through the doorway. The trailer was crammed with boxes and bags. The white Formica counter separating the kitchen and living space was covered with treasures—shiny rocks, plastic prizes from boxes of Cracker Jacks, empty bottles of perfume and Listerine.

The walls were alive with pictures that had been carefully cut from magazines. Springsteen rocked beside a kindly-faced Barbara Bush. Christie Brinkley flashed a winning smile next to a fading portrait of the Supremes in spit curls and pale lipstick.

They were her friends, her companions, from Princess Di to an anonymous model for clean, shiny hair.

"You can sit," Annie told them. "Sit anywhere you want. I have some Cherry Smash and some Oreos."

"That's nice." Clare chose a faded floral cushion while Cam ducked under a Mickey Mouse wind chime. "But you don't have to bother."

"I like company." Annie arranged cookies in a circular pattern on a chipped plate, then poured the sweet cherry drink into three plastic cups. "Mrs. Negley came and brought me some books. I like to look at the pictures." With the grace of habit, she moved around the boxes to serve the drinks. "You can have more."

"This'll be fine," Cam told her. "Why don't you sit down with us?"

"I have to get the cookies first. You're always supposed to offer company something to eat. My mama said." After setting the plate on a box, she settled. "Did you like the parade yesterday?"

"Yes." Clare smiled at her. "I liked it very much."

"The music was good. Good and loud. I wish we could have a parade every day. Afterwards I went to Reverend Barkley's house. They had hamburgers and ice cream."

"Do you remember seeing Clare at the parade, Annie?"

"Sure. I met her friends. You had a black friend and a white friend. Isn't that right?"

"Yes, and you showed us your bracelets. Cam would like to see them, too."

Obligingly, she held out her arm. "I like pretty things."

"These are pretty." He slid aside plastic, gold-plated links, and painted metal to examine the silver bracelet. "Where did you get this one?"

"I found it."

"When did you find it?"

"Oh, sometime." She smiled, twisting her wrist back and forth so that the bracelets jingled. "Before yesterday."

Cam battled back impatience. "Did you have

it the day I drove you home in my car? Do you remember the day we listened to Billy Joel on the radio?"

Annie's eyes clouded, then brightened. " 'It's Still Rock and Roll to Me.' I like that song. I know all the words."

"Did you have the bracelet that day?"

"Yes, yes, indeed." She ran her fingers lovingly over the letters. "I found it a long time before that. Before the roses were blooming and after the leaves came out."

"Okay. Can you tell me where you found it?"

"On the ground."

"Here, in town?"

She frowned. "No." She remembered, but she couldn't tell him about the secret place. No one was supposed to know about that. Uneasily, she pulled her arm back and reached for a cookie. "Just on the ground. See a pin, pick it up. I pick up lots of things. Do you want more to drink?"

"No, thank you." Clare leaned forward to take her hand. "Annie, it could be important that you remember where you found this bracelet. I thought maybe because you liked it so much you might remember where. You must have been very happy when you found it."

She squirmed in her chair and began to stutter a little, like a child called on to recite before the class. There was a faint ring of red around her mouth from the Cherry Smash. "I just found it

somewhere. Somewhere or other. Finders keepers. I find lots of things. It's okay to pick them
up because people just drop them and leave
them right on the ground."

"All right." It was obvious to Clare that they
were only going to agitate her. "I like your pictures."

Annie's nervous hands stilled. "I put them up,
and I have company all the time. But only people who smile. No, sir, no sad faces. I made a
special book with pictures so I can look through
it at nighttime."

"I made something just today. Would you like
to see it?"

"Yes." Annie folded her hands politely, even
though she would rather have talked about her
pictures. "You make statues."

"Sometimes."

"Miz Atherton says you make statues of naked
people." Annie blushed and giggled. "Isn't Miz
Atherton funny?"

"She's a riot," Cam murmured. "Clare makes
bracelets, too."

"Really?" Annie's eyes widened. "You do?"

Clare reached in her pocket. "Today I made
this."

"Oh." Annie drew out the words into a sigh
as she ran a gentle finger along the metal. "It's
pretty. It's the prettiest ever."

"Thank you. Do you see the letters?"

Annie bent closer and giggled. "A–N–N–I–E. Annie."

"That's right. Now look at this." She took Annie's arm again to hold the bracelets side by side. "This one is different. It says something different."

Frowning, Annie studied both. "I don't know."

"This one doesn't say Annie, but this one does. The first one doesn't belong to you."

"I didn't steal it. My mama said it was bad to steal."

"We know you didn't steal it," Cam said. "But I think I might know who it belongs to."

"You want me to give it back." Her mouth began to quiver. "It's mine. I found it."

"You can keep the one I made."

She calmed instantly, like a baby with a pacifier. "Like a present?"

"Yes, it's a present, but it would help us if you would give us the other."

Annie turned her head from side to side, humming under her breath as she considered. "Yours is prettier."

"It's yours." Clare slipped it over her wrist. "See?"

Annie lifted her arm to watch the sunlight glint off the metal. "Nobody made me a bracelet before. Not ever." She gave a little sigh as she slid Carly's from her wrist. "You can have this one."

"Annie." Cam put a hand on her arm to get her attention. "If you remember where you found it, you come and tell me right away. It's important."

"I find lots of things. I find them all the time." She smiled with her old, guileless eyes. "Do you want another cookie?"

"What are you going to do now?" Clare asked as they drove away from Annie's trailer.

"Call the Jamisons."

She reached out to touch his arm and knocked the metal file to the floor. "It's too bad she couldn't remember where she found it."

"There's no telling what she remembers. You were a big help, Clare. I appreciate it."

"I wish we'd found the girl instead of the bracelet."

"So do I."

Clare turned to stare out of the window. "You don't think you're going to find her."

"There's no evidence—"

"I'm not talking about evidence." She looked back. "I'm talking about instinct. I could see it in your face when you put the bracelet in your pocket."

"No, I don't think I'm going to find her. I don't think anyone's going to find her."

They drove the rest of the way in silence. In the driveway they got out of opposite sides of the car. She went to him, sliding her arms around his waist, laying her head on his shoulder.

"Why don't you come in, let me fix you some coffee and a couple of eggs?"

"I like the thought of you cooking for me."

"I guess I kind of like it myself."

"I've got work, Slim." He kissed the top of her head before he broke the embrace. "I'm going to have to settle for carry-out from Martha's."

"I'll be around when you're finished."

"I'm counting on it."

Clare waited until she had waved him off before turning to go into the house. She followed the sound of voices into the kitchen.

"I don't like it," Angie insisted. "When it happens that often, it's deliberate."

"What?" Clare pushed through the door and studied the trio around the kitchen table. "Something going on?"

"Where's Cam?" Angie countered.

"He's going back to his office. Why?"

"Angie's a little spooked." Blair guzzled coffee and tried to clear his brain. The hangover was down to a miserable thud-bump-thud. "The phone rang last night."

"The phone rang three separate times last night," she corrected. "And each time I answered, whoever it was hung up."

"Kids," Clare decided and headed to the coffeepot.

"One kid, maybe." Angie tapped her foot in agitation. "That kid across the street."

"Ernie?" With a sigh, Clare leaned back against the counter and sipped her coffee. "Why would you think that?"

"The second time it happened, I got up. There was a light on in the top window of his house."

"For God's sake, Angie."

"Yesterday at the parade, he was staring at you."

"That's it then. I guess we'll have to drag him out in the street and shoot him."

"Don't take it lightly," Jean-Paul told her. "The boy is trouble."

"The boy is just that. A boy."

"He's toying with Satanism," Jean-Paul insisted, and Blair choked on his coffee.

"What?"

"Ernie's got a pentagram," Clare said, "and Jean-Paul's seeing demons."

"I see a troubled, and perhaps dangerous, boy," the Frenchman said tightly.

"Hold on." Blair held up a hand. "What's this about a pentagram?"

"An inverted pentagram." Jean-Paul frowned over his coffee. "The boy wears it, flaunts it. And he watches Clare."

Blair set his cup aside and rose. "Clare, I think you should talk to Cam about this."

"Don't be ridiculous. There's nothing to talk about. And God knows Cam has enough to do without adding demon-busting to the list. I'm going to work." The screen slammed behind her.

"How much do you know about Satanism?" Blair asked Jean-Paul.

"Only what I read in the papers—enough to make me uneasy about this boy."

"Tell him about the cat," Angie insisted, glancing toward the garage.

"What cat?"

She leaned forward, hurrying on before Jean-Paul had a chance to explain. "Someone left a dead cat—a headless cat—outside the back door. Clare insists it was dragged there by some stray dog, but I don't think so—it wasn't mangled." She sent an uneasy glance toward her husband. "Jean-Paul looked it over when he—when he got rid of it."

"It was decapitated," he told Blair. "Not mauled, as an animal might do. Beheaded."

Nodding grimly, Blair rose. "Keep an eye on her. I need to make some calls."

Chapter 20

"WHY THE HELL DIDN'T she tell me?" Cam demanded when Blair sat across from him in the sheriff's office.

"I don't know. I wish I did." Blair's mouth was a thin line from tension. "I'd like to get a look at that kid, too. A good, long look."

"I'll deal with Ernie."

"You might want to deal with this." Blair tapped a finger on the fat file he'd brought along. "I went up to the newspaper in Hagerstown. Did a little digging in the morgue. And I called the *Post*, had them fax me some articles on Satanism. I think you'll find it interesting reading."

Cam flipped open the file and whistled

through his teeth. "We're a long way from D.C."

"A lot of places are. It doesn't stop this kind of crap from going on."

Mutilated livestock, disemboweled house pets. Cam paged through the slick fax sheets, disgust surging in him. "We ran into this now and again when I was on the force. Ritual circles in some of the wooded areas, symbols carved into trees. But here?" His eyes lifted to Blair. "Christ, we grew up here. How could this be going on without our having a clue?"

"For the most part this kind of group is careful, real careful." He rose and went to the coffeepot. "You want some more of this nuclear waste?"

"Yeah." His gut had told him something was very wrong almost from the beginning, when he'd stared down into that small empty grave. "Biff, though," he said. "That was sloppy. No." His eyes glittered up at Blair. "Not sloppy. Arrogant."

"I'll tell you what I get from this." Blair poured more coffee into Cam's cup. "They don't think like other men. They don't feel like other men." As he sat again, the chair squeaked with his restless movements.

Cam pulled over an ashtray. "Tell me, like a reporter."

"Okay." He settled back, steepled his hands. "I

think arrogant was a good choice of words. It's a mistake to believe that they're stupid. It's not all junkies and psychopaths and rebellious teenagers in cults. Some of this stuff talks about doctors, lawyers, college professors being involved, often highly placed within the cult, too."

Cam had gleaned that much himself but wanted to hear the logic. "How do they get involved?"

"The groups are well organized. There's networking, recruiting. Part of the appeal is the secrecy, the smugness of belonging to a group that's outside society's normal bounds." As he talked, Blair was afraid he understood the allure all too well. "They live for pleasure, a lot of sick pleasure. Getting off with animals. Christ, with kids. And power—a lot of it comes down to power." He spread out the sheets. "Some don't believe they can conjure up demons, but they belong for the indulgences. Sex. Drugs. The thrill of killing." He glanced over as Cam watched him. "You can see from a couple of these articles that we aren't always talking about killing sheep and dogs. Sometimes they get in deeper. Runaways are a good target."

Cam thought of Carly Jamison with a sick feeling of acceptance. Then of Biff. "Do they kill their own?"

"Why not? This isn't your average men's club,

Cam, and some of these people believe, deeply, fervently, that Satan will give them whatever they want if they follow the path. I've got all kinds of stuff here, from what they call the dabblers right on up to the big boys. But from a couple of kids lighting a black candle and playing a record backward to La Vey—what pulls it together is power. It all comes down to power."

"I've been reading quite a bit, too," Cam said. "What I'm getting is that there are different type of cults. The high-profile ones are big into indulgence and ceremony but reject any kind of ritual sacrifice."

"Sure." Blair nodded and found himself stifling a nervous laugh. Here they were, good old friends, discussing devil worship and ritual murder over bad coffee. "But there are others. I need to do more checking, but from what I can gather, that's your most dangerous group. They take what they want from the books, from the traditions, and make their own. They go back to the ancients, when blood was the only way to appease and—and cajole the gods. They form where they please. They don't seek attention, they hide from it. But they find each other."

"How do we find them?"

"I'm afraid," Blair said, and he no longer had the urge to laugh, "that we may not have to look very far." Restlessly, he dragged a hand through his hair. "But I'm a political reporter, Cam. I don't know whether that's an advantage or an obstacle."

"I'd imagine a cult would be lousy with politics."

"Probably." He let out a long breath. Did one campaign for the job of high priest? he wondered. Gather votes by kissing babies and slapping palms? Jesus. "There's too much I don't know. I've got a line on a couple of people back in D.C. who'll talk to me. You know there are cops who specialize in this sort of thing?"

"We don't need a story."

"You've got one," Blair shot back. "But if you think I'm into this because of some fucking byline—"

"Sorry." Cam held up a hand, palm out, then used it to soothe the headache brewing behind his eyes. "Knee-jerk. It's my town, goddammit."

"Mine, too." Blair managed what passed for a smile. "I didn't realize how much it was still my town until this. I want to talk to Lisa MacDonald, Cam. Then I'll do what I can from here. But before long I'm going to have to go back to D.C., do some legwork on this."

"All right." He had to trust someone. In the town he thought he knew so well, he was afraid there was no one else to trust. "I'll call her and clear it. Be easy with her. She's still fragile."

"She'd be dead if it wasn't for Clare." Carefully, a little too carefully, he set down his coffee. "I'm scared for her, Cam, I'm scared real deep. If this Ernie character belongs to a cult and he's obsessed with her—"

"He won't get near her." The soft, controlled statement was in direct opposition with the heat in Cam's eyes. "Count on it."

"I am counting on it." Pushing the mug aside, he leaned closer. "She's the most important person in my life, and I'm trusting her to you after I go. By God, you'd better take care of her."

Ernie's fingers trembled as he held the slip of paper. He had found it in the visor of his truck at the end of his shift at the Amoco. At last it was coming together.

The risk he'd taken out at Dopper's farm, the ugly sickness and revulsion he suffered after he'd butchered the black calves had all been worth it. He would be joining them.

May 31, 10:00. South end
of Dopper's Woods.
Come alone.

Tonight, was all he could think. Tonight he would see, and he would know, and he would belong. He folded the paper and slipped it into the back pocket of his jeans. When he started the truck, his hands were still trembling. His leg shook as he pushed in the clutch.

On the drive home, his nervousness turned into cold, clearheaded excitement. He would no longer be an onlooker, he thought, no longer have to content himself with spying through his telescope. He would belong.

Sally saw him drive up and was out of her car before Ernie had pulled to the curb in front of his house. Her smile of greeting faded as soon as he looked at her. His eyes were dark, cold.

"Hi . . . I was just driving around, and I thought I'd come by."

"I got stuff to do."

"Oh, well, I can't stay anyway. I've got to get over to my grandmother's. Sunday dinner, you know."

"So go." He started toward the door.

"Ernie." Hurt, Sally trotted after him. "I just wanted to ask you about the party again. Josh is bugging me to go with him, but I—"

"So go with him." He shook her hand off his arm. "Stop hanging on me."

"Why are you being like this?" Her eyes had already filled, in reflex. He watched the first tear fall and felt a stirring of remorse that he quickly smothered.

"Being like what?"

"Mean to me. I thought you liked me. More than liked me. You said—"

"I never said anything." And that was true. "I just did what you wanted me to do."

"I wouldn't have let you . . . I would never have done those things with you unless I thought you cared about me."

"Cared about you? Why the hell should I? You're just another slut." He watched her face go dead pale before she sat down on the lawn and sobbed. Part of him was embarrassed. Part of him was sorry. Part of him, the part he concentrated on, watched her with calculated indifference. "Get out of here, will you?"

"But I love you."

Again something stirred, and again he squelched it. He reached down to pull her to her feet just as Cam drove up. Ernie let his hands dangle at his sides and waited.

"Problem here?"

"Not mine," Ernie said.

After flicking a glance over the boy, Cam bent down to Sally. "Hey, honey. Did he hurt you?"

"He said he doesn't care about me. He doesn't care at all."

"Then he's not worth crying over." Gently he held out a hand. "Come on, now. You want me to drive you home?"

"I don't want to go home. I want to die."

Cam glanced up and felt relieved to see Clare crossing the street. "You're too young and pretty to want to die." He patted her shoulder.

"What's going on?" Clare looked from one face to the other. "I saw you drive by," she said to Cam.

"Sally's pretty upset. Why don't you take her over to the house and . . ." He made an inadequate gesture.

"Sure. Come on, Sally." Clare put an arm around the girl's waist to help her up. "Let's go to my house and trash men." She shot Cam a last look and led the weeping girl across the street.

"Nice going, champ," Cam said to Ernie.

To the surprise of them both, Ernie blushed. "Look, I didn't do anything. She was bugging me. I never asked her to come around. It's not against the law to tell some stupid girl to take a hike."

"You're right there. Are your parents home?"

"Why?"

"Because I want to ask you some questions. You might want them around when I do."

"I don't need them."

"Up to you," Cam said easily. "You want to talk in the house or out here?"

He jerked his head, a single defiant gesture that sent his hair flying back. "Here."

"Interesting piece of jewelry." Cam reached out to touch the pentagram, and Ernie closed a hand over it.

"So?"

"It's a Satanic symbol."

Ernie's lips curved in a leer. "No kidding?"

"You into devil worship, Ernie?"

Ernie kept smiling, kept stroking the pentagram. "Isn't a person's religion covered in the Bill of Rights?"

"Yeah. Yeah, it sure is. Unless the people practicing that religion break the law."

"It's not against the law to wear a pentagram."

At a nearby house, someone started a lawn mower. The motor coughed and died twice, then caught in a steady purr.

"Where were you last Monday night between one and four A.M.?"

His stomach jumped, but he kept his eyes steady. "Asleep in bed, like everybody else in this frigging town."

"Ever try your hand at animal sacrifice, Ernie?"

"Can't say I have."

"Can you tell me where you were last Tuesday night, about ten-thirty, eleven?"

"Yeah." With a grin, Ernie glanced up at the top window of the house. "I was right up there, balling Sally Simmons. I guess we finished about eleven. She left a few minutes later, and my parents came home from the pizza parlor about eleven-thirty. That should cover it."

"You're a lousy little sonofabitch."

"That's not against the law either."

"No, it isn't." Cam took a step closer so that they were eye to eye. There was a faint film of sweat on the boy's brow. Cam was gratified to see it. "You're my favorite kind of bug to squash, and I'm not that long out of practice. Make a wrong move, you little bastard, and I'll be on you like a leech, sucking you dry."

"Is that a threat?"

"That's a fact. If your alibi doesn't check out by even five minutes, we're taking this down to the office. You'd better dig one up for Monday night, too." He closed his hand over Ernie's pentagram. "Stay away from Clare, stay far away. If you don't, there isn't a god in heaven or hell who'll protect you from me."

With his hands clenched into fists, Ernie watched Cam walk away. He'd have more than that, he thought. After tonight, he'd have whatever he needed.

"I thought he loved me." Sally hiccuped into the soft drink Clare had poured her. "But he didn't care at all. He never cared, he only . . . He said such awful things to me."

"Sometimes people say awful things when they're fighting that they're sorry about later."

"It wasn't like that." Sally took another tissue and blew her nose. "We weren't fighting. He wasn't even mad, just cold. He looked at me like—like I'd crawled out of a hole. He said—he said I was a slut."

"Oh, baby." She closed a hand over Sally's and thought about what she would say to Ernie at the first opportunity. "I know that hurts."

"I guess I am, too, because I did it with him." She covered her face with the tattered tissue. "He was the first one. The very first one."

"I'm sorry." Near tears herself, Clare put her arms around the girl. "I wish I could tell you that what he said doesn't matter, but it does to you. And it will for a while yet. But being intimate with Ernie doesn't make you a slut. It only makes you human."

"I loved him."

Already past tense, Clare thought, grateful for the resilience of a teenage heart. "I know you thought you did. When you really fall in love, you'll see the difference."

Sally shook her head, hair swinging. "I don't ever want to care about another boy. I don't want anybody to be able to hurt me like this ever again."

"I know what you mean." Every woman did, she thought. "The problem is you will care." She took Sally by the shoulders, drew her back. The girl's face was blotched from weeping. Her eyes were swollen and red. And so young, Clare thought. She took a fresh tissue and gently dabbed at the tears. "There's something I'd better tell you, though. Something every woman should know about men."

Sally sniffed. "What?"

"They're all assholes."

With a watery chuckle, Sally wiped her eyes.

"They are," Clare insisted. "They get older and become older assholes. The trick is to avoid coming in contact with the one guy who will make you fall in love with him despite it. Otherwise, you'll end up married for fifty or sixty years before you realize you've been fooled."

Sally laughed just as Angie walked through the kitchen door. "Oh, I'm sorry." Angie noted the girl's tear-streaked face and started to back up.

"No, that's all right." Clare motioned her in. "Angie, this is Sally, and she and I were just discussing why the world would be a better place without men."

"That goes without saying. Except for sex and killing roaches, they really have no purpose."

"Parallel parking," Clare put in, pleased that Sally had laughed again.

"Auto repairs." Sally rubbed her cheeks dry with her hands. "My dad's really good at auto repairs."

"That's true." Clare considered a moment. "But a woman can always buy a manual."

Sally sighed and ran a fingertip down her glass. "I feel pretty stupid, acting the way I did."

"You have no reason to."

She swallowed and stared down at the table. "I can't tell my mother about the things Ernie and I did."

"Do you think she'd be angry?" Clare asked.

Sally shook her head. "I don't know. She's really great to talk to. We've had all the discussions. You know. It's not like she expected I'd stay a virgin forever, but . . . I can't tell her what I did with Ernie."

"I guess it's for you to decide." She heard Cam pull up in the drive. "Here comes Sheriff Rafferty."

"Oh." Sally covered her face. "I hate for him to see me like this. I look awful."

"Why don't I show you where to wash your face?" Angie suggested. "A little lipstick and eye drops should do the trick."

"Thanks." On impulse she hugged Clare. "Thanks a lot, both of you."

She hurried out just as Cam walked in. "Where's Sally?"

"Tidying up so you wouldn't see her with red eyes and a runny nose. You talked to Ernie?"

"Yes, I talked to him."

"I don't know what got into him, saying things like that to Sally, but I've got a good mind to have a few words with him myself."

"Stay away from him." He cupped a hand under her chin. "I mean it."

"Now, wait a minute—"

"No. I'm not asking you, I'm telling you. Until I'm sure he's clean, you keep away from him."

"Clean? What are you talking about?"

"Why the hell didn't you tell me about the cat?"

"Cat?" She edged back a little. "What does that have to do with anything?"

"It may have a hell of a lot to do with everything. Don't pull away from me, Slim."

"I'm not." She was. "I don't want to," she amended. "There are things I have to work out. Okay?"

"No, it's not okay." He caught her chin in his hand again, studied her a moment, then let his hand drop away. "But it'll have to do for now. I need to talk to Sally." He swore under his breath, knowing the harder he pushed the more inclined Clare would be to push back. He could already see it in her face, the faint, stubborn line between her brows, the tension in her jaw. "Slim . . ." He sat, taking both her hands in his. "It's important. I wouldn't ask you otherwise."

"You said you weren't asking, you were telling."

"Okay." He smiled a little. "I wouldn't tell you if it wasn't important."

"And maybe I'd be less inclined to tell you to go to hell if you'd explain."

Cam pinched the bridge of his nose. "I will, as soon as I can." He glanced up as Sally came back into the kitchen.

"I guess you want to talk to me," she said, and linked her hands together.

Cam rose to offer her a chair. "How are you feeling?"

She stared down at her feet, then at the table. "Embarrassed."

"Don't be." He smiled at her so gently that she had to bite her lip to keep from crying all over again. "I once had a fight with Susie Negley right at the counter of Martha's Diner."

"Susie Negley?" Sally said blankly.

"She's Sue Knight now."

"*Mrs. Knight?*" Sally stopped staring at the table to stare at Cam as she tried to imagine her stiff-spined English teacher with the sheriff. "You used to . . . with Mrs. Knight?"

"When she was sweet sixteen. And she slugged me, nearly knocked me off the stool. *That* was embarrassing."

She giggled, and the sheen of tears faded from her eyes. "Mrs. Knight hit you? Really?"

"Don't let it get around. I think people have almost forgotten."

"No, they haven't," Clare said as she rose. "It just makes him feel better to think so. Why don't I leave you two alone?"

"Can't you—" Sally bit her lip again. "Can't

she stay? I already told her and . . . will it be all right?"

"Sure." Cam looked up at Clare and nodded. "I need to ask you some questions. You've known Ernie for a long time?"

"Since middle school."

"Does he get along with the other kids?"

It wasn't the line of questioning she'd been expecting and she frowned. "Well, he doesn't get into fights or anything. This time . . ." She looked at Clare. "This time was my fault, really. I came by, and I guess I made a scene because I wanted him to feel about me the way I felt— thought I felt," she corrected, "about him. I don't want him to get into trouble, Sheriff. He isn't worth it."

"Good going," Clare murmured and toasted Sally with a Diet Pepsi.

"He's not in trouble." Yet. "Who does he hang around with?"

"Nobody really."

"He doesn't sit with a particular group in the lunchroom?"

"No, he kind of keeps to himself."

"He drives to school, doesn't he?"

"Yes."

"Does he ever have anybody in the truck with him?"

"I've never seen him give anybody a ride." That was funny, she realized. Kids were always piling into each other's cars. But nobody ever rode shotgun with Ernie.

It wasn't what Cam wanted to hear. If Ernie was involved with what had been going on in Emmitsboro, he wasn't acting alone. "You've been with him a lot over the past few weeks."

The flush started at her neck and rose slowly to her cheeks. "Mr. Atherton assigned partners for a chemistry project. Ernie and I were working on it together."

"What did he talk about?"

She moved her shoulders. "He doesn't talk much." It occurred to her then that Ernie had never talked like Josh—about school, about his parents, other kids, sports, movies. He'd let her do all the talking, then had led her upstairs to his room.

"Did you ever talk about the things that have been going on, like Biff Stokey's murder?"

"I guess we did, some. I remember Ernie saying that Biff was just an asshole." Her blush turned fiery. "I'm sorry."

"It's okay. Did he say anything else?" Mortally embarrassed, she shook her head. "Did he ever ask you about the night you and Josh were in the cemetery?"

"Not really. But Josh told everybody, and he kept telling everybody until it got really boring. Josh just doesn't let things go, you know?" And she hoped he still wanted to go to the party with her.

"Sally, were you with Ernie last Monday night?"

"Last Monday?" She looked up gratefully as Clare refilled her glass of Pepsi. "No, I baby-sit for the Jenkinses every Monday."

"And Ernie didn't come by? You didn't go over to his house after you were finished?"

"No. The Jenkinses live right next door to us, and if I had a boy over, my mom would get really hyped. They don't usually come home until about eleven."

"How about Tuesday?"

"Tuesday?" She looked away and picked up her glass.

"Were you with Ernie Tuesday night?"

She nodded, then put down the glass without drinking. "I was supposed to be over at Louise's house, studying, but I went to Ernie's. His parents work at night."

"I know. Can you tell me what time you got there and what time you left?"

"I left Louise's just before ten, so I got there a few minutes later. It was after eleven when I left."

"Are you sure?"

"Yes, because I was supposed to be home at eleven, and it was almost eleven-thirty when I got there, and my father was ticked."

"Okay." The little bastard couldn't be in two places at once, Cam thought. But he wasn't willing to let go quite yet. "You've seen that pendant Ernie wears?"

"Sure, he used to wear it under his shirt, but . . ." She realized too late what that implied, and looked down at the table again.

"Do any of the other kids wear one?"

"No. I don't think so. Nobody's really into that kind of thing."

"What kind of thing?"

"You know, Satanism and stuff."

Cam felt Clare stiffen beside him but concentrated on Sally. "But Ernie was?"

"I guess. He had the pentagram. He had black candles in his room. He liked to light them and listen to black metal."

"Did you ever ask him about it?"

"I asked him once why he was into that kind of thing, and he just smiled and said it was a game. But . . . I didn't think it was a game to him. I said I'd seen on television how cults killed people, even babies, and he said I was gullible, that was just society's way of putting down something they didn't understand."

"Did he say anything else about it?"

"Not that I remember."

"If you do, will you come and tell me?"

"All right."

"Do you want me to drive you home?"

"No, I'm okay." She pressed her lips together. "Are you going to talk to my parents?"

"If I have to talk to them about any of this, I'll tell you first."

"Thanks." She gave him a weak smile, then turned to Clare. "You and Angie were really great."

"We have to stick together."

Sally nodded as she stood. "I, ah . . . Ernie has a telescope in his room," she blurted out. "I looked through it once when he left me alone for a minute. I could see right into your bedroom window." She blushed again. "I thought you should know."

Clare struggled to keep her face blank. "Thanks."

"I'll see you around."

"Come back any time you want." Clare let out a long, quiet breath after Sally had gone. "I guess I'd better start pulling down the shades."

"The little sonofabitch."

Clare clamped a hand on Cam's before he could rise. "What are you going to do, punch him out? Not only are you twice his age and half again his weight, but you've got a badge that says you're not allowed to."

"I'll take it off."

"No, you won't. And if nothing else, that bombshell Sally dropped will get you what you want. I'll stay away from him." She leaned forward, framed his face with her hands, and kissed him. "But I appreciate the thought."

"Start locking your doors."

"He's not going to—" She broke off, gauging the temper in his eyes. "All right. Now, do you want to tell me what brought on that line of questioning with Sally?"

"Missing graveyard dirt, what looks like a ritual killing, and the attack on Lisa MacDonald. The headless black cat on your back door."

"You can't seriously believe that one unhappy kid is on some kind of rampage for Satan."

"No, I don't. But I have to start somewhere."

Restless, she rose to pace to the window. The lilacs were blooming, damn it. There was a nest of starlings in the eaves, and the grass needed mowing. That was the way things were supposed to be. The way they had always been. She wouldn't accept that there was something undulating beneath the calm surface.

But she thought of the books in her night table drawer. For one horrid instant, she could see her father sprawled on the terrace, broken, bleeding, beyond hope.

She rubbed her hands over her eyes as if to erase the image. "It's absurd. The next thing you'll tell me is that the Emmitsboro Ladies Club is actually a witches' coven that meets every full moon."

He put his hands on her shoulders and turned

her to face him. "I'm telling you that there's something sick in this town. I'm going to find it and cut it out. Right now Ernie Butts is the only lead I've got."

Again she thought of the books, her father's books. God, her father. She couldn't bring herself to speak of it. But there was something else, something that perhaps meant nothing but wouldn't be such a complete betrayal.

"I didn't think anything of it at the time," she began and had to give herself a moment before her voice steadied. "The day you found Biff, and we went out to your mother's. . . ."

His fingers tensed on her shoulders. "What about it?"

"I stayed with her after the doctor gave her a sedative. I just kind of wandered around. There were books in, well, I guess you'd call it Biff's den. I wanted something to read. Mostly there was just pornography and men's adventures. But—"

"But?"

"I found a copy of *The Satanic Bible.*"

Chapter 21

JANE STOKEY SPENT EACH DAY cleaning and packing. After the eggs were gathered and the stock seen to, she settled into one room of the rambling farmhouse. Much of it would be sold at auction. She'd already had Bob Meese out to give her a bid on the mahogany dining room set that had been her grandmother's. The big and little server, the china cupboard, the extension table meant for large families with lots of children, the scarred and treasured chairs. They had all meant something to her once. Over the years, the shellac had turned black, and the surfaces wouldn't hold much of a shine, but the dining set had been her pride and joy. And a bone of contention between her and Biff.

He had wanted to sell it. It was one of the few things she'd had the will to refuse him.

Now he was getting his wish.

She would have no room for heavy old furniture in Tennessee. Her sister didn't want it. Cam had his own. Jane had no daughter to pass the tradition down to. It would end with her.

She didn't think about that. Didn't allow herself.

It would cost too much to truck it south, too much to store it. The plain fact was she didn't have the heart to hold on to it now that she was alone.

She went through the drawers, separating linens into a box to sell or a box to take. Her mother's damask tablecloth with its spot of cranberry sauce that hadn't washed out from some Thanksgiving years before. The lacy runner that had been a wedding present from Mike's aunt Loretta. She had once starched and pressed it so lovingly; now it was limp with age and disuse. There were the napkins with the fancy R in the corners that she had embroidered herself.

She folded them into her takeaway box like a secret.

From linens she moved to glassware, wrapping the candlesticks, the candy dishes, the single champagne flute that had survived thirty years.

One box filled, and she started on a new one,

thinking, How things do collect after thirty-odd years. With competent hands she wrapped pieces of her life in newspaper for other people to pick and paw through. And here was the platter Mama had bought from the traveling salesman with the carrot red hair and the white, white grin. He'd said it would last a lifetime, but Mama had bought it because of the pretty pink flowers around the edges.

A tear fell on the newsprint as Jane wrapped it.

She couldn't take it all with her. She couldn't. What would a woman alone do with so much? Why, every time she washed or dusted them, she would be reminded that there was no one to care.

She would buy herself some new dishes, like the ones she'd seen in the JC Penney catalog. There was no reason to fill cupboards and closets with things she didn't need. Why, she couldn't think what had made her keep all of it for so long. Dust collectors, Biff had called them. He'd been right, too. She'd spent hours chasing the dust from them.

She wrapped a small china cat and slipped it guiltily into her takeaway box.

The knock on the door made her jolt. Jane brushed off her apron, smoothed down her hair before she went to answer. She sincerely hoped it wasn't Min Atherton again, come to poke around the house with the excuse of being a concerned friend and neighbor.

Jane nearly laughed at the thought. Min had been a nosey busybody since the day she could talk. If she weren't married to James, no one would give her the time of day. The surge of regret and envy came swiftly. Min might have been an irritant, like a speck of dust in the eye that wouldn't tear out, but she had a husband.

Jane opened the door to her son.

"Mom." He could think of nothing in his life he regretted more than what he was about to do. "I need to talk to you."

"I'm busy, Cameron." She was afraid he had come to talk about the farm. She'd waited for him to come and complain that she was selling. But he hadn't complained. He hadn't said a word about it. "Settlement's in three weeks, and I've got the whole house to pack up."

"In a hurry to get rid of it?" He held up a hand, cursing himself. "That's your business. But I need to talk to you. It's about Biff."

"Biff?" Her fingers went to the buttons of her blouse and began to twist. "Did you find out something? Do you know who killed him?"

"I need to talk to you," he repeated. "Are you going to let me come in?"

Jane stepped back. Cam noted that she'd already started on the living room. There was nothing left but the sofa, the TV, and a single table and lamp. There were dark squares on the faded wallpaper where pictures had hung, a faint outline on the floor where the rug had lain.

He wanted to shout at her, to shake her and demand that she think. It was part of his life she was packing away. But he wasn't here as her son. She didn't want him to be.

"Why don't you sit down?" He gestured to the sofa and waited. "I need to ask you some questions."

"I've already told you everything I know."

"Have you?" He didn't sit but studied her. "Why don't you tell me about Biff's interests."

"Interests?" Her face went blank. "I don't understand."

"What was he into, other than drinking?"

Her mouth was a thin, straight line. "I won't have you speaking ill of him in his own house."

"This was never his house, but we'll leave that alone. What did he do with his time?"

"He worked the farm."

Like hell, Cam thought, but left that, too, alone. "His free time."

"He liked to watch the TV." She groped, fumbling to find a grip on a man she'd lived with for more than twenty years. "He liked to hunt. He'd never let a season go by without getting a deer."

Or two, Cam thought. He'd dressed them illegally in the woods, bypassed the check-in station at the market, and sold the meat.

"Did he read?"

Baffled, she blinked at Cam. "Some."

"What kind of things did he read?"

She remembered the magazines she had found, and burned, in the shed. "The things men read, I suppose."

"What about religion?"

"Religion? He didn't have one. He was raised Methodist, I think, but he always said church was a waste of a good hour every week."

"How many times a week did he go out?"

"I don't know." She began to huff. "I don't see what this has to do with his murder."

"Was there any particular night he always went out?"

"I didn't keep track of the man. It wasn't my place."

"Then whose was it? Who'd he go out with?"

"Different people." Her heart was beating too loud, but she didn't know what she was afraid of. "Mostly he'd go out alone and meet Less Gladhill or Oscar Roody or Skunk Haggerty or one of the others. Sometimes they'd play poker or just go to Clyde's." And sometimes he'd go into Frederick and visit a whore. But she left that unsaid. "A man's entitled to relax."

"Did he ever relax with drugs?"

Her color fluctuated, white, then pink, then

white again. "I wouldn't have those filthy things in my house."

"I need to look in his den."

Her color changed again, to a dull red. "I won't have it. I won't. You come here, after the man's dead and can't defend himself, and try to say he was some kind of drug fiend. Why aren't you out looking for whoever killed him instead of coming here and slinging dirt?"

"I am looking for whoever killed him. Now, I need to look through his things. I can do it this way, or I can get a court order. It's up to you."

She rose, very slowly. "You'd do that?"

"Yes."

"You're not the boy I raised." Her voice shook.

"No, I guess I'm not. I'd like you to come with me. If I find anything, I want you to see where and how it was found."

"You do what you have to do. Then I don't want you coming back here anymore."

"There's nothing to come back to."

He followed her stiff back up the stairs.

He was relieved she hadn't started on Biff's den yet. It was exactly as Clare had described it. Cluttered, dusty, scented with stale beer.

"I take it you didn't come in here much."

"This was Biff's room. A man's entitled to his

privacy." But the dust embarrassed her almost as much as the magazines piled on the floor.

He started in one corner, working silently and systematically. In a drawer with shotgun shells and matches, he found a package of Drum, filled with about an ounce of grass.

He looked at her.

"That's just tobacco."

"No." He held it out for her to look at. "It's marijuana."

There was a quick, dull pain in the center of her stomach. "It's Drum tobacco," she insisted. "It says so right on the bag."

"You don't have to take my word for it. I'll send it to the lab."

"That won't prove anything." She began to ball and unball the skirt of her apron. "Somebody gave it to him—like a joke. He probably didn't even know what it was. How would he know?"

He set the bag aside and continued to search. Inside the hollowed-out stand for the stuffed squirrel he found two vials of cocaine.

"What?" Jane put her fingers to her mouth. "What is it?"

Cam opened a vial, touched a wet fingertip to the powder and the powder to his tongue. "Cocaine."

"Oh, no. My God, no. It's a mistake."

"Sit down. Come on, Mom, sit down." He led her to the chair. Part of him wanted to hold her and tell her to forget all about it, to put it right out of her mind. Another part wanted to shake her and gloat. *I told you what he was. I told you.* He set those parts aside, the two halves of her son.

"I want you to think, tell me who used to come here. Who would come upstairs here with Biff?"

"Nobody." She looked at the vials Cam still held in his hand, then away with a kind of horror. She didn't understand drugs, unless they were the kind Doc Crampton gave you for the stomach flu or those twinges of arthritis. But she feared them. "He didn't let anybody come in here. If he had a poker game, he would lock the door first. He said he didn't want those guys poking around in his stuff. He'd just sit up here by himself."

"Okay." He took a chance and squeezed her hand, but got no response. "I have to keep looking."

"What difference does it make?" she murmured. Her husband had been unfaithful to her. Not just with a woman. She could understand another woman, especially one who took money. But he had been unfaithful with those little tubes of powder. And *that* she would never understand.

He found a few more stashes. All small quantities, obviously for personal use. If he'd been selling, Cam thought, he hadn't been doing it from here.

"Did you ever see Biff with a large amount of cash?"

"We never had money," she said wearily. "You know that."

"How did he come up with the down payment for the Caddy?"

"I don't know. I never asked."

He went through the paperbacks on the shelves and found a stack that dealt with Satanism, cult worship, and ritual sacrifices. Two of them were straight porn, with obviously staged photographs of naked women being tortured by men in masks. Others were serious works on devil worship.

Setting the worst of them aside, he brought the rest to the chair. "What do you know about these?"

Jane stared, with a glassy kind of horror, at the titles. Her Catholic background reared up and grabbed her by the throat. "What are they? What are they doing here? How did they get in my house?"

"They were Biff's. I need you to tell me if you knew anything about them."

"No." She folded her hands on her breasts,

afraid to touch them. This was much worse even than the drugs. "I've never seen them. I don't want to see them. Put them away."

"Do you see this?" He pointed to the pentagram on the cover of a book. "Did Biff have one of them?"

"What is it?"

"Did he have one?"

"I don't know." But she remembered the things she had found in the shed. "What does it mean?"

"It means that Biff was involved in something. It could be why he was killed."

She pushed out her hands to ward him off but couldn't find the strength to rise. "He was a good man," she insisted. "He wasn't a churchgoer, but he wouldn't blaspheme this way. You're trying to make him into some kind of monster."

"Goddamn it, open your eyes." He all but shoved the books into her face. "This was his idea of a good time. And this." He grabbed one of the other books and tore it open to a full-color scene. "And I don't think he just read about it. Do you understand? I don't think he just sat up here snorting coke and looking at dirty pictures. I think he went out and practiced this stuff."

"Stop it! Stop it! I won't listen."

Now he did grab her, he did shake. But he didn't have it in him to gloat. "Why are you protecting him? He never made you happy, not one single day of your life. He was a sick, sadistic sonofabitch. He ruined this farm, he ruined you, and he did his damnedest to ruin me."

"He took care of me."

"He made you an old woman. A scared, beaten old woman. If I hated him for nothing else, I'd hate him for what he's done to you."

She stopped struggling to stare. Though her mouth worked, there were no words.

"You used to laugh." In his desperate and angry voice, there was a trace of a plea. "Damn it, you used to care about things, about yourself. For the past twenty years, all you've done is work and worry. And when you went to bed at night, too tired to care anymore, he was out lighting black candles and sacrificing goats. Or worse. God help us. Or worse."

"I don't know what to do." She began to croon, rocking back and forth. "I don't know what to do." Jane believed in Satan, deeply, superstitiously. She saw him as a serpent, slithering in the Garden, as a dark angel, taunting and tempting Christ, as the king of a fiery pit. In her heart was a cold terror that he had been invited into her home.

Cam took her hands again. This time she held on. "You're going to tell me everything you know."

"But I don't know." Tears leaked out of her

eyes. "Cam, I don't. Did he . . . did he sell his soul?"

"If he had one to begin with."

"How could I have lived with him for twenty years and not known?"

"Now that you do, you might start to remember things. Things you didn't pay any attention to before. Things you didn't want to pay attention to."

With her lips tightly pressed together, she looked down at the book that had fallen open on the floor. She saw the naked woman, blood smeared on her breasts. A candle between her legs.

She'd been trained well, trained to be loyal, to overlook, to make excuses. But there had been an earlier training, one that surfaced now to make her fear the Wrath of God and the punishment.

"The shed," she said weakly. "In the shed."

"What's in the shed?"

"I found things. I burned them."

"Oh, Christ."

"I had to." Her voice skipped and shivered. "I had to burn them. I couldn't let anyone see. . . ."

"See what?"

"Magazines. Ones like this." She gestured toward the floor, then looked away.

"Is that all you burned?"

She shook her head.

"What else?"

The shame, the shame all but sickened her. "Candles. Like the ones in the picture. Black candles. And a robe with a hood. It smelled"— she tasted bile in her throat—"like blood. And there were pictures. Snapshots."

Cam's hand tightened on hers. "Of what?"

"Girls. Two young girls. One dark-haired, one blond. They were . . . they were naked and tied up, on the cot in the shed. I tore them up and burned them."

A granite fist closed in his stomach. "You burned the pictures?"

"I had to." Hysteria bubbled in her voice. "I had to. I didn't know what else to do. It was so ugly. I couldn't let people know he'd brought women here, paid them to pose for those dirty pictures."

"If you saw the girls again, or other pictures of them, would you remember?"

"I won't forget. I'll never forget how they looked."

"Okay. I'm going to call Bud. Then you're going to take me outside and show me."

"People will know."

"Yes." He let go of her hands so that she could cover her face with them and weep. "People will know."

★ ★ ★

"What have we got, Sheriff?"

"I don't know yet." Cam looked back toward the house where his mother was standing on the porch wringing her hands. "You brought everything?"

"Just like you said."

"Let's put on the gloves and get to work."

They snapped on thin surgical gloves and went into the shed.

She'd even burned the damn mattress, Cam thought, frowning at the iron frame of the cot. There was little left other than a few tools, lots of dust, and a few broken beer bottles. Hunkering down, Cam searched the underside of a workbench.

"Do we know what we're looking for?" Bud asked.

"I'll let you know if we find it."

"Hell of a way to spend a Sunday." But Bud whistled between his teeth. "I got me a date with Alice tonight."

"Oh, yeah?"

"Taking her to a Mexican restaurant and the movies."

"Shooting the works, huh?"

"Well . . ." Bud colored a little as he ran his fingers lightly over and under the metal shelves. "She's worth it. Maybe you ought to take Clare up to the Mexican place sometime. It's got a real nice atmosphere. You know, pots and paper flowers and stuff. Women go for that."

"I'll keep it in mind."

"Do you figure a margarita's a woman's drink?"

"Not according to Jimmy Buffet."

"Who?"

"Never mind. Try a Dos Equis and keep it to one."

"Dos Equis," Bud repeated to himself, committing it to memory. "I wonder what—shit."

"What?"

"Something sharp here, nearly went through the glove. One of those earrings with a pointy back." Bud held it up, a bit uncomfortable. Everybody knew Biff had fooled around, but it was different when you were the one who found a woman's earring in his toolshed. "I, ah, guess I should bag it."

"Yeah. And this, too." Cam peeled off a bag of cocaine that had been taped to the underside of the worktable.

"Holy shit, is that what I think it is?"

Bud's eyes bulged. If Cam had held up a five-headed toad, he'd have been less amazed. "Jesus, Cam, what are you going to tell your mom?"

"Just tag it, Bud."

"Sure. Yeah." He took the bag, cradling it in his hands as if it were a squirming infant.

Using his flashlight, Cam crawled on his hands and knees, working every inch of the floor. Mixed with the broken beer bottles he found a thin slice of smoky glass. He held it up and peered through it. Prescription. Carly Jamison had been nearsighted. He shifted through the broken glass and found two more pieces.

When they'd finished the search, he stepped out into the sunlight. "Did you bring the Jamison girl's picture?"

"Sure, like you said. It's in the car."

"You go ahead and dust for prints."

"Sure." Bud brightened instantly. It was something he practiced religiously and rarely got to put into use. "I'll get right on it."

Cam took the photograph out of the car and walked toward the house, where his mother still waited. She looked old, he thought, even older than when she had opened the door for him two hours before.

He held out the picture. "Is this the girl in the photograph you found in the shed?"

Jane licked her lips and forced herself to look. It was a pretty face, young and pretty. She had to turn away from it. "Yes."

"Try to think back to around Eastertime. Did you ever see this girl around?"

"I never saw her." Jane looked over his head, toward the fields. "Is she dead?"

"I'm afraid she might be."

"You think Biff killed her."

"He had a part in whatever happened to her. She was in that shed. Tied up, held there."

She thought she'd cried herself out, but the tears began again, pouring from her burning eyes. "I didn't know. I swear on my life I didn't know."

"Who was around here during that time? Who came out and spent time with Biff?"

"Cam, that was weeks and weeks ago. I don't know. How would I remember? I was down with the flu before Easter. Remember, you brought me flowers."

"I remember."

"Biff came and went. There might have been a poker game, or that might have been after Easter." She pushed a hand over her limp hair. "I never paid any mind to that kind of thing. He didn't want me to. What difference does it make now? He's in hell. He sold his soul and sent himself to hell."

"All right." He was beating a dead horse and knew it. "If you remember anything, you call me. I don't want you to talk to anyone about this."

"Who would I talk to?" she said dully. "They'll all find out anyway. That's the way things work."

He let out a sigh. "Do you want to come and stay with me until . . . for a while?"

Surprise registered first. Then shame. "No, I'll be fine here, but it's kind of you."

"Damn it, you're my mother. It's not kind. I love you."

She could barely see him for the tears blurring her eyes. But he looked as she remembered him as a boy. Tall and straight and defiant. Angry, she thought. It seemed that he'd been angry with her since the day his daddy had died.

"I'll stay just the same. It's my home for a little while longer." She started to walk into the house, then stopped. It took the rest of the courage she had left just to turn and face her son again. "When you were five, you got ahold of my good red nail polish. You wrote 'I love you Mom' in big, block letters on the bathroom tile. I guess nothing before or since ever meant so much to me." She looked at him helplessly, hopelessly. "I wish I'd told you that before."

She went inside, alone, and closed the door quietly behind her.

Clare was waiting for him when he got home. She met him at the door, took one look, and put her arms around him.

"We don't have to talk about it." She tightened her grip when he laid his cheek against her hair. "I picked up some pizza. If you'd rather be alone, I'll head home. You can just warm it up when you get around to it."

He lowered his mouth to hers. "Stay."

"All right. Angie and Jean-Paul left about an hour ago. They had to get back to the gallery and said to tell you good-bye."

"Blair?"

"He's decided to hang around for a couple of days." She eased back to study him. "Rafferty, you look like hell. Why don't you go up, have a soak in that magic tub of yours? I'll heat up the pizza and fix you a beer."

"Slim." He closed her hand into a fist and brought it to his lips. "You're going to have to marry me."

"I'm what?"

He didn't really mind the shock in her eyes. "I like the idea of you meeting me at the door and heating up pizza."

She smiled even as she eased away. "Boy, do one good deed, and the guy expects a lifetime."

"Right now I'd settle for company in the tub."

Her smile became more relaxed. "So I can wash your back, I suppose."

"You wash mine, I'll wash yours."

"Deal." She hoisted herself up and wrapped her legs around his waist. "What do you say we heat up the pizza later?"

"I say good thinking."

They went upstairs as the sun began to lower.

Others waited, restless, for sundown.

Chapter 22

At NINE-THIRTY, Rocco's was hopping. Joleen Butts had given up on the idea of closing early when the Hobbs family walked in, all seven of them. The youngest howled around the bottle in his mouth while the other four kids made beelines for the arcade games, their quarters ready. Joleen took the order for three large pizzas, loaded, then went back to sprinkling diced mushrooms on top of shredded mozzarella to the tune of the beeps and buzzes of Super Donkey Kong.

Now all four booths were packed with bodies and pizza in varying degrees of annihilation. Balled-up paper napkins littered the tabletop. Their part-time delivery boy had just taken four extra cheese with pepperoni over to the fire hall. She noted that the youngest of the Hobbs troop was on the loose and was pressing gooey fingers on the glass of the display case as he peered at the soft drinks and candy bars.

So much for a ten o'clock closing, she thought.

In another couple of weeks, after school was out for the summer, they would keep the parlor open until midnight. Kids liked to hang out there, munching on pizza in the wooden booths, popping quarters in Dragon Master. Except her kid, she thought, and slid the pizza into the oven.

He'd rather sit home alone and listen to his music.

She smiled at her husband as he carried two cardboard boxes to the cash register. "Busy night," he murmured and winked at her.

Most were, she thought and began to build a submarine. They had made a success out of this place, just as they had dreamed they would. Since she and Will had been teenagers themselves, they had worked toward this. A place of their own, in a nice, small town where their children would be safe and happy. Their child, she corrected. Two miscarriages after Ernie had drawn the curtain on the notion of a big family.

But they had everything else.

She worried sometimes, but Will was probably right. Ernie was just going through a stage.

Seventeen-year-olds weren't supposed to like their parents or want to spend time with them. When she was seventeen, her major goal in life had been to get out of the house. It was a lucky thing that Will had been out there waiting, just as eager.

She knew they were the exceptions. Teenage marriages were almost always a mistake. But at thirty-six, with eighteen years of marriage under her belt, Joleen felt smug and secure and safe.

Not that she wasn't glad that Ernie didn't seem to be serious about any particular girl. Maybe she and Will had been ready at a tender age to take the big leap, but Ernie wasn't. In some ways, he was still just a child. In others . . .

Joleen pushed back her long brown braid. In others she didn't understand him at all. He seemed older than his father and tougher than nails. He needed to find his balance before he could be serious about a girl, or anything else.

She liked Sally Simmons, though. The fresh face, the polite manners, the neat clothes. Sally could be a good influence on Ernie, bring him out of himself a little bit. That was all he needed.

He was a good boy really. She wrapped the sub and rang it up, with a six-pack of Mountain Dew, for Deputy Morgan. "Working tonight?"

"Nope." Mick Morgan grinned at her. "Just

hungry. Nobody makes a sub like you, Miz Butts."

"I doubled the onions."

"That's the way." She was a pleasure to look at, he thought, with her face all flushed from the ovens, and the white bib apron over her jeans and shirt. She didn't look old enough to have a grown boy, but Mick figured she'd got herself knocked up at a young age and made a go of it. "How's your boy?" he asked as he pocketed his change.

"Fine."

"Graduating next week?"

She nodded. "It's hard to believe."

"Take it easy."

"You, too."

Graduating, she thought, and took a deep breath of air laced with the scents of spices and sauce and sharp cheeses. Her little boy. How often she wished she could go back five years, ten, and find the moment when she had made the wrong turn.

But that wasn't right, she assured herself. Ernie was his own person, and that was how it was supposed to be. She watched, with some envy, as little Teresa Hobbs hugged her father's knees and giggled. Maybe Ernie wasn't outwardly affectionate or full of jokes and good humor, but he kept out of trouble. His grades were steady if not spectacular. He never came home drunk or stoned—as she had certainly done before marriage focused her. He was just, well, deep, she supposed. Always thinking.

She wished she knew what he was thinking.

He was waiting. Ernie knew he was early, but he'd been too psyched to sit at home. His adrenaline was pumping so hard and fast he thought he might explode. But he didn't know he was scared because the fear was so deep, so cold in his bones.

The moon was full. It silvered the trees and sprinkled the fields. He could just make out the Dopper farmhouse in the distance. Close by, cattle lowed.

He was reminded of the last time he had come here. He'd climbed the fence then, the rope and knives he carried in a laundry bag. There hadn't been so much moonlight then, and the breeze had carried a chill.

He hadn't had any trouble cornering the two calves or tying their legs, just the way he'd seen in the movies he watched in ninth grade when he was stuck in agriculture class. He'd hated every minute of ag, but he'd remembered the movies of brandings and birthings and butcherings.

Still, he hadn't known, he really hadn't known, there would be so much blood. Or the sounds they would make. Or that their eyes would roll.

He'd been sick at first and left the carcasses to run into the woods until his grinding stomach was empty. But he'd done it. He'd gone back and finished. He'd proven he was worthy.

Killing wasn't as easy to do as it was to read about. Having blood in a little vial in the drawer was different, much different, than having it splash warm from a vein onto your hands.

It would be easier next time.

He rubbed the back of his hand over his mouth. It had to be easier next time.

He heard the rustle of leaves and turned to look, unaware that there was fear in his eyes— the same kind of rolling fear he'd seen in the calves' eyes. His hand closed over the key in the ignition. For a moment, just one moment, his mind screamed at him to turn it, to throw the truck into reverse and drive away fast. Run away, while there was still time.

But they came out of the woods. Like spirits or dreams. Or devils.

There were four of them, robed and masked. Ernie's throat clicked on a swallow as one of them reached out and opened the door of the truck.

"I came," he said.

"You were sent," he was answered. "There will be no going back."

Ernie shook his head. "I want to learn. I want to belong."

"Drink this."

He was offered a cup. Unsteadily, he climbed out of the truck to take it, to raise it to his lips, to drink with his eyes on the eyes behind the mask of Baphomet.

"Come."

One of the men got into the truck and drove it up a logging trail until it was hidden from the road. They turned, Ernie in the center, and went back into the woods.

They didn't speak again. He could only think they looked magnificent, powerful, walking in the shadowed light, layers of dead leaves rustling beneath the hems of the robes. Like music, he thought and smiled. As the hallucinogen cruised through his system, he felt he was floating. They were all floating, around the trees, even through them. Air parted like water. Water like air.

The moonlight was crimson, and through its haze he saw brilliant colors, magical shapes. The crunching of leaves underfoot was a drumbeat in his blood. And he was marching toward destiny.

Baphomet turned to him, and his face was huge, bigger than the moon's and brighter. Ernie smiled and thought that his own features changed. Into a wolf's, a young wolf's, hungry and handsome and shrewd.

He didn't know how long they walked. He didn't care. He would have walked with them into the pit of Hell. Flames couldn't touch him. He was one of them. He felt it, the power, the glory, swelling inside of him.

When they came to the circle, the others were waiting. Baphomet turned to him. "Do you believe in the might of the Dark Lord?"

"Yes." Ernie's eyes were glassy with the drug and harmless. Not hungry, not handsome, not shrewd, his face was slack and vulnerable. "I've worshiped him. I've sacrificed for him. I've waited for him."

"Tonight, you will meet him. Take off your clothes."

Obediently, Ernie pulled off his Nikes, his Levi's. He stripped off his Black Sabbath T-shirt until he wore only the pentagram. A robe was slipped over him.

"You will not have a mask. Later, when you are one of the few, you will choose your own."

The voice came to Ernie's ears, low and stately, like a funeral march or a record played on the wrong speed. "I've studied," he said. "I understand."

"You have more to learn."

Baphomet stepped into the circle. The others closed around it. When Ernie took his place, he saw the woman. She was beautiful, draped in a red robe, her hair loose and glossy. She was smiling at him. Even as he hardened beneath his own robe, he recognized her.

Sarah Hewitt had participated in the ceremonies before. For two hundred dollars, all she had to do was lie naked on a slab of wood and wait until a few nut cases went through their ridiculous routine. There was a lot of chanting and calling up the devil. The devil, for Christ's sake. It was all an excuse to ball her. For two hundred, she didn't care if they wanted to wear masks and shake their naked butts at each other. 'Course, sacrificing goats was pretty sick, but boys would be boys. In any case, tonight looked like a special treat. She'd recognized Ernie and figured he might add something to the night's entertainment.

The kid was stoned, she thought, and would probably pop off before they got to the good part. But she could bring him around again. She was good at it.

And she had been relieved to be told to come tonight. She'd made a mistake talking to Cam. Sarah was well aware that people paid for mistakes.

The bell was rung, the candles were lit, and the flame was set in the pit. Sarah slid a hand down the center of her robe and let it slither from her shoulders. She held the pose a moment, knowing eyes were on her. In the spotlight of the moon, she walked over to spread herself on the slab.

The high priest raised his arms. "In the name of Satan, king and ruler, I command the Dark Forces to bestow their infernal power upon me. Open wide the gates of Hell and grant me all I ask. We rejoice in the life of the flesh. We seek and demand its pleasures. Hear the names!"

Ernie shuddered as the names were called. He knew them, had studied them. Had prayed to them. But for the first time, he wasn't alone. And his blood was hot, melting the lingering fear in his bones, as he repeated them with the coven.

The cup was passed. Ernie wet his dry mouth with the tainted wine. The flames from the pit seemed to tower, alive, snapping greedily. His flesh burned.

He watched the high priest. The image of the sculpture Clare had created imposed itself over the reality. She knew, he thought, and yearned for her. She knew.

The sword was taken up to call out the four Princes of Hell.

The power was like a shaft of ice speared into him. The heat and cold vacillated like a sexual dance. He shook with it as he joined in the chant.

"We bring a new brother to You tonight,

Master. We offer You his heart, his soul, his loins. Youth is blessed. Youth is strong. His blood will mix with ours in Your glory."

"*Ave*, Satan."

He held out a hand, gesturing Ernie into the circle. "Do you come to this place of your own will?"

"Yes."

"Do you embrace the Dark Lord as your Master?"

"Yes."

"Do you give your oath now, to hold sacred this place? To give yourself over to the Law?"

"I swear it."

Ernie barely felt the prick on the index finger of his left hand. Dreamily, he set it against the parchment held in front of him. And signed his name in blood.

"Now you have sworn. Now you have added your name to the few. If you speak of what you have seen this night, your tongue will turn black and fall from your mouth. Your heart will shrivel in your breast to a stone and stop your breath. Tonight, you accept His wrath and His pleasures."

"I accept them."

The priest set hands on Ernie's shoulders and flung back his head. "We ride a sweeping wind, to the bright place of our desires. The joys of life are ours to take. A life of lust is ours to bear. We are men."

"Blessed be."

"I am a thrusting rod with the head of iron. Women crave me."

"We are men."

"I am filled with carnal joy. My blood is hot. My sex aflame."

"We are men."

"All demons dwell within me." He lowered his eyes and his gaze bored into Ernie's. "I am a pantheon of flesh."

"Hail, Satan."

A figure stepped forward, offering the priest a small bone. Taking it, he moved to the altar, leaving Ernie swaying. The bone was placed upright between the altar's thighs. He took the cup from between her breasts and upended it so that the wine spilled over her flesh.

"The Earth is my mother, the moist and fertile whore." He moved his hands over the altar, squeezing, scraping. "Hear us now, Great Satan, for we invoke Your blessing in the pleasures of the flesh."

"Sustain us, Master."

"Desiring all."

"Sustain us, Master."

"Taking what we will."

"*Ave*, Satan."

The goat was brought out, the knife drawn. With the drug and the chants spinning in his head, Ernie fell to his knees. He prayed, to the God he had just forsworn, that he wouldn't be sick.

He was pulled to his feet and his robe stripped from him. The priest put out a hand, dripping with blood, and smeared it over Ernie's chest.

"You are marked with the sacrificial blood. Invoke the Name."

Ernie swayed, mesmerized by the eyes that burned into his. "Sabatan."

"Sabatan!"

The priest moved back to the altar, repeating the exaltation. He took up the bone and turned so that the rest of the coven could pass before her.

"Flesh without sin," he said.

Robes were cast aside, and the chanting grew louder. Ernie could hear nothing else as he was pulled to the altar. He shook his head, struggling to clear it. She cupped her hands around his rigid penis, manipulating it roughly until he shuddered. Beneath the chanting, he could hear her laugh, low and mocking.

"Come on, little boy. Don't you want to show these old farts what you can do?"

And the rage filled him, and the sickness, and the need. He rammed himself into her, driving hard until he saw the mockery fade and pleasure flicker.

He knew they were watching but didn't care. Her hot breath washed over his face. His muscles trembled. Tears came to his eyes as the chanting rolled over him. He belonged.

And when he was finished, he watched others and grew hard again. They took turns with her, greedy, pushing themselves into her, slurping at her flesh. They no longer looked powerful, but pathetic, emptying themselves into the same vessel, showing their flab and flaws in the moonlight.

Some of them were old, he realized. Old and fat, wheezing as they climaxed and collapsed. And his watching became more cynical as the drug wore off and excitement drained. Some masturbated onto the ground, too impatient to wait. They howled, drunk on sex and blood.

Ernie's eyes skimmed over them derisively and met another's. He wore the mask, the head of Mendes. His naked form was trim and pale, and the heavy silver pendant rested against his chest. He didn't dance around the fire, or call to the moon, or fall drooling on the woman. He only stood and watched.

There was power, Ernie realized. In this man it was centered. He knew, he understood. When he moved toward Ernie, the boy trembled at what he might have guessed.

"You have begun."

"Yes. The rite—it was different from what I've read and studied."

"We take what we need. We add what we choose. Do you disapprove?"

Ernie looked back at the altar and the men who climbed over her. "No." That was what he wanted, the freedom, the glory. "But lust is only one way."

Behind the mask was a smile. "You will have others. But this night is done for you."

"But I want to—"

"You will be taken back and will wait to be called. If what you have seen and done is spoken of outside this place, you will die. And your family will die." He turned and went back to the head of the altar.

Ernie was given his clothes and told to dress. Flanked by two robed men, he was escorted back to his truck. He drove for about a half mile before pulling over, turning off the ignition, and jogging back.

He would take what he wanted, he told himself. The rite had not been closed. If he was to join, he was entitled to see it all.

He belonged.

His head throbbed, and his mouth felt sandy and dry. Aftereffects of the drug, he supposed. He would take care not to drink again, but only to pretend. He didn't need his senses clouded, but cleared. Drugs were for fools and cowards.

Though he feared once or twice that he would lose his way, he kept walking. He was certain he had recognized some of the men there tonight, and he intended to make a list in secret. They had seen his face. He was entitled to know theirs. He would not be treated like a child again, not here. He would belong in full, and one day, one day, he would stand in the center of the circle with the goat's head. He would be the one to call up the power.

He could smell the smoke, stenched with the carcass of the goat. Quickly, he crossed the stream where years before Junior Dopper had met his own devil. The sound of chanting came hollowly through the trees. Ernie slowed his steps, crouched and moved forward. There—in the same place a little girl had once hidden, though he did not know it—he watched the rite continue.

They had not donned their robes again, but stood naked. The altar lay limp, sated and sleepy with the glitter of moonlight on her skin.

"Our lust is quenched. Our bodies are pure. Our minds are clear. Our secret thoughts have been channeled into the movements of our flesh. We are one with our Master."

"Hail, Satan."

The priest stood, legs spread, arms outstretched in the center of the circle. His head thrown back, he shouted out an imprecation. Latin? Ernie wondered, licking his lips. Whatever language, it sounded more passionate, more powerful than English.

"Beelzebub, come forth and fill me with Your wrath. Woe to the Earth, for her iniquity was great." He whirled toward the altar. Lazily, Sarah pushed herself up on her elbows.

She knew him, knew his appetites and his secrets.

"You didn't take your turn," she said and shook back her tumbled hair. "Better get in while you can. Your two hours are almost up."

He brought a hand hard across her face. Her head snapped onto the slab. "You will not speak."

She lifted her fingers and rubbed them over her lips where blood spurted. Hate filled her eyes, but she knew if she disobeyed, he would hit her again. Instead, she lay still and waited. She would have her day, she thought. By God, she would. And he would pay a hell of a lot more than two hundred for the slap.

"Behold the whore," he said. "Like Eve she will seduce, then betray. Between her spread thighs lies our pleasure. But before lust, there is the Law. I am the Sayer of the Law. None escape."

"None escape."

"Cruel are the punishments of the Law. None escape."

"None escape."

"The weak are cursed. She who speaks what is secret is damned. That is the Law."

"Hail, Satan."

Even as they crowded around her, Sarah scrambled up. Her arms and legs were grabbed and borne down to the wood.

"I didn't say anything. I didn't. I never—"

She was silenced by another blow.

"The gods of the pit demand vengeance. They hunger. They thirst. Their mighty voices smash the stillness of the air." Turning, he threw something into the pit that caused the flames to leap and roar.

And the chanting began, a murmuring chorus behind his shouted words.

"I am the instrument of annihilation. I am the messenger of doom. The agony of the betrayer will sustain me. Her blood will slake my thirst."

"Please." Writhing, terrified, Sarah looked at the men who surrounded her. It couldn't happen. She knew them, all of them, had served them beer and sex. "I'll do anything you want. Anything. For God's sake—"

"There is no god but Satan."

When her hands and feet were bound, the coven fell back. From his place in the bush, Ernie began to sweat.

"Behold the vengeance of the Master." The priest picked up the sacrificial knife, still dampened with blood. He stepped forward.

Sarah began to scream.

She screamed for a long time. Ernie pushed his hands against his ears to block it out, but the sound reeked, like a scent in the air. Even when he closed his eyes, he could see what was being done to her.

Not a sacrifice. Not an offering. But a mutilation.

With his hands over his mouth, he ran blindly through the woods. But her screams chased after him.

But there was another who did not run. There was one who crouched, animallike on haunches, eyes bright and a little mad. This one watched, this one waited, with the heart pounding and flesh sweating fervor of the damned.

Even when the screams died, their echoing shuddered the stillness. There was one who rocked back and forth, back and forth in an obscene parody of the sex act, hot tears leaking, body quivering. For it was good, so good to witness the Master's work.

The one who watched sniffed greedily at the air, a wolf scenting blood. Soon, the clearing would be empty again, but the blood would remain. For now the woods smelled wild, full of death and smoke and spent sex. And the shad-

ows hid the form hunched in the brush. Whatever gods might have guarded that small clearing had been banished by death and damnation.

"Clare. Baby, come on." Cam pulled her against
him and stroked her hair. She was trembling violently. Disoriented, he fumbled with the sheet
as he tried to wrap it around her.

"I'm okay." She drew in long, steadying
breaths. "I'm okay. It was just a dream."

"That's supposed to be my line." He turned
her face into the moonlight and studied it. It
was pale as water. "Must have been a pretty bad
one."

"Yeah." She ran both unsteady hands through
her hair.

"Want to tell me about it?"

How could she? How could she tell anyone?
"No. No, it's okay, really."

"You look like you could use a brandy." He
touched his lips to her brow. "Wish I had some."

"I'd rather have a hug." She settled into his
arms. "What time is it?"

"About two."

"I'm sorry I woke you."

"Don't worry about it. I've had my share of
nightmares." He settled back against the pillows,
cradling her in the crook of his arms. "Want
some water?"

"No."

"Warm milk?"

"Ugh."

"Hot sex?"

She laughed a little and looked up at him. "Maybe in a minute. I liked waking up and finding you here." She sighed and snuggled against his shoulder. The nightmare was no more than a smear on her mind now. Cam was a reality.

"It's a pretty night," she murmured.

Like Clare, he watched the moonlight through the window. "Great night for camping. Maybe next full moon, you and I could pitch a tent."

"A tent?"

"Sure. We could go down to the river and camp overnight, make love under the stars."

"We could just pull the mattress out on your deck."

"Where's your sense of adventure?"

"It's firmly attached to things like indoor plumbing." She slid onto him. "And box springs." Nipped his bottom lip. "Percale sheets."

"Ever made love in a sleeping bag?"

"Nope."

"Allow me to simulate." He rolled her over and tucked the sheets tight around them. "This way, I hardly have to move to—oh, shit."

Echoing the sentiment, Clare scowled at the ringing phone. She gasped when Cam shifted.

"Sorry."

"No, no, anytime."

"Rafferty," he said into the phone. Then, "*What?*"

"They're killing her," Ernie repeated in a desperate whisper.

"Who?" Hitting the light, Cam struggled out of the sheet.

"She's screaming. She just keeps screaming and screaming."

"Take it easy. Tell me who this is."

He swore as the phone disconnected. Banging down the receiver, he rose.

"What is it?"

"Damned if I know. Probably a crank." But he'd recognized true terror in the voice. "Claimed somebody was getting killed, but he wouldn't say who or where."

"What are you going to do?"

Cam was already reaching for his pants. "There's not much I can do. I'm going to drive into town, look around."

"I'll go with you."

He started to refuse, then stopped himself. What if the call had been a trick to get him out of the house. To get Clare alone. Paranoid,

Rafferty, he thought. But it was better to take no chances.

"Okay. But it's probably a waste of time."

He wasted a full hour of it before heading back home. The town had been silent as a tomb.

"Sorry to drag you out."

"I don't mind. Actually, it's a nice night for a drive." She turned to him. "I wish you weren't so worried."

"I feel like I'm not in control." It was a feeling he remembered too well from his Jack Daniel's days and one he didn't care for. "Something's going on, and I need to . . ." His words trailed away when he spotted a car pulled off the road into the trees. "Stay in the car," he murmured. "Doors locked, windows up."

"But I—"

"You slide over in the driver's seat. If it looks like trouble, I want you to peel out. Go for Bud or Mick."

"What are you going to do?" He leaned across, unlocked the glove compartment, and took out a gun. "Oh, my God."

"Don't get out of the car."

He left her, moving quickly, quietly. She understood exactly what it meant to have your heart in your throat. She couldn't swallow, could barely breathe as she watched him approach the dark car.

He glanced at the plates and memorized the number. He could see figures inside the car and movement. Just as he reached the door, there was a woman's high-pitched scream. He wrenched open the door and found himself pointing his .38 at a man's naked ass.

What was taking so long? Clare wondered. Why was he just standing there? Orders or no orders, she had a hand on the door handle, ready to spring out to his aid. But he had turned away from the parked car and seemed to be talking to a tree. She was nearly faint with relief when Cam started back.

"What happened? What did you do?"

Cam put his head down on the steering wheel. "I just broke up, at gunpoint, the copulation of Arnie Knight and Bonny Sue Meese."

"You—oh, God." With her hands still pressed to her mouth, Clare began to laugh. "Oh, God. Oh, God."

"You're telling me." With as much dignity as he could muster, Cam started the car and headed for home.

"Were they just fooling around or really, you know?"

"You know," he muttered. "You could call it coppus interruptus."

"Coppus. I like that." She threw her head back, then instantly sat up again. "Did you say Bonny Sue Meese? But she's married to Bob."

"No kidding?"

"Well, that sucks."

"I can now guarantee that she does."

"That's disgusting, Rafferty. Bob doesn't deserve to have his wife out in some other man's car at two o'clock in the morning."

"Adultery isn't against the law. That makes it their business, Slim."

"I wish I didn't know."

"Believe me, seeing it is a lot worse than just hearing about it. I'm never going to be able to look Arnie in the face again without seeing . . ." He began to laugh, saw Clare's expression and choked it off. "Sorry."

"I happen to think it's sad. I talked to Bonny just the other day, and she was showing off pictures of her children and talking about drapery fabric. I don't like knowing that all that domestic bliss was just a front so she can sneak out and screw around with Arnie. I thought I knew her."

"People aren't always what they seem. That's just exactly what I'm having to deal with. Besides, I probably just scared the fidelity back into Bonny Sue."

"Once you cheat, you can't take it back." She rolled her eyes. "Christ, I sound self-righteous.

A few weeks in this town and I start thinking everything should be a Norman Rockwell painting. I guess I wish it could be."

"Me, too." He slipped an arm around her. "Maybe, with a little luck, we'll come close."

Chapter 23

CLARE MADE THE TRIP to the hospital at least three times a week. Usually she found Lisa's brother, one of her parents, or a friend sitting with her. But the last person she'd expected to find stuffed into the chair beside the bed was Min Atherton.

"Clare." Lisa smiled. Her injured eye was unbandaged now, and though it was puffy and red, there was no permanent damage. Her leg was still propped in the mechanical cast, with the second surgery scheduled for the second week in June.

"Hello, Lisa. Mrs. Atherton."

"Nice to see you, Clare." But Min looked disapprovingly at Clare's choice of jeans for a hospital visit.

"Mrs. Atherton came by to deliver some flowers from the Ladies Club." Lisa gestured to a copper pot filled with spring blooms. "Aren't they lovely?"

"Yes, they are."

"The Ladies Club of Emmitsboro wanted to show Lisa that the town cares." Min preened. The flowers might not have been her idea, but she had fought tooth and nail for the right to deliver them. "Why, we're all just sick about what happened. Clare will tell you that we're a quiet town with traditional values and decent morals. We want to keep it that way."

"Everyone's been so kind to me." Lisa winced as she moved, and Clare walked over quickly to rearrange the pillows. "Your Dr. Crampton drops by to see how I am and just to talk. One of my nurses is from Emmitsboro, and she comes in every day—even on her day off."

"That would be Trudy Wilson," Min said, nodding.

"Yes, Trudy. And of course, there's Clare." She reached out for Clare's hand. "Someone from the market sent me a basket of fruit, and the sheriff has been here over and over. It's hard to believe this ever happened."

"We're shocked," Min said breathlessly. "I can tell you that each and every person in our town was just shocked and appalled by what happened to you. Why, we couldn't be more upset if it had happened to one of our own girls. Doubt-less it was some crazy person from out of the county." She studied Lisa's open box of choco-lates and chose one. "Probably the same one that killed Biff Stokey."

"Killed?"

Clare could cheerfully have pushed Min's face into the chocolates. "It happened weeks ago," Clare said quickly. "It's nothing for you to worry about."

"No, indeed," Min agreed and helped herself to another chocolate. "You're safe as a bug here. Just as safe as a bug. Did I mention that my hus-band and I made a sizable donation to this hos-pital a few years ago? Quite sizable," she added over a coconut cream. "They put up a plaque with our names on it. This is one of the finest institutions in the state. Not a thing for you to worry about while you're here. And there are some who say Biff Stokey got what he deserved, though I don't hold with that view. Being a Christian woman. Beat him to death," she said, and it was hard to say if the relish in her voice came from the information or the chocolates. "It was a gruesome and horrible thing." She licked a bit of cherry syrup from her finger. "The first murder in Emmitsboro in nigh onto twenty years. My husband's very disturbed about it. Very disturbed. Him being the mayor and all."

"Do you—you think it could have been the same person who attacked me?"

"That's for the sheriff to find out." Clare sent Min a warning look, but the woman just smiled.

"Yes, indeed. We're mighty pleased to have Cameron Rafferty back. 'Course, he was a wild one as a boy. Racing around on that motorcycle and looking for trouble." She laughed and plucked up another piece of candy. "Finding it, too. Why I know there was some who figured he'd end up on the other side of the bars. Can't say I didn't have some concerns at first, but it seems to me if you're looking for a trouble-maker, it makes sense to put another on the scent."

"Cam's had over ten years' police experience," Clare said to Lisa. "He won't—"

"That's true," Min interrupted. "Worked down to D.C. Had some trouble down there, I believe, but we're pleased to have him back. Emmitsboro's not like Washington. I watch the Channel Four news every night and just shud-der. Why, they have a murder down there every blessed day, and here we are with only one in twenty years. Not that we don't have our share of tragedy."

Pop went a butter cream into her continually working mouth.

"I don't think Lisa wants to—"

"I'm sure the child can't help but be interested

in our sad times," Min interrupted. "Clare would be the first to agree about our tragedies, the way her father had that terrible fall some years back. And just last year, the little Meyers boy drank that industrial cleaner. Lost five youngsters five years back in a car wreck—not that it was anyone's fault but their own—and old Jim Poffenburger fell down his cellar steps and broke his neck, of course. All for a jar of watermelon pickles. Yes, indeed, we have our tragedies. But no crime."

"It was so nice of you to drive all the way up here," Clare said firmly. "But I know what a busy schedule you have."

"Oh, I do my duty." She patted Lisa's hand, and her fingers were sticky. "We girls have to stick together. When one of us is attacked, all of us are attacked. The Ladies Club isn't only concerned with bake sales and raffles."

"Please tell the rest of your group how much I appreciate the flowers."

"I'll do that for sure. I'd best be going back to put supper on. A man likes a hot meal at the end of the day."

"Give the mayor my best," Clare told her.

"I will." She picked up her white patent leather purse. "I've been planning on dropping by, Clare."

"Oh?" Clare pasted a smile on her face.

"Now that your . . . friends have gone back to

New York. I didn't like intruding when you had company."

"That's very considerate of you."

"I must say, I was glad they didn't stay longer. You know how people talk."

"About what?"

"After all, dear, that woman *is* black."

Clare gave Min a blank look. "No, really?"

Sarcasm skimmed over Min's head like a balloon. "As for me, I haven't got a bigoted bone in my body. Live and let live, I say. I even had a black girl from over in Shepherdstown come in to do my house once a week last year. Had to fire her for laziness, of course, but that's neither here nor there."

"You're a regular humanitarian, Mrs. Atherton," Clare said tartly.

Min beamed at the praise. "Well, we're all God's children under the skin, after all."

"Sing Hallelujah," Clare murmured, and Lisa had to hold back a chuckle.

"But as I was saying, I was going to drop by to talk to you. The Ladies Club would like you to speak at our monthly luncheon."

"Speak?"

"About art and culture and that sort of thing. We thought we might even be able to get a reporter down from Hagerstown."

"Oh, well . . ."

"If you're good enough for the *New York*

Times, you're good enough for the *Morning Herald*." Min patted her cheek. "I know how important publicity is, being a politician's wife. You just leave it all up to me. Don't you worry about a thing but wearing a pretty dress. You might go by Betty's and let her see to your hair."

"My hair?" Clare ran a hand through it.

"I know how you artists are—bohemian and all, but this is Emmitsboro. Fix yourself up and talk a little about art. Maybe you could bring a piece or two to show off. Might be the paper would take pictures of it for you. Come by the house Saturday, about noon."

"This Saturday?"

"Now, Clare, you remember the Ladies Club has their luncheon the first Saturday of every month. Always has, always will. Why, your mama was chairwoman three years running. Don't be late, now."

"Yes—no—"

"You'll be just fine. Now, you take care of yourself, Lisa. I'll come back and see you real soon."

"Thank you." Lisa waited until Min had departed before grinning. "Maybe I should call a nurse."

Clare blinked. "Are you feeling sick?"

"No, but you look as though you've been run over by a truck."

"In a pansy dress." On a long breath, Clare plopped into a chair. "I hate ladies' luncheons."

Lisa laughed. "But you're going to get your picture in the paper."

"Well, then."

"She's quite a . . . woman," Lisa said.

"Emmitsboro's first lady and resident pain in the ass. I hope she didn't upset you."

"No, not really. She just wanted to gossip. The business about the murder. . . ." Lisa looked down at her leg. "I guess it should make me realize how lucky I am."

"Dr. Su's the best." At Lisa's lifted brow, she continued. "I checked him out. If anyone can get you back in pointe shoes, he can."

"That's what Roy says, and my parents." Lisa smoothed the sheet. "I can't think that far ahead, Clare."

"Then don't try."

"I'm a coward." She smiled a little. "I don't want to think about tomorrow, and I keep trying to block out yesterday. Before Mrs. Atherton came in, this chant kept playing over and over in my head. I tried not to hear it, even though I knew it might mean something."

"A chant." Clare reached for her hand. "Can you tell me?"

"Odo cicale ca. Zodo . . . zodo something. Gibberish. But I can't get it out of my mind. I guess I'm worried something got knocked loose in my brain and the doctors haven't found it yet."

"I think it's more that you're remembering something. Parts of something. Have you told Cam?"

"No, I haven't told anyone yet."

"Do you mind if I tell him?"

"No." Lisa lifted her shoulders. "For whatever good it might do."

"The MacDonald girl is beginning to remember things." Mayor Atherton dipped his fork delicately into his hot apple pie. "Something may have to be done."

"Done?" Bob Meese tugged at the collar of his shirt. It was too tight. Everything was too tight. Even his boxer shorts were binding him. "It was dark. She didn't really see anything. And the sheriff, he's watching her. Real close."

Atherton paused and smiled benignly at Alice when she came over to refill his coffee cup. "The pie is excellent, as always."

"I'll pass that on. Be sure to tell Mrs. Atherton that those flowers the Ladies Club planted in the park are pretty. A nice touch."

"She'll be glad you like them." He forked up another bite of pie, waiting until she moved to her next table. Absently, he tapped his foot to a

Willie Nelson number. "We're not yet sure what she saw," he went on. "And the sheriff is hardly a genuine worry."

Bob took a sip of his coffee and fought to swallow it down. "I think—that is, some of us think, that things are getting a little out of hand. . . ." He stumbled to a halt, struck dumb by the flash in Atherton's eyes. Cold fire.

"Some of us?" Atherton said gently.

"It's just that—it used to be . . ." *Fun* was the word Bob was groping for, but it seemed miserably inappropriate. "I mean, it was just animals, you know. There wasn't any trouble. There was never any trouble."

"You're too young, perhaps, to remember Jack Kimball."

"Well, no. I mean, that was just before my time. But in the last year or two things have started to change." Bob's gaze darted around the room. "The sacrifices—and Biff. Some of us are worried."

"Your fate is in the hands of the Master," Atherton reminded him mildly, as he might remind a recalcitrant student to complete an assignment. "Do you question Him? Or me?"

"No—no. It's just that I—some of us were wondering if we shouldn't ease back a little, let things calm down. Blair Kimball's been asking questions."

"A reporter's curse," Atherton said, with a gentle wave of his hand. "He won't be here long."

"Rafferty will," Bob insisted. "And once it comes out about Sarah—"

"The whore got what she deserved." Atherton leaned forward, his expression pleasant. "What is this weakness I see? It concerns me."

"I just don't want any trouble. I got a wife and kids to think of."

"Yes, your wife." Atherton settled back again, dabbed his lips with a paper napkin. "Perhaps you'd be interested to know that your Bonny Sue is fucking another man."

Bob went dead white, then beet red. "That's a lie! A filthy lie!"

"Be careful." Atherton's expression never changed, but Bob paled again. "Women are whores," he said quietly. "It's their way. Now I'll remind you that there's no turning back from the path you've chosen. You're marked. Others have tried to turn away and have paid the price."

"I don't want any trouble," Bob mumbled.

"Of course not. Nor will we have any but what we make ourselves. The boy will watch Clare and watch her well. Others are watching Lisa MacDonald. And you." He smiled again. "I have two assignments for you. First is to tell those who are discontent that there is only one high priest. Second is to take a particular statue from the Kimball garage and deliver it to our place in the woods."

"You want me to steal that metal thing right from under Clare's nose?"

"Be innovative." Atherton patted Bob's hand. "I know I can depend on your loyalty." And your fear.

Cam put in yet another call to Florida. With a lot of time and perseverance, he'd been able to trace the former sheriff from Fort Lauderdale to Naples, and from Naples to Arcadia, Arcadia to Miami, and from there to a little town near Lake Okeechobee. Parker had moved from one town to the next within a period of six months. To Cam, it looked more like running.

But from what?

"Sheriff Arnette."

"Sheriff Arnette, this is Sheriff Rafferty, Emmitsboro, Maryland."

"Maryland, huh? How's the weather?"

Cam glanced out the window. "Looks like rain coming in."

"Eighty-five and sunny," Arnette put in smugly. "So what can I do for you, Sheriff?"

"I'm trying to track down the man who used

to hold my job here. Name's Parker. Garrett Parker. He and his wife, Beatrice, moved into your territory about a year ago."

"I recollect the Parkers," Arnette said. "They rented a place by the lake. Bought themselves an RV. Said they were going to do some traveling."

Cam rubbed an ache at the back of his neck. "When did they leave?"

"Ain't. Both of 'em buried in Cypress Knolls the last ten months."

"They're dead? Both of them?"

"House burned to the ground. Didn't have no smoke detectors. They was both in bed."

"What was the cause of the fire?"

"Smoking in bed," he said. "House was all wood. Went up like a tinderbox. You say he was sheriff there before you?"

"That's right."

"Funny. He told everybody he was a retired insurance man and they were from Atlanta. You got any idea why he'd do that?"

"Maybe. I'd like to see a copy of the police reports, Sheriff."

"I could do that—if you tell me what you've got cooking."

"There's a chance that the Parkers' deaths might be connected to a murder I've got here."

"That so?" Arnette paused and considered. "Maybe I'll have to have another look-see myself."

"Did they have any visitors?"

"Not a one. Kept to themselves. Seemed to me that the wife wanted to put down stakes and Parker couldn't wait to pull them up. Guess he didn't pull them up in time."

"No, I guess he didn't."

Fifteen minutes later, Cam found Bud ticketing a Buick in the red zone in front of the library. "Don't know why Miz Atherton keeps parking here," he began. "Guess she'll come and strip a few layers off my hide."

"The mayor'll pay the fine. Bud, I need to talk to Sarah. I'd like you to come along."

"Sure." He pocketed the citation book. "She in some kind of trouble?"

"I don't know. Let's walk it."

Bud slicked a hand over his cowlick. "Sheriff, I don't like to . . . I just wanted to say that Sarah's got some problems right now. She and my mom have been fighting a lot lately."

"I'm sorry, Bud, I just need to ask her some questions."

"If she's done something . . ." He thought about the men going up the back stairs into her room. "She might listen to me. I could try to get her to straighten up."

"We're just going to talk to her." They skirted the park, where Mitzi Hawbaker had her youngest on the swing and Mr. Finch walked his Yorkies. "The Ladies Club put in some real nice flowers this year."

Bud looked down at the petunias. He knew Cam was trying to make an uncomfortable situation easier. But it wasn't working. "Sarah's just mixed up. She never got anything she wanted. Guys were always after her, and they weren't much good." He looked at Cam, looked away, and cleared his throat.

"It was a long time ago, Bud. And I wasn't much good."

They got to Clyde's and walked around the back.

"Her car's not here."

"I can see that," Cam murmured. "We'll see what time her shift starts." Cam banged on the rear door of the bar.

"Goddamn it, we're closed. Ain't opening till five."

"It's Rafferty."

"I don't care if it's Christ Almighty wanting a Budweiser, we're closed."

"I don't want a drink, Clyde. I'm looking for Sarah."

"You and half the men in town." Clyde pushed open the door and scowled. From his tiny boxlike office came the theme music for a long-running soap opera. "Can't a man sit for five minutes in peace?"

"What time will Sarah be in tonight?"

"That worthless—" He caught himself because he had affection for Bud. "Supposed to be in at four-thirty. Just like she was supposed to be in at four-thirty yesterday and the day before. She ain't deigned to show up this week."

"She hasn't come in to work?"

"No, she hasn't come in to work. Didn't I just say? She hasn't shown her butt around here since Saturday night." He stuck out a finger at Bud. "You see her, you tell her she's fired. I got the Jenkins girl working her shift now."

"Has she been upstairs?" Cam asked.

"How the hell do I know? I'm one of the few men in town that don't climb those steps." He looked away, sorry to see Bud's face. But, damn it, they'd interrupted his favorite show.

"Do you mind if we look around upstairs?"

"Nothing to me. You're the law, and he's her brother."

"How about a key, Clyde?"

"Jesus H. Christ." He swung away and rattled through a drawer. "You tell her if she don't come up with this month's rent by the end of the week, she's out. I ain't running no halfway house." He thrust the key into Cam's hand and slammed the door.

"That's why I love him," Cam said. "For his cheery smile and sparkling personality."

"It's not like Sarah to miss work," Bud said as

they climbed the stairs. "She's been wanting to save up and move to the city."

"She's been fighting with your mother," Cam pointed out. "Maybe she decided to take a few days to cool off." He knocked first, waited, then slipped the key into the lock.

The single room was almost empty. The rug was in place, a braided oval, ragged around the edges. The pullout bed was unmade, the red polyester satin sheets rumpled. There was a lamp, a dresser with a missing drawer, and a rickety vanity. Dust had settled, and Cam could see the lighter spots where bottles and jars had sat on the vanity top. He opened the closet and found it empty.

"Looks like she cleared out."

"She wouldn't just leave. I know she's been pissed at Mom, but she'd've told me."

Cam opened a drawer. "Her clothes are gone."

"Yeah, but . . ." Bud rubbed his hands over his hair. "She wouldn't just leave, Cam. Not without letting me know."

"Okay, we'll check things out. Why don't you take the bathroom?"

Cam opened the rest of the drawers, took them out, looked behind and beneath. He tried not to think of Sarah as a person, not to remember her the way she had been all those years ago. Or the way she had looked the last time he'd seen her. Odds were she'd gotten fed up and taken off. When she ran out of money, she'd be back.

But as he looked through the empty drawers of the vanity, he kept remembering the phone call on Sunday night.

They're killing her.

Taped to the back of the bottom vanity drawer, he found a wad of bills folded into a Baggie. The sickness in his stomach increased as he counted them out.

"She left half a bottle of face cream and some—" Bud paused in the bathroom doorway. "What's that?"

"I found it taped to the drawer. Bud, there's four hundred and thirty-seven dollars here."

"Four hundred?" Wide and helpless, Bud's eyes focused on the bills. "She's been saving. Saving so she could move. Cam, she'd never have gone away without that money." His gaze lifted to Cam's even as he lowered himself to the edge of the bed. "Oh, Christ. What are we going to do?"

"We're going to call the State boys and put out an APB. And we're going to talk to your mother." He slipped the plastic bag of money into his pocket. "Bud, did Sarah have something going with Parker before he left town?"

"Parker?" Bud looked up blankly, then flushed. "I guess maybe she did. Jesus, Cam, you can't think she went down to Florida to be with Parker. She used to make fun of him. It wasn't like she had a thing for him. It was just that he . . . She was saving," he murmured.

"Did she ever tell you anything about him? Like that he belonged to a club?"

"A club? You mean like the Moose or something?"

"Or something."

"He used to hang out at the Legion. You know that. I'm telling you, she wouldn't have gone to Parker. She could barely stand him. She wouldn't have left here, left her money and her family and gone to Parker."

"No, I know that." He put a hand on Bud's shoulder. "Bud, who else did she sleep with?"

"Jesus, Cam."

"I'm sorry. We have to start somewhere. Was there anyone who gave her a hard time, kept after her?"

"Davey Reeder kept asking her to marry him. She laughed about that. Oscar Roody used to pretend a lot, but he never came up here that I know. Sarah said he was scared of his wife. Lots of others, I guess. She said that most of the upstanding citizens of Emmitsboro and the tristate area had been upstanding in here. She talks like that, but it doesn't mean anything."

"Okay. Why don't we go make those calls?"

"Cam, you think something's happened to her? Something bad?"

Sometimes a lie was best. "I think she probably got riled and headed out. Sarah always acts first and thinks later."

"Yeah." Because he had nothing else, Bud clung to that. "She'll come back when she's cooled off and sweet-talk Clyde into giving her her job back."

But when they left the tiny room behind, neither of them believed it.

Joleen Butts sat at her kitchen table busily making lists. It was the first time in weeks she'd taken an afternoon off. But then, midweek afternoons were slow, and she figured Will could spare her.

It wasn't every day your son graduated from high school.

She was concerned by the fact that Ernie showed no interest in college. But she tried not to make too much of it. After all, she hadn't gone to college either, and things had turned out just fine. Will had pictured Ernie with an MBA and was bitterly disappointed. But then, he'd never really gotten over the fact that Ernie refused to work in the pizza parlor after school.

Both she and Will had built themselves up for

that fall, she decided. They'd worked so hard trying to make a success out of the place so that they could bring Ernie into a thriving business. And he preferred to pump gas.

Well, the boy was nearly eighteen. By his age, she'd certainly dished out plenty of disappointment to her parents. She just wished . . . Joleen set her pen aside. She just wished her son would smile more.

She heard him come in the front and brightened instantly. It had been so long since they had sat and talked in the kitchen. Like the old days, when he'd come home from school and they'd had cookies and worked on long division together.

"Ernie." She heard him hesitate on the stairs. The boy spends too much time in his room, she thought. Too much time alone. "Ernie, I'm in the kitchen. Come on back."

He walked through the doorway, hands stuffed in his jeans pockets. She thought he looked a little pale but remembered he'd been sick on Monday. Just a touch of graduation nerves, she thought, and smiled at him.

"What are you doing here?"

It was like an accusation, but she made her lips curve. "I took a few hours off. I can never remember your schedule. Aren't you working today?"

"Not till five."

"Good, then we'll have a little time." She rose and took the head off the fat, white-hatted ceramic chef that served as a cookie jar. "I picked up some chocolate chip."

"I'm not hungry."

"You haven't been eating well for a couple of days. Are you still sick?" She started to put a hand to his forehead, but he jerked back.

"I don't want any cookies, all right?"

"Sure." She felt she was looking at a stranger whose eyes were too dark, skin too pale. His hands kept sliding in and out of his pockets. "Did you have a good day at school?"

"We're not doing anything but marking time."

"Well . . ." She felt her smile falter and bolstered it up. "I know how that is. The last week before graduation is like the last week before your parole comes up. I pressed your gown."

"Great. I got things to do."

"I wanted to talk to you." She fumbled for her lists. "About the get-together."

"What get-together?"

"You know, we discussed it. The Sunday after graduation. Grandma and Pop are coming down, and Aunt Marcie. Nana and Frank, too, from Cleveland. I don't know where everyone's going to sleep, but—"

"Why do they have to come?"

"Why, for you. I know you only got two tickets for the actual graduation because the school's so small, but that doesn't mean we can't all get together and have a party."

"I told you I didn't want one."

"No, you said you didn't care." She set down the list again and struggled with her temper.

"Well, I do care, and I don't want a party. I don't want to see any of those people. I don't want to see anyone at all."

"I'm afraid you're going to have to." She heard her own voice, flat, cold, uncompromising and realized it sounded just like her own mother's. Full circle, she thought, wearily. "The plans are already made, Ernie. Your father's mother and stepfather will be here Saturday night, along with some of your cousins. Everyone else will get here Sunday morning." She held up a hand, warding off his complaints like a traffic cop holding back cars. Another of her mother's habits, she realized. "Now, you might not want to see them, but they all want to see you. They're proud of you, and they want to be a part of this step in your life."

"I'm getting out of school. What's the big fucking deal?"

"Don't you speak to me like that." She stepped toward him. He was taller by inches, but she had the power of motherhood on her side. "I don't care whether you're seventeen or a hundred and seven, don't you ever speak to me like that."

"I don't want a bunch of stupid relatives

around." His voice began to hitch, and he panicked because he couldn't stop it. "I don't want a party. I'm the one who's graduating, aren't I? Don't I have a choice?"

Her heart went out to him. She remembered what it was like to be trapped in parental borders. She hadn't understood it either. "I'm sorry, but I guess you don't. It's only a couple of days out of your life, Ernie."

"Sure. *My* life." He kicked a chair over. "It's my life. You didn't give me a choice when we moved here, either. Because it would be 'good' for me."

"Your father and I thought it would. We thought it would be good for all of us."

"Yeah. It's just great. You take me away from all of my friends and stick me in some hick town where all the kids talk about is shooting deer and raising pigs. And men go around killing women."

"What are you talking about?" She laid a hand on his arm, but he jerked away. "Ernie, I know that woman was attacked, and it was terrible. But she wasn't killed. Things like that don't happen here."

"You don't know anything." His face was dead white now, his eyes bitter and wet. "You don't know anything about this town. You don't know anything about me."

"I know I love you, and I worry about you.

Maybe I've been spending too much time at the restaurant and not enough with you, just talking. Sit down now. Sit down with me and let's talk this out."

"It's too late." He covered his face with his hands and began to weep as she hadn't seen him weep in years.

"Oh, baby. Honey, come here. Tell me what I can do."

But when she put her arms around him, he jerked away. His eyes weren't bitter any longer, but wild. "It's too late. I made a choice. I already made it, and it's too late to go back. Just leave me alone. Leave me alone, that's what you're best at."

He stumbled out of the house and ran. The louder she called after him, the faster he ran.

Chapter 24

CLARE PUT THE FINISHING TOUCHES
on her sculpture of Alice. It would be the first
piece for the women's wing at the Betadyne. It
showed grace, competence, fortitude, and quiet
determination. She could think of few better
qualities in a woman.

She glanced up once when she heard Ernie's
tires scream on the pavement as he roared down
the street. Her brow furrowed as she heard his
mother calling him. Before Sally had told her
about the telescope, Clare would have been
tempted to drive after him herself, to try to
soothe and smooth over.

Don't get involved, she told herself as she
went back to her work. If she hadn't gotten involved in the first place, she wouldn't feel odd

and uneasy every time she pulled down the bedroom shade.

And she had problems of her own. Contracts and commissions, a relationship that had zoomed out of control, a damn luncheon speech. She blew the hair out of her eyes and looked at her watch. Plus she had to tell Cam about the phrase Lisa had remembered.

Where the hell was he?

She'd gone directly by the sheriff's office on her way back from the hospital, but he hadn't been there. She'd called his house, and he hadn't answered. Out preserving law and order, she supposed, and smiled a little. She'd see him in a few hours in any case, when they were both off duty.

Clare turned off her torch and stepped back. Not bad, she thought, narrowing her eyes. Excitement began to stir as she pushed her goggles up. No, it wasn't bad at all. Perhaps it wouldn't be exactly what Alice had had in mind since the female form was elongated, exaggerated, the features anonymous. It was Everywoman, which was exactly what Clare thought she might title it. The four arms might throw Alice off a bit, but to Clare they symbolized a woman's ability to do her duties simultaneously, and with the same cool-handed style.

"What's that supposed to be?" Blair asked

from behind her and made her jolt. "A skinny rendition of the goddess Kali?"

"No. Kali had six arms. I think." Clare pulled off goggles and skullcap. "It's Alice."

Blair lifted a brow. "Sure it is. I could see that right away."

"Peasant."

"Weirdo." But his smile faded quickly when he stepped into the garage, a stack of books in his hands. "Clare, what's all this?"

One glance had her cheeks heating. "You've been poking around in my room. I thought we settled the privacy issue when we were ten."

"The phone rang while I was upstairs. Your bedroom phone is the closest."

"I didn't realize I'd put the phone in my night-stand drawer."

"I was looking for a pad. I'm doing some research for Cam, and I needed to write some-thing down. But that's not the issue, is it?"

She took the books from him and dropped them on a workbench. "My reading material is my business."

He put his hands on her shoulders. "That's not an answer."

"It's my answer."

"Clare, this isn't a matter of my peeking into your diary and finding out you have a crush on the captain of the football team."

"It was the tight end." She tried to shrug away, but he held firm. "Blair, I've got work to do."

He gave her a quick shake that was both affectionate and impatient. "Listen, I thought it was what's going on between you and Cam that had you so nervous and upset."

"Just nervous," she corrected. "Not upset."

"No, I can see that. But I knew something was bothering you the minute I got here. Why do you think I stayed?"

"Because you're addicted to the way I burn hamburgers."

"I hate the way you burn hamburgers."

"You ate two last night."

"Which should give you a clue to how much I love you. Now where did you get the books?"

The anger went out of her. He could see it melt out of her eyes until they were dark and damp. "They were Dad's."

"Dad's?" His fingers went limp on her shoulders. Whatever he had suspected, whatever he had feared, it had never been this. "What do you mean they were Dad's?"

"I found them in the attic, in the boxes Mom stored away. She'd saved most of his books and some other things. His gardening shirt and his— his broken compass. The rocks he'd collected when he took that trip to the Grand Canyon. Blair, I thought she'd gotten rid of everything."

"So did I." He felt like a child again, confused, vulnerable, sad. "Let's sit down."

They sat on the half step between the kitchen and the garage. "It always seemed, after he died, that she just—put it all behind her. You know." Clare gripped her hands together, holding them between her knees. "I resented that, the way she picked up and went on. I knew—in my head I knew—that she had so many things to deal with. The business falling apart, the awful scandal with the shopping center. The fact that even though it was ruled an accident, everyone wondered if he'd jumped. She just handled everything so well. In my heart I hated her for it."

He slipped an arm around her shoulders. "She had us to worry about, too."

"I know. I know that. It just seemed that she never stumbled, you know? She never faltered or fell apart, so a part of me always wondered if she'd ever really cared. Then I found all those things, the way she'd boxed them up so carefully, keeping all those little junky things that had meant so much to him. I realized, I think I realized, how she might have felt when she'd done it. I wished she'd let me help her."

"You weren't in any shape to help. It was worse for you, Clare. You found him. I never saw . . ." He shut his eyes a moment and leaned his head against hers. "Neither did Mom. We all lost him, but you were the only one who had to see. She stayed up with you all that first night."

Clare looked back at him, then down at her feet. "I didn't know."

"Doc Crampton sedated you, but you kept calling out in your sleep. And crying." When she lifted a hand to Blair, he gripped it hard. "She sat by the bed all night. Everything happened so fast after that. The funeral, then the story breaking about the kickbacks."

"I wish I understood. I wish I understood any of it."

They sat silently for a moment, hip to hip. "Tell me about the books."

"I found them upstairs. You know how Dad used to read anything—everything." She was talking too fast and rose, hoping to slow herself down. "Religion was a kind of obsession with him. The way he was raised . . ."

"I know." Obsessions. Rebellions. Power. Good God.

"Well, he just devoured stuff like that. From Martin Luther to Buddha and everything in between. I guess he was just trying to figure out what was right. If anything was right. It doesn't mean anything."

He rose as well, to take both of her nervous hands. "Have you told Cam?"

"Why should I?" Panic sprang into her voice. "It doesn't have anything to do with him."

"What are you afraid of?"

"Nothing. I'm not afraid of anything. I don't even know why we're talking about this. I'm just going to put the books back in the attic."

"Cam's working on the theory that Biff's death and the attack on Lisa MacDonald might be tied up with a cult."

"That's ridiculous. And even if it has some merit, which it doesn't, it hardly applies to Dad. He's been dead for more than ten years."

"Clare, be logical. This is a small, close-knit community. If there's a cult going on in this town and you found a library on Satanism in somebody's house, what conclusion would you draw?"

"I don't know." She pulled her hands away. "I don't see that it applies."

"We both know that it applies," he said quietly. "Dad is dead, Clare. He doesn't need you to protect him."

"He wouldn't have had anything to do with this kind of thing. Christ, Blair, I read the books, too. I'm not going to go out and sacrifice a virgin."

"You sent Cam out to the farm because you'd seen one book in Biff's den."

She looked up. "You seem to know a lot about what's going on."

"I told you, I'm helping him with research. My point is, you thought that one book was enough to warrant his investigating. And you were right. Do you know what he found?"

"No." She wet her lips. "I didn't ask. I don't want to know."

"He found evidence that Carly Jamison had been held there."

"Oh, God."

"He found drugs, too. And his mother told him she'd burned a black cloak, black candles, several pornographic magazines with a Satanic bent. There's no doubt that Biff was involved with some kind of cult. And it takes more than one person to make a cult."

"Dad's dead," she said again. "And when he was alive, he could barely tolerate Biff Stokey. You can't honestly believe that our father would have had anything to do with kidnapping young girls."

"I wouldn't have believed he'd do anything illegal, either, but I was wrong. We have to face it, Clare. And we have to deal with it."

"Don't tell me what I have to deal with." She turned away.

"If you don't go to Cam with this, I will."

She shut her eyes tight. "He was your father, too."

"And I loved him as much as you did." He grabbed her and spun her around. "Damn it, Clare, do you think any of this is easy to take? I hate thinking there's a chance, even a shadow of a chance, that he might have been involved with something like this. But we have to deal with it now. We can't go back and make everything all right. But maybe, just maybe, if we figure it all out, it'll make a difference."

"All right." She covered her face with her hands. When she dropped them, her eyes were cool and dry. "All right. But I'll go to Cam."

"I figure she just lit out." Mick Morgan sipped coffee and nodded at Cam. "You know how she was. Sarah'd get a bug up her butt and do most anything."

"Maybe." Cam kept typing the report. "Seems odd she'd have left the money behind, though. From what her mother told me, she and Sarah had been fighting about Sarah's little sideline. Sarah told her she wasn't going to be making money that way much longer. Claimed she had some deal in the works that was going to set her up."

"Could be just talk," Mick mused. He didn't like the way Cam was latching on to this. He hadn't figured anyone would think twice about Sarah Hewitt leaving town. "Or could be she'd hooked up with something, and that's why she took off. Odds are she'll cruise back into town in a few days." He set the mug down and sighed. "Women are a mystery to me, Cam, and that's a fact. My wife took off to her mother's for a solid week once 'cause I bitched about her meatloaf. There's no figuring them."

"I'll go along with that." He pulled the sheet out of the typewriter. "But I feel better having the APB out on her. Bud's pretty shook. I might need you to fill in some for the next couple of days."

"Sure thing. He's a good kid, Bud is. Never could figure how come his sister never straightened out. Want me to take Bud's route?"

"Appreciate it. He's staying with his mom. Finish your coffee, though. There's time."

"Don't mind if I do." The chair creaked as he leaned back. "Sure was funny, you finding all that stuff out to the farm. Biff Stokey'd be the last person I'd figure for drugs. Liked his beer, all right, but can't see him sniffing powder up his nose."

"Makes me wonder how well we know anyone. You played poker with him, didn't you?"

"Oh, now and again." Mick smiled reminiscently. "We'd get a group together and get drunk, eat salami sandwiches, and play a quarter limit. Not strictly legal if it comes to it, but nobody squawks about the bingo over at the Catholic church or the tip jars at the firehall on Las Vegas night."

"Drugs?"

The casual question had Mick's brows lifting. "Come on, Cam. You don't think any of those boys would have done that shit around me? Hell, I can't see Roody lighting up a joint. Can you?"

The image had Cam grinning. "No. Fact is, it's hard to see drugs and murder around here. But we've got both."

"I'd say they're tied in. Looks to me like Biff got in over his head and some dealer from the city whiffed him."

Cam gave a noncommittal grunt. "I found out something else odd today. Parker and his wife are dead."

"Sheriff Parker?" Mick sat up straight. His insides began to tremble. "Jesus, Cam. How'd that happen?"

"House fire. They were living on a lake in Florida."

"Lauderdale."

"No." Cam steepled his hands. "They moved from Lauderdale. In fact, they moved quite a bit last year. Zigzagging around the state."

"Itchy feet."

"Itchy something. I'm waiting for the police and fire department reports."

Mick was seeing Parker where Cam sat now, his belly over his belt, and had to bring himself back. "What for?"

"I'll know when I see them." He glanced up as Clare walked in. He shuffled papers on top of the report he'd just typed, then smiled at her. "Hi."

"Hi." She didn't quite manage a smile. "Hello, Mr. Morgan."

"Hey there. Heard you're working on some big deal with a fancy museum."

"Looks that way." She set the bag of books on the desk. "Am I interrupting?"

"Nope." Mick set his mug aside again. One look from Cam had told him the Parker business wasn't for open discussion. "Just chewing the fat."

"I'd like to talk to you," she said to Cam, "if you've got a minute."

"I've got a few of them." He could see trouble on her face and glanced at Mick.

"Guess I'll be going on, then." The deputy stood. "I'll check back in at seven."

"Thanks."

"Nice seeing you, Clare." He gave her a little pat on the shoulder as he moved by her.

"You, too." She waited until he'd closed the door, then dived straight in. "I don't think this means anything. More than that, I don't think it's any of your business. But—"

"Whoa." He held up a hand, then took hers. "Should I suit up?"

"I'm sorry," she said more calmly. "It's just that

I've had a go-around with Blair, and I'm not happy about the outcome."

"Want me to go rough him up for you?"

"No." This time she did smile a little. "I can do that for myself. Cam, I don't want you to think I was keeping this from you. I felt—still feel—that it's family business."

"Why don't you just tell me?"

Instead, she took the books out of the bag and set them on his desk. He looked at them, one at a time. A couple he'd already seen, at Biff's or at the library. While he studied them, Clare lighted a cigarette.

They were old, and obviously well used. Some of the pages were splattered with coffee or liquor stains. Passages were underlined, pages dog-eared.

"Where did you get these?"

She blew out smoke. "They were my father's."

With his eyes on hers, he set them aside. "Maybe you'd better sit down and explain."

"I'll stand up and explain." She took another jerky drag and exhaled. "I found them boxed up in the attic. In my father's old office. I don't know if you were aware, but he was fascinated by religion. All religions. He also had books on Islam, Hinduism, stacks on Catholicism—any other *ism* you can name. Blair seems to think I should have brought these to you."

"You should have."

"I don't agree." She put out the cigarette, snapping it in half. "But since Blair was adamant, I said I would. Now I have."

"Sit down, Slim."

"I'm not in the mood to be interrogated. I brought them to you, and you can make what you like out of it."

He studied her in silence. Her eyes were too bright, her mouth just beginning to tremble. Cam rose from his chair and walked around the desk. As she stood rigid, he put his arms around her.

"I know this isn't easy."

"No, you don't know. You can't know."

"If I had a choice, I'd tell you to take the books and walk away so we could pretend this never happened." He drew back. "I don't have that choice."

"He was a good man. I had to listen to people say terrible things about him once. I don't think I could stand it a second time."

"I'll do everything I can. That's all I can promise."

"I want you to try to believe in him. I want you to see that owning these books, reading them, studying them, even believing in some of what they say wouldn't make him a bad person."

"Then let me try to prove that. Sit down. Please."

She did, stiffly, her hands linked on her lap.

"Clare, did he ever talk to you about these books or what's in them?"

"No, never. He talked about religions. It was a big topic, especially after—after he started drinking. He went back into the church. He was raised Catholic, but he'd had a real attitude about organized religion because of the way he was raised."

"When did he go back to the church?"

"When I was about seven or eight. It became very important to him. Blair and I ended up going to CCD classes and making our First Communion. The whole bit."

"That would have been about twenty years ago?"

"Yeah." She smiled wanly. "Time marches on."

He noted it down, wondering what events he could tie in. "Did you ever wonder why?"

"Sure. At the time I was too young to think about it. And I liked the mass and the music, the priest's clothes. The whole ritual." She stopped abruptly, uncomfortable with her own choice of words. "Later, I suppose I figured that he'd just gotten a little older, put some distance between himself and all the things he'd rebelled against in his upbringing. He'd probably missed the security and the familiarity. He'd have been about the age I am now," she murmured. "Nearly thirty and starting to wonder what the rest of his life would be like. He was worried about Blair and me, too. The fact that we'd had no religious training. He felt as though he'd overcompensated for his parents by going as far in the opposite direction as possible."

"Did he say that?"

"Yes, actually, I remember him saying almost exactly that to my mother. Dad was what my mother called a fretter. Always worrying whether he'd done the right thing or, if he had, whether he'd done it well enough. He tried so hard not to stuff the church down our throats. He wasn't a fanatic, Cam. He was just a man struggling to do his best."

"When did he start drinking, Clare?"

"I don't really know." Her fingers began to twist together on her lap. "It wasn't a sudden thing, more of a progressive one. None of us really noticed at first. I remember him having a whiskey and soda after dinner. Then maybe he'd have two. Then he stopped bothering with the soda."

The misery in her voice had him reaching over to still her hands. "Clare, I've been down that road. I'm the last one who would condemn him."

"I feel disloyal. Can't you understand? I feel like I'm betraying him by talking about his flaws and mistakes."

"He was a whole person. Whole people have flaws. Don't you think he'd have wanted you to recognize them and love him anyway?"

"You sound like my shrink." She rose and walked to the window. "I was thirteen the first time I saw him really drunk. I'd come home from school. Blair had band practice, and my mother was at a meeting. Emmitsboro Boosters or something. Dad was at the kitchen table, crying into a bottle of whiskey. It scared me to see him that way, reeking and sobbing, his eyes all red. He kept telling me how sorry he was. His words were all slurred together, and he tried to stand up. He fell. He just lay there on the kitchen floor, crying and trying to apologize." She brushed impatiently at a tear. " 'I'm sorry, baby. I'm so sorry. I don't know what to do. I can't do anything. I can't change it. I can't go back and change it.' "

"Change what?"

"His drinking, I suppose. He couldn't control it. He didn't think he could change it. He told me he'd never wanted me to see him that way. He was really frantic about that. He'd never wanted me to see, wanted me to know."

"Wouldn't that have been around the time he was making the deal for the shopping center?"

"Yes. And the closer all that came to being a reality, the more he drank. My father was a very uncomfortable criminal. His ambitions might have gotten out of line, but his conscience made him pay."

"I want you to try to think. Did he go out at night with any regularity? Did he go out with someone or a particular group?"

Sighing, she turned back. "He belonged to all kinds of groups, Cam. The Jaycees, the Optimist Club, the Knights of Columbus. He was out quite a bit for meetings, dinners, to show houses after hours. I used to ask to go with him, but he would tuck me into bed and tell me I had to wait until I grew up, then he would make me his partner. One night I snuck into his car—" She broke off, eyes panicked, cheeks paling.

"You snuck into his car?" Cam prompted.

"No, no, I didn't. I only dreamed I did. You can keep the books if you think they'll help. I need to get back."

He took her arm before she could bolt for the door. "What did you dream, Clare?"

"For Christ's sake, Cam, my dreams are certainly my business."

She had the same look on her face, precisely the same look, as when he had pulled her out of the nightmare. "Where did he go that night?"

"I don't know. I was dreaming."

"Where did you dream he went?"

She went limp, seemed to fold into herself when he eased her into the chair again. "I don't know. It was a dream. I was only about five or six."

"But you remember the dream. You still have the dream."

She stared at the books on Cam's desk. "Sometimes."

"Tell me what you remember."

"It didn't happen. I woke up in my own bed."

"Before you woke up?"

"I dreamed I hid in the back of the car. I knew he was going out, and I wanted to surprise him, to show him that I was big enough to be his partner. We didn't go to a house. We were outside. I followed him. It seemed like such an adventure. There was a place, and other men were there. I thought it was a meeting, like the Moose or the Elks, because . . . they all wore long black robes with hoods."

Oh, God, Slim, he thought. What did you see? "Go ahead."

"They wore masks, and I thought that was funny because it wasn't Halloween. It was spring. I hid in the bushes and watched."

"There were other men. Who were they?"

"I don't know. I didn't pay attention. I was looking at my father. They made a circle and rang a bell. There were women. Two women in red robes. One of them took off the robe and lay down on top of something. I was fascinated and embarrassed all at once. There was chanting and a fire. A big fire. I was sleepy, and I couldn't understand it all. The man in the big mask had a sword. It glinted in the moonlight. He would say things, then the rest of the group would say things."

"What things?"

"I couldn't understand." But she had read the books, and she had remembered. "They weren't names I knew."

"Names?"

"Oh, God, Cam, the names in the books. The calling up of demons."

"Okay, take it easy."

She swiped the heel of her hand over her cheek. "I was cold and tired, and I wanted Daddy to take me back home. But I was afraid, and I didn't know why. The man in the mask touched the woman, fondled her. They brought out a goat, a little white goat, and he took a knife. I wanted to run, but I couldn't. I wanted to run away, but my legs wouldn't move. The men took off their robes but left their masks on and danced around the pit of fire. I saw my father. I saw him with blood on his hands. And I woke up screaming, in my own bed."

He pulled her out of the chair to hold her, and his hands were gentle. But his eyes stared over her shoulder and were cold with fury.

"It wasn't real," she insisted. "It didn't happen. I woke up in bed, just as I always do when I have that dream. My mother and father were there."

"Did you tell them about the dream?"

"I couldn't at first. I guess I was hysterical. I remember my father rocking me, stroking my hair and rocking me. He kept telling me it was a dream, just a terrible dream, and that he would never let anything bad happen to me."

Cam pulled her back, looked long and deep into her eyes. "It wasn't a dream, Clare."

"It had to be." Her hands shook. "It had to be a dream. I was in bed. My father was there with me. I know you're thinking about the books. I thought about them too. He must have bought them afterward. He was worried about me, about why I had the dream, and that it kept coming back. He wanted to understand. He was worried about me. For weeks after, he would come into my room at bedtime and tell me silly stories, sing songs, just be there."

"I know he was worried about you. I know he loved you. But I think he was involved in something he couldn't control. Just like the drinking, Clare."

She shook her head, frantic, furious. "I'm not going to believe that."

"Clare, he must have been sick at the thought that you had seen him and what went on. A few years later, you're still having nightmares, he sees that it's not going to stop. And he tries to pull out. He goes back to the religion of his childhood."

"You didn't know him the way I did."

"No, I didn't."

"He would never have hurt anyone. He wasn't capable of it."

"Maybe he didn't hurt anyone but himself. Clare, I don't want to hurt you, but I'm going to have to dig deeper. Part of that will be looking into whatever information is available on the land deal, the shopping center business. And your father's death."

"Why? What possible difference can any of it make now?"

"Because what you saw that night is still going on. Have you told anyone else about your dream?"

"No."

"Don't."

She nodded. "Are we finished?"

"No." He pulled her close again, ignoring her rigid stance. "I'll just wait you out, Slim," he murmured. "You can step back, build a wall, run away, and cover your trail. I'll just wait you out."

"I can't think about you and me right now."

"Yes, you can." He put a hand under her chin, lifting it until their eyes met. "Because when the rest is done, that's all there is. I love you." He tightened his grip when she would have turned away. "Damn it, that's one bit you're going to have to swallow once and for all. I love you, and I never expected to feel this way about anybody. But it's a fact."

"I know. If this could have happened without the rest—"

"It happened. That's the bottom line. I want to know what you're going to do about it."

She put a hand on his cheek. "I guess I'm going to love you back. That's about all I can do right now."

"That'll be fine." He kissed her. "I wish I could fix it for you."

"I'm old enough to fix things for myself. I'd rather have a friend than a white knight."

"How about a friend and a black sheep?"

"It's a nice combination. I wasn't holding this back from you. I was," she corrected before he could speak. "But I was holding it back from myself first. I need to go home and think things through. You'll want to keep the books?"

"Yes. Clare . . ." He brushed the hair back from her cheeks. "We're going to need to talk again, to go over everything you remember in more detail."

"I was afraid you'd say that."

"Why don't we table it for tonight? What do you think about dinner at a Mexican restaurant? They've got pots and paper flowers."

"I think that sounds like a great idea. Can we take your bike?"

"A woman after my own heart."

"I'll be ready by seven." She went to the door, then stopped. "Rafferty, you made it easier than it might have been. I appreciate that."

Alone, he sat at the desk and studied his notes. He was afraid he wouldn't be able to make it easy for long.

Chapter 25

Min Atherton was the kind of woman who kept candles out for a centerpiece with the cellophane still wrapped around them. Almost everything she owned was for show and not for use. She would buy pink or purple candles—her favorite colors—and place them in the genuine brass or crystal holders, where they would stay snug in their clear wrap, never to be lit.

She liked buying things. More, she liked being able to buy things—particularly things her neighbors couldn't afford. Often, she left the price tags on, hoping a guest would take a peek at the base of a vase or statuette. In their place, she would. And did.

Min considered flaunting a responsibility. She

was the mayor's wife, after all, and she had her stature to uphold. She knew they were the most well-to-do couple in town and her husband was devoted to her. Hadn't he bought her a pair of honest-to-God diamond earring clips just last Christmas? One-half carat each, too, counting the baguettes. Min showed them off at the Church of God every Sunday.

She made certain her hair was tucked behind her ears and that she tilted her head from side to side as she solemnly sang the hymns so that the stones would catch the light—and the envy of the congregation.

Her home was crowded with furniture. She didn't believe in antiques, no matter how expensive or valuable they might be. Min liked things new, brand spanking new, so that she was the first to use them. She only bought brand names. In that way she could talk about her La-Z-Boy, her Ethan Allen, or her Sealy Posturepedic as if they were members of the family.

Some of the less charitable people of the community said it was a shame she didn't have less money and more taste.

But Min recognized green-eyed jealousy when she saw it and hugged it to her like a medal of honor.

She loved her big, rambling brick house on Laurel Lane and had decorated every inch of it herself, from the living room with its pink and lavender floral sofa and matching draperies, to the powder room with its wild rose ceramic tile and hyacinth wallpaper. She liked big statues of dancing ladies in ball gowns and men in waistcoats. All of her plants were plastic, but they were tucked into precious containers in the form of woolly sheep and cottontail rabbits.

Min's creativity didn't stop with the interior. Goodness no. Many of the residents of Emmitsboro would never have the privilege of being invited inside the Atherton castle. Min felt they deserved some glimpses of the glamour within.

She had her big striped umbrella table on the patio, with its matching chairs and chaise longue. Since real animals made such a mess, she substituted plastic and plaster ones so that the yard was alive with ducks and squirrels and more sheep.

In the front, opposite her pedestaled moon ball was her pride and joy, a cast-iron stable boy, black-faced, red-liveried, with a permanently sappy grin. Davey Reeder had once done some carpentry work for them and stuck his lunch pail on the statue's outstretched hand. Min had failed to see the humor of it.

Inside and out, Min's home was neat as a pin. For today, the monthly Ladies Club luncheon, she'd even gone down to the florist and bought a centerpiece of lilies and greens. Out of her own pocket. Of course, she'd see that their prissy accountant found a way to deduct it.

A penny saved was a penny left to spend.

"James. James. I want you to come in here and take a look. You know how I value your opinion."

Atherton stepped out of the kitchen into the dining room, smiling and sipping coffee. He studied his wife in her new pink dress and flowered bolero jacket. She'd worn her diamonds and had had Betty give her a rinse and her best bouffant. She'd had a manicure and a pedicure. Her pink toes peeked out of her size ten heels. Atherton kissed her on the tip of her nose.

"You look beautiful, Min. You always do."

She giggled and slapped playfully at his chest. "Not me, silly. The table."

Dutifully, he studied the dining room table. It was fully extended to seat the eighteen expected guests. On the damask cloth were the correct number of Corelle dinner plates with their tiny painted roses. She'd set out little fingerbowls of lemon water, just as she'd seen in a magazine. In the center were the lilies, flanked by the cellophane-wrapped candles.

"You've outdone yourself."

"You know I like things to look nice." Eagle-eyed, she walked over to hitch a hold out of her shell pink brocade draperies. "Why, last month when it was Edna's turn, she used plastic plates. I was mortified for her."

"I'm sure Edna did her best."

"Of course, of course." She could have said more about Edna, oh, indeed she could. But she knew James could be impatient. "I wanted to make today extra special. Some of the ladies are just frantic, James. Why, there was even talk about having a self-defense course—which, as I told Gladys Finch when she brought it up, is very unladylike. I'm just worried about what they'll think of next."

"Now, Min, we're all doing what we have to do." He winked at her. "You trust me, don't you, Min?"

She blinked at him, eyes bright. "Now, James, you know I do."

"Then leave it to me."

"I always do. Still, that Cameron Rafferty—"

"Cameron's doing his job."

She snorted. "When he's not sniffing around Clare Kimball, you mean. Oh, I know what you're going to say." She waved her pudgy hand at him and made him smile again. "A man's entitled to his free time. But there are priorities." She smiled up at him. "Isn't that what you're always saying, James? A man has priorities."

"You know me too well."

"And so I should after all these years." She fussed with his tie. "I know you're going to want to scat before the girls get here, but I'd like it if you'd stay just for a few minutes. The newspaper and the television station are sending people. You wouldn't want to miss the opportunity. Especially if you're going to run for governor."

"Min, you know that hasn't been settled yet. And"—he tweaked her chin—"it's between you and me."

"I know, and it's just killing me not to brag on it. The idea that the party is considering you for a candidate. Not that it isn't richly deserved." She brushed lovingly at his lapels. "All the years you've put into this town."

"My favorite constituent. I'll stay awhile," he said, "but don't set your hopes on the governor's mansion, Min. The election year's some ways off," he reminded her when he saw her face fall. "Let's just take it as it comes. There's the door. Why don't I get it so you can make a grand entrance?"

Clare was late. But it was better than not showing up at all, which is just what would have happened if Gladys Finch hadn't called and asked Clare if she needed a ride. It was hardly a wonder she'd forgotten after she discovered the sculpture missing from the garage.

Kids, she told herself, and wanted to believe it

had been kids playing a prank. But deep inside there was a fear that it was something much more deadly.

All she could do was report the theft, which she would do the minute this damned luncheon was over.

Why that piece? she wondered. Why that nightmare image?

She shook off the thought and concentrated on what she had to do next. Unfortunately, the call from Gladys hadn't come until noon, and once Clare had remembered what the offer of the ride was for, she'd had to dash from the garage to the bedroom and throw on a suit.

She wasn't sure if the short blue skirt and military-style jacket constituted ladies luncheon wear, but it was the best she could do. Even now she was driving with her elbows as she struggled to fasten her earrings.

She could only groan when she spotted the van from the Hagerstown television station. She pulled up behind it and rested her forehead on the steering wheel.

She hated public speaking. Hated interviews, hated cameras aimed in her direction. Her palms were already wet and clammy, and she hadn't even stepped out of the car.

One of the last things she'd done in New York had been to cave in and speak to Tina Yongers's

club. The art critic had put on the pressure—
just as Min had done. And Clare had buckled.
Just as she always did.

No backbone. No spine. You wimp. You
wuss. She pulled the rearview mirror over
and studied her face. Great. She had mascara
smeared under her eyes. For lack of something
better, she spit on her finger and wiped at it.

"You're a grown woman," she lectured herself. "An adult. A professional. You're going to
have to get over this. And no, you are not going to throw up."

It went deep, and she knew it. The fear, the
panic. All the way back to the weeks after her
father had died. All those questions, all those curious eyes focused on her. All those cameras at
the funeral.

This is now. Damn it, this is today. Get your
queasy stomach and jelly knees out of the car.
All of this was bound to take her mind off of
being robbed—and the prospect of Cam's asking her why the hell she hadn't locked the
garage in the first place.

When she climbed out, the first thing she saw
was the moon ball, then the stable boy. A nervous giggle escaped as she started up the walk.

Then there were the lions. She had to stop.
She had to stare. Reclining on either side of the
steps were a pair of white plaster lions wearing
rhinestone collars.

"Excuse me, boys," she murmured and was grinning when she knocked on the door.

While Clare was dealing with the Ladies Club, Joleen Butts sat on a folding chair beside her husband in the high school gym. The commencement address was running long, and more than a few people were shifting in their seats, but Joleen sat still and stiff with tears in her eyes.

She wasn't certain why she was crying. Because her boy was taking another giant step toward adulthood. Because he looked so much like his father had when she and Will had donned cap and gown. Because she knew, in her heart, she had already lost him.

She hadn't told Will about the argument. How could she? He was sitting there with his own eyes bright and pride glowing all over his face. Nor had she told him that she had raced up to Ernie's room when he slammed out of the house, on a frantic search for drugs. She'd almost hoped she would find them so that she would have something tangible on which to blame his mood swings.

She hadn't found drugs, but what she had found had frightened her more.

The books, the leaflets, the stubs of black candles. The notebook crammed with drawings of symbols, of strange names, of the number 666 boldly printed a hundred times. The diary that told, in minute detail, of the rituals he had performed. Performed in that room, while she slept. The diary that she had closed quickly, unable to read further.

She had hardly closed her eyes since that day, wondering and worrying if she would find the courage and wisdom to approach him. Now, as the names of the graduating class were called, as the young men and women filed in a stately march to the stage, she watched her son.

"Ernest William Butts."

Will had the video camera on his shoulder, but his free hand groped for his wife's. Joleen took it, held it. And wept.

In a daze Ernie walked back to his seat. Some of the girls were crying. He felt like crying himself, but he didn't know why. In his hand was his ticket to freedom. He'd worked for twelve years for this single piece of paper so he could go where he wanted. Do as he chose.

It was funny, but Los Angeles didn't seem so important now. He wasn't sure about going there anymore, about finding others like him. He thought he'd found others like him here. Maybe he had.

You have been marked with the sacrificial blood.

But that had been a goat. Just a dumb goat. Not a person. He could hear her scream, and scream and scream.

As the graduation procession marched on, he had to force himself not to press his hands to his ears and run from the gym.

He couldn't afford to bring attention to himself. Beneath his gown his body sweated, the deep acrid sweat of fear. Around him, other graduates were beaming or misty-eyed. Ernie sat stiff and stared straight ahead. He couldn't make a wrong move. They would kill him if he did. If they knew that he had seen. If they suspected that he had panicked for a moment and called the sheriff.

He wouldn't make that mistake again. Ernie took slow, even breaths to steady himself. The sheriff couldn't do any good. No one could stop them. They were too powerful. Mixed with his fear came a quick jolt of dark excitement. He was one of them. Certainly the power was his as well.

He had signed his name in blood. He had taken an oath. He belonged.

That was what he had to remember. He belonged.

It was too late for Sarah Hewitt. But his time was just beginning.

★ ★ ★

"No word on her yet. Sorry, Bud."

"It's been more than a week since anybody's seen her." Bud stood beside his cruiser, looking up and down the street as though his sister might pop out of a doorway, laughing at him. "My mom thinks maybe she lit out for New York, but I . . . We ought to be able to do more," he said miserably. "We just ought to be able to do something."

"We're doing everything," Cam told him. "We got an APB out on her and her car. We filed a missing persons report. And the three of us have talked to everyone in town."

"She could've been kidnapped."

"Bud." Cam leaned against the hood. "I know how frustrated you must be. But the fact is, there was no sign of forced entry, no sign of a struggle. Her clothes and personal items were gone. Sarah's thirty years old and free to come and go as she pleases. If I called the feds and yelled kidnapping, they'd never go along."

Bud's mouth set in a stubborn line. "She'd have gotten in touch with me."

"I think you're right. That's what my gut tells me. But the facts don't. All we've got are the facts. We're not going to stop looking. Why don't you go down to Martha's, have Alice fix you a decent cup of coffee?"

He shook his head. "I'd rather work. I saw

that report you're working on. The stuff on cults that Blair Kimball's looking into for you."

"That's just a theory. We don't have anything solid." And he didn't want Bud, or anyone else, looking over his shoulder while he investigated the possibilities.

"No, but if we've got something weird going on around here, I could follow up. All that stuff we found out at Biff's shed—and the way Biff was killed. We're saying it's all tied together. Maybe Sarah's being gone is tied in, too."

"Don't make yourself crazy." Cam put a hand on Bud's shoulder.

Bud's eyes, desperately tired, met Cam's. "You think it could be all tied together."

He couldn't hedge. "That's what I think. But thinking and proving's two different things."

When Bud nodded, his face no longer looked quite so young. "What do we do now?"

"We start all over again."

"With Biff?"

"No, with the cemetery."

Sometimes men gather together for reasons other than poker or football, or a Saturday night beer. Sometimes they meet to discuss interests other than business or farming or the women they've married.

Sometimes they gather together in fear.

The room was dark and smelled of damp—a place where secrets had been shared before. Spiders skittered along the walls and built intricate webs to trap their prey. No one would disturb them there.

Only three met. They had belonged the longest. Once there had been four, but the other died in flames, among palm trees and quiet waters. They had seen to that.

"It can't go on."

Though voices were hushed, nerves rang loudly.

"It will go on." This was the voice of assurance and of power. The high priest.

"We've done no more than what was necessary." This was the soothing tone, the calming one. Beneath it was a quest for power, a thirsty ambition to ascend to the position of high priest. "We have only to keep our heads. There have to be some changes, though."

"It's all coming apart around us." Restless fingers reached for a cigarette and match, despite the disapproval of the others. "Rafferty's digging deep. He's sharper than anyone bargained for."

This was true, and the slight miscalculation was annoying. But nothing that couldn't be dealt with. "He'll find nothing."

"He already knows about Parker. He got that idiot sheriff down there to reopen the case."

"It was unfortunate that Garrett chose to speak so freely to a whore. And unfortunate that the whore alerted our good sheriff." With a fussy movement, James Atherton waved aside the smoke. It wasn't the law that concerned him. He was above the law now. But the quiet, reasonable man beside him who spoke of change was a worry. "But, as they have paid the price, there is nothing to lead the sheriff to us. Nothing but our own stupidity."

"I'm not stupid." The cigarette glowed, revealing Mick Morgan's frightened eyes. "Shitfire, that's my point. I've been a cop long enough to know when another one's on the scent. We figured wrong when we thought he wouldn't care squat about Biff. He's got a line on everyone in town."

"It hardly matters, since everyone of importance is well alibied."

"Maybe it wouldn't, if he hadn't found all that stuff out at the farm." Mick rammed a fist on the rickety table. "Goddamn it, Biff took pictures. Sonofabitch must've been crazy to take pictures of them."

There was agreement, but no panic. He was much too powerful to panic. "The pictures were destroyed."

"But Jane Stokey saw them. She's already identified the one girl. I tell you Rafferty isn't going to let go. God*damn* Biff."

"Biff was a fool, which is why he's dead. If we made a mistake, it was in not realizing how large a fool he was earlier."

"It was the drink," the other man said sadly. What was left of his conscience mourned the death of a brother. "He just couldn't handle drink."

"Excuses are for the weak." This was said sharply and brought both of Atherton's companions to silence. "However, the pieces of evidence the sheriff found there that linked the girl to Biff, link her only to Biff. In the end, it will be a dead man who will be accused of her abduction and murder. I've already taken steps to assure that. Do you doubt me?"

"No." Mick had learned not to. He looked from one man to the other and knew he, and others, were caught in their tug-of-war for control. "It's hard, you know? I gotta work with Bud every day. I like Bud, and he's just sick about his sister."

"We're all sorry for the family," the second man said. "But what was done had to be done, though it could have been accomplished with less—relish." He looked hard at Atherton. "She has to be the last. We have to move back to where we were. When we began more than two decades ago, it was a way of seeking knowledge or exploring alternatives, of empowering ourselves. Now we're losing our way."

"What we were is what we are," Atherton stated and linked his long fingers. He kept his smile to himself. He was enough of a politician to recognize a campaign speech. But he understood, as his opponent refused to understand, that sex and blood were what held the group together. And always would. "The Master demands blood."

"Not human blood."

"We will see."

Mick wiped the back of his hand over his mouth. "It's just that before Biff, we never killed one of our own."

Atherton steepled his hands. "You're forgetting Jack Kimball."

"Jack Kimball was an accident." Mick lit one cigarette from the butt of another. "Parker and me just went up to talk to him, maybe scare him a little so he wouldn't mouth off about the shopping center deal. We didn't mean for anything to happen to him. It was an accident."

"Nothing is an accident. The Master punishes the weak."

Mick only nodded. He believed it, deeply. "Jack should've toughened up, we all knew it. I guess I figured when he died, we'd cut out our weak link. But he could still be a problem."

"How do you mean?"

"That's why I asked for this meeting. Cam's looking into the land deal."

There was a sudden, terrible silence broken only by Mick's uneven breathing and the patient gnawing of a field mouse. "Why?"

"I figure because of Clare. The other day she came into the office, tight as a spring. Right after, I find out he's making calls to the county courthouse, asking for access to the records."

A moment's pause. The faint drumming of fingers on wood. "There's nothing for him to find."

"Well, I know we covered our tracks real good, but I figured you ought to know. If he ties any of that business to us—"

"He won't. In your position as deputy, you should be able to steer him in another direction. Perhaps what we need is some new evidence."

"Evidence?"

"Leave it to me."

"I was thinking . . ." Mick tried to choose his words carefully. "With Cam poking around like he is, and the town so edgy, we might postpone the next couple of ceremonies. Maybe until Lammas Night. By then—"

"Postpone?" Atherton's voice was no longer hushed, but sharp as a scalpel. "Postpone our rites because of fools and weaklings? We post-

pone nothing. We yield nothing. We fear nothing." Gracefully, he rose to tower over the other
men. "We will have our *messe noir* on schedule.
And we will demand that His wrath fall on
those who would persecute us."

It was after four when Clare dragged herself into
the house. She went straight to the refrigerator,
popped open a beer, and chugged half of it. It
helped wash the taste of cranberry parfait punch
out of her mouth.

She stepped out of her shoes as she walked
from the kitchen to the living room. "Blair?
Blair, are you home? Guess not," she muttered
into her beer when there was no answer. She
shrugged out of her jacket and tossed it in the
direction of a chair. She started upstairs, tilting
the beer with one hand and unbuttoning her
blouse with the other.

When she heard the movement above her
head, she swallowed slowly. A creak, the sound
of something heavy being dragged. Silent in her
stocking feet, she moved to the top of the steps.

The attic door was open. Her heart sank a little at the idea of Blair going through those
boxes of memories as she had.

But when she stood in the doorway, it was
Cam she saw, not her brother.

"What are you doing?"

Cam looked up from the box he was emptying. "I didn't hear you come in."

"Obviously." She stepped inside the room. Her father—those pieces of his life—had been uncovered and stacked on the floor. "I asked what you were doing."

"Looking for something that might help." He sat back on his heels. One look at her face warned him he'd better go carefully. "Your father might have had something else. A notebook. Some papers."

"I see." She set the half-finished beer aside to pick up the gardening shirt. "Got a search warrant, Sheriff?"

He struggled for patience and at least found understanding. "No. Blair gave the go-ahead. Clare, are we going to cover the same ground again?"

She shook her head and turned away. Slowly, with infinite care, she refolded the shirt and set it down. "No. No, go through every scrap if it'll help put this aside once and for all."

"I can take the boxes home, if it would be more comfortable for you."

"I'd rather you did it here." She turned back. "Sorry for the bitch routine." But she didn't look at the boxes. "This is the best way, and it helps that you're the one doing it. Do you want some help?"

It was a nice feeling to be able to admire as well as love her. "Maybe. I haven't found any-thing." He rose to go to her. "What did you do to your hair?"

She reached a hand to it automatically. "I cut it a little."

"I like it."

"Thanks. So, where is Blair?"

"He was with me earlier. We ran into Trudy Wilson. She was in her nurse's uniform."

"Oh?"

"Well, Blair's tongue was hanging out. Guess he goes for crepe-soled shoes, so I left him in Trudy's capable hands." Cam glanced down to where Clare's blouse gaped open. "Have you got anything on under that?"

She looked down. "Probably not. I got dressed in a hurry."

"Jesus, Slim, it makes me crazy always won-dering whether or not you're wearing under-wear."

She smiled, toying with the last two fas-tened buttons. "Why don't you find out for yourself?"

He picked her up and had just carried her down the attic steps when Blair met them on the landing.

"Oops."

Cam gave him a narrowed look. "There's that way with words again."

"Sorry. I, ah, just came by to tell you I have a date."

"Good for you." Clare tossed the hair out of her eyes. "Want me to wait up?"

"No. I'm going to take a shower." He started down the hall. "By the way, you're on in about fifteen minutes."

"On what?"

"TV. Alice told me. And if you two could wait to play Rhett and Scarlett until after I'm done, I'd appreciate it." He closed the bathroom door.

"TV?"

"Oh, it's nothing." Clare went back to nuzzling Cam's neck. "That Ladies Club thing."

"I forgot. How'd it go?"

"It went. I stopped feeling nauseated when I saw the white reclining plaster lions."

"Excuse me?"

"The white reclining plaster lions. Where are we going?"

"Downstairs, to the TV."

"You don't want to watch, Cam. It's silly."

"Of course I want to watch. Tell me about the lions."

"These incredibly ugly statues in front of the Athertons'."

"There are a lot of incredibly ugly statues in front of the Athertons'."

"You're telling me. I'm talking about the guard lions, at their ease. I kept imagining them springing off the stoop and devouring all the plastic ducks and wooden sheep, and chasing that poor stable boy up a tree. It was hard to take the whole business too seriously after that. Cam, I really hate to watch myself on television."

"Okay." He set her down. "Then you can get me something to drink while I watch. Did you wear that blouse?"

"Yes."

"Like that?"

She wrinkled her nose and began doing up buttons. "Of course not. I unbuttoned it completely for TV."

"Good thinking. Why were you feeling sick before the lions?"

"I hate public speaking."

"Then why did you do it?"

"Because I'm a spineless wimp."

"You've got a spine. I know, because you go crazy when I nibble on it. Make it a Coke or something, okay? I'm on duty."

"Sure, I live to serve." She slunk off to the kitchen while he fiddled with the TV dial. When she came back, he was settled on the couch, his feet propped on the coffee table. "Sorry, I didn't make popcorn."

"That's okay." He pulled her down with him.

"I really don't want to watch."

"Then close your eyes. I bet you knocked 'em dead, Slim."

"There was polite applause." She propped her feet beside his. "Mrs. Atherton made me come all the way back here for a sample of a work in progress. Which—shit—I just remembered. I left it there."

"What was it?"

"A wood carving. Arms and shoulders. Yours, by the way."

"Oh, God."

His very genuine distress made her grin. "I think some of the ladies recognized you, too. There was some definite snickering. But mostly they wanted to know if I ever carved flowers or children. I think the arms and shoulders made them uncomfortable because without a head it made them think of decapitation, when what I was trying to express was male strength and elegance."

"Now I'm nauseated."

"You haven't even seen it yet." She hesitated briefly, knowing how upset he would be, then decided to confess. "Cam, someone stole one of my sculptures. The nightmare work."

He didn't move, but she sensed him go on alert. "When?"

"Had to be between last evening and mid-morning. I think kids—"

"Bullshit."

"All right, I don't know what I think. All I know is that it's gone."

"Did they break in?"

"No." She stuck out her chin. "Yell if you want. I forgot to lock the garage."

"Damn it, Clare, if I can't trust you to lock a door, I'm going to have to put you in a cell."

"I'll lock the damn thing." It was easier to be annoyed with him than to dwell on having her work taken. On having someone close enough to steal it away. "I'll put in an alarm system if it'll make you happy."

"Move in with me." He cupped a gentle hand on her cheek. "Make me happy."

The little hitch in her stomach forced her to look away. "I don't need protective custody."

"That's not what I'm talking about, Slim."

"I know." She let out a shaky breath. "Just be a cop on this one, Rafferty. Go find my statue." After a moment she forced herself to look back at him. "Don't push, please. And don't be mad."

"I'm not mad. I'm worried."

"It's going to be okay." She snuggled back against him and was sure of it. "Let's take a little time off and watch me make a fool of myself for the viewing public. Oh, God, here it comes. Cam, why don't we—"

He put a hand over her mouth.

"A star of the art world comes to the county,"

the anchorwoman announced. "Clare Kimball, renowned sculptress . . ."

"Ugh. Sculptress!" she managed behind Cam's palm.

"Shut up."

". . . today at the home of Emmitsboro's mayor. Miss Kimball is a native of Emmitsboro who made her mark in the Big Apple."

"Any art is an expression of emotion." As Clare's face filled the screen, she moved Cam's hand from her mouth to her eyes. "Sculpture is often more personal, as the artist is directly linked to the work through touch and texture."

"You look great."

"I sound like a geek. Once a nerd, always a nerd."

"No, you sound great, too. I'm impressed. Is that me?"

She peeked out between his fingers and saw the wood carving. "Yeah."

"It's not so bad," he said, pleased.

"It's brilliant." She widened the space of his fingers to get a better look.

"A sculpture," her television image went on, "is often a tangible piece of the artist's feelings, memories, hopes, disappointments, dreams. It's a way of liberating reality, expanding it, or duplicating it, with a live model or your own imagination."

"Can we at least turn off the sound?"

"Shh!"

"Whether the mood is violent or romanticized or stark depends on the artist's mood and the medium employed. My work is a part of me, sometimes the best part, sometimes the darkest. But it always reflects what I see or feel or believe."

They switched back to the studio.

"Happy now? I sounded so frigging pompous."

"No, you sounded honest. Do you sculpt from dreams, Slim?"

"Sure, sometimes. Look, I've already done one interview today." She slid her arms around him, danced her fingers up the nape of his neck. "I thought we were going to make out."

"In a minute. The nightmare piece that was stolen, did it come out of the dream about your father?"

"Maybe. I don't know."

"You could sketch what you saw that night, couldn't you?"

"God, Cam."

"You could."

She closed her eyes. "Yes, I could."

Chapter 26

CHIP DOPPER WOULD RATHER have been working under a tractor than riding on one. He'd never cared for haying, even his own fields. And here he was, at six-goddamn-thirty in the morning, cutting hay for Mrs. Stokey. But his ma had laid down the law—the one about good neighbors and Samaritans. And when Ma laid down the law, everyone jumped.

The worst part, as far as Chip was concerned, was that it was boring. Acre after acre, cutting and baling, with that half-wit July Crampton riding behind him on the big baler.

July was third or fourth cousin to Alice, the result of some fevered inbreeding. He was somewhere near thirty, irritating as hell, from Chip's viewpoint, but harmless, with a solid bantam rooster body and a slack, permanently sunburned face. Right now he was happy as a frog with a bellyful of flies, riding and stacking and singing. He sang dumb songs from the fifties, before either of them had been born. Chip figured he might have handled the whole thing better if July had picked up some Roy Clark, but there he was, grinning like an asshole and singing about taking out the papers and the trash.

Jesus.

"Christ Almighty, July, what the hell kind of song is that?"

" 'Yakety-Yak,' " July sang, grinning.

"You always was a dick," Chip muttered.

It wouldn't be so bad, Chip thought, riding along with the baler humming under him— 'cept the engine could use some work. It was warm and sunny, and the hay smelled sweet. July might've been three bricks shy of a load, but he was doing the dirty work, hauling and stacking. He'd be the one with hay splinters.

The idea gave Chip some satisfaction.

No, it wouldn't be so bad, he mused, circling back to his original thought, if he'd've thought to bring his radio with him. Then he could've drowned July's sissy voice right out.

Anyway, he was making a little extra money. Just a little, he thought, with just a shade of resentment. Ma wouldn't let him charge Mrs.

Stokey more than half the usual price. But still, with the extra he could relax some. The baby needed those damn corrective shoes. Christ, babies needed every damn thing. But he smiled, thinking of his little girl with her mama's curly hair and his eyes.

It sure was something, being a father. After eleven and a half months, Chip felt like a veteran. He'd been through sleepless nights, roseola, teething, muddy diapers, and inoculations. Now his little girl was walking. It made him glow with pleasure and pride when she held out her arms and toddled toward him. Even if she was a bit pigeon-toed.

His slightly foolish smile changed to a look of curiosity, then disgust.

"What the hell is that smell?"

"I thought you cut one," July said and giggled.

"Christ!" In defense, Chip began breathing through his teeth. "It's making my eyes water."

"Something dead." July pulled out a bandanna and held it over his mouth. "Woo-ee. Something *real* dead."

"Sonofabitch. Stray dog or something musta crawled off and died in the hay field." He stopped the baler. The last thing he wanted was to look for some maggoty dog, but he couldn't afford to run over it with the baler either. "Come on, July, let's find the damn thing and haul it off."

"Maybe it's a horse. Smells as bad as a horse. Could call the dead wagon."

"We ain't calling no dead wagon until we find it."

They hopped off the baler. Chip took a page out of July's book and tied a bandanna around his nose and mouth. The stench was worse on the ground, and he was reminded of the day he'd been playing by the railroad tracks and had come across what was left of a dog that had had the bad luck to get flattened by the freight train headed toward Brunswick. He cursed and breathed shallowly behind the cloth. It wasn't an experience he wanted to repeat.

"Gotta be right around here," he said and started into the uncut hay. It was unpleasant, but not difficult to follow the scent, which reared up like a big, squishy green fist.

As it was, Chip almost tripped over it.

"Jesus Christ Almighty." He pressed a hand over his already covered mouth and looked at July.

July's eyes were bulging out of his head. "Shit, oh shit, oh shit. That ain't no dog." He turned away, coughing and gagging, then began a shambling run after Chip, who was already racing over the freshly cut hay.

★ ★ ★

Thirty minutes later, Cam stood at the same spot. His breath hissed out between his teeth. After ten years on the force, he thought he'd seen everything a man could see. But he'd never come across anything as bad as this.

She was naked. Death hadn't robbed her of her gender, though it had taken nearly everything else. He judged her to be of small to medium build. Age wasn't possible to determine. She was ageless now.

But he thought he knew. Even as he took the blanket he'd brought from the car and covered her, he thought that Carly Jamison would never party down in Fort Lauderdale.

His face was pale, but his hands were steady, and he only thought once, fleetingly, that a shot of Jack would go down real smooth just about then. He walked across the field he'd once plowed in his youth to where Chip and July waited.

"It was a body, just like we told you." July was hopping from foot to foot. "I ain't never seen a dead body, 'cept my Uncle Clem, and he was laid out in his Sunday suit down to Griffith's. Chip and me, we was haying your ma's field, just like we told you, then we smelled it—"

"Shut the fuck up, July." Chip passed a hand over his sweaty brow. "What do you want us to do, Sheriff?"

"I'd appreciate it if you'd go into the office

and give your statements." He took out a cigarette, hoping the taste of smoke would clean his
mouth. "Did either of you touch her?"

"No, sir. Nosirree." July hopped again. "Shit,
she was a mess, wasn't she? Did you see all them
flies?"

"Shut the fuck up, July," Cam said without
heat. "I'll call in, make sure Mick's there to take
your statements. We may need to talk to you
again." He glanced toward the house. "Did you
say anything to my mother?"

"Sorry, Sheriff." Chip shifted, shrugged. "I
guess July and me weren't thinking proper
when we ran into the house."

"It's all right. It'd be best if you gave your
statements right away."

"We'll drive in now."

With a nod, Cam went up the steps and into
the house, where his mother waited.

She all but pounced. "I told them it was just a
dog or some young deer," she began, twisting
her apron. Shadows haunted her eyes. "Neither
one of those boys has a lick of sense."

"Have you got any coffee?"

"In the kitchen."

He walked past her, and she followed, a
sour sickness in her stomach. "It was a dog,
wasn't it?"

"No." He poured coffee, drank it down hot
and black, then picked up the phone. For a mo-

ment he hesitated, the receiver cool in his hand, the image of what he had left in the field twisting in his mind. "It wasn't a dog. Why don't you wait in the other room?"

Her mouth worked, but the words wouldn't come. Pressing her lips together, she shook her head and sat while he called the coroner.

Clare was downing a breakfast Twinkie and contemplating her sketches for the Betadyne Museum. She wanted to get started on the outdoor piece. It had been nudging at her for days. She could already see it, completed, glowing copper, an abstract female form, arms lifted, with the circling planets just above the fingertips.

When the phone rang, she walked back into the kitchen and answered with a mouthful of cake and cream. "Hello?"

"Clare? Is that you?"

"Yeah. Angie, hi. I've got my mouth full."

"What else is new?"

"You tell me."

"I sold your *Wonderment Number Three* yesterday."

"No kidding? Well, that's cause for a celebration." She opened the refrigerator and pulled out a Pepsi. "How's Jean-Paul?"

"He's fine," Angie said, smoothly lying. Neither of them were fine since Blair was keeping them updated on all the news in Emmitsboro. "How are things there?"

"The corn crop looks good."

"Well, we can all sleep easy now. Clare, when are you coming home?"

"Actually, Angie, I'm beginning to think I am home." Time to drop the bomb. "I'm considering selling the loft."

"Selling it? You can't be serious."

"I'm heading that way. You can't say my work has suffered because I've changed my view."

"No, no, it hasn't." But it wasn't Clare's work that concerned Angie. It was Clare. "I don't want you to do anything rash. Maybe you should come up for a few weeks, think things over."

"I can think here. Angie, don't worry about me. I'm fine. Really."

Angie bit her tongue and asked a question she already had the answer to. "Has Cam got a lead on who attacked that woman?"

"He's working on a theory." Deliberately, she turned away from the view of the terrace. "You're not going to tell me I'd be safer in New York than here."

"Yes, I am."

"I'm sleeping with a cop, so relax. I mean it," she said, anticipating an argument. "Angie, for the first time in years, I'm starting to believe I can make it work—a real relationship, a sense of place and purpose. I don't care how corny that sounds, I don't want to blow it."

"Then move in with him."

"What?"

"Move in with him." And then you won't be alone, in that house. "Pack up your things and set up housekeeping with him."

"Did I miss a step here?"

"Why should you live in separate houses? You're already sharing a bed. And damn it, I'd sleep better at night."

Clare smiled. "Tell you what, I'll give it serious consideration."

"Just do it." Angie took a slow, cleansing breath. "I had a meeting with the rep for the Betadyne."

"And?"

"They approved your sketches. Get to work."

"That's great. Angie, if you were here, I'd kiss Jean-Paul."

"I'll do it for you. Get started, girl."

She didn't waste time. By that afternoon, she'd made fair headway on the infrastructure. There were some inconveniences. The garage wasn't tall enough to handle the twenty-foot sculpture, so she had to move her work area to the driveway and bless the mild weather. Standing on a stepladder, she welded and riveted. Occasionally a crowd gathered to watch and comment, then move on. Kids parked their bikes at the curb and hunkered down on the grass to ask her questions.

She didn't mind the interruptions or the audience. But she did have a bad moment when she saw Ernie standing in his front yard, watching her.

At one point, she gave one of the young art connoisseurs five dollars to run to the market for cold sodas. He pedaled off while Clare took a moment to show her new students the proper way to fire a torch.

"We saw you on TV." One of the girls looked up at her with awe and admiration. "You looked real pretty, just like a movie star."

"Thanks." Clare hitched up the strap of her overalls and grinned. That was the beauty of small towns, she thought. It was so easy to be a star.

"Is Miz Atherton's house really all pink?"

"Just about."

"How come you wear that funny hat?"

"So my hair doesn't catch on fire."

"Them's men's shoes," one of the boys put in.

"Them's my shoes," Clare corrected. "For safety, though I do consider them quite a fashion statement."

"My daddy says that women are trying to be

men all the time these days. Taking over men's jobs 'stead of staying home like they's supposed to."

"He says that, does he?" Clare wanted to ask if his daddy's knuckles scraped the ground when he walked, but she decided against it. "That's a very interesting opinion as we approach the second millennium." After rolling her shoulders, she pulled off her skullcap and sat on the stepladder. "It's too nice a day to debate sociosexual theories. Besides, you'll ram straight into reality soon enough. Anybody got a candy bar?"

The boy popped up. "I could go get some. If you got some money."

"We'll settle for Twinkies. There's a box in the kitchen, on the table. Go on through the garage."

"Yes, ma'am." He was off like a shot.

"What in the wide world is that, Clare?"

Clare glanced down and waved at Doc Crampton. He was carrying his black bag, obviously going to or coming from a house call in the neighborhood.

"We can call it a skeleton." Chuckling, she got down from the ladder and walked over to kiss his cheek. "Who's sick?"

"The little Waverly girl has the chicken pox." Still baffled, he studied the maze of metal. "I guess I pictured you whittling wood or patting clay."

"That, too, sometimes."

He turned to her, put on his doctor's face. "You didn't make that appointment."

"I'm fine. Really fine. I just wasn't at my best that night."

"It was a shock for you. Lisa tells me you visit her often."

"I can say the same about you. You don't change, Doc."

"Too old to change." He sighed a little, hating to admit that age was slowing him some. "You're doing proud with Jack's flowers."

"It makes me feel closer to him when I garden." She followed his gaze back to the lawn, where the annuals and perennials flashed out of green grass. "You were right before, about my having to forgive him. I'm coming closer to it, being here." She worried her lip for a moment.

"What is it, Clare?"

She checked her audience and noted the boys were involved in wrestling and devouring Twinkies. "I'd really like to talk with you about it, about some things I found out. Not here," she said. Not here with her father's delphiniums waving behind her. "Once I think it through a little more, can I come see you?"

"You can always come to me."

"Thanks." Just knowing it relieved her. "Listen, I know you've probably got to go stick a hypodermic in somebody. I'll call you."

"See that you do." He shifted his bag. "Jack would have been proud of you."

"I hope so." She started back to her ladder. "Hey. Tell Alice I'm up for another pizza bash." With a last wave, she started back to work.

Clare was just lighting a cigarette when the boy on the bike—Tim, Tom, no, Todd, she remembered—came racing down the street, a carton of soft drinks strapped to the back of the seat.

"You made good time," she commented, climbing down.

"I heard about it at the market." Todd's voice was breathless with excitement and exercise. "July Crampton came in. He came right in and told us."

"Told you what?"

"About the body. Him and Chip Dopper found a dead body over in the Stokeys' hay field. They was baling hay, you see? Baling it for Mrs. Stokey 'cause she's widowed and all. July Crampton said they nearly ran right over it."

The rest of the kids gathered around him, shouting out questions and adding to his sense of importance. Clare sat on the grass.

She was still there thirty minutes later when Blair drove up. He got out of the car and walked over to sit beside her.

"I guess you've heard."

"The afternoon bulletin." She plucked a blade of grass. "Have they identified the body?"

"No. Apparently whoever— Well, she'd been dead awhile."

The tender blade bent in her fist. "She?"

"Yeah. Cam seems to think it might be the body of a young runaway who passed through here back in April."

Clare closed her eyes. "Carly Jamison."

"He didn't mention a name. The coroner's doing an autopsy. Cam's already sent Mick Morgan up to Harrisburg for dental records."

Clare watched the shadow of a bird circling overhead. "It just won't stop, will it? A little while ago, I was working out here, and there were a bunch of kids around. The boy down the street was out washing his car and playing the radio. I give a kid a few bucks to go get sodas, and he comes back and tells me there's a dead body in the Stokeys' hay field." She watched as a bee hovered over her impatiens. "It's like looking at two pictures, and one got imposed over the other. A darkroom mistake."

"I know it's bad, Clare. The way it looks, Biff picked the girl up, killed her, and dumped her body in the field. Maybe he meant to take care of it later, maybe he was just plain crazy."

"Either way, he's dead, too."

"Yeah, he's dead, too. But it looks as if this

murder is going to be laid right at his door. In a way, that might be a blessing."

The bird settled in a weeping cherry and began to sing. "How?"

"Because it would have to mean he acted on his own. If there had been a group, a cult, as Cam was thinking, they wouldn't have left the body on the property like that. It's not the way they operate. Groups like that cover their tracks."

It made sense. She wished she could have left it there. "That doesn't explain who killed Biff."

"He was obviously into drugs. Maybe he didn't pay his supplier, screwed up a deal. There's not much forgiveness in that line." With a sigh, he leaned back on his elbows. "I'm not big on the crime beat. I'll take graft and corruption over murder any day."

"When are you going back?"

"Soon. My editor wants me to follow up on what's happening here, since I'm a hometown boy. But once the body's identified and I can file the story, I'm out of here." There were people he needed to talk with, face to face. As long as there was a chance of a cult—one his father might have been tied to—he would dig. Since digging meant leaving Clare, he was putting all his faith in Cam. "You going to be okay?"

"Sure."

He studied the metal frame she'd designed. "Reproducing the Statue of Liberty?"

"No. Possibilities." She studied it herself, comforted by it. "I want to show that sometimes your reach doesn't have to exceed your grasp."

"It looks like you're planning on the long haul."

Dropping her chin on her knees, she studied the marigolds glowing orange in the yard across the street. There was a dog barking deeply, monotonously. The only sound on a balmy afternoon.

"It wasn't such a long trip back from New York after all."

"What about the trip from here to there?"

She moved her shoulders. "You can hold off on finding tenants for a while."

He was silent a moment. "Cam's nuts about you."

"Oh, yeah?" She looked over her shoulder.

"I never would've figured the two of you together. But . . . I guess what I want to say is that I think it's great."

She leaned back on her elbows and watched the puffy clouds glide across the sky. "So do I."

Cam paced the pale green corridor outside the autopsy room. He'd wanted to go in—no, he hadn't wanted to go in, he corrected. But he'd felt he should. Dr. Loomis had politely but firmly requested that he wait outside. And keep out of the way.

The waiting was the worst. Especially since he knew in his heart, in his gut, that he would be putting in that call to the Jamisons in Harrisburg before the day was over.

He had an itch for a cigarette and opted to scratch it despite the signs thanking him for not smoking. He didn't see how the residents could be offended.

Morgues were quiet places, even peaceful in a businesslike way. And a business was just what it was, he thought. The business of living, followed by the business of dying. For some reason, they never bothered him the way cemeteries did.

Here, people were still people somehow.

He couldn't say he cared for the smells, the scents of pine cleaner and heavy antiseptics not quite hiding something nasty underneath. But he could think of this as a job. Someone was dead, and he had to find out why.

Loomis came through the swinging doors, still drying his pink and scrubbed hands. He wore a lab coat with an identification tag, and a surgical mask dangled by strings from his neck. All that was missing, Cam mused, was a stethoscope. But then, it wasn't Loomis's job to listen for heartbeats.

"Sheriff." Dr. Loomis tucked the paper towel neatly into a waste can. He gave Cam's cigarette a mild look of disapproval, but it was enough to have Cam extinguish it in the dregs of the coffee in his plastic cup.

"What can you tell me?"

"Your Jane Doe was a Caucasian between fifteen and eighteen years of age. My estimate is that she's been dead for about a month, no longer than two."

They were six weeks past the first of May, Cam thought. Six weeks past May Day Eve. "How?"

"Death was induced by a severed jugular."

"Induced." Cam tossed the cup into the waste can. "That's quite a word."

Loomis merely inclined his head. "The victim was sexually assaulted prior to death. By all indications, violently and repeatedly. Her wrists and ankles had been bound. We're running tests on blood types. I can't tell you, as yet, if she had been drugged."

"Put a rush on it."

"We'll do our best. You've sent for dental records?"

"They're on their way. I have a missing person, but I'm holding the parents off."

"I think that's best under the circumstances. Could I buy you another cup of coffee?"

"Yeah. Thanks."

Loomis led the way down the corridor. Meticulously, he counted out change and slid coins into a vending machine. "Cream?"

"I'm taking it black these days."

Loomis handed Cam a cup, then pushed more coins into the slot. "Sheriff, this is a very shocking and difficult case, and I realize that it also has some personal connection for you."

"I played in those fields as a child. I baled hay with my father where that girl was found. And my father died there, crushed under his own tractor on a pretty summer afternoon. Yeah. I guess that's personal enough."

"I'm sorry."

"Forget it." Annoyed with himself, Cam rubbed the bridge of his nose. "I've got evidence that my mother's husband had held that girl in a shed. That girl, and maybe others. Now it looks as though he raped her, killed her, and tossed her body in a field."

Whatever Loomis thought was a secret behind his mild eyes. "It would be your job to prove that, but it's mine to tell you that the body was not in that field for weeks."

Cam stopped with the cup partway to his mouth. "What do you mean it wasn't in the field?"

"It was certainly found there, but it was put there fairly recently."

"Wait a minute. You just said she'd been dead a couple months."

"Dead and buried, Sheriff. That body has been in the ground for several weeks. My estimate is that it was exhumed and placed in that field no more than two or three days ago. Perhaps even less."

He wanted to take it slow. "You're telling me that someone killed that girl, buried her, then dug her up again?"

"There's no question of it."

"Give me a minute." He turned to stare at the green walls. It was worse somehow, worse than her abduction, her rape, and her murder that someone had violated her even after death. "Sonofabitch."

"Your stepfather may well have murdered her, Sheriff, but as he's been dead for several weeks himself, he wasn't the one who put her in the field."

Cam's eyes narrowed. He drank coffee now without tasting it. The muscles in his stomach hitched as he turned back to face the coroner. "Whoever did wanted her to be found, and to be found there."

"I'm forced to agree. From my viewpoint, it was a very clumsy maneuver. But then, your average lay person might not be aware of the scope of forensic medicine." Loomis sipped delicately from his cup. "It's highly possible that it was assumed the evidence would be taken at face value."

"Your profession is underrated, Dr. Loomis."

Loomis gave a small smile. "Sadly true."

When Cam came out of the hospital, the sun was setting. It was nearly fourteen hours since he had gotten the call from Chip Dopper. He wasn't just tired, he was drained. When he saw Clare sitting on the hood of his car, he stopped, waiting for her to slide off.

"Hey, Rafferty." She walked to him, put her arms around his waist, and hugged. "I thought you could use the sight of a friendly face."

"Yeah. Yours is the best one. How long have you been here?"

"Awhile. I went up and visited Lisa. I rode in with Blair." She eased back to study his face. "He wanted to interview the coroner." Dozens of questions raced through her mind, but she couldn't ask them, not now. "You look beat. Why don't you let me drive you home?"

"Why don't I?" He took the keys out of his pocket, then squeezed until the metal scraped his hand. His eyes changed from weary to furious in the space of a heartbeat. "You know what

I want? I want to beat the hell out of something. Pound the shit out of it."

"We could wait for Blair to come out. You could kick him around."

With a half laugh he turned around. "I gotta walk, Slim."

"Okay, we'll walk."

"Not here. I want to get the hell away from here."

"Come on." She took the keys. "I know the place."

They drove in silence, Cam with his head back and his eyes closed. Clare hoped he was asleep as she juggled her memory for direction. When she stopped the car, she continued to sit, saying nothing.

"I haven't been here in a long time."

She turned, studying him in the soft evening light. "I always liked coming to City Park. We'd bring a bag of Saltines and feed the ducks. Got any crackers?"

"Fresh out."

Inspired, she reached for her purse and searched through it. "Let 'em eat cake," she said, holding up a spare Twinkie.

There was a pond in the center of the park. Clare remembered how they would float a tree out on a raft at Christmastime, where it would twinkle mystically over the water. She had come there with her parents, on school field trips, with dates. Once she had come there to sit alone on a bench, overcome with pleasure when one of her sculptures had been placed on exhibit at the nearby art museum.

As they walked, fingers linked, the big leafy trees insulated them against the sound of traffic.

"Smells like rain," she murmured.

"By tomorrow."

"I guess we need it."

"It's been a pretty dry spring."

She looked at him. They both smiled with the easy understanding of lovers. "Want to try politics next?"

He shook his head and, putting an arm around her shoulders, drew her closer to his side. "I'm glad you were there when I came out."

"So am I."

"It's funny, I didn't think about cruising by the nearest bar. First thing I thought about was getting in the car and driving fast, maybe finding some asses to kick." On her shoulder his fist curled, uncurled, then settled. "It used to work."

"So what works now?"

"You do. Let's sit down." He chose a bench and kept her close while he watched the water. Ducks paddled, noisy and optimistic, to the edge. Clare unwrapped the Twinkie and began to toss small hunks. The light gentled to purple.

"Was it Carly Jamison?"

"Yeah. The dental records came in late this afternoon. Her parents . . . there wasn't much I could do for them."

She watched the ducks scramble and fight. "They're here then?"

"They came in about an hour ago. I can't sit."

She got up with him, walking, waiting for him to speak again.

"I'm going to find out who killed that girl, Clare."

"But Biff—"

"He was part of it. He wasn't all of it." He stopped, looked down at her. She could see the anger in his eyes and, beneath it, a pain that wrenched at her own heart. "Somebody tossed her into that field. My field. Like she was nothing. I'm going to find out who it was. Nobody's going to do that to young girls in my town."

Looking out to the water, she wiped her sticky fingers on her jeans. "You still think that this is part of some kind of cult."

He put his hands on her shoulders. "I want you to make that sketch. Clare, I know what I'm asking, but I need you to remember everything, every detail of that dream, and write it down." He tightened his grip. "Clare, she was killed somewhere else. Just like Biff. She was killed somewhere else, then put there, where we'd find her. Maybe you can help me find out where."

"All right. For whatever good it'll do."

"Thanks." He kissed her. "Let's go home."

Chapter 27

SHE DIDN'T WANT TO REMEMBER. Clare knew it was cowardly, but she didn't want to call it up in her mind. For more than twenty years, she'd tried to block it—through force of will, the occasional tranquillizer, and hours of therapy. Never once had she deliberately re-created the picture in her mind. Now she had been asked to put it on paper.

She'd procrastinated, making excuses to Cam and to herself. At night she lay awake, fighting sleep, afraid her subconscious would rear up and accomplish what she was stubbornly resisting.

He didn't press her, not out loud. But then, he'd been so swamped with the investigation, he'd had little time to be with her at all.

The rain had come, as Cam predicted. It had

fallen solidly for two days and two nights. Still, at the market, the post office, down at Martha's, people talked about the water table and the possibility of water restrictions again this summer. When they weren't talking about that or the Orioles' chances at a pennant this year, they were talking about murder.

Clare's outdoor sculpture was put on hold. She piddled around the garage as she hadn't for weeks, unable to settle on a substitute. She moved listlessly from project to project, studying sketches, making more. In the back of her mind, her promise to Cam continued to nag.

It was just that the house seemed so empty. At least that's what she told herself. With Blair back in D.C. and the rain falling and falling and falling, she felt so isolated. So alone.

Why hadn't that ever bothered her before?

Because she'd never jumped at shadows before. Never checked and rechecked her locks or analyzed every creak and groan of a board.

When she caught herself staring out her window at the skeleton of her sculpture yet again, she swore and snatched up the sketchpad she'd tossed on the sofa.

She would do it and do it now. Get it out of her mind.

Her pencil in one hand and the pad on her lap, she sat with her eyes closed and tried to take herself back.

She could see her father puttering around his roses. Tapping the stakes, the garden stakes, into the softened ground.

She could see him lying on the terrace, impaled by them.

Clare shook her head, gritted her teeth, and tried again.

On the swing now, soft summer night. Gliding, her head resting on his arm. The scent of sweet peas and grass and Old Spice.

"What do you want for your birthday, cutie pie? A girl deserves something special when she turns thirteen."

"I want my ears pierced."

"Why do you want to put holes in yourself?"

"All the other girls have pierced ears, Dad. Please."

Further back, she had to go further back. Autumn. Planting tulip bulbs. Spicy smoke from leaves burning. A pumpkin on the porch ready to carve.

"Clare Kimball!" Her mother's voice. "What are you doing outside without a sweater? For heaven's sake, you're eight years old. You should have more sense."

Her father winking at her, running a fingertip down her chilled nose. "You run in and get one. And don't track any of this mulch in the house, or your mother'll put us both in the doghouse."

Still further back. She could almost hear Dr.

Janowski telling her to relax, breathe deeply, let her conscious mind surrender to her subconscious.

"But I want to go. You never take me with you. I'll be good, Daddy. I promise."

"You're always good, cutie pie."

Crouching down to scoop her up and kiss her on the neck. Sometimes he would swing her around and around. She liked that, the giddy dizziness. Fear and excitement. *Don't let me go. Don't let me go.*

"This is just boring stuff, for big people."

"But I want to go. I like to see the houses." Pouting. Bottom lip trembling. Sometimes it worked.

"I'm going to show a big one on Sunday afternoon, and you can go with me. You and Blair, too, if he wants."

"Why can't I go now?"

"Because it's too late for little girls to go outside. It'll be dark soon. Look at you. You've already got your nightgown on." Carrying her into her room. Dolls and colored pencils. "Come on now, be a good girl and kiss me good night. When you're bigger, you can be my partner. Kimball and Kimball."

"Promise?"

"Promise. Sweet dreams, Clare."

The door closing. Nightlight glowing. Getting up to listen. Daddy's talking to Mommy. Quiet, very quiet. Putting a doll in the bed and creeping downstairs. Out the side door and into the garage.

Wouldn't he be surprised to see she was big enough? She was good enough? Hiding in the backseat and holding back giggles with her hands.

The car starting, rolling out of the drive.

They drive and drive and it's getting dark. Hunched on the floor of the backseat, she sees the stars begin to pop out of the sky. Daddy drives fast, like he does when he's afraid he's going to be late.

The car slows, bumps. Stops. Daddy gets out of the car, opens the trunk.

Holding her breath. Holding it as she pulls up the handle. Peeks through the crack. He's walking away. The house must be there, in the trees. Hurrying after, silent in her bunny slippers.

It's dark in the trees, and he doesn't look back.

But there isn't a house. Just a place. A place with no more trees where the men stand in their black robes. Daddy takes off his clothes—that makes her giggle—and puts on a robe like the others. They wear masks, so maybe it's a party. But it's not trick-or-treat. Scary masks, like bulls and goats and mean dogs. But Mommy told her that masks are just for playing pretend, so she isn't scared.

They stand in a circle, like a game. Ring-around-the-rosy. She giggles at that, the idea of the men dancing in a circle and falling down. But they stand very quietly, not speaking at all.

A bell rings.

Clare jolted up. Heart racing, she stared around the living room. Both pad and pencil lay on the floor where she had dropped them. Maybe she was too good at this, she thought, pressing the heel of her hand to her brow. When the bell rang again, she bolted out of her seat before she realized someone was at the door.

She blew out a breath, a long one, before she went to answer. When she opened it, she saw a woman starting back down the steps. "Hello?"

"Oh." A dark-haired woman stood hesitating in the rain. "I thought you weren't home."

"I'm sorry. Come on in, you're getting soaked."

"I was just— Did I wake you?"

"No." Clare got a better look at the face under the wet hat. Mid-thirties, she judged, quietly pretty with big, dark eyes as the outstanding feature. "Rocco's, right?"

"Yes. I'm Joleen Butts."

They were both pale, for different reasons, and both tried to smile. "Would you like to come in?"

"I don't want to disturb you. I just . . . Yes, yes, I'd like to come in."

Inside, Joleen looked around for a moment. Clare had already started to fill the hallway. There were tables with bowls and flowers, prints and posters on the walls she'd picked up at yard sales and flea markets. The floor where Joleen stood, dripping, was bare.

"Let me take your coat."

"I'm sorry to disturb you in the middle of the day. You're probably working."

"Actually, the rain's got me down." She took Joleen's coat and hat and laid them over the newel post. "Would you like some coffee, tea?"

"No, no, don't bother." Joleen twisted the long strand of colored beads she wore. "I, ah, noticed your work outside."

"It looks pretty strange right now." Feeling a little as if she were guiding a child, Clare showed her into the living room. "The noise isn't bothering you, is it?"

"Oh, no. No, it's interesting to see—what you do. I'm afraid I don't know very much about art."

"That's okay, I don't know much about making pizza. You make a great one."

"Thank you." Joleen stared around the room, wishing with all her heart that she had never come. "It's an old family recipe. My maiden name's Grimaldi."

"That explains why Ernie has Italian eyes. Sit down, please."

Joleen lowered herself slowly to the sofa. "You know Ernie, then?"

"Yes. We got to know each other when he was modeling for me."

"Modeling? Modeling for you?"

"Didn't he tell you?" Joleen's long, silent stares were making her uncomfortable. Clare reached for a cigarette and lighted it before continuing. "I used his arm for a clay piece."

"His arm?"

Clare blew out smoke. "Yes, I liked the look of youth and virility. It turned out very well."

"I—I see."

"I wish he'd told you. Actually, I wondered why you didn't come take a look. I have some pictures. I take them of my work for my portfolio, but it's not quite the same as seeing the sculpture itself."

"Miss Kimball, are you having an affair with my son?"

Clare choked, coughed up smoke. "What?" Eyes huge, she pounded on her chest. "What?"

"I realize you might think it's none of my business, but Ernie's only seventeen. He'll be eighteen in November, but I feel I have a right to know as long as he's a minor—"

"Wait, wait, wait." Clare held up a hand. "Mrs. Butts, Joleen, I sculpted Ernie's arm, talked to him, gave him a couple of soft drinks.

That's it. That's absolutely it. I don't know where you got the impression that—"

"From Ernie," Joleen interrupted.

Staring, Clare leaned back on the couch. "That's just crazy. You're saying that Ernie told you that he and—that we . . . oh, God."

"He didn't tell me." Joleen rubbed her chilled hands together. "He wrote it down. I was cleaning his room." Looking away, Joleen pressed her lips together. She didn't lie well. "And I found some things he'd written. About you."

"I don't know what to say. I really don't. Except that I never . . ." She dragged a hand through her hair, wondering how to put it. "I realize you don't know me, and as Ernie's mother you would be inclined to believe him before me. But I swear to you, there was never anything physical, romantic, or sexual between your son and me."

"I believe you." Joleen looked down at the hands twisting in her lap. She couldn't control them—just as she had come to realize she couldn't control her son. "I think I knew all along. I told myself I was going to come over here to protect my baby, but I . . ." She looked up again, damp-eyed and defeated. "Miss Kimball—"

"Clare," she said weakly. "I think you should call me Clare."

"I want to apologize."

"No." Staggered, Clare rubbed at her temple. "Please don't. I can only imagine how you must've felt, thinking that I . . . I'm surprised you didn't break down the door and rip my eyes out."

"I'm lousy at confrontations." Joleen swiped at her wet cheeks. "I guess I'm lousy at mother-hood, too."

"No, don't say that." For lack of something better, Clare gave her shoulder a helpless pat. "Ernie's just confused."

"Could I have one of your cigarettes? I gave them up, but—"

"Sure." Clare picked one up and lighted it herself. At the first drag, Joleen shuddered.

"It's been five years." She took another, greedy. "Clare, I wasn't cleaning Ernie's room. I was searching it." She closed her eyes. The smoke made her a little dizzy, but it helped loosen the knots in her stomach. "I swore I would never invade my child's privacy. My mother used to look through my drawers, un-der the mattress. She thought it was her duty to be sure I wasn't up to something. I swore when I had a child, I would trust him, give him space. Yet I went up to his room twice in the last week, going through his things like a thief. I was looking for drugs."

"Oh."

"I didn't find any." Joleen smoked in long, hungry puffs. "I found other things." Things she couldn't speak of. "What he wrote about you . . . I think you have a right to know. It was very explicit."

The chill started in Clare's stomach and worked its way from there. "I don't suppose it's unusual for a boy to develop a fantasy or even a kind of fixation on an older woman."

"That may be. You might not be as kind if you'd read this stuff."

"Joleen, have you thought about counseling?"

"Yes. I'm going to talk to Will, my husband, tonight. As soon as we can find a therapist, we're all going in for counseling. Whatever's wrong with Ernie, with our family, we're going to fix it. They mean everything to me."

"The pentagram that Ernie wears. Do you know what it means?"

Joleen's eyes wavered once, then steadied. "Yes. We're going to take care of that, too. I'm not going to let him get away from me, Clare. No matter how hard he tries."

Cam came home after dark, his steps dragging. He'd been a cop long enough to know that paperwork, repetition, and monotony were often the biggest part of the job. But it was hard to be patient when he felt that he was right on the edge of breaking through.

He was grateful to see Clare's car in front of his house and the light in the window.

She was dozing on his couch, a paperback novel on her lap and the stereo up too loud. Cam pressed a kiss to her hair and thought how nice it would be to curl up beside her and tune everything out for an hour.

When he turned the radio down from blast to mellow, she sat straight up, looking like an owl who'd been startled by a beam of sunlight.

"I guess I made too much quiet," he said.

"What time is it?"

"Little after nine."

"Mmm." She rubbed her eyes. "Did you eat?"

"That's a very wifely question." He sat beside her, changed his mind, and stretched out, laying his head in her lap. "I think I had a sandwich." On a long, long sigh, he let his eyes close. "God, you smell good. How was your day?"

"You go first."

"Long. The rest of the tests came in on Carly Jamison. She'd taken—more likely been given—barbiturates. Loomis released her body to her parents."

Knowing small comforts were sometimes the best, she brushed at the hair over his brow. "I wish there was something I could do."

"I went out to see Annie again. Got nowhere." He curled his fingers around Clare's. "I can't seem to find anyone who saw that girl in or around town, just like I can't find anyone who saw Biff on the night he was killed."

"Maybe you should let it go for tonight. Start fresh tomorrow."

"The longer it takes, the colder the trail." He opened his eyes. "Clare, you know I've been looking into the land deal your father was involved in. And I've found out something strange. Most of the paperwork is missing."

"What do you mean?"

He sat up and rubbed his hands over his face. "I mean it's gone. There's a deed from the Trapezoid Corporation to E. L. Fine, Unlimited."

"I don't understand."

"Trapezoid was the company that originally bought the land, through your father. They sold it again, within a month, to the developers. Then Trapezoid was dissolved. I can't find any names."

"There have to be names. Who owned it?"

"I haven't been able to find out. All the documentation is gone. The deed was signed by an agent in Frederick, and he's been dead for five years."

"What about the other company, the one that owns it now?"

"Solid as a rock. Holdings all over the East Coast, specializing in malls and shopping centers. The transaction was handled over the phone and by letter. Almost immediately after the grand opening, it came out that your father had bribed inspectors and two members of the planning commission. And that he had misrepresented the deal to his client by claiming the land was sold for seven hundred an acre, when it had actually been sold for twelve hundred. With the Trapezoid Corporation folding their tents, Kimball Realty took all the heat. Your father wasn't around to confirm or deny."

"What are you saying?"

"I'm saying it's strange that all the paperwork on Trapezoid seems to have vanished. That there's no record of who worked with your father on the other end. Kimball Realty's records were confiscated during the investigation, but no one, no one at all from Trapezoid was ever implicated. Doesn't that strike you as unusual?"

"It struck me as unusual that my father would be involved in anything illegal."

"It's hard for me to buy that he was involved alone. Clare, cults form for several basic reasons. The biggest is power. Power requires money. At five hundred an acre, somebody made a lot of money on this deal. Were you in trouble financially when your father started drinking?"

"No, the business was doing very well. We

were talking about taking a family vacation to Europe. Both Blair and I had college funds, substantial ones. No." She shook her head. "Kids know when their parents are worried about money. Mine weren't."

"Yet your father risked his business, his reputation, his family's security on this one deal. He'd never done anything unethical before. Why then?"

She rose. "Don't you think I've asked myself that same question for years? It didn't make sense. It never made sense."

"Maybe he did it for a reason other than personal gain. Maybe there was outside pressure. Maybe he wasn't given a choice."

"I appreciate what you're doing. What you're saying. But would you think this way if it was someone else's father?"

It was a question he had already asked and answered for himself. "Yes. Because it doesn't add up." His eyes followed her as she wandered the room. "I'll tell you what I figure. He was involved with something, maybe out of defiance toward his upbringing, maybe out of curiosity. Whatever, he was in over his head. Something made him pull out, and he felt strongly enough about it that he went back to the church. But you can't just pull out, because you know names and faces and secrets. So you continue to do what you're told to do, and you start to drink."

"You're circling right back around to the cult."

"That's the root. You, Clare, see something you weren't meant to see, twenty years ago. A few years later your father juggles a deal that everyone who knew him would say was totally out of character. And when he's dead, he's the only one the finger points at. Parker's the sheriff, which makes it pretty handy."

"Parker? You think Parker was in on this whole business?"

"I think he was in on it right up to his fat neck. Maybe his conscience started to eat at him or maybe he just couldn't think straight when the blood drained out of his head into his dick, but he tells Sarah Hewitt things best kept to himself. He's losing it, and he packs up, leaving his cushy job, his home, his security. A few months later, he's dead."

"Dead? You didn't tell me he was dead."

"I'm telling you now. What do we have since then? A kid hitches the wrong ride a couple miles outside of town, and she's dead. Somebody kills Biff and dumps her body in the field so it looks like he did it all by himself. And he's not around to say different. Lisa MacDonald is attacked. Sarah Hewitt disappears, after she drops hints to me about Parker."

"And the books," Clare murmured.

"Yes, the books. I can't see Biff and your

father having the same taste in reading material without a reason."

"No," she said faintly. "No, neither can I."

"And if they were both involved, others are, too. Carly Jamison was murdered, Clare. I don't think she was the first, and I'm dead scared she's not going to be the last."

Saying nothing, she got up, went to her tote bag and took out a sketch pad. She brought it to the couch and handed it to him. "I did these this afternoon."

Cam opened it. The first page was a drawing of robed figures standing in a circle. It was almost reverent. He wondered if she knew. In silence he turned the pages, studying each one. A woman spread on a slab of wood, a cup between her naked breasts. A single figure, robed, with the mask he recognized from his research as the Goat of Mendes.

"Was this your father?"

"No. He wore another mask. A wolf."

He studied another drawing. One man stood with his arm raised while the others faced him and the woman. Beside them flames rose out of the ground. Another drawing showed a small goat, a knife held at its throat.

Clare turned away then.

After a brief glance back at her, he continued through the pad. She'd drawn the men, masked and naked, circling the fire while another copulated with the woman. Cam focused on the man in the wolf's mask, the blood dripping from his fingers.

She was only a baby, he thought, and had to force himself not to shred the drawings into pieces.

"Do you know where this place is?"

"No." She faced the window, looking out into the wet, dreary night.

"The way you've drawn it, it looks like a clearing."

"There were trees. A lot of trees, I think. Then it all just opened up. It seemed like a very big place, but that could have been because I wasn't."

"After this last scene you've drawn, what happened?"

"I don't know. I woke up in bed."

"Okay." He went back over them, searching for details she might not even be aware of including. One of the men she'd drawn was short, stout with a thick neck. It could have been Parker. Maybe he just wanted it to be Parker.

"Clare, when you drew these, were you just relying on impressions, or were you able to picture it all clearly?"

"Both. Some things are very vivid. The night was clear, lots of stars. I could smell the smoke. The women had very white skin. Some of the men had farmers' tans."

He looked up sharply. "What?"

"Farmers' tans. You know, brown faces and necks and forearms." She turned back. "I didn't remember that until today. Some of them were pale all over, but it was still spring. The one in the goat mask—the one in charge—he was very thin, milky pale. The way you are when you don't get any sun."

"What about voices?"

"The one in charge, his was very powerful, authoritative, mesmerizing. The others were always mixed together."

"You've drawn thirteen figures. Is that right?"

"Did I?" She walked over to look over his shoulder. "I don't know. I didn't think about it, really. It just came out that way."

"If it is, and our theory is right, at least three of these men are dead. Sheriff Parker, Biff, and your father. That means, to hold the number, they'd have recruited three more. Where is this place?" he murmured.

"Somewhere in the woods. Lisa ran out of the woods."

"We've been over every foot of Dopper's Woods. Bud and Mick and I, and men we drafted from town. We split up into three groups over two solid days and combed every inch. Nothing."

"It would take ten times that number to search every wooded area in this part of the county."

"Believe me, I've thought of that."

She glanced over his shoulder at the sketches again. "I guess this wasn't as much help as you'd hoped."

"No, it's plenty of help." He set the pad aside before reaching up for her hand. "I know it was tough on you."

"Actually, it was purging. Now that it's done, I won't have to think about it. I can get back to work."

"When this is over, I won't be bringing the job home with me and dragging you into it." He brought her hand to his lips. "That's a promise."

"You didn't drag me into this. It's beginning to look as though I've been in it for a long time. I want to find out what my father did or didn't do, and put it behind me. Maybe that's one of the reasons I came back."

"Whatever the reasons, I'm glad you're here."

"Yeah, me, too." She made an effort to shake off the mood. Putting her hands on his shoulders, she began to rub the tension from them, smiling when he let out a satisfied *ah.* "Anyway, I'd be really disappointed if you didn't bring the job home. How else will I keep on top of all the gossip?"

"Yeah. Well, this afternoon Less Gladhill's girl spun out coming around to Main from Dog Run and creamed Min Atherton's Buick."

"See?"

"Between the two of them, they had traffic backed up from one end of town to the other. Min was standing in the intersection directing traffic in a plastic rain hat and white galoshes."

"I'm sorry I missed it."

"When you marry me, you'll have a direct line to the pulse of Emmitsboro."

"First you have to build a garage, though."

"What?"

"A garage," she said, bending over the back of the couch to nip his earlobe. "I have to have a place to work, and I've already figured out you'd be annoyed if I set up in the living room."

He swung an arm back, hooked her, and pulled her over the couch on top of him. "Is that a yes?"

"First I see the plans for the garage."

"Uh-uh. That was a yes."

"It was a conditional maybe," she managed before he closed his mouth over hers. His hands were already busy. With a gasping laugh, she shifted over him. "I guess it was more of a probably."

"I'm going to want to make babies."

Her head shot up. "Now?"

He pulled her back again. "For now we'll just practice."

She was laughing again when they rolled off the couch onto the floor.

Part Three

—

He who has understanding,
let him calculate the number of the beast,
for it is the number of a man.
—Revelation

Chapter 28

*A*S WHORES WENT, Mona Sherman was a crackerjack. Since the age of fourteen, she'd been earning a living by selling her body. She liked to think that she performed a public service. And performed it well. She took pride in her work, running her business by the creed that the customer was always right.

Like a good utility man in baseball, Mona could—and would—do whatever was requested. For twenty-five an hour. Straight or kinky, rough or smooth, bottom or top, as long as the pay was right Mona was your girl. Satisfaction guaranteed.

In her own way, she considered herself a feminist. After all, she was a businesswoman who set her own hours and made her own choices. She figured her street experience would have earned her an MBA.

Mona had her own corner and a steady stream of repeat customers. She was a likable woman, friendly before, during, and after business transactions. With ten years of experience under her garter belt, she knew the importance of customer relations.

She even liked men, regardless of build, personality, or staying power. With the exception of cops. She hated them on principle—the principle that they interfered with her inalienable right to make a living. If she chose to make that living with her body, it was her business. But cops had a way of hauling you in whenever they got bored. She'd had the shit beat out of her in holding once and placed the blame squarely on the cop who had stuck her in there.

So when she was offered a hundred times her going rate to pass a mixture of lies and truth on to a cop, Mona was more than happy to oblige.

She had gotten half the cash up front. It had been delivered to her post office box. Being a good businesswoman, she'd slapped the money into a six-month CD so it would earn solid interest. With it, and the second half, she planned to spend next winter in Miami. On sabbatical.

She didn't know who the money was from, but she knew where it was from. Through her professional relationship with Biff Stokey, Mona had earned a few extra bucks getting gang-banged by a bunch of loonies in masks. She knew that men liked to play all sorts of weird games, and it was nothing to her.

As agreed, she'd contacted Sheriff Rafferty and told him she had information he might be interested in. She arranged to meet him at the scenic overlook off 70. She didn't want a cop in her room. She had her reputation to think of.

When she drove up in her battered Chevette, he was already there.

Not bad-looking, for a cop, Mona mused, and ran through her lines again in her head. She had them cold. It made her smile. Maybe she'd try Hollywood instead of Miami.

"You Rafferty?"

Cam looked her over. She was leggy and slim in her off-duty outfit of shorts and a tube top. Her hair was cropped short, with the tips bleached platinum. She might not have looked her age if it hadn't been for the lines carved around her eyes and mouth.

"Yeah, I'm Rafferty."

"I'm Mona." She smiled, reached in the little red purse that hung from a strap between her breasts, and took out a Virginia Slim. "Got a light?"

Cam pulled out matches, struck one. He

waited until a family of four walked by, squabbling as they headed for the rest stop facilities. "What have you got to tell me, Mona?"

"Was Biff really your old man?"

"He was my stepfather."

She squinted her eyes against the smoke. "Yeah. There sure ain't any family resemblance. I knew Biff real well. He and I had what you could call a close business relationship."

"Is that what you'd call it?"

He was a cop, all right. Mona held the cigarette out, tapped ashes delicately on the ground. "He'd roll into town now and again, and we'd party. I'm real sorry he's dead."

"If I'd known you were so close, I'd have invited you to the funeral. Let's get to it. You didn't ask me to meet you out here just to tell me Biff was a regular."

"Just paying my respects." He was making her nervous, as if she were an actress on opening night. "I could use a cold drink. They got machines back there." She sat on the stone wall with the mountains and valley spread sedately at her back. Cocking her head and giving him a sultry look, she said, "Why don't you buy me a drink, Rafferty? Make it a diet. I gotta watch my figure."

"I'm not here to play games."

"I'd talk better if my mouth wasn't so dry."

He reined in impatience. He could play this

two ways. He could be a hard-ass, stick his badge in her face and threaten to take her in for questioning. Or he could get her the damn drink and let her think she was leading him by the nose.

Tapping the filter of the cigarette against her teeth, Mona watched him walk away. He had cop's eyes, she thought. The kind that could spot a hooker even if she was wearing a nun's habit and saying Hail Marys. She was going to have to be careful, real careful if she wanted to earn that other twelve-fifty.

When he came back with the Diet Coke, Mona took a long, slow sip. "I didn't know whether to call you or not," she began. "I don't like cops." She felt more confident, starting with the plain truth. "In my business, a girl's got to look out for herself first."

"But you did call me."

"Yeah, 'cause I couldn't stop thinking. You could say I wasn't giving my clients my full attention." She took a deep drag, blew smoke out through her nostrils. "I read in the papers about what happened to Biff. It really shook me, his getting beat to death that way. He was always real generous with me."

"I bet. So?"

She tapped her cigarette again. The family walked by, to pile wearily into their station wagon and head north. "Well, I just couldn't put it out of my head like I wanted to. I kept thinking about poor Biff suffering that way. It didn't seem right. You know, he was into some pretty bad business."

"What kind of bad business?"

"Drugs." She inhaled slowly, watching him. "I'm going to tell you, I don't hold with that shit. Maybe a little grass now and again, but none of the hard stuff. I've seen too many of the girls burn themselves out. I got respect for my body."

"Yeah, it's a temple. What's the point, Mona?"

"Biff did a lot of bragging about his sideline, especially after he was, like, satisfied. Seems he had a connection in D.C., a Haitian. And Biff, he was the mule."

"The Haitian have a name?"

"Biff just called him René and said he was a real high roller. Had a big house, fancy cars, lots of women." She was cruising now and set the can aside on the wall. "Biff wanted all that, he wanted it bad. He said if he could make a score, a big one, he wouldn't need René. The last time I saw him, he said he was moving out on his own, that he had a shipment and was going to deal it himself and cut René out. He bragged about how maybe we'd take a trip to Hawaii," she said, deciding to embellish. She'd always wanted to go to Hawaii. "Couple days later, I read about how he was dead. Biff, I mean."

"Yeah." He studied her. "How come you waited so long to contact me?"

"Like I said, I don't have any use for cops. But Biff, he was a good guy." Mona tried to bring tears to her eyes, for effect, but couldn't quite manage it. "I read how they're saying he raped and killed some kid. But I don't buy it. How come Biff would rape a kid when he knew he could pay for a woman? So, I start thinking, maybe this René guy whacked them both, and since Biff was a good customer and all, I thought I ought to tell somebody."

It sounded neat, very neat and tidy. "Biff ever talk to you about religion?"

"Religion?" She had to hold back a smile. It was a question she'd been told to expect and told how to answer. "Funny you should ask that. This René was into some weird shit. Devil worship, Santa—Santer—"

"Santeria?"

"Yeah, that's it. Santeria. Some Haitian thing, I guess. Biff thought it was great. Real spooky and sexy. He brought some black candles up to the room a couple of times, and I'd pretend like I was a virgin. We'd do a little bondage." She grinned. "You get what you pay for."

"Right. Did he ever talk about doing a real virgin?"

"Virgins are overrated, Sheriff. When a man's putting down cash, he wants experience. Biff liked some unusual stuff, athletic, you know? A virgin's only going to lie there with her eyes shut. If I were you, I'd get a line on this René."

"I'll do that. You keep available, Mona."

"Hey." She ran a hand down her hip. "I'm always available."

Cam didn't like it. Not one bit. The D.C. police had run a make on the Haitian for him. René Casshagnol a.k.a. René Casteil a.k.a. Robert Castle had a rap sheet that would stretch to the Caribbean. He'd done time, once, for possession, but none of the other charges had stuck. He'd been arrested or questioned on dozens of charges, from distribution to gunrunning, but he was slick. He was also vacationing in Disneyland at the moment, and it would take more than the word of a hooker to extradite him.

Why would a big-time drug dealer kidnap and kill a runaway? Because of his religious deviations? Maybe, Cam mused. He couldn't ignore the obvious. But would a man with the Haitian's experience make the clumsy mistake of exhuming the body to point the finger at someone else? It didn't fit. A man like René would know too much about police procedure.

In any case, Cam could still spot a plant. His next order of business was to find Mona's connection to Carly Jamison's murderer.

Cam took out a file to read it over again. It was the middle of June, and the weeks were moving too damn fast. He was closing the file again when Bob Meese came in.

"Hey, there, Cam."

"Bob. What can I do for you?"

"Well, I got this curious thing." He scratched the top of his balding head with his index finger. "You know I bought a lot of stuff from your mama—furniture, some lamps, and glassware. Ah, she get off to Tennessee all right?"

"She left yesterday on the train. Is there a problem with any of the stuff you bought?"

"I couldn't say as it was a problem. I was cleaning up that chest of drawers—already got somebody interested. That's a real fine oak piece. 'Bout 1860, I'd say."

"It's been in the family."

"It needed a little work." Bob shifted uncomfortably. He knew how touchy some people could be about selling family pieces. He had to play this cagey for a number of reasons. "Anyhow, I was taking the drawers out to sand them up some, and I came across this." He took a small book out of his pocket. "Found it taped to the bottom drawer. Didn't quite know what to think of it, so I brought it in."

It was a passbook, Cam noted when he took it. A savings account in a Virginia bank. He read the names over twice.

Jack Kimball or E. B. Stokey. The first deposit, a whopping fifty thousand, had been made the year before Kimball's death. The year, Cam thought grimly, that the land had been sold for the shopping center. There had been withdrawals and more deposits, continuing after Kimball's death and up until the month before Biff's.

Bob cleared his throat. "I didn't know Jack and Biff had, ah, business together."

"It sure looks that way, doesn't it?" The account had swelled to more than a hundred thousand and had shrunk to less than five with the final withdrawal. "I appreciate your bringing this in, Bob."

"I figured it was best." He edged toward the door, anxious to spread the word. "I guess if Biff was alive, he'd be in a shit pot of trouble."

"You could say that." Eyes moody, Cam looked up to study the antique dealer. "I don't suppose it would do any good to tell you to keep this to yourself?"

Bob had the grace to flush. "Well now, Cam, you know I can keep my mouth shut all right, but Bonny Sue was standing right there when I come across it. No telling who she's told already."

"Just a thought," Cam murmured. "Thanks again." He leaned back in his chair, tapping the book against his palm and wondering how he was going to show it to Clare.

Clare got home at dusk, angry, frustrated, and miserable. She'd just spent the better part of an hour with Lisa's surgeon. The second operation was over, and Lisa's leg was in a conventional white cast that had already been signed by her family, friends, and most of the staff on the third floor.

She would be going back to Philadelphia within the week. But she would never dance professionally again.

No amount of arguing or pleading with Dr. Su had changed his prognosis. With care and therapy, Lisa would walk without a limp, even dance—within limits. But her knee would never stand up to the rigors of ballet.

Clare sat in her car at the curb in front of her house and stared at the sculpture taking shape in the drive. A woman reaching for the stars and gaining them.

Oh, fuck.

She looked down at her hands, slowly opening, then closing them, turning them over. How would she feel if she could never sculpt again? Could never hold a mallet or a torch or a chisel?

Empty. Dead. Destroyed.

Lisa had lain in that bed, her eyes filled with pain, her voice strong.

"I think I knew all along," she'd said. "Somehow it's easier being sure than wondering. Hoping."

But no, Clare thought as she slammed out of the car. It was never easier to lose hope. She stopped under the sculpture, staring up at it in the waning light. It was only a hint of a shape, long, slender, graceful arms lifted high, fingers spread. Reaching. But she saw it completed, and the features of the face were Lisa's.

She could do that, Clare thought. She could give the statue Lisa's face, and her grace and her courage. And maybe it wouldn't be such a small thing. Casting her eyes back to the ground, she walked into the house.

The phone was ringing, but she ignored it. She didn't want to talk to anyone, not yet. Without bothering with the lights, she moved through the kitchen to the living room and thought about escaping into sleep.

"I've been waiting for you."

Ernie rose, a shadow in the shadows, and stood waiting.

After the first jolt, she steadied, facing him adult to child. "People usually wait outside until they're invited in." She reached over to turn on the lamp.

"Don't." He moved quickly, covering her

hand with his. She found it sweaty cold. "We don't need the light."

Her annoyance was laced with the beginnings of fear. She reminded herself that the windows were open and a few good screams would bring neighbors. And he was a kid. She slid her hand from under his. Sexually frustrated, mixed up, but still a kid.

Not a murderer. She wouldn't believe that. Didn't dare.

"All right, Ernie." She moved casually and put the couch between them. "What's this about?"

"You were supposed to be the one. The way you looked at me."

"I looked at you the way a friend would. That's all."

"You were supposed to be the one," he insisted. She was his hope. Maybe his last. "But you went with Rafferty. You let him have you."

The pity that had been creeping into her heart iced over. "My relationship with Cam isn't open for discussion. It's my business."

"No. You were mine."

"Ernie." Patience, she told herself. Patience and logic. "I'm ten years older than you, and we've only known each other a couple of months. We both know that I never did anything to make you think I was offering more than friendship."

He shook his head slowly, continually, his eyes

dark and fixed on hers. "You were sent. I thought you were sent." A whine came into his voice, the music of youth, and softened her.

"Sent? Ernie, you know that's not true. You've built something that never existed out of your imagination."

"I saw the statue. The statue you made. The high priest. Baphomet."

Shaken, she took a step back in denial. "What are you talking about? Did you steal it?"

"No, others did. Others know what you know. You've seen. So have I."

"Seen what?"

"I belong. There's nothing I can do now. I belong. Don't you see? Can't you understand?"

"No." She laid a hand on the back of the couch. "I can't. But I'd like to. I'd like to help you."

"It was supposed to make me feel good. It was supposed to give me anything I wanted."

The whining turned to tears, but she couldn't make herself step forward and comfort him. "Ernie, let me call your parents."

"What the hell for?" Tears turned to rage. "What do they know? What do they care? They think they can make everything all right by making me go to a psychiatrist. All right for them, maybe. I hate them, I hate them both."

"You don't mean that."

He pressed his hands to his ears, as if to block

out her words and his own. "They don't understand. Nobody does, except—"

"Except?" She took a step toward him. The whites of his eyes glowed in the shadows. She could see the sweat beaded over the upper lip he only had to shave once a week. "Sit down, Ernie. Sit down and talk to me. I'll try to understand."

"It's too late to go back. I know what I have to do. I know where I belong." He turned and ran out of the house.

"Ernie!" She raced after him, pausing in the middle of her yard when he jumped into his truck. "Ernie, wait." When he speeded past her, she looked frantically down the street. His house was dark. Clare swore and darted to her own car. She hadn't been able to change things for Lisa. Maybe she could help Ernie.

He turned onto Main, and she lost him. Slapping the heel of her hand against the wheel, she circled around, scooting down side streets searching for his truck. Ten minutes later, she was ready to give up, figuring the best thing she could do was go into Rocco's and relate the incident to his parents.

Then she spotted the truck, parked in the rear lot of Griffith's Funeral Home. Clare pulled in beside it. Great, just great, she thought. What was he doing? Breaking into a funeral parlor?

She didn't bother to weigh the consequences.

She would go in and get him out, as quickly and quietly as possible. Then she'd turn him over to his parents.

The rear door was unlocked, and she opened it, fighting back her natural distaste for entering a place where death was a daily business. She sent out a quick prayer that no one had died lately and slipped inside.

"Ernie?" she whispered, her voice sounding hushed and reverential as it floated downward. The delivery entrance, she supposed, looking down the flight of iron steps. "Damn it, Ernie, why here?"

Abruptly, she thought of the symbolism. Coffins and candles. Clare was well aware of the statistics on teenage suicide. Ernie was a prime candidate. Torn, she stood at the top of the stairs. She wasn't a doctor. She wasn't trained. If she couldn't stop him . . .

It would be better to go find Cam, she decided, though it made her feel like a squealer. Doc Crampton might be an even better choice. As she turned toward the door, a sound from below made her hesitate. Why would the boy listen to a cop—especially one he'd decided to hate? And he certainly wouldn't pay any attention to a small-town G.P. If it was just an adolescent temper tantrum, how much harder would it be for Ernie to have a cop pick him up? She remembered his tears and his desperation, and sighed.

She would just go on down and see if she could find him first. Trained or not, she could talk to him, and with luck and perseverance calm him down. Slowly, letting her eyes adjust to the dark, she descended the stairs.

Voices. Who the hell could Ernie be talking to? she wondered. Chances were that Charlie was working—oh, God—and the boy had run into him. She would try to explain, cajole, smooth over, then get Ernie back to his parents before there was any real trouble.

No, not voices, she realized. Music. Bach played on an organ. She supposed Charlie preferred the reverential music to set the mood for his work.

She turned into a narrow corridor. Light was thrown by wall sconces, but was overwhelmed by shadows. There was movement again, murmuring under the music. Clare reached out with a hesitant hand and parted a long black curtain.

And the gong sounded.

There was a woman lying on a platform. At first Clare thought she was dead, so pale was her skin in the flowing candlelight. But she shifted her head, and Clare knew, with an even more primitive horror, that she was alive.

She had her arms crossed over her naked breasts and gripped a black candle in each hand. Between her spread thighs was a silver cup, covered by a paten on which lay a small round of black bread.

There were men, a dozen of them, in long, hooded robes. Three of them approached the altar and made a deep bow.

A voice was raised, intoning Latin. Clare recognized it and began to tremble.

But it wasn't right, she thought, swaying a bit with the first shock. There had been trees and a fire and the smell of smoke and pine. Her knuckles were bone-white against the black curtain, and she stared. The voice, the one she remembered from her dream, filled the stark little room.

"Before the King of Hell and all the demons of the Pit, before this, my brotherhood, I proclaim that Satan rules. Before this company, I renew my allegiance and my vow to honor Him. In return I demand His assistance for the fulfillment of all my desires. I call upon you, Brothers, to do the same."

The men flanking him spoke in unison, repeating the vow.

It was true, Clare thought, horrified, as the celebrant and his deacons continued in Latin. All of it was true. The dream, her father. Sweet God, her father. And all the rest.

"Domine Satanas, Rex Inferus, Imperator omnipotens."

The celebrant took up the paten, raised it to chest level, where a heavy silver pentagram rested against his robes, and recited the profane words in a long-dead language. He replaced it, repeated the gesture with the cup, then set that down as well, back between the woman's slim white thighs.

"Mighty Lord of Darkness, look favorably on this sacrifice we have prepared for You."

The scent of incense, sweet and heavy, took her back to the long, formal High Masses of her childhood. This, too, was a mass, she thought. A black one.

"Dominus Inferus vobiscum."

"Et cum tuo."

Her body was sheathed in ice. She shuddered from it, willing herself to move, to step back, to run; unable to pull her rigid hand away from the curtain. The music droned on, dreamlike. The incense spun thickly in her head. The celebrant lifted his arms, palms downward. He called out again, his voice rich and full and hypnotic. And she knew. Though her mind rejected it, she knew the voice and the face that went with it.

"Salve! Salve! Salve!"

The gong rang three times.

And she fled.

She didn't think about moving silently, being cautious. The panic that gripped her demanded that she run, escape. Survive. It had been the same that night so many years ago, when she had scrambled like a rabbit through the woods, back to her father's car. She had lain there, shivering with shock, until he found her.

The lights in the corridor floated around her, silent and secret, casting the steps into deeper shadow. For an instant, she thought she saw her father, standing at the base of them, his eyes filled with sorrow, his hands stained with blood.

"I told you not to come, cutie pie. It's not a place for little girls." His arms reached out for her. "It's just a dream, a bad dream. You'll forget all about it."

As she raced toward him, the image faded. She bolted through it, sobbing, and up the metal stairs. She knew the taste of hysteria. Its chalky flavor clogged her throat, gagging her, as she pushed against the exit door.

She was trapped. The sweat that had beaded on her skin began to run in rivers as she pushed against the door. Her own whispered pleas roared in her head. They would come for her. They would find her. And she would die, as Carly Jamison had died. They would take up the knife and, as if she were a small, terrified goat, slice it across her throat.

A scream bubbled up to her lips, then she

found the latch and stumbled out into the night. Blind fear took her across the dark parking lot. Breath heaving, she clung to a tree, pressing her wet cheek against the bark.

Think, think, damn it, she ordered herself. You have to get help. You have to get Cam. She could run to his office, but her legs no longer felt as if they could carry her. He might not be there. She would go to his house. Safe, it would be safe there. Somehow, between the two of them, they would make everything right again.

She looked over and saw her car, gleaming red beside Ernie's truck. She couldn't leave it there. Didn't dare. She took a step back, and the wave of revulsion struck like a fist. Clare gritted her teeth against it and kept walking. She would get in her car, drive away, drive to Cam's house, and tell him what she'd seen.

When the beam of headlights cut across her, she froze like a rabbit.

"Clare?" Dr. Crampton leaned his head out the window of his car. "Clare, what in the world are you doing there? Are you all right?"

"Doc?" Weak with relief, she darted to his car. Now she wasn't alone. "Thank God. Oh, thank God."

"What is it?" He pushed up his glasses and focused, noting her pupils were dilated. "Are you hurt, ill?"

"No. No, we have to get away." She sent a

quick, desperate look toward the rear entrance. "I don't know how much longer they'll be down there."

"They?" His eyes, behind the glint of his glasses, were filled with concern.

"In Griffith's. Down in the basement. I saw them. The robes, the masks. I used to think it was a dream, but it wasn't." She held up a hand, trying to stop herself. "I'm not making sense. I need to get to Cam. Can you follow me?"

"I don't think you're in any shape to drive. Why don't you let me take you home?"

"I'm fine," she told him when he stepped out of the car. "We can't stay here. They've already killed the Jamison girl and probably Biff. It's dangerous." Her breath hissed as she felt the prick of a needle on her arm.

"Yes, it is." There was regret in his voice as he sent the drug screaming into her bloodstream. "I'm very sorry, Clare. I tried very hard to protect you from this."

"No." She struggled away, but her vision was already wavering. "Oh, God, no."

Chapter 29

IT WAS A DREAM. In dreams you didn't really feel anything, and voices floated in and around your head. She had to open her eyes and wake up. Then she would find herself curled on her sofa, groggy from a late nap.

But when she was able to lift her heavy lids, she saw a small room, draped in black. The symbol of Baphomet leered down at her. Panic struggled with the drug so that she tried to move her weighted limbs. Her wrists and ankles were bound. The scream that ripped through her mind came through her lips as a moan. Since she couldn't be heard, she had no choice but to listen.

"She can't stay here." Charlie Griffith paced on the other side of the platform. His hood was thrown back now, revealing his mild brown hair and worried eyes. "Damn it, it isn't safe for any of us as long as she's here."

"Let me worry about safety. I always have." The mayor ran his long, bony fingers along his silver pendant. His smile was faint, even mocking, but Charlie was too wound up to notice.

"If Doc hadn't been so late and run into her right outside—"

"But he did," Atherton pointed out. "We're protected. How could you doubt it?"

"I'm not—I don't—it's just that—"

"Your father helped form our brotherhood." Atherton laid a hand on Charlie's shoulder, more in restraint than comfort. "You were the first of the new generation. I depend on you, Charles, for your good sense, your discretion, and your loyalty."

"Of course, of course. But holding a service here is entirely different than keeping her here. I have to think of my family."

"We all think of our families and of each other's. She'll be moved."

"When?"

"Tonight. I'll see to it myself."

"James . . ." Charlie hesitated, afraid his words would show not only his fear, but his doubts. "You have my loyalty, as you have for more than ten years when my father brought me to be initiated. But Clare . . . I grew up with her."

As if in benediction, Atherton grasped Charlie's shoulders. "Destroy before you are destroyed. Is this not the Law?"

"Yes, but . . . if there was another way."

"There is only one way. His way. I believe she was sent. We know there are no accidents, Charles, yet she came here tonight. I believe her blood will purify, will make clean the smear that her father tried to mark us with so many years ago. She will be the sacrifice to appease Him for the betrayal of one of our own." Atherton's eyes glittered in the shadowy light, with delight and with hunger. "Your son, it will not be long before he joins us."

Charlie wet his lips. "Yes."

"Take comfort in that, knowing that the next generation will prosper and succeed through His power. Go, and leave this to me. I want you to contact the others, see that they're calm and quiet. On the night of the solstice, we'll meet and sacrifice, and grow stronger."

"All right." There was no other way, and the Law left no room for guilt or conscience. "Do you need any help?"

Atherton smiled, seeing that he had once again overpowered the weak. Domination was his drug of choice. "Mick will be all the help I need."

Atherton waited until Charlie slipped through the curtain before turning to Clare. He knew

she was conscious and listening. It pleased him.
"You should have left the boy alone," he said.
"He's already mine." Bending, he took her face
in his hand, turning it from side to side. "Still a
little glassy-eyed," he observed, "but you understand well enough."

"I understand." Her voice came to her ears as
if through a tunnel. "It's been you, all these
years. You killed that poor girl."

"Her, and others. The Master demands His
sacrifice."

"You don't believe that. You can't."

He pursed his lips as he often did before lec-
turing one of his classes. "You'll find that it isn't
what I believe that matters, but what they believe. They'll spill your blood without a second
thought because I tell them to."

"Why?"

"I enjoy it." He stripped off his robe, then
laughed at the horror in her eyes. "Oh, no, I
don't intend to rape you. I haven't the time or
the inclination. But it wouldn't do for the
mayor to be seen in anything other than a
proper suit." He began to dress, casually, pulling
boxer shorts up his skinny legs.

"It isn't working anymore." She twisted her
wrists ruthlessly but only succeeded in scoring
her flesh with the rope. "You've made too many
mistakes."

"Mistakes have been made, certainly. And

corrected." He shook out his white Arrow shirt, perusing it for wrinkles. "The first one was your father. He was a disappointment to me, Clare. A grave one."

"My father never killed anyone. He wouldn't have been a part of this."

"Oh, indeed he was." Atherton meticulously did up his buttons, from bottom to top. "A very important one. Such a bright and ambitious man, thirsty for knowledge. When he became one of us, the fever burned so hot in him, he was like a brother to me." He sat on a three-legged stool to pull up his black support socks. "His turning away hurt me deeply. And for him to go back to some useless religion with its powder-puff God. . . ." Sighing, he shook his head. "Where did it get him? I ask you, where? It got him a bottle and a false sense of righteousness. All because he wasn't ready to move on with us, to seek higher power."

Ever the teacher, he placed his hands on his hairy thighs and leaned toward her. "Human sacrifice is hardly my invention, my dear. It's been around since time began. For the very simple reason that man not only needs to spill blood but thrives on it." He regarded her. "Yes, I can see it appalls you, as it did Jack. But, ask yourself honestly, is your disgust merely a knee-jerk reaction?"

She could only shake her head. "How many? How many people have you killed?"

"Numbers are irrelevant, don't you think? The first sacrifice was a test that everyone passed but your father. And the woman was only a whore, after all. Killing her was symbolic. Perhaps if I had discussed it with Jack first, explained the reasoning, he wouldn't have reacted so strongly, so negatively. Well, I blame myself for that."

He reached over and picked up his dark trousers with their knife pleats. "You could say Jack left me for a woman, though our relationship was spiritual, never physical. He left me and ran back to his rosaries and his cold, sexless God. And I forgave him." Atherton stood, zipped, then reached for his belt. "He couldn't afford to betray me and risk his family. We had taken a vow, a blood vow. Jack did what he was told, for as long as he was able."

"You threatened him."

"He understood the rules before he was marked. It was the land deal that seemed to push him over the edge. I can't understand why. He told me he would no longer be part of it. And it was only money, you see. A transaction guaranteed to make us wealthy and more powerful. But Jack was crawling deeper and deeper into that bottle and couldn't think clearly."

Through despair she felt a glimmer of hope. "He was going to tell. He was going to tell about you and this, and everything."

"Oh, yes. I believe he was. Or at least he hoped to find what he considered the courage to do so." Atherton picked up his gray-and-burgundy-striped tie and slipped it under his collar. "Parker and Mick went to see him, to try to convince him how foolhardy it would be for everyone involved. From what I'm told, Jack simply wouldn't listen. He went quite wild, violent. There was a fight, and, well, you know the rest."

"They killed him," she whispered. "My God, they killed him."

"Now, you can hardly blame Parker or Mick for the fact that your father left those stakes out on the terrace. He might very well have lived through the fall, you know. I like to think of it as justice." He completed the knot in his tie, smoothed it with his hands. "I still miss him." Sighing again, he picked up his suit jacket. "Now I see your coming back, your coming here, as a circle. I made mistakes with Jack. He should have been treated like any other traitor, but I let my affection for him get in the way. I'll have to rectify that mistake with you."

"You murdered my father."

"No, my dear, I wasn't even there."

"You murdered him," she repeated. She struggled against the rope. She wanted to bite, scratch, claw. Calmly, Atherton picked up a square of cloth and neatly folded it into a gag.

"I'm afraid you'll have to be quiet while we transfer you."

"Go to hell."

"There is no hell." He smiled, closing the gag over her mouth. "Except the one we make."

Stoically, Mick carried her up the steps and out to her car. Clare writhed and bucked, but to no avail. When he dumped her in the passenger seat of her own car, she swung out with her banded hands. He took the blow on his shoulder in silence, then strapped her in.

"It was careless of you to leave the keys in the car." Atherton climbed into the driver's seat. "We may be a small rural town, but young people might find it difficult to resist the temptation of this car. A Japanese model, isn't it?" he continued conversationally as he fastened his seat belt. "I believe strongly, at least publicly, in buying American." Atherton turned the key. "But I can appreciate the sense of power. It won't be a long drive, Clare, but try to make yourself comfortable."

He cruised out of the parking lot, turned left away from Main Street, and headed out of town. For his own amusement, he toyed with the radio until he came to a classical station.

"An excellent machine," he said. "Handles

beautifully. I envy you. Of course, it wouldn't do for me to be seen driving such an expensive vehicle. Political aspirations mean I must continue a more subtle lifestyle." He imagined himself in the governor's mansion. "My money goes into Swiss accounts—and land, of course. Jack taught me the value of land. And it's so pleasant just to have it. Naturally, I indulge Min's wishes whenever possible. Her tastes are very simple, really. A man couldn't ask for a more supportive wife. Sexually, if I might say, she's a bit rigid. But paying for a whore is a small price for a solid, successful marriage. Wouldn't you say? Oh, of course, you can't say."

He reached over and tugged off her gag. "You can scream if you like. You won't be heard."

She didn't bother. With her hands tied in front of her and strapped to her body by the seat belt, she couldn't even attempt to grab the wheel. Perhaps that was best, she thought. She might not survive a car crash. And she was determined to survive. The best she could hope for was to keep him talking and to pay very close attention to the direction they were taking.

"Your wife—she knows?"

"Min?" He smiled affectionately, tolerantly, at the thought. "Now, now, we won't discuss my Min. One of our basic rules is not to involve our wives and daughters. You might say we have a very exclusive men's club. You might consider that both sexist and unconstitutional. We prefer to think of it as selective."

"Dr. Crampton. I can't believe that he would be a part of this."

"One of our founding members. It's unlikely you know that he had a bit of a problem with drugs in medical school." He gave her a brief glance. "As you should be aware, people are not always what they seem. Though the good doctor has been giving me a bit of trouble of late, it's nothing I can't deal with. In time." And it would give him great pleasure to deal with Crampton as he had dealt with Biff. Once done, there would be no one left who'd dare to question him. "It isn't difficult to find men who want a different way," he went on. "Particularly when that way offers sex, money, drugs, and a taste of power."

They were climbing now, up a steep, winding road that cut through largely undeveloped land. Woods closed in on either side. Atherton tapped the accelerator and pushed them up to fifty.

"A wonderful car. It's a shame to destroy it."

"Destroy it?"

"George at Jerry's Auto Sales and Repairs sees to such matters for us. We'll strip it first. It should make up for the worthlessness of Sarah Hewitt's tired old Chevy."

"Sarah? You—"

"It had to be done, I'm afraid. She knew more than it was wise for her to know."

"And Biff."

"Executed." He smiled. There was new power here, he discovered, in being able to speak with impunity of things he had done. "Quite simply, he could no longer control his drinking or his drug habit. He broke the Law by attacking one of our own, then publicly fighting with the sheriff. A pity. He was one of the first to accept the power of a true sacrifice. He had a pure selfishness I admire. He wanted Jane Rafferty, and Mike Rafferty was in the way. He killed him."

"Biff killed Cam's father?"

"A bold and brilliant move. I believe he knocked Mike unconscious, then using chains and a lever pulled the tractor on top of him. Risky. But what is life without risk? Then he was there to comfort the grieving widow."

She shifted, sickened. Her foot scraped across the metal file that had lain forgotten on the floor since the trip to Annie's trailer. With her heart pounding dully, Clare nudged it between her feet. "Your cult is nothing but an excuse to murder."

"Not an excuse at all." He turned onto a dirt road and was forced to slow down to navigate the bumps and turns. "But a way. A way to take and to have. Every member of our group has what he wants, what he needs, and more. We grow daily. In small towns and large cities. Thirty years ago, I was an unhappy draftee in the army. While stationed in California, marking time until I was discharged and would be able to start the rest of my dull, unhappy life. I was introduced to a sect, a fascinating group, but disorganized. I began to see how, with care and persistence, a religion such as theirs could be turned into a satisfying and profitable business. After all, look at the wealth and power of the Catholic church. I took what I needed from them, and from other similar groups, and when I came home I sought out others. Does it surprise you that it's easy to entice solid citizens?"

"It disgusts me."

Atherton chuckled. "Ah, well, not everyone can be a convert. I had big hopes for Cameron, but he proved to be a disappointment. I'm afraid he'll have to be disposed of." He caught her look of blank horror and laughed. "Oh, don't worry, I doubt we'll need violence. Political pressure should be enough to move him out and along. I've already planted seeds that will have him looking elsewhere for Biff's murderer. I don't have anything to fear from Cameron. As long as that remains true, he's safe enough. Well, here we are."

The road had cut through the mountain, perhaps a half mile straight up. They'd stopped in front of a high gate. Atherton hummed along with Chopin as Mick climbed out of the car behind them and walked up to unlock the gate and swing it open.

"I've just had a thought," Atherton said as he drove through. "You won't be using that burl now. It's a pity. I had looked forward to seeing what you would do with it."

Clare had quietly worked the file up to her ankles. "Are you going to kill me here?"

"Why no, of course not. As Jack's daughter, you're entitled to some ceremony. I've even decided to discourage the sex rite. In honor of his memory." He stopped in front of a small, squat cabin. "We'll make you as comfortable here as possible, until the solstice."

"I'm going to be sick." She slumped, keeping the file tight between her calves. When Mick opened her door, she allowed her head to loll forward. "Please, I'm going to be sick."

"Push her head between her knees," Atherton said as he opened his own door.

"Take it easy, Clare." Mick unbuckled the seat belt. "I'm sorry about all of this. There's nothing else we can do." He pushed her head down.

She gripped the file in her hands, then swung it up. Blood spurted out of his chest. He stumbled back, so her second swing only grazed his thigh. "You killed my father, you bastard!"

When he fell to his knees, gasping, she tried to

struggle out of the car. Pain exploded in her head. She collapsed at Atherton's feet.

Where the hell was she? Cam walked through Clare's house for the second time that afternoon. He didn't want to panic. She could have gone for a drive, for a visit to a friend. She could have gotten the bug to go on one of her flea-market frenzies.

Why hadn't she called?

The note he'd left on the kitchen table after dropping by the night before—and waiting two hours—was still there. Her bed was rumpled, as it always was. It was impossible to know if she'd slept in it. Her purse was there. But she often left that behind, stuffing money into her pockets and popping into the car.

Maybe he'd pushed her too hard with the sketches and she needed some time alone.

But damn it, the last time they'd been together, it had been perfect between them. He sat at the kitchen table, trying to fight off a black uneasiness, and remembering the last night they'd spent together.

Lying on the living room rug, arms and legs tangled. Bonnie Raitt playing on the stereo. A breeze, tipped with summer, had drifted in through the windows, along with the call of a whippoorwill.

"Why did you change you mind?" he'd asked her.

"About what?"

"About marrying me."

"I didn't change it." She'd rolled over, folding her arms on his chest and resting her chin on them. "I made it up." He remembered how she'd smiled. Her eyes had been dark, like gold in an old painting. "My first marriage was a really dismal failure. It made me gun-shy. No—" She'd taken a breath, as if determined to be accurate. "It made me insecure. I thought I was doing everything right, but I wasn't."

"That kind of thing is never one person's fault."

"No, we both made mistakes. My biggest was that I didn't care enough. When things started to fall apart, I just let it happen. Pulled in emotionally. It's been a habit of mine since my father died. It's a very elemental equation. Don't care too much equals don't hurt too much. It doesn't work with you."

"So you're going to marry me because I messed up your equation."

"Simply put." She'd pressed a kiss to his throat. "I love you so much, Cam." He'd felt her lips curve against his skin. "You'd better get to work on that garage."

He hadn't seen her since.

Restless, he rose to walk into her garage. Her

tools were there, ready to be picked up. Piles of sketches littered the worktable. Wood chips were scattered on the floor.

If she drove up now, she'd laugh at him for worrying. And she'd be right. If he wasn't so edgy, he wouldn't have given a second thought to the fact that she wasn't home. But the interview with Mona Sherman still nagged at him. He was just so damn sure he was being set up.

Mona Sherman had been lying. Or at least there had been enough lies mixed in with the truth that he was having a hard time telling one from the other. First he had to prove she was lying, then he had to find out why.

But that didn't have anything to do with Clare, he told himself. Clare was out of it. He would make sure it stayed that way.

Ernie watched Rafferty walk back to his car and drive away. Like the child he wished he could be, he climbed into bed and pulled the covers over his head.

When Clare woke, it was dark. She couldn't tell if it was night or day because the windows were all shuttered tight. Her head throbbed, dull as a toothache. When she tried to shift, she found that her hands and feet were tied to the iron rungs of a bed.

In blind, dry-mouthed panic, she fought against the rope, pulling and twisting until the pain sliced through the fear and had her weeping into the musty pillow.

She didn't know how long it took her to gain some control. It didn't seem to matter. She was alone. At least Atherton wouldn't have the satisfaction of seeing her fall apart.

Atherton. The dutiful mayor of Emmitsboro. Her father's friend. The dedicated science teacher and faithful husband. His was the voice she had heard so many years ago, calling out demonic names. His was the hand she had seen lift the knife to slaughter.

All these years, she thought. He'd been quietly serving the town. And quietly destroying it.

Dr. Crampton. Her father's best friend, her own surrogate father. She thought of Alice with jagged despair. How would Alice ever get over it? How would she ever accept it? No one, Clare thought, understood better than she herself what it was like to lose a father.

Chuck Griffith, Mick Morgan, Biff Stokey. How many more?

Ernie. She closed her eyes, grieving as she thought of his mother.

But there was still a chance for Ernie. He was

afraid, and the fear was healthy. Maybe, just maybe, she could find a way to convince him to help her.

She wondered if she'd killed Mick. She prayed she had. The bitter venom of hate stirred and helped clear her head. Yes, she prayed to God she'd killed him. Atherton would have to work to explain a dead deputy.

The tears had passed and so, she was grateful, had the panic. Carefully, she turned her head to study the room.

It was no bigger than ten by twelve and smelled of stale, humid air. Occasionally, she could hear a skittering sound and tried not to think about what was making it.

There was a table and four chairs. A few cigarette butts littered the floor around them. She understood she was feeling better when she pined for a quick drag from one of the butts.

A disgusting thought but a normal one, she decided.

How the hell was she going to get out?

She twisted one way, then the other, hissing at the pain, and discovered they hadn't even left her enough mobility to sit up. Her wrists were already raw and bleeding. She had to pee.

Clare nearly succumbed to a bout of hysterical laughter and forced herself to lie still and concentrate on breathing until it passed.

The sound of a car engine broke her control

again. She was screaming for help when the door opened and Dr. Crampton came in.

"You'll only hurt yourself, Clare." He propped the door open with a rock so that the sunlight and fresh air could pour through. She blinked against it. He had his medical kit in one hand, and a McDonald's takeout bag in the other. "I've brought you some food."

"How can you do this? Dr. Crampton, you've known me all my life. I grew up with Alice. Do you know what it's going to do to her when she finds out what you've done? What you are!"

"My family is my concern." He set both bags on a chair, then dragged it to the bed. He hated this, despised it. Once he had wrested control from Atherton, they would go back to the pure way. There would be no more mistakes. No more waste. "You've injured yourself." He clucked his tongue as he examined her wrists. "You're courting infection."

She had to laugh. "So, you make house calls to your victims. Keeping us alive for the sacrifice. You're a real humanitarian."

"I'm a doctor," he said stiffly.

"You're a murderer."

He set the bags on the floor, then sat. "My religious beliefs don't infringe on my dedication to medicine."

"This has nothing to do with religion. You're sick and sadistic. You rape and kill and enjoy it."

"I don't expect you to understand." In his competent way, he opened his bag and took out a fresh syringe. "If I were a murderer, I would kill you now, with an overdose." His eyes remained patient, even kind. "You know I couldn't do that."

"I don't know anything about you."

"I'm what I've always been." He took cotton to dab on antiseptic. "Like the others, I have opened myself to possibilities and renounced the so-called Christian church, which is based on hypocrisy and self-delusion." He pushed up his glasses, then held the syringe up, squirting out a bit of the drug to test.

"Don't." Her eyes fixed on the needle. "Please, don't."

"I've seen great things, Clare. I know, believe me, I know that a man's salvation can't be based on self-denial, but on indulgence and vitality." He smiled at her, but his eyes glittered with a fervor she didn't want to understand.

"This will make you feel better. Trust me. When you're calm, I'll dress your wounds and help you eat. I don't want you to be in pain or to worry. It'll all be over soon."

She twisted, screaming, but he clamped a hand on her arm and slid the needle gently under her skin.

★ ★ ★

Time drifted, misty and dreamlike. Docile with the drug, she sat unresisting while Crampton cleaned and dressed her wrists and ankles. She even thanked him, with a blank, polite smile, when he fed her the hamburger.

In her mind she was a child again, sick with the flu, dressed in her nightgown with the dancing kittens on it. She went with him, floating, when he took her outside to urinate. He tucked her back into bed and told her to sleep. Obediently, Clare closed her eyes. She didn't feel him tie her again.

She dreamed of her father. He was crying. Sitting at the kitchen table, crying. Nothing she could do or say seemed to comfort him.

She dreamed of Cam, of making love to him on the kitchen floor, aching with need, stunned with pleasure. Her body was slick with sweat and naked as it slid over his.

Then she was tied to a slab, no longer hot with needs but cold with fears. And it was Ernie who mounted her.

When she woke, she was chilled with drying sweat. Nauseated from the drug, she turned her face into the pillow. But she was too weak even to pray.

"She hasn't been seen since yesterday morning." Cam rubbed a hand over his face as he talked to the state police. "Her house was unlocked, nothing was taken. Her clothes, her jewelry, her tools, all her I.D. are still there." He paused to drag smoke into his already raw throat. "I've contacted her brother, her friends. No one's heard from her." He fought against a sickness in his gut as he detailed her description. "White female, aged twenty-eight. Five ten, about a hundred fifteen pounds. Red hair, medium short, with bangs. Amber eyes. No, not brown. Amber. No scars. She could be driving a new model Nissan three hundred, red. New York license number Baker Baker Adam four-four-five-one."

He made the trooper repeat everything. When he hung up, Bud Hewitt was standing by the doorway. "Half the town's out looking." Feeling inadequate, Bud glanced at the coffeepot. "Want some?"

Cam figured his blood was already ninety percent caffeine. "No, thanks."

"You call the press?"

"Yeah. They'll be running her picture." He rubbed his hands over his face again. "Fuck."

"You ought to get some sleep. You've been at this for better than twenty-four hours." Bud slipped his hands in his pockets. "I know how you feel."

Cam looked up then. "I know you do. I'm

going to drive around some more. You man the desk?"

"Sure. Hell of a time for Mick to get sick. We could use him."

Cam only nodded. "I'll be in radio contact." The phone rang, and he pounced on it. After a brief conversation, he hung up. "The warrant came through to check Mona Sherman's bank records."

"Want me to take it?"

"No. I've got to do something. I'll check in about a half hour from now."

In double that, he was pounding on the door of Mona's apartment.

"All right . . . Christ. Wait a goddamn minute." She opened the door, sleepy-eyed, still tying a thin, flowered robe around her waist. Before she could speak, Cam shoved the door open and slammed it behind him.

"We're going to talk."

"I already told you what I know." She dragged a hand through her tousled hair. "You got no right busting in here."

"Fuck my rights." He pushed her into a chair.

"Hey. One call to my lawyer, pal, and you can lose that tin badge of yours."

"You go ahead and call him. You might want to mention accessory to murder."

Watching him warily, she pulled the robe back

over her shoulder. "I don't know what you're talking about."

"Ever done real time, Mona?" He put his hands on the arms of the chair and leaned toward her. "I'm not talking about a night or two in county. I mean the real thing. Ten to twenty in Jessup."

"I ain't done nothing."

"You made a couple of hefty deposits. Smart thinking to lock them into CD's. You're a real financial wizard."

"So?" Her tongue slid out over her lips. "Business has been good."

"The first one was made the day before you talked to me. The second one, the day after. Hell of a coincidence."

"Yeah." She reached for the pack of cigarettes beside her. "So?"

"Where'd you get it?"

"Like I said—" She choked off the words when he slid a hand around her throat and squeezed.

"I'm a busy man, Mona, so let's not waste time. Why don't I tell you how it went? Somebody paid you to throw a new scent in my path. All that bullshit about some Haitian doing Biff because he'd queered a drug deal."

"Biff was a mule, just like I told you."

"I figure he moved it, all right. That's about all

he had the brains for. The rest is shit. Now tell me who paid you to talk to me."

"I came to you on my own. I wanted to help is all."

"You wanted to help." He stood back, then kicked over the table. The lamp crashed to the floor. "You wanted to help," he repeated, shoving her back when she tried to dart out of the chair. "They didn't tell you about me, did they? About this problem I have. I was a cop down in D.C. for a long time. Had to give it up for a nice quiet job in a small town. Know why?"

She shook her head. He didn't look like a cop now. He just looked mean.

"Well, I have this control problem. When someone starts lying to me, it makes me crazy." He picked up a nearly empty bottle of Jim Beam and threw it against the wall. Glass exploded and released the ripe scent of liquor. "I just start breaking things. And if the lying keeps up, I lose it. One time I threw a suspect out a window." He glanced over at the window behind her convertible sofa. "We're on the third floor here, aren't we?"

"That's bull. I'm going to call my lawyer." She scrambled up to grab for the phone. "You're crazy, that's all. I don't have to take this crap."

"Right and wrong." He clamped a hand over her wrist. "I'm crazy, all right. But you're going to take it. Let's see how far you can fly." He dragged her toward the window while she struggled and shouted. She managed to grab the sill and fall to her knees. "I don't know who it was. I don't."

"Not good enough." He hooked an arm around her waist.

"I don't. I swear. He just called. He told me what to say and mailed me the money. Cash."

Cam hunkered down beside her. "I want a name."

"Biff's the only name I knew. He was a customer, just like I said." She inched away until her back was to the wall. "Couple years back, he told me about this, well, kind of club or something. Said they'd pay me two hundred for the night. So I went."

"Where?"

"I don't know." Eyes wide, she tumbled down to one elbow. "I swear I don't. I was blindfolded. It was kind of kinky, you know? Biff picked me up, and we drove out of town, into the country. Then he stopped and blindfolded me, and we drove some more. After a while we had to walk. In the woods or something. He didn't take the blindfold off until we got to this place. They did rites and stuff there. You know, Satanism. But mostly it was just a bunch of guys who wanted some ass and thrills."

"I want descriptions."

"They wore masks. The whole time. I never knew none of them but Biff. It was weird, sure, but the pay was good. I went back every couple of months."

"Okay, Mona." He helped her up, though she cringed back. "Let's sit down. You're going to tell me all about it."

Chapter 30

ALICE TIDIED UP the kitchen for lack of anything better to do. Behind her Blair paced back and forth. It had been a long week, she thought, for everyone. No one believed that Clare had just lit out. That was fine for someone like Sarah Hewitt, but not Clare. It didn't make sense.

The big sculpture she'd been working on was still standing out in the drive. Like a sign. People walked by it and stopped and traded speculations on a daily basis. Min Atherton had even taken Polaroid pictures of it and showed them off at Betty's.

The mayor had called a special town meeting, offering a reward. It had been a moving speech, too, Alice remembered. All about taking care of your own and looking out for your neighbor. The mayor could talk as good as a tent evangelist. There'd hardly been a dry eye in the town hall.

Except for the sheriff. He'd been dry-eyed. And haggard, she thought now. It was clear that he hadn't been doing much sleeping or eating in the six days since Clare had disappeared. He'd gotten up at the end of the meeting to answer questions from the townspeople and the reporters who had crowded the small auditorium. Not just local people either, Alice reflected, but big-city reporters from D.C., New York, and Philadelphia.

She ran the dishcloth under the water, then wrung it out to wipe off the counters. The air was hot and still, the temperature more suited to August dog days than June. But no one had thought to turn on the air conditioner. Clare's mother and her new husband were staying at the house, and so were the LeBeaus. Nobody complained about the heat.

She glanced over at Blair and felt a kinship that had already replaced the longtime crush.

"I could fix you something to eat," she offered. "A sandwich maybe, or some soup."

"Thanks. Later maybe. I thought Angie and Jean-Paul would be back by now."

"They'll be along." She spread the cloth over the lip of the sink. It was a helpless feeling, not being able to offer more than ham on rye or Campbell's chicken and rice. "It doesn't do any good not to eat. I could fix something up. The others'll be hungry when they get back."

He started to snap but stopped himself. Alice was as hollow-eyed and jumpy as the rest of them. "Fine. That's fine." They both rushed into the garage at the sound of a motorcycle. Before Cam could climb off, Blair was beside him.

"Anything?"

"No." Cam rubbed his gritty eyes, then swung his rubbery legs off the cycle. He'd been riding most of the day, down back roads, over old logging trails, covering ground that had already been covered and covered again.

"I'm making sandwiches," Alice said. "You come in and have one before you go again. I mean it, Cam. You need fuel just like that machine of yours."

Cam sat down on the cycle again as Alice hurried back in. "How's your mother?" Cam asked Blair.

"Worried sick. She and Jerry are driving around." He looked helplessly at the sculpture that towered behind them. "Like everyone. Christ, Cam, it's been almost a week."

He knew exactly how long it had been, to the hour. "We're doing a house-to-house, search and interviews. Now that Mick's on his feet again, it'll go easier."

"You don't really believe someone's holding her in town."

"I believe anything." He looked across the street, to the Buttses' house. That one he would search personally.

"She could already be—"

"No." Cam's head whipped around. His eyes, shadowed and weary, sharpened. "No, she's not. We start here, and we spread out, and we go over every inch of these hills." Cam looked down at the ground. "I didn't take care of her."

When Blair didn't respond, Cam understood his friend thought the same thing.

Blair stood where he was, struggling to be calm as Cam lighted a cigarette. His research had gone well. Too well. He knew much too much about what could be happening to his sister. What might have happened already. He couldn't afford to break down now. "I'd like to go out on the next search. I know you've got experienced men, but I know the woods around here."

"We can use everyone. Have to use everyone," Cam corrected. "I just don't know who I can trust." He looked up at the sun. It was straight up noon. "Do you know what today is?" He turned his head again and looked at

Blair. "It's the summer solstice. I didn't realize it until I heard it on the radio."

"I know."

"They'll meet tonight," he murmured. "Somewhere."

"Would they take a risk like that, with the search and the press?"

"Yeah. Because they want to. Maybe they need to." He swung onto the bike again. "There's somebody I've got to see."

"I'll go with you."

"It's better that I go alone. It's a long shot." He kicked the engine. "I'll let you know."

"It's outrageous. Absolutely outrageous."

"I'm sorry, Miz Atherton." Bud had his cap in his hands, running the brim through his fingers. "It's procedure, is all."

"It's insulting, that's what it is. Why, the very idea of your coming into my home and searching all over it, as if I were a common criminal." She planted herself in the doorway, floral bosom trembling. "Do you think I've got Clare Kimball tied up in the basement?"

"No, ma'am. No ma'am. And I sure do apologize for the inconvenience. It's just that we're looking through every house in town." He gave a little sigh of relief as the mayor came down the hall.

"What's all this?"

"An outrage. Why, James, you won't believe what this boy wants to do."

"We're conducting a house-to-house search, Mr. Atherton, sir." He flushed. "I got the proper warrants."

"Warrants!" Min plumped up like a broody hen. "Did you hear that, James? Warrants. The very idea."

"Now, Min." He put a soothing hand on her shoulder. "This has to do with Clare Kimball's disappearance, doesn't it, Deputy Hewitt?"

"Yes, sir, Mayor." Bud always preened a bit when Atherton called him Deputy Hewitt. "It's nothing personal, and I'll be in and out in just a few minutes. Just have to take a look around and ask you some questions."

"You step a foot inside this house, I'll take a broom to your behind, Bud Hewitt."

"Min." Atherton gave her shoulder a gentle squeeze. "The man's only doing his job. If we don't cooperate with the law, who will? You come right on in, Deputy, go through from attic to cellar. No one in town wants to get to the bottom of what happened to Clare more than my wife and myself."

He gestured Bud inside, and the deputy took a strategic step so that the mayor was between him and Min. "I appreciate it, Mr. Atherton."

"Our civic duty." His eyes and voice were grave. "Can you tell me how things are going?"

"We ain't found a trace. I'll tell you, Mr. Atherton, the sheriff's worried sick. Don't think he's slept more'n an hour at a stretch since it started."

"It must be a dreadful strain on him."

"I don't know what he'll do if we don't find her. They were talking marriage, you know. Why, he'd even called up an architect about building Clare a studio over to his house."

"Is that so?" Min's gossip glands went into overdrive. "Could be the girl got cold feet and ran off."

"Min—"

"After all, James, she already failed at one marriage. It wouldn't be the first time a woman just up and took off when the pressure built up."

"No . . ." Atherton stroked his bottom lip gravely. "No, I suppose you're right." He waved the thought away, hoping it had taken root. "We're holding up Deputy Hewitt. Start anywhere you like. We have nothing to hide."

Annie wasn't in her trailer. Nor could Cam find her in any of her usual haunts around town. The best he could do was have a neighbor promise to see that she stayed put when she got back.

He was running in circles, he thought as he headed back to town. Chasing his tail just like they wanted him to. He knew more than they realized. He knew that the passbook with Kimball's and Biff's names had been a plant. What he didn't know was whether Bob Meese had found it or had merely been following orders.

He knew that rituals were held on a regular basis. At least monthly, from what Mona had finally told him. But he didn't know where.

He knew there were thirteen men involved, from Clare's sketch and Mona's corroboration. But he didn't know who.

So when you added it all up, he thought as he pulled up in front of Ernie's house, you still got zero.

The worst was that he couldn't afford to share what he did know with anyone, not even Bud or Mick. Even in a town as small as Emmitsboro, thirteen men could hide easily.

He hoped Ernie would answer the door. He was in the mood to choke some answers out of the boy. But it was Joleen Butts who answered.

"Mrs. Butts."

"Sheriff?" Her eyes darted behind him. "Is something wrong?"

"We're conducting a house-to-house search."

"Oh, yes. I heard." She twisted her beads. "I guess you can get started. Excuse the mess. I haven't had a chance to pick up."

"Don't worry about it. Your husband's been a big help with the search party."

"Will's always the first to volunteer, the last to leave. I guess you'll want to begin upstairs." She started to lead him up, then stopped. "Sheriff, I know you've got a lot on your mind, and I don't want to sound like an overanxious mother, but Ernie . . . he didn't come home last night. The therapist says it's a very common behavior pattern, given the way Ernie feels right now about himself and his father and me. But I'm afraid. I'm afraid something might have happened to him. Like Clare." She rested her hand on the banister. "What should I do?"

Cam was on his way back out of town when he passed Bud's cruiser. He signaled, then stood, straddling his bike as Bud backed up and leaned out the window.

"Where's Mick?"

"Supervising the search on the other side of Gossard Creek." Bud wiped his sweaty forehead with a bandanna. "I had radio contact about twenty minutes ago."

"Did you finish the house-to-house?"

"Yeah. I'm sorry, Cam."

Cam looked out, over a field of corn. There was a haze of heat hovering like fog. Above, the sky was the color of drywall. "You know that kid, Ernie Butts?"

"Sure."

"The truck he drives?"

"Red Toyota pickup. Why?"

Cam looked back at Bud, steadily. He had to trust someone. "I want you to cruise around, keep your eye out for him."

"Did he do something?"

"I don't know. If you spot him, don't stop him. See what he's up to, but don't stop him. Just contact me. Just me, Bud."

"Sure, Sheriff."

"I've got another stop to make." He checked the sky again. It was the longest day of the year, but even that didn't last forever.

As Cam parked in front of Annie's trailer, Clare tried to claw her way out of the sticky mists the drug coated over her mind. She recited poetry in her head, old Beatles lyrics, nursery rhymes. It was so hot, so airless in the room. Like a coffin. But you were cold in a coffin, she reminded herself. And she'd already soaked through the sheets that day.

She wasn't certain how much longer she could take lying in the dark. How much time had passed? A day, a week, a month?

Why didn't someone come?

They would be looking. Cam, her friends, her family. They wouldn't forget her. She'd seen no one but Doc Crampton since the night she'd been brought there. And even then she wasn't certain how many times he had sat beside the bed and popped a drug in her veins.

She was afraid, not only for her life but for her sanity. She knew now that she was too weak to fight them, whatever they did to her. But she was desperately afraid she would go mad first.

Alone. In the dark.

In her more lucid moments, she plotted ways to escape, then expose them all and clear her father. But then the hours would pass in that terrible, dark silence, and her plans would turn into incoherent prayers for someone, anyone, to come and help her.

In the end, it was Atherton who came. When she looked up and saw him, she knew she wouldn't spend another night lying in the dark. It was the shortest night of the year, for everyone.

"It's time," he said gently. "We have preparations to make."

It was his last hope. Cam stood in front of the empty trailer. His last hope centered on the chance that Crazy Annie knew something. And if she knew, she would remember.

It was a crap shoot, and he wouldn't even have the chance to roll and come up seven if she didn't get home.

It came down to this, him and a sixty-year-old woman with an eight-year-old's mind. They weren't getting a hell of a lot of outside help. He hadn't been able to prove conspiracy or ritual slayings. All he had proven was that Carly Jamison had been held in a shed, murdered, buried, and exhumed to be placed in a shallow grave in a hay field. The fact that a dead man had had an accomplice didn't prove cult killings—not as far as the State boys or Feds were concerned. They'd helped in the search for Clare, adding men and helicopters. But even with them, he'd turned up nothing.

Time was running out. He knew it. The lower the sun dipped in the sky, the colder he became, until he wondered if by nightfall his bones would be brittle as ice.

He couldn't lose her. And he was afraid because the thought of it was so abhorrent that he had rushed and fumbled in his search for her and made one tiny miscalculation that could cost Clare her life.

Three steps behind, he thought, and falling through.

He hadn't forgotten how to pray, but he'd taken little time for it since his first decade, when there had been CCD classes and mass on Sunday, monthly confessions with strings of Our Fathers and Hail Marys to cleanse his youthful soul of sin.

He prayed now, simply and desperately as the first streaks of red stained the western horizon.

" 'Beyond the sunset, O blissful morning,' " Annie sang happily as she toiled over the hill. " 'When with our Savior heav'n is begun. Earth's toiling ended, O glorious dawning; Beyond the sunset when day is done.' "

She dragged her bag behind her and looked up, startled, when Cam raced the last yards toward her. "Annie, I've been waiting for you."

"I've just been walking. Gosh Almighty, it's a hot one. Hottest day I remember." Sweat had stained her checkered dress from neck to hem. "I found two nickels and a quarter and a little green bottle. Do you want to see?"

"Not right now. There's something I want to show you. Can we sit down?"

"We can go inside. I can give you some cookies."

He smiled, straining for patience. "I'm not really hungry right now. Can we just sit down on the steps there, so I can show you?"

"I don't mind. I've been walking a long way.

My dogs are tired." She giggled at the expression, then her face lit up. "You brought your motorcycle. Can I have a ride?"

"Tell you what, if you can help me, I'll take you out real soon, all day if you want."

"Really?" She petted the handlebars. "You promise?"

"Cross my heart. Come on, Annie, sit down." He took the sketches from the saddlebag. "I have some pictures to show you."

She settled her solid rump on the yellow stairs. "I like pictures."

"I want you to look at them, look at them very carefully." He sat beside her. "Will you do that?"

"I sure will."

"And I want you to tell me, after you've looked at them, if you recognize the place. Okay?"

"Okeedoke." She was grinning widely when she looked down. But the grin faded instantly. "I don't like these pictures."

"They're important."

"I don't want to look at them. I have better pictures inside. I can show you."

He ignored his rapidly beating pulse and the urge to grab her by her poor wrinkled neck and shake. She knew. He recognized both knowledge and fear in her eyes. "Annie, I need you to look at them. And I need you to tell me the truth. You've seen this place?"

She pressed her lips tightly together and shook her head.

"Yes, you have. You've been there. You know where it is."

"It's a bad place. I don't go there."

He didn't touch her, afraid that no matter how he tried to keep his hand easy, his fingers would dig right through her flesh. "Why is it a bad place?"

"It just is. I don't want to talk about it. I want to go in now."

"Annie. Annie, look at me now. Come on. Look at me." He forced himself to smile when she complied. "I'm your friend, aren't I?"

"You're my friend. You give me rides and buy me ice cream. It's hot now." She smiled hopefully. "Ice cream'd be good."

"Friends take care of each other. And they trust each other. I have to know about this place. I need you to tell me."

She was in an agony of indecision. Things were always simple for her. Whether to get up or go to bed. Whether to walk west or east. Eat now or later. But this made her head ache and her stomach roll. "You won't tell?" she whispered.

"No. Trust me."

"There are monsters there." Her voice continued to whisper through her wrinkled lips. An aged child telling secrets. "At night, they go there and do things. Bad things."

"Who?"

"The monsters in the black dresses. They have animal heads. They do things to women without clothes on. And they kill dogs and goats."

"That's where you found the bracelet. The one you gave to Clare."

She nodded. "I didn't think I should tell. You're not supposed to believe in monsters. They're just on the TV. If you talk about monsters, people think you're crazy, and they lock you up."

"I don't think you're crazy. And no one's ever going to lock you up." He touched her then, stroking her hair. "I need you to tell me where the place is."

"It's in the woods."

"Where?"

"Over there." She gestured vaguely. "Over the rocks and through the trees."

Acres of rocks and trees. He took a deep breath to keep his voice even. "Annie, I need you to show me. Can you take me there?"

"Oh, no." She got up, spry from panic. "No, indeedy, I don't go there now. It'll be dark. You can't go there at night when the monsters come."

He took her hand to still the jingling bracelets. "Do you remember Clare Kimball?"

"She went away. Nobody knows where."

"I think someone took her away, Annie. She didn't want to go. They may be taking her to that place tonight. They'll hurt her."

"She's pretty." Annie's lips began to tremble. "She came to visit."

"Yes. She made this for you." He turned the bracelet on her wrist. "Help me, Annie. Help Clare, and I swear to you I'll make the monsters go away."

Ernie had been driving for hours. Away from town, in circles, out on the highway, and back on the rural roads. He knew his parents would be frantic, and he thought of them, for the first time in years, with real regret and need.

He knew what tonight would mean. It was a test, his last one. They wanted to initiate him quickly, finally, so that he would be bound to them by blood and fire and death. He'd thought of running away, but he had nowhere to go. There was only one path left for him. The path that led to a clearing in the woods.

It was his fault that Clare would die tonight. He knew it, had agonized over it. The teachings he had chosen to follow left no place for regret or guilt. They would wash him clean. He craved that, thought only of that as he turned his truck around and headed for his destiny.

Bud passed the Toyota, glanced at it absently, then remembered. Swearing under his breath, he turned around and reached for the radio.

"Unit One, this is Unit Three. Do you copy?" He got nothing but static and repeated the call twice. "Come on, Cam, pick up. It's Bud."

Shit on a stick, he thought, the sheriff was off the air, and he was stuck following some kid in a truck. God knew where, God knew why. Annoyed or not, Bud followed procedure and kept a safe distance back.

It was dusk, and the taillights of the pickup gleamed palely red.

When the truck turned off the road, Bud pulled over and stopped. Where the hell was the kid going? he wondered. That old logging trail led straight into the woods, and the Toyota wasn't a four-wheel drive. Hell, the sheriff had said to see what the kid was up to, so that's what he'd have to do.

He decided to go on foot. There was only one road in and one road out. Grabbing the flashlight, he hesitated. The sheriff might say it was cowboying, Bud thought as he strapped on his gun. But with everything the way it was, he wasn't going into the woods unarmed.

When he reached the start of the logging trail, he saw the truck. Ernie stood beside it, as if waiting. Thinking it would be his first-time-ever genuine stakeout, Bud crept back and crouched low in a gully.

Both he and Ernie heard the footsteps at the same time. The boy stepped forward, toward the two men who came out of the woods. Bud nearly betrayed himself by calling out when he recognized Doc Crampton and Mick.

They hadn't bothered with masks, Ernie thought, and was pleased. He shook his head at the cup with drugged wine.

"I don't need that. I took the oath."

After a moment Crampton nodded and sipped from the cup himself. "I prefer a heightened awareness." He offered the cup to Mick. "It will ease that twinge. That chest wound's healing well enough, but it's deep."

"Damn tetanus shot was almost as bad." Mick shared the drug. "The others are waiting. It's nearly time."

Bud stayed crouched until they had disappeared into the trees. He wasn't sure what he had seen. He didn't want to believe what he had seen. He glanced back toward the road, knowing how long it would take him to go back and try to contact Cam again. Even if he succeeded, he would lose them.

He crawled out of the gully and followed.

★ ★ ★

They'd taken her clothes. Clare was beyond embarrassment. She hadn't been drugged. Atherton
had told her, privately, that he wanted her fully
aware of everything that happened. She could
scream and beg and plead. It would only excite
the others.

She'd fought when they dragged her to the altar. Though her arms and legs were stiff and
weak from disuse, she'd struggled wildly, almost
as horrified to see the familiar faces surrounding
her as to recognize what was happening.

Less Gladhill and Bob Meese tied down her
arms, Skunk Haggerty and George Howard her
legs. She recognized a local farmer, the manager
of the bank, two members of the town council.
They all stood quietly and waited.

She managed to twist her wrist so that her fingers gripped Bob's.

"You can't do this. He's going to kill me. Bob,
you can't let it happen. I've known you all my
life."

He pulled away and said nothing.

They were not to speak to her. Not to think
of her as a woman, as a person they knew. She
was an offering. Nothing more.

Each, in his turn, took up his mask. And became her nightmare.

She didn't scream. There was no one to hear,
no one to care. She didn't cry. So many tears

had been shed already that she was empty. She imagined that when they plunged the knife into her, they would find no blood. Only dust.

The candles were placed around her, then lighted. In the pit, the fire was ignited, and fed. Shimmers of heat danced on the air. She watched it all, eerily, detached. Whatever hope she had clung to through the days and nights she had spent in the dark was snuffed out.

Or so she thought, until she saw Ernie.

The tears she hadn't thought she had now sprang to her eyes. She struggled again, and the ropes scraped harmlessly against her bandages.

"Ernie, for God's sake. Please."

He looked at her. He'd thought he would feel lust, a raw and needy fire inside the pit of his belly. She was naked, as he'd once imagined her. Her body was slender and white, just as it had been when he'd caught glimpses of her through her bedroom window.

But it wasn't lust, and he couldn't bear to analyze the emotion that crawled through him. He turned away and chose the mask of an eagle. Tonight, he would fly.

However immature her mind, Annie's body was old. She couldn't go quickly, no matter how Cam urged, pleaded, and supported. Fear added to the weight of her legs so that she dragged her feet.

The light was fading fast.

"How much farther, Annie?"

"It's up ahead some. I didn't have my supper," she reminded him.

"Soon. You can eat soon."

She sighed and turned, as instinctively as a deer or rabbit, taking a path overgrown with summer brush.

"Gotta watch out for them sticky bushes. They reach right out and grab you." Her eyes darted right and left as she searched the lengthening shadows. "Like monsters."

"I won't let them hurt you." He put an arm around her waist, both for support and to hurry her along.

Comforted, she trudged ahead. "Are you going to marry Clare?"

"Yes." Please God. "Yes, I am."

"She's pretty. When she smiles, she has nice white teeth. Her daddy did, too. She looks like her daddy. He gave me roses. But he's dead now." Her lungs were starting to trouble her so that she wheezed when she walked, like a worn-out engine. "The monsters didn't get him."

"No."

"He fell out the window, after those men went up and yelled at him."

He looked down but didn't slacken pace. "What men?"

"Was that another time? I disremember. He left the light on in the attic."

"What men, Annie?"

"Oh, the sheriff and the young deputy. They went up and then came out again. And he was dead."

He swiped sweat from his brow. "Which young deputy? Bud?"

"No, t'other one. Maybe they went up to buy a house. Mr. Kimball, he used to sell houses."

"Yes." His skin turned icy beneath the sweat. "Annie, we have to hurry."

Bud stood in the shelter of the trees and stared. He knew it was real, but his mind continued to reject it. Alice's father? How could it be? His friend and partner, Mick?

But he was seeing it with his own eyes. They were standing in a circle, their backs to him. He couldn't see what they were facing, and was afraid to try to move closer. It was best to wait and watch. That's what the sheriff would have him do.

He wiped a hand across his mouth as the chanting began.

★ ★ ★

It was like the dream. Clare closed her eyes and drifted between past and present. The smoke, the voices, the men. It was all the same.

She was in the bushes, hiding, watching herself. This time she would be able to run away.

She opened her eyes and stared up at the seamless black sky, crowned by a floating crescent moon. The longest day was over.

She saw the glint of a sword and braced. But it wasn't her time. Atherton was calling the Four Princes of Hell. She wished they would come, if there were such things, and devour him for his arrogance.

She turned her head away, unable to look, refusing to listen. She thought of Cam and the years they wouldn't share, the children they wouldn't make. He loved her, and now they would never have the chance to see if love was enough. To make it be enough.

He would find them. Stop them. She was sure of it, or she would have gone mad. But it would be too late for her. Too late to talk to her mother again, to make up for the coolness and distance she'd put between them. Too late to tell the people who mattered that her father had made mistakes, had taken wrong turns, but hadn't been a thief or a murderer.

There was so much she'd wanted to do. So much left to see and touch. But she would die like this for one man's ego and others' blind cruelty.

The rage built up in her. They had stripped her naked, of clothes, of dignity, of hope. And of life. Her hands balled into fists. Her body arched as she screamed.

Bud's hand went to the butt of his gun and stuck there, trembling.

Cam's head reared up, and the fear that shot through his veins was hot and pulsing. "Stay here." He shook off Annie's clinging hands. "Stay here. Don't move." He had his weapon out as he raced through the trees.

Atherton raised his knife toward the sky. He'd wanted her to scream. He'd yearned for it, sweated, the way a man yearns and sweats for sexual release. It had infuriated him when she'd lain still, like a doll already broken. Now she writhed on the altar, skin gleaming with sweat, eyes full of fear and anger.

And the power filled him.

"I am annihilation," he cried out. "I am vengeance. I call upon the Master to fill me with His wrath so that I might slash with keen delight His victim. Her agony will sustain itself."

The words buzzed in Ernie's ears. He could barely hear them, could no longer understand

them. The others swayed around him, capti-
vated. Hungry for what was to come. It wasn't
hunger that crawled through Ernie's gut, but a
sickness.

It was supposed to make him feel good, he reminded himself. It was supposed to make him
belong.

But he saw her, struggling, terrified. Screaming
and screaming as Sarah Hewitt had screamed. It
made him ill with pity. How could he belong if
he felt such things? How could he be one of them
when what they were about to do revolted him?
Frightened him.

She shouldn't have to die.

His fault. His fault.

Her eyes met his once, pleading. In them, he
saw his last hope for salvation. With a cry that
was both pain and triumph, he lurched forward
as Atherton brought the knife down.

Clare felt the body fall over hers. She smelled
the blood. But there was no pain. She saw
Atherton stumble back. Groaning, Ernie slid
from her and crumpled on the ground.

Snarling in fury, Atherton raised the knife
again. Two shots rang out. One caught him in
the arm, the other full in the chest.

"Don't move." Cam held his weapon firm, but
his finger trembled on the trigger. "I'll send
every fucking one of you to hell."

"Sheriff—it's Bud." Bud stepped forward, arms shaking. "I followed the kid. I saw— Christ, Cam, I killed a man."

"It's easier the second time." He fired into the air as one of the men turned to run. "Take another step, and I'll show my deputy here just how much easier it is. On your faces, all of you. Hands behind your heads. Bud, the first one of them that moves, kill him."

Bud didn't believe it would be easier the second time. Not for a minute. But he nodded. "Yes, sir, Sheriff."

Cam was with Clare in three strides, touching her face, her hair. "Oh, God, Slim, I thought I'd lost you."

"I know. Your face." In reflex she tried to reach out to him but was held down by the rope. "It's bleeding."

"Briars." He pulled out his pocket knife to cut the rope. He couldn't break down, not yet. All he wanted was to hold her, to bury his face in her hair and hold her.

"Take it easy," he told her and stripped off his shirt. "Put this on." His hand trembled as it stroked over her skin. "I'm going to get you out of here as soon as I can."

"I'm okay. I'm okay now. Ernie. He saved my life." And his blood was wet on her skin. "Is he dead?"

He bent down, checked for a pulse, then tore

the ripped robe aside. "No, he's alive. He took most of it in the shoulder."

"Cam, if he hadn't jumped over me . . ."

"He's going to be all right. Bud, let's get these bastards tied up."

"One of them's Mick," he murmured, shamed that he was fighting tears.

"Yeah. I know." He tossed over the rope that had been used on Clare. "Let's get it done, then you take Clare back and call the State boys. Bring them here."

"I want to stay with you." She closed a hand around his arm. "I need to stay with you. Please."

"Okay. Just go sit down."

"Not here." She looked away from the altar. "There's more rope over there." Where they had stripped her. "I'll help you tie them." Her eyes lifted, glittered. "I want to."

Unmasked, bound, they looked pitiful. That was all Clare could think as she knelt beside Ernie, holding his hand and waiting for Bud to get back with the state police and an ambulance.

"I can't believe Annie brought you here."

"She was terrific. She'll be getting quite a charge from riding with Bud with the siren going." He glanced down at Ernie. "How's he doing?"

"I think I stopped the bleeding. He's going to need help, but he's going to be okay. I mean really okay."

"I hope you're right." He reached down to brush his fingers over her hair. Just to touch. "Clare, I have to check the other one."

She nodded. "It's Atherton," she said flatly. "He started it all."

"Tonight, it's finished." He walked around the altar. Atherton lay facedown. Without pity, Cam turned him over. The chest wound was mortal; he didn't doubt it. But breath still hissed out of the opening of the mask. When he heard Clare behind him, he rose quickly and turned to shield her from the body.

"Don't protect me, Cam."

"You're not as strong as you think you are." He lifted one of her hands and touched the bandaged wrist. "They hurt you."

"Yes." She thought of what she had learned, of how his father had died. "They hurt us all. Not anymore."

"Do you think it's over?" The question rasped obscenely through the mask of the Goat of Mendes. "You've done nothing. You've stopped nothing. If not you, your children. If not them, their children. You didn't get the head. You never will." Fingers curled like claws, he made a grab for Clare, then fell back with a rattling laugh and died.

"He was evil," Clare whispered. "Not crazy, not ill, just evil. I didn't know that could be."

"He can't touch us." He drew her back, then closed her tightly in his arms.

"No, he can't." She heard the sirens echo in the distance. "Bud was quick."

Cam pulled her back just to look at her face. "There's so much I have to tell you. So much I have to say. Once I start I don't know if I'll be able to stop. It's going to have to wait until we're done with this."

She closed her hand over his. Behind them, the fire was going out. "We've got plenty of time."

Two weeks later, wearing mourning black, Min Atherton boarded a train going west. No one came to see her off, and she was glad of it. They thought she was slinking out of town, shamed by her husband, shocked by his actions.

She would never be shamed or shocked by her James.

As she maneuvered herself and her one huge bag back to her compartment, she blinked away tears. Her dear, dear James. Someday, somehow, she would find a way to avenge him.

She settled on the wide seat, thumping her bag beside her before folding her hands on her generous lap for her last look at Maryland.

She would not come back. One day perhaps she would send someone, but she would not be back.

Still, she sighed a little. Leaving her house had been difficult. Most of her pretty things would be shipped, but it would not be the same. Not without James.

He'd been the perfect mate for her. So thirsty, so malleable, so anxious to pretend he was the power. She smiled to herself as she took out a fan to cool her heated flesh. Her eyes glittered. She hadn't minded playing the woman behind the man. So satisfying to wield the power over them all without any of them—not even James really—understanding who had been in charge.

He'd been no more than a dabbler when she had taken him in, taken him over. Interested and angry, but with no clear idea of how to use that interest and anger for more.

She'd known. A woman knew. And men were only puppets, after all, to be led where a woman chose by sex, by blood, by the offer of power.

A pity he had become so bold and careless at the end. Sighing, she fanned herself more briskly. She had herself to blame, she supposed, for not stopping him. But it had been exciting to watch him spin out of control, to risk all for more. Almost as exciting as the night all those years ago when she had initiated him. She, the goddess of the Master, and James her servant.

It was she, of course, who had started it. She who had looked beyond the accepted and grabbed those dark promises with both hands. She who had ordered the first human sacrifice. And had watched, oh, and had watched from the shadows of trees as blood was spilled.

And she who had felt the power of that blood and craved more.

The Master had never granted her fondest wish—the wish for children—but He had given her substitutes. He had shown her greed, the most delicious of the deadly sins.

There would be other towns, she thought, as the train's whistle shrilled. Other men. Other victims. Whores with fertile bellies. Oh, yes, there would always be more.

And who would look to her, the poor Widow Atherton, when their women disappeared?

Perhaps she would choose a young boy this time. A lost, angry boy like Ernie Butts—who had turned out to be such a disappointment to her. No, she would not search for another James but for a young boy, she thought comfortably. One she could mother and guide and train to worship both her and the Dark Lord.

As the train pulled slowly away from the station, she slipped a hand down her bodice, closed her fingers over the pentagram.

"Master," she murmured. "We start again."

About the Author

Nora Roberts, one of the world's most successful and best-loved novelists, has more than 201 million copies of her books in print, including the *New York Times* bestsellers *Remember When*, *Birthright*, and *Chesapeake Blue*. Ms. Roberts lives in Maryland.

LIKE WHAT YOU'VE SEEN?

If you enjoyed this large print edition of
Divine Evil, look for other Random House
Large Print books available from Nora Roberts.

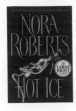 **Hot Ice** (hardcover)
0-375-43167-5 ($21.95/$32.95C)

Brazen Virtue (hardcover)
0-375-43112-8 ($18.95/$28.95C)

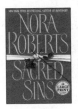 **Sacred Sins** (hardcover)
0-375-43066-0 ($18.95/$28.95C)

The Villa (hardcover)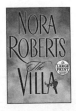
0-375-43103-9 ($25.95/$37.95C)

Large print books are available wherever
books are sold and at many local libraries.

All prices are subject to change. Check with your
local retailer for current pricing and availability.
For more information on these and other large print titles,
visit www.randomlargeprint.com.